Praise for *And Now the Light is Everywhere*

'A vivid, involving and beautifully written story'

JOSEPH O'CONNOR

'Classic story-telling bathed in a generous light ... it moves so confidently between lives and epochs it easy not to realise at first how cleverly it's put together, how effectively the different stories intersect and echo. It's poignant and funny, and marks Lucy out as an exciting and ambitious writer of real talent'

ANDREW MILLER

'A book that draws you in and holds you till the very end'

ANNE GRIFFIN

'*And Now the Light is Everywhere* is a page-turner, with a clever plot and a range of engaging characters ... MacRae's writing is sensitive and accurate, rising to passages of brilliance at the right moments. A wonderfully accomplished first novel'

JAMES ROBERTSON

'An eloquent novel. I was captivated by the story telling, the landscape, the brilliant dialogue and the wonderfully vivid characters'

MARGOT LIVESEY

L.A. MacRae was born in St Andrews, Scotland. Her first novel *And Now The Light Is Everywhere* was longlisted for the Caledonian Novel Award 2021. She now lives in the Isle of Skye with her family and animals.

L.A. MACRAE

And Now the Light is Everywhere

HODDER &
STOUGHTON

First published in Great Britain in 2024 by Hodder & Stoughton
An Hachette UK company

This paperback edition published in 2025

The authorised representative in the EEA is Hachette Ireland, 8
Castlecourt Centre, Dublin 15, D15 XTP3, Ireland (email: info@hbgi.ie)

1

Image used p.10 Shutterstock

A CIP catalogue record for this title is available from the British Library

Paperback ISBN 978 1 399 70749 7
eBook ISBN 978 1 399 70747 3

Typeset in Plantin Light by Hewer Text UK Ltd, Edinburgh
Printed and bound in Great Britain by Clays Ltd, Elcograf S.p.A.

Hodder & Stoughton policy is to use papers that are natural, renewable
and recyclable products and made from wood grown in sustainable
forests. The logging and manufacturing processes are expected to
conform to the environmental regulations of the country of origin.

Hodder & Stoughton Limited
Carmelite House
50 Victoria Embankment
London EC4Y 0DZ

www.hodder.co.uk

To my parents, who taught me to read and to love stories.
To my sister, and the worlds we created when we were small.

Thig trì nithean gun iarraidh, an t-eagal, an t-iadach 's an gaol

Three things come without asking – fear, envy and love

Nighean Fhir na Rèilig,
Fhir a Dhìreas am Bealach
The Daughter of the Laird of Rèilig,
You Who are Climbing the Pass

Netta

Our names are pressed in the black-bound Bible like dried flowers. On opening, the filmy page whispers beneath the light and the air.

In the front of the book concerned with the preservation of the soul, here is proof of each fleshly, if fleeting, existence. Most of us are here, set down in the hands of our fathers. We are woven in stems of ink. We are unfurled offshoots from the familial branches of begetting and becoming: sons, daughters, sisters, brothers, husbands, wives. Incomings, outgoings. Legitimacy, apparent or otherwise, is the sap which binds us all together, the short-lived and the long-lasting jostling for space.

It is true that history does not relate every relation, but I, Netta, am here:

Janet MacArthur, born 1st January 1920.

As it was for my twin sisters Fern and Bella, and for Angus John, the long-awaited son, my first squalling sight of the world was the upstairs bedroom of our family home of Crois na Coille, a room so low my father could stand up straight only in its centre. Back when there were four of us, Crois na Coille was our broad kingdom: the squat cottage with its whitewashed walls and its meagre rectangle of ground before it, huddled in the lee of the yellow hill.

As children we were taught not to write in books unless

they were school jotters. My siblings and I would situate ourselves upon the insides of the front covers, beneath our names:

Carrabhal School,
Carrabhal,
Argyllshire,
Scotland,
The Earth,
The Milky Way,
Etcetera.

Only lazy scholars use *etcetera*, Miss Grimond would tut. Undeterred, we carried on regardless, just as I insisted on writing with my left hand despite muttered prophecies of deviance and delinquency. We did not think much of Miss Grimond, with her widow's peak, her red running nose and her strange aversion to violence.

When Fern and Bella last opened the Bible, it was to record the death of Angus John, our little brother. There was some mild bickering over whether it was respectful to use biro, and then there was the question of me: of whether to fill the blank space next to my date of birth. A question mark was suggested by Fern but swiftly rejected by Bella. For of all the querulously quick and the definitely dead in this family, I am one whose whereabouts is unknown.

In this uncertain state, I join a motley selection of familial waifs and strays. In the space of a few lifetimes we fade from missing-person mysteries into tales that trail into the unknown. Those who once searched for us pass on. And so some of our endings are lost forever, our beginnings our only legacy: an inked name in an opened book.

Monday 16 March 1998

Fern

Fern MacArthur stoops to strike a match on the back step. She touches the flame to the cigarette held between her creased lips and the tip burns red with her indrawn breath. She shakes the match out and tilts her chin back, sighing smoke. She stares up at the yellow hill.

They had all grown up in its shadow: she and Bella, Netta, Angus John. Fern thinks of the path that winds over the hill, of the caves that hold centuries of stories in their dark mouths. Her brother had known the hill path well. He'd trudged it, knee-deep in winter drifts, stotted bleary-eyed among the whin and gorse during spring lambing, and swaggered over it in late summer to the harvest dance at Altnaglas.

Angus John will always be a boy to Fern, supple-limbed and striding, setting the field-covering pace of his youth. And Netta will always be twenty-six, dark hair on the collar of her pale mackintosh and the scent of Shalimar, the last day Fern saw her.

Latha na beinne: the day of the mountain. One of their father's expressions. Fern had always taken it to mean death, but now she isn't so sure. She'd been reminded of it in the final weeks of her brother's life, as his mind travelled to the places his legs could no longer take him. It is two weeks since Angus John went from being, in Bella's words, 'poorly' to 'very poorly'. He asked for their mother. Bella and Fern kept watch as their brother's life slipped through the cracks in his breath.

Fern sat closest to the door, her twin sister at the head of the bed, her broad, work-swollen fingers encircling Angus John's wrist. The bedside table was piled with large-print Westerns. *Solitude's Lawman* was uppermost, bent sickle-seamed on the top of the stack.

In the final hours Angus John's breathing was ragged, irregular, and when it stopped for some time Bella would look up, whereupon another breath would rasp forth, a low growling rattle. Fern found herself wishing for his final illness to be over almost as strongly as she wished it had never begun. She had to excuse herself three times to stand in the kitchen and wait, her fingers pressing her face.

When it was over, Bella placed her brother's arm back by his side and rose to turn the dark-spotted mirror to the wall. Fern leaned forward to touch Angus John's cheek. His skin was warm and his eyes were closed. Bella hauled the sash window open, and the wind slammed the door shut on the other side of the room.

Bronchial pneumonia, the doctor wrote on the death certificate. Bella took him downstairs at the end of his visit, but Fern remained where she was. She picked up *Solitude's Lawman* from the pile of books and opened it where her brother had left off.

'Those will have to go back to the library van,' Bella said on returning upstairs. She had stood on the threshold of the room, looking in. Their brother had never been late with a library book in his life, and Bella evidently saw no reason to sully his record in death.

That day, the hill had glowed in the gold of deep winter sun. But today the land is pale and betrays nothing. It is an in-between time, spring still hibernating beneath layers of ancient rock. The gorse will come soon.

We only get a certain number of springs, Fern thinks, and this one will be my seventy-fifth, if I'm saved.

Fern doesn't really believe in predestination, not the way her father had, anyway. Without it, he would say, who would be saved? She can still hear his voice to this day, asking his children solemnly, one after the other: *Are you saved? And are you?*

The radio in the kitchen plays out the closing jingle of the weather report. Fern hears a car drawing up, the crunch of footsteps that sets the dogs barking, then a rapping at the front door. She stubs out her cigarette, tucking it behind her ear, and backs into the house, closing the door behind her. She hisses to the dogs to be still. Good news seldom enters in through the front door. Those on social visits know to come around the back.

She hears Bella moving around upstairs. Her sister has set to rearranging every single item in the house, it seems. Today it is the turn of the linen press: each item being re-ironed and refolded and returned to its place. Fern adjusts the combs in her hair, preparing to answer the door. Her sister calls downstairs that it's the postman. Fern makes her way down the corridor, weaving through the fronds of the dogs' tails. She opens the door.

'You're not the usual one,' she says to him.

The usual one would disappear if he turned sideways; this man's square frame is a bristly silhouette in sudden sunlight. Fern has to squint at him in the glare and sidestep into his shadow. He is carrying a parcel a little larger than a shoe box.

'I'm just covering. I do the other side, normally.' The postman taps the box with a thick finger. 'MacArthur?'

'It is.' Fern settles her glasses on her nose and looks down. Handwritten, the label, badly smudged, with no post code. A red and blue sticker bearing the words *Air Canada*. Her heart strikes a blow.

'Been round the houses a bit.' The postman sets his burden down gently on the step. He walks back to his van and drives away with a crunch of gears.

7

Fern stands for a few seconds, staring down at the parcel, at the Canadian postmark from a month ago. She hears the prattle of jackdaws in the rowan tree by the gate, the end of a tune from the radio she can't quite grasp. She stoops and lifts the package, and goes inside.

Bella sits down in the opposite chair. She says nothing. Fern nudges knives and spoons aside with the bottom of the box, placing it in the middle of the table. She turns it to show her sister the label and Bella stops, a spoon dangling from her fingers. They look at each other. Jinky, the orphan jackdaw tamed by their brother, hops from slat to slat on the pulley above their heads. Fern knows Bella's face better than she knows her own, but after all these years living together she finds her sister's expression hard to decipher. She almost looks fearful.

'We'll open it, will we?' Fern says, her voice high and bright, as if humouring a recalcitrant child. She springs into action, delving in a kitchen drawer to unearth 'the scissor', black-handled tailoring shears that belonged to their mother. She makes to hand them to Bella, but Bella shakes her head impatiently, as Fern had known she would – *never pass a blade,* their mother would say, *it'll sever the friendship.* So Fern wields the squeaking shears, sawing through the bindings of tape and cardboard to reveal another box inside. She slits the Sellotape seam of the second box to expose another: sturdy, with a lid which Fern removes.

Inside is a small envelope sitting on top of a folded piece of white cloth. She picks them both out, weighing the softness of the material in her hands. A silk scarf. She looks from the scarf to her sister, expecting to meet her eye, but Bella has turned away to take up a serving spoon and a rag.

Fern sighs, and turns her attention to the envelope. It is heavy, too heavy to contain only paper. She slides her finger under the flap and looks inside before gently shaking out the contents. A small wad of photographs falls and spills out on the table top.

'Bel,' she says, 'would you put down that spoon for a minute?'

The first images are black and white. A bridal party, a formal studio portrait, everyone stiffly arranged on high-backed chairs. Fern stirs the pile with a finger, turning one of the photographs the right way up. Across the table, Bella leans forward. She says nothing.

The picture under Fern's finger shows a young woman with dark hair holding two kittens. It looks windy. Fern strains to see the landscape behind her but it is a wash of grey. Not how she imagined Canada, but she has always found it hard to reimagine black and white photographs in their true colours. She turns it over again in case anything has been written on the back, but there is nothing. When she raises her eyes she sees Bella is looking too, now, and so she moves around the table to stand beside her, gently prodding another picture under her sister's nose. A group in a boat, fishing rods slung over the sides like spider legs. A black dog a blur in the stern. They peer at this one for some time.

'Perhaps,' Bella says at length, in a small voice. 'Perhaps it is her.' She puts down the spoon and wipes her hand down the side of her housecoat.

'There's a note,' Fern says.

With both hands, Bella pushes herself slowly away from the table, her chair squawking backwards on the tiled floor. She turns herself side-on to the table, burying her hands in her lap and leaning over them. Beside her, Bree, the oldest collie, gets to her feet and shakes herself loudly.

Fern watches the dog moving arthritically across the kitchen to slump down in front of the Rayburn with a wheezing sigh. 'Och, Bella,' she says. 'Do you not want to look at this?'

Bella does not move.

It is just a scrap of lined paper; Fern can see that before she unfolds it. She smooths it beneath her fingers.

Dearest Angus John,

I thought you might like to see these. I'd always hoped to return, and tell you about my 'new' life, as it was then. But it would seem that time is against me, and this may be the only way I can.

— As we used to say —

Once more across the water, MacArthur!

The clock on the dresser ticks. Fern realises she still has the scarf tucked in the crook of her arm. She holds it to her face. Powdery and exotic-smelling. The white of her sister Netta's neck in the rain and her cold fingers in Fern's hand as they said their goodbyes. The scent from the little amber bottle, the label gold and blue.

The rest of the melody comes to Fern unbidden. The years unroll as easily as a spool of thread, tangling as they loosen. It is the song they used to crank from the gramophone in the best room, and the words, too:

Pale hands I loved beside the Shalimar
Where are you now? Who lies beneath your spell?

She turns back to the table. 'And where are you now?' she murmurs, scarcely audible even to herself. She looks to the kitchen window as if her long-lost sister Netta might be walking up the path.

Beyond the house, the yellow hill shivers in its thin winter coat. Every mountain has its day.

Tuesday 17 March 1998

Anna

I wake up in my mum's Fiesta with the car keys clenched in my fist. My cheek is squashed against the fabric of the seat and there is a patch of drool on the shoulder of my jacket. The sky is a grey smudge edged by the glow of dawn, so I know it's early, but the dashboard clock hasn't worked for years. I rub my face, feeling the imprint of the upholstery on my skin. I would guess it's about six.

I always used to set my alarm for six when we lived in Beveridge Place. Even though it's been three years since I moved out, I can remember each step in order when I wake every day at the same time: boiling water over a teabag which balloons and falls like a tiny lung, the little rhyme I used to count out Mum's medication before loading everything on to the tray with Elvis and his sneer on it. Then up the stairs, avoiding the creaky boards, the bits where the carpet tacks could snag a bare foot, trying not to spill tea on the King's quiff.

But that was then; neither of us lives like that now. I lean forward to look up at my stepfather's house through the car window, but it's blind to the world: curtains drawn, no lights. Bruce bought this house and moved my mum here when he married her. A smart bungalow, in case her MS gets too bad to manage stairs one day. It's right at the top of the development, looking down the hill on all the neighbours. Knowing my stepfather as I wish I didn't, I expect this only added to the appeal. From up here I can see the town of Barnadine laid out below, a crosshatch of shop fronts and new house builds.

I open my hand. The car keys have left pink and white rivets in my palm. It is attached to a leather fob with a sparkly disc that reads *Life is a Series of Moments Called Now*. Mum used to like all that sort of stuff; the walls of the double upper we shared were covered in reasons to be cheerful. But No. 5 Beveridge Place is a place of the past now, like the caravan before that, and, as of yesterday, the third-floor flat on Killearn Street where Liam Bell and I briefly lived together.

Headlights flare on the wet road in front of the bungalow, and my brother Jamie's battered pickup pulls into view. I stretch and lean forward stiffly to pull the locking peg up and open the Fiesta's door. Getting out of the car, I nearly fall as my legs flood with pins and needles. It was pins and needles that sent Mum to the doctor, all those years ago. Tingling and burning on the tips of everything, she'd said to him: hands, feet, face.

I stalk down the short driveway towards the pickup. When I pass Bruce's new BMW, I grit my teeth and score the tip of the car key all the way along that slick, smug bodywork.

Yesterday afternoon I stood by the sofa and looked down at Liam, asleep on his back. The living room was dim; he rarely bothered to open the curtains. Light from the TV was casting a rippling glow on his face. The remote lay on the floor beside a couple of empty cans.

Bending down, I edged a cushion out from under his curled hand. I held it a couple of inches above his sleeping face, blotting out the light. How easy it would be to press it down and hold it there? I'd probably have to kneel on his arms. I leant over his sleeping body with care and placed the cushion back on the other end of the sofa. I put the note down on top of it and moved quietly from the room and down the corridor.

His fluorescent jacket glimmered by the door. I removed two tenners from the inside pocket, slid them into my jeans and unhooked my coat from the next peg. Then I picked up my bag, opened the door gently and left the flat.

Outside. The late afternoon sun white-gold. The ancient Fiesta, which Mum had given me to bring to Glasgow when she stopped being able to drive, was parked on the other side of the road. The door opened with a creak, shedding rust on to the pavement. Old car smell and the cold night air. I put my hand out to adjust the rear-view mirror. It was shaking. I rubbed my eyes and slammed both hands down on the wheel. On the street in front of me a scraggy cat froze on top of a bin. Something shot out from beneath a sagging pile of bin bags and the cat gave chase.

What a waste, to spend your life chasing a rat as if it were a prize. I am sick of myself.

The engine turned over a few times before it started. There was a tape sticking out of the machine. I poked it back in and music flooded the car: Waylon Jennings in the middle of 'Highwayman'. The tape was so overplayed that the music swelled and faded as if borne aloft on a high wind. I let off the handbrake and pulled away down the dark street, heading west. This time I would not be coming back. I would begin myself again, leaving for the last time.

Jamie's hair is shorter, and he looks to have grown thinner in the face since I last saw him, but most of all he's wearing a suit. And, for some reason known only to himself, sunglasses. Together they look bloody awful but I won't tell him that.

He grins and opens his arms as I walk towards him. I hug him fiercely, one arm around his neck and one under his jacket, wrapped around his ribs.

'You look bloody awful,' he says into my hair.

'And you look like one of the Blues Brothers,' I reply. 'The skinny one.' I lean my forehead into his shoulder. He smells of frying and fags, top notes of Davidoff's Cool Water. As if he were still nineteen. I fight the urge to hold him tighter.

'Hey,' he says. He pries me off, peering into my face, shaking his head. 'Hey. You OK?'

I nod and sniff, holding the back of my hand to my nose. 'Fine.'

Jamie opens the pickup's passenger door and shoos me into the cab. The seats are scattered with newspapers, drink cans and tools.

'See you cleaned up for the occasion.' I shift some menacing-looking pliers and a Styrofoam box filled with old lettuce on to the floor so I can sit down.

'Aye.' He's not really listening, scrubbing at the misty windscreen with his sleeve and squinting through the small space he has cleared. We leave the bungalow behind and he accelerates as the road broadens, winding out over the flat grazing land that surrounds Barnadine. He catches my eye in the mirror. 'So,' he says, 'what was all that about, then.'

'What?' I say, although I know.

Jamie sighs. 'I saw you, getting out of the Fiesta. Did you sleep in there last night?'

I tip my head upside down and pull my fingers through my hair. 'Can we stop at the petrol station? I need to get changed. Brush my teeth.'

'I'm guessing you and Bruce had a barney.'

I say nothing.

'Did you sleep in the car?'

'Nowhere else, was there?'

'Not true,' he says. 'They have an airbed now. They were talking about it last time I was in.'

'Lilo,' I say, lifting my head, and he sniggers.

'Now you are joking me.'

'I wish.'

'*The* lilo?'

16

'The happy holidays lilo,' I say. 'Which leaks.' The lilo dates from one disastrous 'family' holiday to Cyprus not long before Bruce and Mum got hitched.

'You'd think they were trying to tell you something,' Jamie says.

I lean my forehead against the window. 'You would.'

The bungalow's spare bedroom has become Bruce's *home office*, which means he has his brand-new Compaq in one corner and his Scalextric set taking up the entire floor space.

'I'd rather sleep in the car,' I say to Jamie, who is whistling tunelessly through his teeth. Jamie likes to make it clear that he finds the whole me-Mum-Bruce thing petty. Of course he doesn't get it. He wasn't there for those last few years in Beveridge Place, the years when Mum and I muddled along just about coping, before Bruce cruised into her life. Bruce Langlands of the quarry and the fish farm, her saviour in a suit, her beard-netted champion, come to sweep her off her tingly pincushion feet. From that moment on it had been clear there was no place for me in their cosy pairing: my mum, and the man who'd once been Dad's best mate.

I once heard Mum describe my and Bruce's relationship as 'complicated'. But it's not. It's dead simple. I can't stand him.

'Lena, how is Lena?' I ask, stretching back in the seat, feeling my shoulders relax for the first time in twenty-four hours.

'Lena's grand.' He meets my eyes in the mirror and smiles, the smile that always got him out of trouble when we were kids.

Lovely Lena, three years older than me. Lena, who always says exactly what she thinks in her cautious, creative English, who has eyes the colour of aloe vera and wears her silvery blonde hair wrapped around her head in plaits. Lena who rests absent-minded, careful hands on her belly, now, because the youngest member of our family floats inside. I doodle a love heart on the steamed-up glass.

'They might be a redhead.' I picture a toddler with freckles and hair the colour of a pumpkin.

'I hope so,' he says.

'Not many of them in our family.'

'Well, there's always the Prawn, no?'

'Wish you wouldn't call her that,' I say. Ever since Jamie hit the teenage years and refused to call her *Mum* in public, Mary Rose had become *the Prawn*. 'And anyway, she's auburn.'

I picture her sitting at the table yesterday, swishing a spoon through her tea silently, not touching the edges. Never before had I seen her with painted nails.

We're heading out on the high road to Lecknish, and the road is curving up the hill. The Forestry has been felling pines all along this strip, and we both fall silent for a minute. I wonder if he, like me, is thinking about Dad, or the search party, at least: flashlights flickering on ridged tree bark, and the fear of finding what they were looking for. I turn my palms upwards to the growing light. My skin is dry and pale. I try to remember which are the lines for life, heart and fate, but I can't.

Jamie is reaching up, taking something from the flap of the sun visor. 'Here,' he says. He hands me a piece of paper without taking his eyes off the road. 'You might be able to tell me what this is.'

I look. It's his handwriting, or what passes for it, torn from a pad of lined paper. The words are pressed tight on the page in his small, blocked writing.

THE MERCILESS MACDONALD FROM THE WESTERN ISLES OF KERNS AND GALLOWGLASSES IS SUPLIED AND FORTUNE ON HIS DAMMED QUARREL SMILING SHOWED LIKE A REBELS HORE

I think of a school trip to Glasgow, when I was about fourteen. We had been so high up in the theatre that a load of my classmates had complained of vertigo. I'd been seated with a giant pillar in front of me and Ross Fraser behind me making fart sounds and sticking sweetie wrappers to my back.

'You're still boycotting punctuation,' I say.

'Eh?'

'There's an apostrophe in *rebel's*. And you've spelt *whore* wrong. And *supplied*. And *damned*. Eejit.'

'Yeah, yeah.'

'It's Shakespeare. The Scottish play.'

'Ah.'

'You don't know which one that is, do you?'

He shrugs. '*MacRomeo and Juliet*,' he says, and actually laughs. Well, no one else was going to. 'Go on tell us, then. I can see you're dying to.'

'I'm not going to say it.'

'Well.' He pulls into a passing-space to let a post van past; it's been tailgating us for the last five minutes. 'It's the engraving on my latest commission.'

'Hope you spelled it right there, then.' I hold up the page again. 'This thing here.' I point at the symbol. 'The triskele.'

'Tricycle?'

'Triskele.' I'm not actually sure how to pronounce it. I've only seen it written down. 'Do you recognise it?' I ask.

'Nup.'

'Honestly?'

'Och, just tell me,' he says. 'And stop showing off.'

'It's cut into all those rocks up there.' I nod up towards the big hills on our right. 'Those rings and spirals. You know the ones. Like a snake eating its tail. Life and death. Rebirth. Eternal return. They've been there forever.'

'Ah. Druids,' he intones, in his Spinal Tap voice. He brakes for a bend. '*In ancient times . . . hundreds of years before the dawn of history . . .*'

I sigh. 'You're going to do the whole thing, aren't you.'

He is staring straight ahead. '*. . . lived an ancient race of people. The Druids.*' He leans back, smirking, before lurching forwards. '*No one knows who they were. Or . . . what they were doing.*'

'Cut!' I look down at the paper once more before folding it up and putting it on his lap. 'Good for you, though. Another sword in the bag.'

Jamie grins. 'In the scabbard, you mean.'

'You'll be kitting out an army of medieval re-enactment weirdos soon enough.'

'In my dreams. But that's the plan, aye.' He tucks the paper back under the visor. 'Need more commissions like this one, I'm telling you. Got to replace this old shagger before it falls apart on me once and for all.' He taps the pickup's steering wheel, nods towards the radio. 'Anyhow. Shall we see what's on the airwaves this fine morning?'

On the radio Morrissey is singing 'Sweet and Tender Hooligan'. We throw our heads back to squall along at the tops of our voices. *In the midst of life we are in death, etcetera, etcetera, etcetera.* Jamie turns up the dial, shouts at me over the music, shaking his head. 'Debt.'

'It's death!' I protest. An ongoing debate.

'Definitely debt.'

'Both, then.'

'Oh, and happy birthday for last week by the way,' Jamie says. 'Meant to send you a card but didn't know the address of your halls.'

'Doesn't matter,' I mumble. I hunch down in my seat to unzip my bag, pretending to look for something. He doesn't know about Killearn Street; no one does apart from me and

Liam. It was Liam who wanted to keep it that way. And because I am a pathetic excuse for a person, I let him make up all sorts of reasons as to why this was.

Etcetera etcetera, etcetera. Twenty-one, I think, young enough to hope for your time again twice over. Old enough to die young, like Liam's brother Barry last summer. Old enough to know better, as his sisters said to me after his funeral, those three permed, pale Furies afloat on dark grief, sucking down the Bacardi in more or less perfect unison.

I don't ask Jamie to stop but he does anyway, as I knew he would, in the wide layby at the foot of the hill. He switches off the engine and cranes across me, peering upwards.

'Well, she's still there,' he says.

The caravan sags about fifty metres from the road, as yellow as an old toenail. In front of it, on levelled ground, a rickle of weed-encrusted blocks mark the foundations that Dad laid for the house he never quite built. A jumble of crates, buoys and broken creels are scattered in the field beyond, poking through the tussocks of grass and rushes. The rusted skeleton of the shed he used for the cars is the same colour as the dead bracken, and looks as if it has become one with the land.

'Will we?' I ask, and he nods.

We walk up the hill side by side, not speaking. The air is quiet, broken only by the mewing of a buzzard somewhere high and far.

The caravan door is padlocked.

'Remember the bathroom window?' I say. 'Might still be slidey.'

It is. The Perspex is ingrained with bright green mould but slips out of the frame just as it used to. I scramble through and the whole structure shakes as I stumble to find my feet. This place; this land of before.

'Anna! Christ's sake. You'll take the whole place down.' My brother hasn't followed me; he's already inside.

'How the heck did you get in?' I ask in dismay.

'Welcome to the workstation.' He weighs the padlock and key in his hand.

'You locked it? You've been working here?'

'In a fashion,' he says. 'Need somewhere, don't I?'

'But—' I stop. Where to even start? 'We'd best not stay long.'

He moves ahead of me. 'Just a minute. I've the dirk to pick up. The commission I was telling you about. I'm due to hand it over tonight, after the funeral.'

I follow him, careful where I put my feet, feeling the creak and give of the floor as I tread on it. A tin of Swarfega teeters by the twisted sink. I wonder if it was Dad's. I can still remember the mineral smell of it, the way it left your hands bleached and dry as chamois.

'Sorted.' Jamie's voice floats through from the other end of the caravan, where he's standing by the big window holding a Woolworth's bag.

'Let's see it, then,' I say, but he shakes his head.

'I don't want to show it to anyone till I hand it over. It's bad luck, Macbeth.'

I make a face at him and he puts his palm to the wall panels that droop like wet cardboard. 'It'll be wrecked soon, this place,' he says. 'One more bad winter will do it. Fucking waste.'

I look into the second bedroom. There is a pile of ashes on the red-carpeted floor. 'Did you have a fire in here?' I point, incredulous.

'Yeah, right, Anna.' He comes up behind me. 'That's been there since last summer. Yooves.'

'We were youths not so long ago,' I say.

'Remember how we used to say we'd burn it down, build the house?'

22

'Wonder why we didn't.'

Mum is especially frightened of fire. One night, years ago when the caravan was still *home*, we'd been driving over the hill, just the two of us, and seen thick smoke gathered in the sky over the ridge. She had started forward over the steering wheel with a cry. Oh, my God, she'd said. He's finally done it. He's set the whole bloody thing ablaze.

But when we arrived the caravan was unharmed. It was just Dad and a few of his Forestry pals standing around a burning boat on the other side of the road. He'd taken Mum in his arms and danced her slowly around the flaming pyre, and he'd sung 'Ring of Fire'.

When Dad died, Mum had him cremated.

I go to the seat beneath the window and kneel gingerly on the mildew-specked cushions. The view from up here sweeps down to the sea and it is still magnificent. Dad got the plot from Jerome Mondegrene, owner of the Altnaglas estate. He had all sorts of plans for the house, but they never got further than some taut lines of twine and a few blocks on the ground in front of the caravan.

Jamie sits down beside me, runs his thumbnail along the windowpane's dirty seam. 'Anna,' he says at length. 'I want to show you something.'

'Yeah? What?'

He lays a Polaroid photo down on the table in front of us. The first thing I see is the girl. You can't not see her: she blazes out of the picture despite the dodgy exposure. Permed blonde hair glimmering in the light of the flash, lots of skin on show. Breasts unfeasibly large for her slim frame, barely contained by a halterneck top. She is sitting forward on a sofa, her head tipped sideways and nestled into a man's neck.

The man is our dad. He is lean-faced, handsome, half turned from the camera as if someone has just called his name.

His arm is around the girl. He's wearing a blue shirt with the sleeves rolled up. I remember that shirt, how it felt against my cheek.

'Where did you get this?' I say.

Jamie drums his fingers on the table. 'Bruce.' He looks at me, then taps the photo. 'What do you think?'

I stare at him. 'I'm seeing what you're seeing. It's a picture of Dad with some stranger.'

'I wish I hadn't seen it,' he says.

'You haven't shown this to Mum, have you?'

'Christ, no.'

'Do you think Bruce would've?'

'Don't think so. I know you think he's a walloper but he thinks the world of her. And they were pals, him and Dad.'

'Why would he want to give it to you?'

'We were talking, the other night. About, you know, me becoming a dad and that. We'd had a few. I was asking him – I don't know, just some stuff about Dad. Bruce thought he had some photos, but . . . when he looked it was just this one he could find. Said he didn't know where it came from.'

I look down at the photo again despite myself. 'It's a party or something, is it?' There are a few figures standing to the left of the sofa but I don't recognise any of the blurry faces.

'Dunno.' Jamie takes the photo from me, lifts it to his face.

'I hate it,' I say.

Jamie puts it down again, taps one of the shadowy figures near Dad and the girl. 'Know who this is?'

'Who?'

'That's Jerome Mondegrene. That's who I'm delivering the dirk to, tonight.' Jamie indicates the bag beside him. 'Small world, eh?' He blows air through puffed cheeks.

I shake my head. 'We both know Dad wasn't exactly a saint. I wouldn't read too much into it. And I think I know what we can do with this.'

I pick up the photo and Jamie doesn't stop me as I tear it in half, splitting the pair apart, and then into quarters. I wedge the pieces into an empty Coke can, crush the can flat and put it into my pocket.

'There.' I feel the need to wipe my hands down the front of my parka. 'Now. Have you everything you need?'

'Yeah.' He sounds glum. I watch him as he picks the seal on the window again, peers out through the murky glass. I can tell there is something else on his mind.

'Is there something else?' I ask.

He turns back from the window, looks up at me like a wee boy. 'I'm sorry for showing you that,' he says.

'It's fine.' My voice sounds brisker than I feel. 'Let's get out of here.'

He doesn't move, not yet. He looks out of the window. 'It gets to me sometimes, you know? Not because of Dad, but what it means for me, I suppose. For the future. How do you be a dad?' His eyes flick up but don't quite meet mine. 'Our dad was – well, in the end, he was kind of shit, wasn't he? And I don't want to be shit, Anna.' He sighs. 'It's not like he didn't try. I know that. It was like . . . he tried too hard. Always knocking his pan in for this, that or the other. For – well, for fuck all, really.'

'Don't say that.'

'Aye, well it's true, isn't it?' He gestures around the caravan. 'Living here, the four of us all jammed in, not that we cared at the time, you and me, but . . . kids don't, do they? It's later you look back, you remember. He just never got the finger out, did he? All his dreams and charm and Mum loved him, I know she did, but it was like she just lost the will, in the end. To keep believing in him. And she was probably right.' Jamie sighs, tugs at his shirt collar. 'So I just keep thinking, waiting on our wee one to be born, will I really be that different? What if these things are, I dunno, in the blood?

25

Bound to repeat themselves, like the tricycle thing you were telling me about, that I've engraved on to this.' He holds the bag containing the dirk aloft. 'Eternal return, wasn't that what you said?'

'No,' I say firmly. 'That's not the way things are. It's certainly not the way they have to be. You work for yourself, and you work hard. You and Lena have your flat; in a few years you'll be able to get somewhere bigger. You'll be an amazing father when the time comes. All the good bits of Dad, without the . . .' I hesitate. 'Without the mess,' I say in the end. 'He was always working for someone else, wasn't he? Under someone else's thumb. You're not like that. You just keep going as you are. You stand on your own two feet.' I nudge him off the bench. 'Come on.'

'Aye.' He stands up. 'You're probably right, Anna.' He doesn't sound quite convinced.

'I am. Now scoot. We've got somewhere we need to be. You can't be late to a funeral.'

'Right enough.' He slides his eyes sideways at me, the hint of a smirk. 'Better late than dead on time.'

'Not funny.' I swing on my heel, as delicately as I can to avoid going through the floor, and we exit, through the door this time, Jamie replacing the padlock with a click.

On the drive to the church we don't talk very much. We stop at the petrol station and I manage to change and wash my face in the tiny toilet. Jamie buys fuel and a chocolate bar for me, but the first bite adheres itself tackily to the roof of my mouth, making me feel sick, and he ends up eating most of it. I drink bottled water and we listen to the radio. I find my thoughts drifting to Liam, to him waking up in the flat next to the envelope I left for him, and then, to stop thinking about that, I think about yesterday evening, when I arrived at Bruce's bungalow in the Fiesta.

'You know you're welcome to stay with us, here,' Mum said. 'You know that, don't you, Anna?' She was leaning on the door handle, watching as I hunted through my old chest of drawers, searching for something dark to wear to the funeral. There was a note of pleading in her voice.

I said nothing, running a pair of black tights through my hands. She sighed and turned to make her way back to the kitchen. I wedged a dress into my bag and followed her.

In the kitchen a breeze was blowing through the open window and Mum was juggling a carton of milk, a stick and a cigarette.

'Thought you'd stopped that.' I took the milk from her and topped up the two mugs of tea on the countertop.

'Ah, milk's never done anyone any harm.' She snatched a drag of her cigarette, turning her head away to blow smoke out of the window before stubbing it out. I had almost forgotten the way she could make me feel like a fussy old woman and a perverse teenager at the same time. A knack all of her own. I watched her raise her mug carefully towards her lips, blowing tiny tidelines across the top of her tea. The mug was emblazoned with the words *Be strong. You are never alone.* I wondered how those statements were connected.

I excused myself to go to the pink-tiled bathroom, and on my way back to the kitchen I heard the sound of a car outside and then Bruce's voice in the kitchen. I lurked in the hallway. Mum's voice was low, Bruce's not so much.

'No, she's not staying,' Mum was saying. 'She's going down to Crois na Coille to stay with Fern and Bella.'

I heard Bruce grunt, and Mum say something I didn't catch, and then Bruce's voice again, louder. 'For pity's sake,' he was saying. 'She needs to get a job, or do *something*, instead of playing house with old wifies in the back of beyond. She'll just keep drifting, Rosie,' he said.

27

I hated that he called her *Rosie*, as if she was a sodding Cabbage Patch kid. Her name was Mary Rose. When had she become so passive? When Bruce bought her the house, the physiotherapy treatments? Or back when he had first asked her out to dinner and ordered her meal for her?

'First the job at the council. Then the care home. Then nursing. I even offer her the chance to work in the office, but that's not good enough either.'

I took a deep breath. There was no point in hiding, so I moved down the corridor.

'It's yourself.' Bruce stood in the kitchen doorway.

I looked past him, to the kitchen table where Mum was stirring another cup of tea. 'Excuse me.' I stepped forward.

He moved aside a fraction. 'Anna.' His voice was thick with the tone of patient reasoning I can't abide, freighted with sham warmth. 'Will you not just stay with us for a few days?' He knew fine I'd heard all he had to say already. 'I can get someone to show you the ropes in the office,' he carried on. 'We could do with a hand.'

I shook my head, kept moving, not looking at him. My bag was by the door. If I could just reach it, I could get out of here without a fight. Jamie says I spoil for a brawl whenever Bruce and I are together, but this isn't so. I avoid them; he enjoys them.

'Here,' he said. His voice changed, as I knew it would. 'Look at me. I'm speaking to you. It's polite to reply when someone's talking to you.'

I turned, fixed my eyes on his ferrety eyebrows. 'I'd rather wipe arses than work in your shitey fish factory,' I said.

He said nothing, just shook his head, drawing in his breath sharply as if appalled, and started to chunter on about manners and respect for the family. Bruce dislikes swearing around women. He'll actually say *sugar* not *shit*.

'Listen to yourself,' I said, when I'd heard enough. 'You're not Don Corleone.'

'Anna.' My mum, sounding a weary note from the table. I'd let her down once again. I pounced on my bag and edged out into the corridor.

'Anna,' Bruce called. My name was certainly getting bounced off the walls this evening. 'Come back here.'

I pulled the door closed. 'Piss off,' I said to the carpet.

Outside the house I walked down the driveway, unsure of what to do. I thought about calling Jamie, but I knew he'd be working. Slowly, I stood up, feeling in my pocket for the Fiesta's keys.

Feeling lonely and foolish, I walked back up the drive, quietly, and opened the car door. I climbed in and sat in the driver's seat, breathing deeply. It wasn't as if I could go anywhere. That arsehole had boxed me in.

Cars line the road for half a mile either side of the church. Jamie finds a space to park and we join the straggling lines of mourners making their way to the service.

I feel small and cold in my black dress and Barely Black tights, purchased earlier under the watchful eyes of Maggie Gilmour who would have known fine well what day it was. They call Maggie 'the Bleep'; she beams gossip around the village as if by satellite.

Bruce's BMW is parked close to the church wall and Jamie and I hover awkwardly in the graveyard while Bruce helps Mum into the church. One of the car's back tyres is bulging against a sunken tombstone. I silently apologise to the late Ebenezer Campbell (departed this life April 22nd 1761, *Memento Mori*).

The air in the packed church is heavy with mothballs and lilies. We sit near the back, Jamie and I. People in front of us swivel around to check on who is coming in.

The minister's fuchsia lipstick transgresses the boundaries of her actual lips. As soon as she begins to speak, I can tell that

29

this won't be the sort of service that celebrates my great-uncle Angus John's life, but one which asks which sinner will be next. I wonder how Fern and Bella will feel about that. I fix my eyes on the war memorial plaque on the wall above my head and count the number of MacArthurs.

The wind lifts hair and clothing as we file outside for the burial after the service. I can't remember the last time I wore a dress; I struggle to keep hold of its hem as it billows above my knees.

I will lift up my eyes unto the hills, from whence cometh my help. When the minister commits Angus John down into the earth I feel the press of tears, and tilt my head back to watch rooks and ravens making noisy, ragged circles in the gap of grey sky above us.

Jamie is on my left, studying his grazed knuckles as he pleats them into some vague shape of a prayer. Next to him, I can see the rubber end of Mum's stick and beyond that, the large shiny toes of Bruce's black brogues. With a glimmer of satisfaction, I note that my stepfather is standing in a small puddle.

Earth scattering on wood, the croak and whoop of crows, the promise of rain, and the service is at last at an end. My great-aunts Fern and Bella are positioned by the church door to shake each mourner's hand in turn.

'I think we've had the best of the day,' mutters Fern. She holds my hand in both of hers and casts a suspicious look heavenwards. The proper rain begins as the mourners pile back into cars or start the long walk back up the road. Most are making for the bar of the Tayfillan Hotel, intent on measuring out Angus John's long years in short glasses.

I avoid Mum and Bruce on the way out, brushing my hand gently against Ebenezer Campbell's stone nestled crookedly in the nettles. The plush of moss is dense beneath my fingertips. *Memento Mori.* Not much chance of forgetting, certainly not today.

The saloon bar of the Tayfillan is heaving, talk rippling in waves. I try to breathe through my nose as I wait my turn at the crowded bar. The steamy air is laden with the contesting odours of sandwiches, spirits, cigarettes and damp clothing, threatening to turn my already queasy stomach. By the time I thread my way back from the bar with a glass in each hand, the table where I left Jamie is empty. Through the small window beside my chair I can see him out in the car park, bending his face over what I imagine is a flame cupped behind another man's hand. The two of them are huddled out of the rain beside the cab of the pickup. I know for a fact my brother doesn't even smoke, unless it's an excuse to escape awkward social situations.

I sit. I sniff the top of my drink but don't drink it, and stare over the rim of the glass to the bar, where what is left of my family are gathered. Bruce is droning on to a local building contractor with cauliflower ears. Beside him, Mum has propped herself against a bar stool, neither quite sitting nor standing, like a jazz singer. Only one stick with her today, and beautiful still: her thick hair the colour of dried blood with only a glint or two of grey around the roots. She is sipping what looks like soda and lime. Her face is arranged into the careful kind of blankness adopted when walking past some- one making a scene in the street. I think, briefly, about going over and putting my arms around her, just letting the thought slide through my mind, knowing I won't.

I'm about to rap on the whorled glass to get Jamie's atten- tion when I hear my name called and turn to see Fern coming towards me, her arms outstretched, a cigarette in one hand and a small glass of stout in the other. I step forward into her arms and hug her, the usual impression of embracing a birdcage. She is wearing black like the other mourners, but then she always does. I can see the comb furrows in her raked-back hair.

We sit down at the table. I mumble my condolences again and Fern leans across the table towards me. She flexes her fingers over mine, her skin dry and calloused, cool as a bird claw. She says how pleased she is to see me.

'It's good to see you too,' I say, and feel again the small spike of tears. I'd forgotten how the pupil of Fern's right eye isn't quite round, but spreads a little into the faded blue iris, like spilled ink.

She asks how things are and I tell her fine, thanks. I don't want to talk about myself and it seems silly to ask how she is, so instead we talk about Angus John. I learnt about seven types of knot from him, I tell her. And I remember him always turning up with fish, and watching *The Searchers* and *Rio Bravo* with him and his dog Mac on rainy afternoons while he drank tea and darned his own socks.

'Always good with a needle,' Fern sighs. 'They teach you that, in the navy.' She smiles at me, lifts my hand and brings it back down to the table with a gentle thump, as if putting a stopper in the subject. 'And now.' Her voice shifts, business-like. 'Anna. If your offer still stands to help us out, with his things, we'd be very grateful.'

'Yes,' I say. 'I want to. If there's room for me.'

'Always!' Fern nods. 'Well. We'll find room, of course. Although, that does bring me to something I wanted to tell you.' She leans forwards. 'You may have heard me talking of William Croke, the folklore collector who visited us many moons ago, when Bella and I were just scraps of girls. He wrote down our mother's stories.'

I tell her I think I do. In truth Fern has mentioned him almost every time we have spoken recently.

'Aye,' she says. 'Willie Croke.' She smiles as she says his

name again. 'Hadn't heard from him for years. But he wrote to me when he heard about Angus John. He was hoping to make it today, only there was some conference in Dublin, he was giving the keynote speech – of course he retired years ago, but in name only, it would appear. Anyway.' Fern squeezes my hand tightly. 'This is the thing, Anna. He's visiting us. He'll be coming to stay.' She lets go of my hand, sits back with a giggle that veers into a cackle and takes a sip from her glass although there's nothing but foam left in the bottom. Her eyes flicker to the bar and back to me. 'Tomorrow!' she says.

'Tomorrow,' I echo lamely.

'That's right,' she says. 'And not just him. He's bringing a young man with him. A – whatchamacallit – a *protégé*.'

I raise my eyebrows politely and feel my heart begin to sink.

'Aye.' Fern taps the back of my hand meaningfully as if delivering Morse code. 'A young man from Ireland. A rising star in his field, apparently. Brains. A musician, too, I believe. Willie was waxing lyrical about him. A real chip off the old block, he was saying. He's completed his PhD on – ah, I can't remember, something to do with *sean-nós* singing, or was it cows . . .' She breaks off, shakes her head. 'Ach, the old memory deserts me. But here's the thing. He's writing a book about the professor, this young lad. And so they're going on a field trip of sorts, I suppose. Retracing the professor's steps all those years ago. And you know this, Anna? Willie said that top of his list of places to visit was Crois na Coille. The things that man can remember about our mother, about his time with our family, when we were young. He must have a mind like an encyclopaedia. Anyway. As I was saying, this young man's not much older than you, I shouldn't think. A fine musician. All-Ireland champion. We'll be in for a treat. And you never know, eh, Anna? You just never know.'

'Mm,' I mumble. We've been here before; I have a suspicion that Fern's idea of 'not much older than you' will mean pushing forty, and 'brains' will doubtless equal the social skills of a guinea pig. I smile at her over-zealously to hide my dismay. I had been thinking of Crois na Coille as I remember it, when Jamie and I used to visit as children. Not exactly visit, in fact – boarded out. For us it was always a house of holidays, of freedom from school. And I would have a job to do, this time, helping my great-aunts sort through Angus John's possessions. I'd looked forward to a place devoid of strangers with whom it would be necessary to make small talk, to be polite, to trot out the same old spiel when they enquired what I'd been doing, what my plans were *next*. Playing host to an aged academic and his earnest understudy had not been part of this vision.

Even as I'm thinking this, I feel the pinch of my selfishness. What right do you have, says the irritatingly virtuous big sister in my head, to expect to have them all to yourself? Rarely do Fern and Bella accept help with anything, and yet, when I'd mentioned letting me know if they needed a hand clearing Angus John's house, they'd jumped at the offer with such enthusiasm and gratitude that I knew this really was a big deal to them.

'Looking forward to it,' I lie. I imagine us sitting around in the evening, the professor asking questions I'd need a dictionary to answer while a bespectacled cardigan aficionado drones interminable ballads with his finger in his ear.

Fern beams, then looks up suddenly, to where her name is being called from the bar by a small man in a paint-splashed boiler suit I hadn't seen at the funeral.

'Give me a minute, Anna.' She winks at me, pats my hand as she stands up.

'Is she alright?' It's Jamie, appearing at my right shoulder as if from nowhere, wolfish in step with a sheepish grin. Always

34

approach from the right, he used to say to me, when we were small and sneaky.

I nod and push his pint across the table.

'You're going to stay with them, then,' he says. His voice points down at the end of the sentence, a statement not a question.

'Planning to.'

'You should. Get out of the rut.'

'It's not a rut,' I say flatly. I take a sip of tepid orange juice that makes my throat shudder.

'It's not like you can't stay with us,' he says. 'Any time. It's just—'

'No, God no. It's far too tiny, your flat. And you two have enough coming your way. Honestly. It's fine, Jamie.'

We sit in silence for a minute. I try not to let myself stray into the spare bits of other people's conversations all around us. 'It's weird being back,' I say. 'I could *hear* them staring, in the church.'

Jamie lets out a snort of laughter. 'Ach, try living here.' He drains his pint and looks up at a girl passing our table with a tray, nods to her. 'Lovely. Cheers.' He takes two sausage rolls from the tray, putting them both in his mouth together. Then he turns his head, chewing, and scans the room before leaning closer to me.

'You know what I was thinking about in there, in the church?' he says. 'Bella's stories. Remember? All the old stuff like that?'

'Stuff like that, yes.'

'Some of those stories. Scared the living crap out of us, didn't they? This is the one I was thinking of.' Jamie swallows, stares up at the ceiling. He's cut himself shaving the underside of his chin. 'That one where the wee girl's on her own in the house,' he says, 'and her grandfather's corpse is outside trying to get in through the door.'

'*Grandfather is rising*,' I say. 'Yeah, I remember.'

'That was it!' Jamie snaps his fingers and the girl with the tray is over to us in a flash. Sandwiches, this time. Jamie laughs and looks shamefaced. 'Sorry. Wasn't – summoning you. But I will, thanks. Want one, Anna?' He waves a squashed-looking triangle at me. 'Ham.'

'Tempting, but no, thanks.' I take another sip of my juice and my mouth fills with saliva. I put the glass down. 'I hate this stuff.'

'Why did you order it, then?' Jamie gives me a quizzical look. 'Vodka-orange, is it?'

I shake my head. 'Just orange.'

'Not drinking, no?'

'No.' I turn my eyes away from his quizzical look.

'Not pregnant, are you?'

'Bloody hell, Jamie.' I sit bolt upright. 'Someone's not having a drink so they must be up the duff?'

'Alright, Anna.' He shakes his head at me, makes downward motions with his hands. 'Keep your hair on. I was only joking.'

'It's not funny.' I push my chair back and stand up. 'Back in a minute. Got to pee.'

Jamie nods, scanning the room beyond me.

The saloon bar is contained within an ugly flat-roofed extension but the rest of the hotel is Victorian, built for the visitors who came here to shoot and fish. I haven't been in since I worked here for a few brief months, the summer I turned sixteen. Both Mum and Dad worked here in the sixties, Dad ghillying on the loch and serving behind the bar, Mum waitressing. It was where they met.

I go straight past the toilets and find myself in the broad entrance hall. There's no one about; I climb the stairs that lead to the bedrooms, resting my hand on the polished banister. Somewhere I can hear a radio and the hum of a hoover. There's a scent of fish and chips drifting from the kitchens as

I go higher, looking for the picture that Dad always used to take us to see.

It's a small photograph in a blue frame. The colours are a little garish – Kodachrome, I remember my dad telling me. He is a young man in a flat cap holding an enormous salmon. His right hand supports the fish under its tail, his left cradles the long, sinuously bulging body beneath its gigantic gills. He stands next to two older men, both of whom are wearing plus-fours, with pipes in their mouths. On his other side there is another young man about the same age as him, thicker-set. Only my dad, the salmon-bearer, is unsmiling. His expression is almost reverent.

I realise with a shock that I'm now older than he was when the picture was taken. The script below the photograph reads: *Record Salmon at Loch Leck. Landed by Jerome Mondegrene, Esq. Weight 51lb. 42 inches long and 18½ inches in girth. Largest rod-caught salmon on record at Loch Leck, 15th of June 1959. Also in attendance, Maj. I. Saltcoats, Hotel Proprietor.*

No mention of Donnie MacArthur, the lowly ghillie. I lean forward to look more closely at my dad's face: his dark features and the firm set to his jaw distinct beneath the cap. *Such a good-looking man*, I have often heard people say, sometimes wistful, sometimes wry.

The salmon's face is ancient, something palaeontological in those flat planes and curves. It is as if the proximity of boy and fish are just a trick of the light, a film figment captured in a second. Dad's image in the Polaroid Jamie showed me in the caravan, taken over twenty years later, slides into my mind like an opening drawer. I mentally shove it closed.

A squeak of noise behind me makes me turn around. A small girl with plaits like a pretzel is standing in the middle of the corridor, grinning at me.

'Hello,' I say.

She stares wordlessly for a minute. She is perhaps five or six years old. Suddenly she dodges forward and nudges my hip, none too gently. 'Hide and seek!' she squeals. 'You're it! Cover your eyes and count to ten!' And she's off, scampering down the corridor and up the stairs at the end, turning around once to shout, 'No cheating!'

I count to ten, quietly, and then walk slowly to the end of the corridor, back past Dad and the giant fish. I can imagine it's a good place for hide and seek; I'd have thought the same as a child. But now I look around and see a building full of hazards, steep drops and places a small person could get trapped and never be found.

I call out, in a low voice. 'Who else is playing, sweetheart? I've got to go.'

Nothing. I stop and listen. I pace the corridor for a minute, and then shout, more loudly, 'I'm going now,' and take the stairs down the other side of the landing. As I do, I hear running feet on the floor above and expect to see her appearing, but nothing, just quietness again, and so I make my way downstairs. I put my hand up to my breastbone, pushing my fingers into the triangular space at the apex of my ribcage. Oh, God.

Back in the bar I find Jamie keen to be off. We search out Fern and Bella, to say goodbye.

'But you'll be coming soon, Anna?' Fern has moved on to whisky. She takes my left hand; Bella reaches out and takes the other. 'Come down tonight,' Fern is saying. 'Why not?'

'Is it not . . .' I look around, the other funeralgoers dispersing '. . . a bit soon?'

Jamie absent-mindedly picks up another sausage roll from a discarded tray and takes a bite.

'Not at all.' Fern presses my hand. 'Seize the moment. We could all be gone tomorrow.' She's definitely had a few.

'Great,' I say, out loud. 'Lovely. Thank you.' I turn to Jamie. 'Would you be OK to take me down on your way off?'

'Where's your stuff?' he asks.

'All in this bag.'

'Light enough to travel.' Fern nods approvingly. She squeezes my hand and I squeeze back and smile brightly, thinking how weighed down I feel.

Jamie

The car park was slick with water. Jamie parked and sat looking through the wet glass of the pickup's window. The dirk lay on the passenger seat in a plastic bag. He leaned over and picked it up, tucking the bundle inside his jacket. Then he opened the door.

Bruce's BMW was parked at the far end. Jamie felt raindrops trickling from his hair on to the exposed skin on the back of his neck. He took the car park in three strides with his head down and put his shoulder to the double doors of the Balsterrick Care Home.

The doors swung open into a reception papered in aggressive florals, but it was the smell of the place that hit him first: institutional disinfectant and yesterday's mashed potato.

His stepfather was striding down the gaudy corridor towards him. Like Jamie, Bruce was still in the suit he had worn to the funeral that afternoon.

'Here he is, boys, here he is!' Bruce was announcing to no one in particular. He smoothed his hair back with a hand the size of a dinner plate.

'Thanks for coming,' Jamie said.

'My pleasure, lad.' Bruce slapped his shoulder. 'Let's be seeing it, then, eh? Didn't forget to bring the thing, I hope.' He gave a taut little chuckle.

The residents' sitting room area could be seen through the half-open door in front of them, done up for the occasion with purple streamers. Jamie unbuttoned his jacket and took out the bag.

'A Woolworth's bag.' His stepfather cocked an eyebrow.

'Yeah, well. Raining, isn't it?' Jamie unwrapped the plastic.

Even beneath the hallway's muted lamps, the dirk's blade shimmered. Bruce bent his head over it and Jamie twisted the weapon slightly, edge-on to the light so his stepfather could better take in the malachite-set hilt, the slim, double-fullered blade. Everyone looks at a knife or a sword face-on, Duncan Robertson had told him, in his workshop off Edinburgh's Royal Mile. Don't you be doing that. Look at it from the side, to get the measure of it. The edge, the taper.

Bruce clapped a hand on Jamie's shoulder again. 'Well, there's it, now,' he said. 'Very nice, aye. Must say, thought it would be a bit – eh – bigger. Funny, that.' He beamed as if bestowing a compliment. 'Should make the old boy happy, eh?'

It wasn't really a question. Bruce was already moving on, towards the reception desk. 'Right we are,' he was saying. 'Grand. I'll just let them know we're here.' He slammed a palm down on the desk bell and raised his voice to a bellow. 'We're here!'

They waited until a stout woman appeared and told them that if they wouldn't mind taking a seat they'd be shown in as soon as everything was ready. When she left, she closed the door to the residents' living room behind her.

They sat. Jamie placed the dirk in its leather scabbard on his lap and put his hands on his knees, palms down. Bruce's brogues jigged on the linoleum. There were muffled squawks and scrapes from the room beyond. Bruce whistled the first phrase of 'Colonel Bogey' through his teeth, three times over, and then, mercifully, fell silent.

Waiting, thought Jamie. My life's a bloody waiting room at the moment. He folded his arms: clad in black polyester, they looked so unfamiliar he could almost make himself believe they belonged to someone else. One of the Blues Brothers, Anna had said. He'd phone her tomorrow, he told himself, see how she was getting on at Crois na Coille with the great-aunties, where he'd dropped her earlier.

It was bloody roasting in here. He ran two fingers around his collar to loosen it. The shirt was on the tight side of fitted and the suit was definitely too big, especially across the chest. Trying the suit on early that morning, Jamie had had his reservations, but Lena had insisted he looked *very handsome*. She had brushed him down with Sellotape wrapped around her fingers.

Lena would have been with him today, but her mother had been visiting from Vilnius and Lena was going to the airport to see her off. Jamie had found Ugne's visit akin to holding in a fart: there were only so many tea rooms and shopping trips to Mothercare that could distract her from fussing around their tiny flat folding things and tutting into overflowing cupboards. Originally she had planned to stay for the baby's birth, only three weeks away now, but Lena's father was having a hip replacement around the same time, so she was flying home today.

'She says you have been born in a trolley-bus,' Lena had informed Jamie when he had asked what Ugne was muttering, before adding helpfully, 'It is because you are never closing doors behind you.' Lena spoke English emphatically, as if she found the smooth edges of more conventional conversation slightly absurd.

'You can tell her I was born in a Swift mobile home, if that explains things,' Jamie had said, to which Lena had not replied. Jamie sometimes wondered who Lena was when she spoke in Lithuanian, her native language, but guessed he might never find out. Languages were not his strong suit.

It had been ten minutes now and still no sign of the double doors opening. The jiggle in Bruce's left foot had spread to his right and Jamie gritted his teeth. Christ, he thought. How much longer? He inspected his nails, wondered if he had time to take a piss.

He wished he could have shown the dirk to Angus John before he died. It was his great-uncle who had sparked his interest in all this. When Angus John was a child, he had found two eighteenth-century swords wrapped and hidden within an old stone wall. One had been claimed by Sir Kenneth Mondegrene, who owned the land where they were found, but Angus John had kept the other, and kept it secret for some years. As an adult, he'd thought he'd better come clean about the find, but by that time Sir Kenneth had been dead for years and the land had long since been sold to the Forestry Commission. Jerome Mondegrene, Sir Kenneth's heir, had made gracious overtures about allowing the finder to keep his find, and Angus John had even written a piece for the local paper concerning the discovery.

Jamie had been ten years old when his great-uncle had shown him the sword for the first time. A basket-hilted back sword, he'd said. It had a single-edged blade like a slim knife. The leather wrapping was still intact on the handle. There were tiny hearts and circles cut out of the hilt and the blade had been etched with delicate swirls, now rubbed and worn. A Jacobite sword, Angus John went on. Hidden here after Culloden, perhaps, but by whom, God only knew. This was Campbell country. He'd offered it to Jamie to hold, and Jamie could remember distinctly the lightness, the balance. The beauty.

That sword was now in Jamie's possession, and had become his object of study. With Duncan Robertson's help he'd learned to make broadswords, rapiers, claymores and dirks: five pieces to date. This was his sixth.

The door to the residents' room opened. Finally. A lumpy man in a purple shirt and tie introduced himself as the manager and ushered them in. The chairs were arranged in a horseshoe shape. At the far end of the room there was a long table laid with platters of food and glasses. Jamie was reminded of the funeral he'd just come from, and had the distinct impression that today had been in the wrong order.

Big band music played a little too loudly and there was a rumble of chat; he thought he could hear someone hooting softly like a wood pigeon. He and Bruce stood awkwardly near the table. Jamie felt awkward, at least. He eyed the sandwiches and wished they could get on with it.

And then, at the other end of the room, a second door clicked open and a tall, heavy-set man in a dark suit stepped into the room. He was followed by the woman from reception, who indicated one of the spare seats, but the man took up a stance near the back of the room, arms crossed. He caught Jamie's gaze and held it for a microsecond. Jamie was sure he'd seen the man's face before and was about to ask Bruce when the music was abruptly cut off. Faces turned towards Jamie and Bruce, and Jamie realised with a sinking heart that they were about to be *announced*.

'. . . So pleased, that you could join us today for some celebrations. Our very special guests . . .' The manager, sweat darkening his purple armpits, had taken up a position at the front of the room, while the receptionist appeared by Bruce's side. She would introduce them to Jerome Mondegrene, 'the birthday boy', she said, with a bright smile. She said *birthday boy* slightly under her breath, as if it was faintly impolite.

Jamie followed her until he could see the occupant of the green armchair, a white-haired man wearing a tweed suit.

'This is Mr Jerome Mondegrene,' she chirped.

There was a scarlet handkerchief in the old man's breast pocket. He was staring fixedly through the gap in the heavy, drawn curtains. In profile Jamie could see his thin face, the skin etched with lines like a relief map. He found himself following the old man's gaze, to the view beyond the window which looked out on to the lower slopes of the yellow hill, only a stone's throw from the care home itself.

'Come around the front when I say.' The woman was hissing at him now, in a stage whisper. 'He's not long woken and he's deaf, see, bad neck.'

She addressed the old man in sprightly tones, all teeth and eyebrows. 'A gift,' she said. 'A very special birthday gift, from an old friend of yours.'

'Eh?' Mondegrene jerked his head upwards. His eyes showed his age, Jamie thought, the rims pink and sunken within shadows as purple as bruises.

'Friends,' the woman said. 'They've brought you a present. I think you'll recognise it.'

'Friends, eh?' Mondegrene barked. 'Few of them this side of the turf.'

She gave a tinkly little laugh as if he'd said something flirty. 'It's a very special gift,' she sailed on, 'made by a very talented young man. A surprise!'

'Too old for surprises. What is it?'

'The Mondegrene Dirk, sir.' This from Bruce, breaking in as he stepped forward with a determined set to his jaw. 'A replacement, for the one that was sadly lost.' Bruce twisted his shoulder, motioning to Jamie to come forward, before turning back to Mondegrene. 'Bruce Langlands, sir,' he introduced himself. 'The quarry at Ballantarbert. We supplied the aggregate for your driveway a few years back. Sir.'

Jamie half expected him to click his heels.

'The what?'

'I – run the quarry. And Langlash Fisheries. On the Carrabhal road.'

'Eh?'

'The FISH FARM,' Bruce blared. 'SIR.'

From behind, Jamie watched the back of his stepfather's

neck darkening until it nearly matched the purple curtains. He rolled his lips in on themselves. *Do-not-laugh*, he told himself. He balled his hands into fists, sinking his nails into his palms. *Do-not-fucking-laugh*.

'I'm not deaf, Sonny Jim!' Mondegrene banged his hand down on the arm of his chair in time with his words. 'Fish farms, bloody lice factories, yes. What's this about a gift, then?'

Bruce repeated his piece about the Mondegrene Dirk and the old man's face shuddered like a horse seeing off a fly.

'So it's been found, eh?'

'Not exactly, sir,' Bruce replied, 'but Jamie here has made—'

'Good riddance to old Balmoral tat, that's what I say. Haven't seen that thing in years. Hung on the dining room wall like the blasted Sword of Damocles. What in the buggering blazes am I going to use this one for? Close combat? Perhaps I could take the cook in this place hostage.' Mondegrene let out a seal bark of laughter, and across the room an elderly lady squealed out in response. 'Bad luck, that thing,' he continued, swivelling stiffly to face Jamie. 'Always was, always wa—'

He stopped speaking, his head and shoulders turning as one, his lips drooping open. The inside of his mouth was a dark place. 'Donnie MacArthur,' he said, in a low voice, 'as I live and breathe.'

The world seemed to shimmer slightly in front of Jamie's face. 'No . . .' he started, and felt heat flare up his scalp. 'It's—'

'I know you fine well,' Mondegrene's hoarse whisper interrupted him. 'Step up here, MacArthur.'

Jamie took a reluctant step forward. 'I'm—'

'His son, sir.' Bruce was waving a hand in front of his chest as if to erase the case of mistaken identity. 'Donald's son, Jamie. The spit of his dad, isn't he, but? His son. He's the one who's made this, sir. Very skilled, as you can see.' Bruce nodded at the dirk Jamie was carrying and Jamie held it out towards Mondegrene. The old man leant forward and Jamie

46

caught a blast of his breath, fusty and sweet like old clothing, before he reached out a shaking hand to take the dirk. He weighed the weapon in his palm, squinting at the writing engraved on the blade and giving a low rumble of laughter.

'The same.' Mondegrene looked up at Jamie, a smile bending one side of his mouth. 'Eh? Eh? And you. The same old blood, eh?'

Jamie opened his mouth without a clue what to say. The old man's crêpey hands on the dirk quivered and then the weapon tumbled from his grip, sliding first on to his lap before hitting the carpet with a dull thump.

'Careful,' Mondegrene said. 'Careful, MacArthur.' He lifted his head up, and his eyes slid away from Jamie as he turned to the room at large, to a sea of aged faces, blank expressions and lolling heads. 'He never used to be dead, Donnie MacArthur.' Mondegrene paused. 'He used to be careful.'

At the back of the room, Jamie saw the man in the dark suit open the door, noiselessly, and leave.

'Strange bugger, the old fellow,' Bruce was saying. 'Always has been.' He grunted with laughter. 'The stories of Altnaglas House, back in the day. Some place for a party, if you get my drift.'

They had dropped into the Legion for a drink on the way home – Bruce's idea. His stepfather was swallowing his half-pint with one eye on his wristwatch. He paused for a second time, looking at Jamie. 'You won't be brooding on it, eh?'

'No.' Jamie caught his reflection in the mirror behind the bar, his head tracing out an unsteady triangle in response, somewhere between a shake and a nod. I should have known, he was thinking, I should have been prepared. He swirled the last inch of lager in the base of his glass.

'What is it they say?' Bruce belched and started patting his pockets, preparing to leave. 'Age doesn't come by itself. He's

47

confused, that's all. A bit of a shock for you, son, but no surprise, really. I did warn you, when you got the commission through.' Bruce picked up his keys from where they sat on the bar. 'Ready for—' His eyes flicked to the door, then back to Jamie. 'Hold on a second. There's someone you'd better meet first. This way.' And Bruce was off, motioning to Jamie to follow.

Jamie pushed himself away from the bar and rubbed his face, feeling the drink opening out inside him. Replacing the empty glass on the bar, he saw himself in the mirror again. It was hard not to keep looking at yourself once you started, he thought, in the same way that you couldn't help but be drawn to a television when it was on. He tried not to stumble as he followed Bruce. He hoped he was still OK to drive. He should go now, he knew, before it seemed like a good idea not to. Edging past a bunch of lads hunched over the fruit machine by the door, he murmured hello and goodbye at the same time. Get home to Lena, he repeated to himself. It was that or stay and get plastered with Shockie Campbell and his mullet-haired pal McFadge, and risk his entire fee from the dirk on spinning grapes and cherries.

But he'd reached Bruce by then and was being pulled by the shoulder. Bruce's voice was strident, his eyes flicking from side to side as he spoke. In front of them was the tall, broad man from the care home who had left early. Dark jacket, a white shirt. In his sixties, Jamie reckoned, perhaps older. He had a heavy, impassive face and slicked-back, silvering hair, the colour not yet drained from his thick brows and moustache.

'Jamie,' Bruce was saying, 'let me introduce you to the man who made today possible. Geordie Gilroy. It was his idea to have you make something for old Mondegrene, and he put up the money for it too. I don't think you've ever met?'

Jamie shook his head and Geordie Gilroy took his hand,

48

stretching his thumb briefly over Jamie's knuckle. 'You did well today,' he said. The voice was like that of a headmaster. Jamie couldn't quite place his accent. 'Better than I expected.'

Jamie turned to try and get a read of his face, but the light was behind the big man and he found it was hard to meet his eyes. 'Thanks,' he said. 'Thanks for the opportunity. It was a real challenge.'

'No doubt it was, no doubt,' Geordie Gilroy replied. 'I've heard you came straight from a funeral. My condolences.'

'Aye,' Jamie said. The back of his neck had started to prickle. He could still feel the slithery touch on his hand and had to stop himself from wiping it on his shirt. The man seemed to position himself so he absorbed the light. 'Thanks,' he said again. 'And if you're ever interested in commissioning another dirk or sword or anything, I'd be more than happy to take on the job.'

Jamie looked over to Bruce, who was nodding enthusiastically, smiling while backing away towards the door, evidently as keen to leave as Jamie himself. 'Well, then,' Bruce was saying, 'many thanks again. We'll be seeing you.'

Geordie Gilroy nodded at Jamie with a short smile. 'Can see you're in a rush to get away there, anyway,' he said. 'Somewhere important to be, Donnie-boy?' He stopped, held up a finger. 'Jamie, of course. My apologies. I knew your father. I'll be seeing you again.' He turned back towards the bar.

'Who the hell was that?' Jamie asked Bruce as he followed on into the car park, the doors of the Legion swinging closed behind them.

'I told you. Geordie Gilroy,' said Bruce. 'You'll have heard the name, eh? Bit of a heavy roller. Used to be police. Involved in a few business ventures, you could say, over the years. Tight enough with old Jerome Mondegrene. I think he fancies himself as a bit of a laird down the line. Didn't I mention him before? Sure I did.'

No, thought Jamie, you didn't. But he said nothing.

'A lot of fingers in a lot of pies. He's not the sort to take up with lightly, but I've known him for years.' Bruce shot Jamie an awkward smile. 'I knew how helpful some extra cash could be for you at this time, lad. Thought it was a chance for you to pull yourself up a little and you did well, very well, but that's that. Geordie's been on at me to introduce you. Maybe I shouldn't have, but that's it done anyway.'

'Right,' said Jamie. 'No, thanks. I appreciate it.'

They reached the BMW. A big stripe of a scratch ran along the two doors on the driver's side. 'What happened here?' Jamie asked.

Bruce growled in his throat, shaking his head. 'Keyed in the driveway last night, can you believe it,' he said. 'Little fu – fudger was lucky I didn't catch them, I tell you. No respect. I'm having it seen to tomorrow.' He paused, patting his hand clumsily on Jamie's shoulder. 'You are like him, you know,' he said. 'Your dad.' He lowered himself into the car seat and shook his head, looking up at Jamie with his eyes narrowed as if trying to sharpen the image. 'Back in the day. 'Spect you've been told that before.'

Jamie shrugged. He hadn't. His dad had been a right good-looking bastard, everyone said so – tall, dark-haired, the lot – and no one had exactly rushed to make the comparison before.

He watched Bruce drive away. An overstuffed Corsa pulled up in the space the BMW had left, and four women of varying ages and shades of blonde hair emerged from its interior. One of them made for him, holding an unlit cigarette like a torch, high heels twisting in the gravel.

''Scuse me,' she was saying. ''Scuse me. You got a light?'

Jamie nodded, dug in his pocket for matches, and she giggled and motioned her pals over. Her skin had an orange tinge; her dress was tight and gleamed dully like the underside of tinfoil. It made him think of fish fingers.

He struck a match and all four of them pushed cigarettes against the flame, but still it took a while till they were all sorted, and his fingertips started to singe.

The door of the pub opened, and was held open.

'Ta.' The foil-wrapped one beamed at him. 'See you in there, hon.'

A man moved away from the door of the pub. Jamie knew exactly who it was. He started to walk towards the pickup, patting his pockets for his keys, and realised that Geordie Gilroy had fallen into step with him, on his left-hand side.

'It's yourself, MacArthur,' he said. 'Still here. Thought you were in a hurry to get away.'

Jamie nodded.

'As it turns out,' Geordie Gilroy carried on, 'I wanted a word with you anyway, just the two of us. I do have another job in mind, as it happens, but I'm not looking to hang around waiting for it. Would you manage another piece for me in a week?'

Two pieces of paper, stapled together in the top corner, were thrust under Jamie's nose. He looked down. There were words on the top page under the heading 'ENGRAVING'. Jamie flicked the top sheet over and found himself staring at a detailed diagram of a forty-two-inch claymore with a wheel pommel, and a crossguard whose straight, forward-swept arms had quatrefoil terminations.

He looked at it carefully, momentarily forgetting where he was and what had just happened. From what he could see in the dimming light the design was simple enough, but he knew from experience that simplicity was a particular type of challenge in itself.

'Any problem, here, MacArthur?' His name used again.

'Not a problem, as such.' He tried to keep his voice casual, as though this was a perfectly normal client meeting. 'Not really. It's a great piece. I've seen a sword like this before, some place.' He paused, still looking at the paper. 'It should be possible,' he said, and congratulated himself on his nonchalance before he realised what his words actually meant. 'Did you say a week? I've got a blade that would be perfect but there's a lot of craft in bringing this to life. And the thing is, it could be pricey, like. I mean—'

An envelope planted in his hands stopped him mid-sentence. 'That'll get you started. When you're done, we'll be in touch, and get you squared up.'

The envelope was heavy in Jamie's hand.

'Right you are.' Geordie Gilroy stopped abruptly for a second, before moving off again. 'Next week.'

They'd taken a few steps together when the man spoke again, quietly. 'Your car's over there, son,' he said, casting him off in the right direction. 'And here. A boy your age needn't be cutting about with a box of matches.'

He handed Jamie something, a small, rectangular piece of metal, and walked away. Jamie looked down at the object in his hand. It was a fancy Dupont lighter, a nice heft to it, silver. He turned, frowning, and made his way back to the pickup, opening up the envelope. It was full of banknotes, right enough, twenties and fifties, with a folded piece of paper holding them together.

His pickup was open, keys in the ignition. Sloppy, Jamie told himself. Although if this piece of junk were stolen he'd find it pretty soon, because the thief would need to stop every few miles to let the bloody engine cool down.

In his rear-view mirror Jamie saw the lights of another car driving away. He riffled through the notes. One thousand. The paper holding them together was an unused payment slip, with a name written in biro. *G. Gilroy, Kilchroan Lodge, Lecknish.* Then the last six digits of a local phone number.

Jamie put the notes back into the envelope. He sparked the flint of the lighter. As the small flame leapt up, he saw that the casing was engraved with three interconnected spirals, carved crudely on to the metal. The same spirals Jamie himself had etched, painstakingly, on to the replica of the Mondegrene Dirk. When the flame died he flicked the cab's overhead light on. The spirals were the same as those on the diagram he had just been given.

He glanced over at the paper again and started the engine. First thing to do was to get home. No point in leaving the pub this early if he didn't make it home until after midnight.

Lena was back from the airport and getting ready to go to work when Jamie got home. She was perched on the table that separated the kitchen from the sofa and the telly, plaiting her hair. The TV screen was full of lions. He paused in the doorway, watching her. She never usually had the telly on.

'It was snakes before,' she said, as if to explain. 'There was a snake that ate itself. It swallowed its own tail and died.'

'Probably thought its tail was an enemy,' said Jamie. 'Another snake.' He came fully into the room, dumped the contents of his pockets on the table. The lighter slid, came to a stop by the edge. He went up behind Lena and put his arms around her and rested his chin on top of her head. She was holding up a wee mirror to her face, turning it this way and that. Her cheeks were glittery with make-up.

'I wish you wouldn't sit on that table,' he said. 'The legs are all shonky.'

She tutted, wriggling round in his arms to kiss him on the cheek, and he tightened his grip on her as the table legs creaked. 'You are fussy like an old man,' she said. 'Chairs next month, we agreed.'

'What's wrong with the sofa?'

'So,' she said, as if she hadn't heard him, 'you are drinking. Did the old man like his fancy knife?'

53

Jamie blew air through his cheeks. 'Don't think he cared one way or the other, to be honest.' He turned to the fridge. 'Have you eaten?'

She shook her head. Jamie found a tin of tomato soup in the cupboard and stirred it round in the pan on the hotplate. Working two jobs, office admin in the nine-to-five and waitressing four evenings a week, she often ran out of time to eat.

'The old guy. Jerome Mondegrene. He thought I was my dad,' he said.

He stuck his finger in the soup to test it before pouring it into two mugs and passing one to Lena. She took it and blew on it, eyebrows raised. 'He knew him?'

'My dad used to do some work for him, I knew that. Ghillying and driving and that, for the estate. It was just – weird. You know.' Jamie realised he had travelled the length of the kitchen and back again. He shoved his empty mug into the sink and stayed there for a second. 'Bruce said he's just old,' he said. 'Maybe he'd had a few drinks, on his birthday. Who knows?'

'So, his memory is gone,' she said. 'Perhaps he decides he is wanting to replace the entire collection. Good for you, no?' She smiled at him.

He stood behind her and put his arms around her shoulders again, his lips on the back of her head. 'I did get some more work, actually,' he said. He rested his chin on the top of her head. Her plaited hair was as solid as rope. 'But that's an even weirder story.'

'This?' she said. He looked down. She was pointing at the diagram he'd brought in from the pickup.

'Aye. He wants it done in a week.'

She made a sharp noise of surprise. He craned round to see her face, quietly turning face-down the slip which had Gilroy's name on it. He wasn't entirely sure why, only that the man wasn't someone he wanted to be discussing with Lena. The feeling of unease from their meeting had still not worn off.

'A week?' she was saying. 'It is too much, no?'

'Well, it's a big piece, yeah. But quite a simple job. Should be.'

'A lot of work, you always say. More than you think.'

'I know.' He leant over her shoulder again, shook out the contents of the envelope.

'How much?'

'A grand.'

She huffed. 'Only?'

'No, that's the deposit.' I bloody hope, he thought. He kissed her cheek. 'It should be fine. It will be fine. I have to, don't I?'

'There is no *have to* about anything,' she said.

'I wish that was true.' There was *have to* about everything, he thought. Particularly now. 'And Lena, keep this to yourself, aye?'

She twisted around, frowning. 'You ask me this, but you know nothing.'

'I'm just saying.'

'And who would I tell?' Her top lip was orange from the soup.

He shrugged. His eyes rested on the lighter, teetering on the edge of the table. She hadn't asked about that, but why would she? He picked it up, put it back in his pocket.

She ducked free from his arms. 'I have to get to work.'

He filled a glass of water and drank it, watching her gather her things to leave. Dressed all in black, her hair plaits the colour of condensed milk.

'You look beautiful,' he said, and she sniffed.

'Oh, I am getting so fat!' She laughed. 'Soon I will be like Christmas pudding, rolling down the street.'

Soon you'll have our baby, he thought. 'I'll pick you up,' he said.

'No, Martin gives me lift,' she said.

'Aye, right. I'll pick you up.' He kissed her on the way out of the door. 'And mind you tell Martin this week's your last. If he has a problem with that, he can talk to me.'

She grinned, raising an eyebrow. 'You big-talking man.' A fair June Carter impression.

'You've got – orange. Just here.' He tapped his own top lip.

'Ah!' She swiped the mirror from the table, scrubbing her mouth with the back of her hand. When she left he filled another glass of water and watched her walk down the road outside.

He used to be careful, Donnie MacArthur. He swallowed. What a day.

He drained his glass, climbed over the back of the sofa and settled himself in front of the television, but the lions were gone.

Saturday 11 June 1977

Angus John

An Argyll Childhood: Recollections of a Discovery
The *Barnadine Star* is grateful to Mr. Angus John MacArthur,
Carrabhal, for providing us with this interesting and lively
account of an intriguing discovery made on An Cnoc Buidhe, the
Yellow Hill, as a child. – Ed.

*The land around us is sown with stories. There is said to be gold in
the yellow hill that sweeps up behind Crois na Coille, a glint in the
veins of the earth. There is said to be a sleeping warrior in the
hump-backed hillock between the byre and the hill. As we children
were growing, we heard all these tales from our mother. But what I
found was hidden in the old mossy dyke that ran like a spine down
the hillside, and she had never said a word about that.*

*I found it because I was hiding. I was hiding because I was the
youngest, and always ended up in the minor role: watchman and
lookout. I remember it was very early spring, and cold still, when
the sun was behind the clouds. We had played all day in the
shadow of the storm-stripped hill. Lapwings whooped and whirred
above the dark ground. All day we had charged up and down the
uneven ridges of the hillock that bristled with grey grass. The
Fortress, we called it. Despite the chill it had been a day to glory in,
and now, at its close, three children were running circles on the
lower slopes of the yellow hill, dragging branches and throwing
sticks. The shadows had advanced on the bright afternoon, but the
children had not yet noticed. Their cheeks were red, and the sweat
chilled their backs.*

Three children; there had been four until a little time ago, but I had slipped away following my sudden demise at the hands of my sister Netta. I had been instructed by my sister that dead men don't move, and that I was to wait until the others had finished their game. But the game had moved on, and, crawling on my belly like a slow-worm, I reached the stone dyke. Concealed behind the wall, I made my way up the hill, the fox terrier, my constant companion, scurrying up and down sniffing and blowing for rabbits, her nose to the ground. Halfway up the hill, I raised my head and looked back down the way I'd come.

The terrier was scrabbling at an old burrow in the side of the wall. I did not want her to go under and become trapped, so I hauled her out backwards. She was not for stopping, however, and as I went in after her once more, my elbow caught a loose jutting stone and it shifted, showering down a stream of earth and dust. And down came something else. It landed on the ground with a great thud. It gave me a great shock.

It was twice the length of my arm. It was bound in sacking, with what looked like old copper wire, turned blue with age. Touching it left the stain of peat on my fingers. The metal wire was tricky to remove, but then the first layer of sacking fell away to reveal another layer, and another. The final layer, a finer material, was pale and dry. I peeled it back slowly, and revealed something I had only seen pictures of in books at school.

I had uncovered nothing less than two genuine, bona fide Jacobite swords, their blades rusted but whole, their hilts basket-shaped and decorated with hearts.

You may imagine that I was much taken aback. I stood looking down at my find for some time, before my mother's voice called us in from the hill. I called my dog to me before gathering the swords and their wrappings, and I started down the hill to the house, bearing my buried treasure in

Wednesday 18 March 1998

Anna

The end of Angus John's article is lost where the newspaper cutting has been torn at the bottom. Tucking the fragile paper back into the manila folder where I found it, I look up through the living room window at the yellow hill where he found the swords. It's nice to finally get a chance to read this after all those years of protest and dismissal. Och, away and waste your time on something else, he'd said once, when I'd asked to read his piece in the *Barnadine Star* about the two Jacobite swords. A shame. I'd have liked to tell him how much I enjoyed it.

'It shouldn't be too much of a job clearing Angus John's house,' Fern had said this morning at the kitchen table.

'What do you mean?' Bella had called, from the door where she was feeding the dogs. 'His house is *full* of rubbish!'

After breakfast I had walked up the track armed with black plastic bags and a hoover, to start work. Angus John's house is smaller than I remember it. But the hallway is still yellow, the floor an ancient lino in varying shades of brown.

My great-uncle was a mountain of a man, given to prolonged silences. I was a little nervous of him, when I was a child. He built this house himself when he'd retired from the merchant navy, on the small patch of flat ground up the hill from Crois na Coille where they'd all grown up. A one-bedroomed Dorran house, it had arrived in bits on a lorry. He just had to bolt them together. Took him a couple of weeks once the foundations were laid.

As a child, I had liked the idea that a house could be screwed together like Meccano. If it was that easy, I'd wondered, why did Dad never get round to it? He could have ordered one just like this, perhaps a few more bedrooms for us all.

I leave the living room and go into my great-uncle's bedroom. I haven't been in this room before, I realise, only glimpsed it through a half-open door. It contains a single bed, a chair, a bedside table and a cupboard. Angus John never married, living alone with his dog Mac. After Mac passed away there was Jinky, the jackdaw he tamed, who roosted each night on the towel rail in the bathroom. Bella and Fern take care of the little bird now. I open the cupboard. There's a strong smell of mothballs and old pipe smoke. I lift a tweed jacket from a hanger and it presses heavy and scratchy in my arms.

When I have finished clearing the rails, laying all the clothes on the bed before putting them in bags, I return to the living room. I think of the great distances Angus John travelled by sea in his lifetime, the tattoos etched on his skin in far-off ports, and how the extent of his travelling towards the end of his life became confined to the narrow path between his chair and the television. There are Haynes car manuals piled up on the sideboard, a car jack tucked under the uncomfortable-looking spare chair in the corner.

I begin to put things into boxes. Everything is from some-where. So many souvenirs and keepsakes. Ashtrays from the model village of Bourton-on-the-Water and Robert Burns's cottage in Alloway. Newspapers neatly folded and stacked in order. Separate piles for the *Trout and Salmon Magazine*.

As evening draws on, I turn on the radio on his Pioneer hi-fi. The only station it seems to pick up is Radio 2. I work away until I hear a car coming up the track. A brown Volvo is parking in the yard at Crois na Coille. It must be later than I realise, and I said I'd help Fern and Bella set out the almost

64

exclusively beige buffet they have prepared for the visitors arriving this evening.

'He's just passing through, the professor,' Fern had said at the breakfast table that morning. She made him sound like a ghost sliding through walls. I had crunched toast to hide my grin and wondered who she thought she was kidding. All the smiling, humming to herself. 'I dare say he won't stay long. We'll just be one of many, won't we, Bel? Eh? The ones that are left.'

'You see, Anna?' Bella had raised an eyebrow as she drew a circle around an advertisement for ferrets in the *Oban Times*. 'Those who last long enough become leftovers.'

The door shakes the walls as I close up Angus John's house. I pull on an old fleece and feel my thumb make a break for it through a hole in the armpit. In the garden I brush my way past overgrown bushes from which I remember picking black-currants in summer.

Fern

'They've arrived,' Bella is calling from the kitchen.

Fern knows this. She has watched the Volvo bumping its way up the track. It is not me he is coming to see, she reminds herself, but Bella, the one who got all our mother's stories. I got the education and Bella got everything else. And I've never begrudged her that.

She scrabbles for her other glasses as the car door opens and two young people emerge. A blonde girl and a tall young man. Fern watches as the wind whips the girl's gleaming hair into her face, as she catches the flying strands in her fist, flipping her head back. The young man turns as she does this, leans on the roof of the car to say something to her. She laughs and they both turn to look up at the house. Very handsome, the pair of them, Fern thinks. Full of the confidence of youth and beauty.

She peers beyond them to get a look at the passenger seat and her pulse stabs in her wrist. There he is, the professor of the long songs and the tall tales, unfurling himself from the car, his hair white now but as wayward as ever. He waves boldly in the direction of the house, smiling broadly. He hasn't changed really, not a bit. The fair-haired girl springs forward to take his arm and Fern sees his age as he is walking, rolling like an old sailor.

The love of my past life, she thinks.

Fern goes to the front door to let them in. She steps down the hallway, glancing at her reflection in the mirror on her way past. She opens the door, and he is there, standing on the doorstep and beaming, his hand already outstretched.

'Oh, Fern, my dear,' he says. His voice alone could bring her nearly to tears. 'It's wonderful to see you.'

She shakes his hand, saying his name – his full name, chirruping words of welcome, and the professor's gaze shifts, looking over her shoulder and down the corridor.

'And where is Bella?' he says.

Anna

In the porch of Crois na Coille I lean unsteadily on an old hobby horse to take off my shoes, trying to avoid pitching headlong into the firewood that is piled in the cramped space. There are voices coming from the kitchen and I hover in the hallway. I feel dusty and tired. My hair is tangled; I pull it free from its elastic band, shake it upside down.

When I lift my head, Fern is in the kitchen doorway. 'Willie,' she is saying, to someone out of sight. 'Come and meet my great-niece, Anna.'

I'd really like to wash my hands and face before I'm introduced but it's too late: an elderly man with a furze of silvery hair is already emerging behind her.

'Very good to meet you, Anna, very good,' he says. He is well spoken: halfway Irish, halfway English.

'Thank you,' I say, idiotically, my head nodding as he shakes my hand up and down. His face is finely carved and his eyes are watery and blue. There is a pipe tucked into the breast pocket of his tweed jacket. I haven't a clue what to say to a university professor, but luckily Fern is fussing over him.

'Now,' she is saying to him, 'your journey. You'll be tired.' Her voice is a touch blurry; there is a high flush in her cheeks.

'Fern, for goodness' sake.' Bella's voice, calling from further inside. I step across the threshold of the kitchen, where she is opening the top plate of the Rayburn, upending the coal scuttle into the firebox and sending sparks shooting upwards. 'Come on in, Anna,' she calls without looking up. She rinses

68

her hands under the sink before resting both palms on the stovetop for a brief moment.

Fern manoeuvres me over to the table, where a young woman and a man are sitting. They are deep in conversation, heads bent together over cups of tea. He is dark-haired, she very fair. I falter for a second, momentarily disconcerted. Fern never said anything about a girl as well, especially not one who wouldn't look out of place in a Tommy Hilfiger advert. There is not, I register with slight dismay, a cardigan to be seen. My heart sinks. I wonder if it's too late to lose the fleece, decide it probably is.

'This is my Anna,' Fern says to the girl, 'and – I'm so sorry, dear, I've forgotten your name.'

'Erin,' she says. She has an American accent. She's very pretty indeed, fresh-faced and golden.

'Nice to meet you,' I say.

'And this is John Teelin,' says Fern, a hand on the man's shoulder. 'You'll remember. The musician.' She all but digs me in the ribs.

John Teelin levels the cup he has been drinking from, places it down on its saucer and stands up, holding out a formal hand in greeting. He is tall and lean, perhaps three or four years older than me. His eyes beneath his dark hair are a clear grey. I vaguely wish my hair and clothes were cleaner.

'Nice to meet you,' I repeat. He smiles, or at least one corner of his mouth lifts, and he sits down again just as I am reaching out awkwardly to shake his hand. Fern has bustled off and I am left standing in front of the pair, as mute and motionless as a scarecrow. I lower my half-raised hand, folding it beneath my other arm.

A brief silence hums heavy on my ears, and then, 'I can't tell you how excited we are to meet Bella,' says Erin. She flashes me a smile and looks over to the professor, who is raising a whisky glass to Bella where she sits in her chair like the

Queen of Sheba. 'We've heard so much about her,' Erin goes on. 'Haven't we, John?' She touches his elbow where it rests on the table, squeezes it.

'We have, yeah,' he affirms. He is Irish like the professor, his accent a good deal stronger. I try to imagine him singing with a finger in his ear but the image won't quite present itself.

Mumbling something about helping out, I make a beeline for Fern, who is now on tiptoe with her head in the cupboard, raking for fresh glasses on the top shelf. I join her in pouring tea and whisky, buttering slices of bread. After handing around the plates I sit down on a low chair by the stove, drawing my knees up to my chin and hugging my arms around them. That it has been only slightly over thirty-six hours since I woke up in the car seems incomprehensible. It feels like a week at least.

I think again of Liam, wonder what he is doing at this moment. The thought shrivels, acidic, in my stomach. I imagine Angus John's house, the half-empty rooms, the half-filled boxes. I fight the urge to rest my head on my knees. *Be a pebble on a beach*, Ceri Talbot used to say to us, the ill-fitting assortment of teenagers who went to Young Carers' meetings in the Barnadine Mission Hall after school on a Wednesday, when we could manage. *You are being rocked by the waves. They break over you but they do not harm you. They flow around you but they do not move you. Be a pebble on a beach.*

By the time everyone is on their third round of drinks, Fern has taken up residence on the ancient green chair beside John Teelin, sipping whisky and smoking as politely as she can. They are talking in low tones; I can't hear what is being said. Erin is hanging on every word that passes between the professor and Bella, who are deep in conversation, running through a list of everyone who has died since his last visit.

Beside me on the wall, the calendar is showing last month; I flip it over, thinking of the stories I have heard about the professor's visits to Crois na Coille nearly half a century ago.

'Just us now, really,' Bella is saying, sounding quite cheerful about it. 'Isn't it, Fern?'

'I was very sorry to hear about your brother,' says the professor. 'May the Lord receive his soul.' The words so often uttered strike a particularly sombre tone. There is a small murmur of sound from Fern and Bella draws her lips into her mouth and sits back in her chair. The room seeps into a silence which rises up slowly and threatens to stretch, before the professor breaks it once more.

'Now forgive me for asking, but – Netta – is she ...?' He trails off. I listen to the clock ticking on the dresser: an empty, ruthless sound.

'Not a word from her,' says Bella briskly.

He nods. 'It's sometimes the way, with the ones that go abroad. My brother, now, scarcely a word and it was to America he went, whether he made good or—'

'John!' Fern exclaims in scandalised tones, making John Teelin sit up straight with a start. 'Your glass is empty!' She hurries to refill it.

The professor tilts his head and pours the remainder of his drink down his throat with his little finger lifted. 'And have you any livestock nowadays?' he enquires of Bella.

'Not like in the old days,' Fern calls across the room.

'We even had to let the goats go,' says Bella.

'I think we only kept them for so long because they reminded us of our mother, eh, Bel?'

And with the mention of their mother the talk turns to the last time the professor stayed, collecting old songs and stories when the twins were teenagers. As the evening wears on I drift on the lulling tide of talk, refilling glasses, handing out sandwiches. Each morsel of food and drink is praised by the professor. 'Wonderful bread,' he says, waving a sandwich in Bella's direction. 'Made by your own fair hand, no doubt.' He must have never tried Mother's Pride before.

'What about a bit of music?' Fern is already halfway across the room to fetch the melodeon that belonged to Angus John. She perches on the edge of her chair to play 'The Conundrum'.

'Fern, I believe you have been practising since we last met,' Professor Croke says as she squeezes the tune to a close, and she throws her head back and laughs delightedly.

'Will you play us something, John?' the professor turns to John Teelin. 'You want to hear this man playing,' he announces to the room at large. 'A treat. Go on now. Give us a tune.'

Amid general consensus that this would be exactly the right thing to do, John Teelin unfolds himself from his chair and leaves the room to fetch his fiddle from the hall. We all watch quietly as he removes the instrument from its case and tunes it, running his thumb across the strings to produce muffled sprigs of sound. He takes his time. Our anticipation does not seem to make him nervous. He is evidently used to playing to an audience. When he is ready he tucks the instrument under his arm and then, looking across the room, he says, 'I'll play if someone dances.'

Erin, for whom this is clearly meant, giggles and protests, and he shrugs. 'Suit yourself, so.' He lifts the fiddle to his shoulder and runs the bow across it, releasing a cloud of white rosin like steam. Then he starts to play, leaning back against the table, the liquid trembling in the glasses behind him.

The pace in the room seems to slow as the music gathers its stride, settling into a rhythm, and I feel my spirits and my shoulders lift as the sound holds the air around it snug within its grasp. It is a reel he is playing, but I lose count of how many parts there are as the notes course freely and strut across one another. His shirtsleeves are rolled up to his elbows and I can see the tendons working in his forearms, yet his fingers on the strings hardly seem to be moving. He makes the playing of it look effortless, his dark head tilted, his ear held close to the sound he is driving from the wood, high and fluid and fast.

The music lifts into a different tune and key. Erin rises from her chair with easy grace and starts to dance, not the poker-backed, rigid-armed Irish dancing I have seen on television, all ringlets and ruffles, but something looser and more liquid. Her feet shuffle and snap on the floor; her arms occasionally lift and fall. She makes eye-contact with no one. John Teelin watches her feet, as if the music he plays can tug and steer her toes. I could watch them and listen forever, but it is over far too soon and when they finish I realise I have forgotten to breathe steadily. The room erupts into sudden congratulatory noise.

'"The Glen Road to Carrick",' the professor is saying, clapping John Teelin so vigorously on the shoulder I fear for the instrument. 'Up Donegal. Some tune, that is.'

I wonder where Carrick is, and just how long has it been since I last listened, properly, to music as it is played, not just the bleeding from the radio or television set? Erin resumes her seat, pink-cheeked, and I am about to ask whether anyone would like a top-up or a refill when an expectant hush falls quite suddenly, and I raise my head to discover everyone is looking at me.

'Give us a song, Anna,' Fern is saying. 'Go on.'

'Oh, no.' I say. 'No. I don't sing.'

'No? You used to. Her mother was a lovely singer,' Fern proclaims to the professor, who is sitting on the floor now, propped against the wall. He is cradling an empty tumbler and looks a bit glassy-eyed. I turn my eyes down, staring at the floor tiles and shaking my head, but I can still feel the expect-ant silence. I feel as if I would rather strip naked than try to remember one of the songs my mother used to sing. I haven't sung since I was a child, when Dad was with us, and I won't be starting again tonight.

'She's alright.' John Teelin speaks quietly, hooking his leg around his chair to pull it back into position. He leans over to

73

place his fiddle on the table, laying the bow carefully on top. 'Too early for songs, maybe.'

'You know something?' Erin chips in. 'That reminds me of a story. The man who came to the house with no tale to tell.' She leans over to Bella, who is sitting quietly with her hands in her lap. 'Do you know that one?'

'Ah, Bella. "The Man Who Had No Story".' The professor tops up his glass and settles himself more comfortably on the floor. 'The kist that opens.'

I edge a fleeting glance at John Teelin and meet his eyes for a second before turning quickly to Bella like everyone else, feeling blurry and shapeless in his considered, faintly pitying gaze.

'I did hear of something like that from my mother,' Bella is saying. Her voice is husky, like the needle of a stylus sliding before settling into the groove of a record. She pauses, clears her throat. 'But the night's too young for stories, surely?' She looks around the room, assured of being told that no, now is just the perfect time.

'There was a man who lived not far from here,' she says, 'and he would go every night to a house where stories were told, but he himself had no story to tell.'

I tell myself I shouldn't, I tell myself I won't, and then I take the Croft sherry bottle and tip a couple of inches into an empty glass. I hold the alcohol in my mouth for a few seconds before swallowing it, letting it kindle and glow.

The professor is leaning back, his eyes half-open yet watchful as a drowsy dog. Erin is nodding enthusiastically, regarding Bella with practised awe, occasionally shifting her gaze to John Teelin beside her.

It's a story I know well. Fern's itching for a cigarette, I can tell; her right hand is almost rolling an imaginary paper. Bella's voice wraps around me like smoke. The story's words infuse the strange images that flow into my mind as I close my eyes and set my thoughts adrift. I'm almost sure I'm not asleep: it seems to me that I can hear Bella's voice and have a perfect awareness of what is happening, but when I open my eyes the room is empty.

It takes a second to orientate myself. There are voices in the passageway. Someone has put a blanket over my legs. I push it to one side and ease myself up, go to the doorway. The professor is standing by the open front door saying something to Fern, and Erin stands on his other side with a hand on his arm. She turns around when she hears me.

'Anna,' she says. 'You were sleeping like a baby; it seemed a shame to wake you.'

Outside the air is clear and cold. John Teelin is leaning against the wall of the house, a cigarette glowing at his lip.

'If that's OK with you, Anna?' Fern is saying.

'Sorry,' I say, turning. 'What was that?'

'The boys are going to take the bed and sofa at Angus John's,' Fern says. 'So you'll be alright for Erin to stay here with you in the spare room?'

Oh, no, I think. 'Of course,' I say out loud. 'No problem.'

Fern hands John Teelin a torch and he flicks it on. There are tiny creases in the skin at the corners of his eyes as he takes a final draw on his cigarette before grinding it beneath his foot. Bella lifts the latch on the byre door and the three collies flow out and fawn around first her feet and then mine, whimpering. I bend down and stroke the old one's silky head and ears. Her eyes are cloudy now.

Above us the skies are clear and star-studded. I remember my dad pointing out constellations to me, showing me how to follow the tip of the plough to find Polaris, the North Star. Tonight the plough appears to be upside down, but it doesn't matter. Imagine tilting the pan up as if you're pouring it out, my dad said. It's five star lengths away from there. As I look, my eyes adjust and more and more stars become visible, until the darkness itself becomes a glimmering mass of light.

You could never see so many stars in the city, I think, not above the streetlamps. *There are more stars up there than grains of sand on every beach and every desert in the world,* I remember Dad telling me. Holding his hand to keep myself tethered to earth, I would stare upwards, mute, enjoying the sensation of this ungraspable sense of enormity.

'Goodnight, Anna.' The professor is standing in the yard behind me. His voice makes me jump.

'*Oidhche mhath,*' I say without thinking. Goodnight. It is the memory of my dad that brings with it the Gaelic words and phrases he used every day without the need to ever teach us exactly what they meant.

John Teelin comes over, takes the professor's arm in preparation for the walk up the track to Angus John's house. He nods at me, and repeats what I have said in Irish. I assume it's Irish. It is a more sinuous-sounding phrase, slippery but still recognisable. The pair walk up further up the hill, the torchlight bobbing ahead of them. I look up at the sky again, but the light from the torch has destroyed my night vision.

Back indoors, I climb the steep stairs, stopping to look in the mirror that hangs midway up on the wall. The half-light from the hallway passage deepens the shadows under my eyes.

'I'm sorry, Anna.' Fern stands at the bottom of the stairs looking up at me, her arms wrapped around her body like a small child. 'About the singing. I apologise.'

'I just couldn't,' I say. 'I couldn't remember the words.'

Fern steps up to me, places both hands on my shoulders and squeezes. 'The fault is mine,' she says. 'I was carried away. Tonight was like – was like it was a long time ago. I shouldn't have pressed you. Only one thing worse than a young fool, and that's an old fool.'

'You're not.' I slide my arms around her slim frame and lay my head on her shoulder. 'You're not any kind of fool.'

We say goodnight. Fern kisses me on the cheek. Bella, passing us with a tray of spent glasses, kisses her fingers and holds them to my forehead like a munificent priest. I should offer to wash up but I am so tired.

'I'll do those in the morning,' I say. 'Please leave them for me.'

The stairs bend up like a dog-leg. I can hear the sound of the tap running in the bathroom. Erin must be in there, so I go into the twin bedroom and lie down fully clothed on the bed I slept in last night. The lampshade is casting tiny squares of light on to the ceiling, and I narrow my eyes until it is a gentle blur. I hold on to the bed on both sides as if it is a ship's bunk. There is a swimming sensation in my stomach, but I can't tell if it's sickness or fatigue or both. Lately I've felt my body becoming unknown to me, mysterious, full of the possibility of betrayal. One drink tonight and I'd felt as if I was committing a cardinal sin.

It's been three weeks since I realised that I could be pregnant. I should have done a test a fortnight ago, when I was a week late. I would have talked to Liam, but by that point I was finally realising that there was nothing more to say. Not after I had seen him with someone else; not after he had once more proved to me that, outside the flat, he did not see me as a part of his life in the wider world and never would.

When I had first joined him in his dad's flat in Glasgow, it had been exciting, even desirable, to feel that our story existed solely within a bubble of secrecy. The bubble did not burst. Instead it became a vacuum. Sealed in, isolated, I became like a gardener who tends a maze, outfoxed by my apparent liberty and ensnared in the sense that this was a situation of my own devising. Liam and I never went out together. I don't believe that, in all our time together, even when we shared the same flat, he even mentioned my name to another living soul.

77

You said you wanted this, he would say to me. This is what we are. No one else has what we have. If you don't like it you can fucking leave.

Later there would be tears, professions of love, self-recrimination, threats of harming himself. And then the cycle would begin again, as he went out and stayed out, did what he wished, never told me where he was, only that he would come back to me. *My other half*, people said about their partners. Living with Liam was a true half-life.

'Jeez, you're about a foot away.'

I open my eyes with a start. Erin is tiptoeing across the floor. She's wearing pyjamas printed with cartoon owls and her blonde hair is scooped up into a topknot. She gets into her bed from the bottom and crawls up to the pillow end. 'This is like Craggy Island,' she grins.

I can't help smiling. 'Is *Father Ted* big in America?'

'I'm Canadian!'

'Oh. Right. Sorry. Sorry.'

'Well. Scottish on my dad's side,' she says. 'Oh, he would die to be here right now.' She lies on her back and stretches her hands out in front of her, spreads her fingers. 'He would just die and go straight to heaven. He's been working for years researching the family bloodline. He's got just about everyone accounted for, all the way back to, like, 1800.'

'Uh-huh.' My eyes have closed again. I can see red circles wheeling beneath the lids.

'Oh, yeah,' she carries on, 'he's really big into it. Mom, not so much. But he got a new computer, down in the basement, and they get along just fine now.'

'That's good,' I murmur.

She's quiet. I breathe out slowly and deeply. In the silence I think about telling her that her dancing was very good, but my face is lazy and will barely move. I roll on to my side and let my body sink. Peace.

'Ah! I just can't sleep!' There's a kind of bounce from the other bed. I hear her push herself upright, propping herself against the headboard. 'That story Bella told tonight. That was something, to hear that. I mean, not on a tape or whatever, but, you know. *Live.* You grew up here, right?'

'Kind of.' I stay as still as I can.

'Oh, you're so lucky,' she says. 'Growing up with all of this around you.'

'S'pose,' I say. My voice sounds thick in my ears, as if I am dredging up words from the deep downhill darkness I am finding when I close my eyes.

'Oh, come on, Anna,' she is saying now. 'I can just picture it. My brothers, playing outside in the woods? My mom cooking on that old stove downstairs? My dad chopping wood by the back door? I mean . . .'

I feel a bit bad about what I'm going to say, but God, I need sleep. 'Actually, we lived in a caravan. And my dad died when I was eight.'

Silence. Then I hear her draw breath. I fight the urge to apologise.

'I'm glad you've had a nice time,' I say. 'It's a beautiful place.' I pull the blanket up to my chin. 'See you in the morning. Night.'

June 1960

Donnie

Donnie MacArthur stood behind the bar in front of a row of seven clean tumblers. The eighth was cradled in his hand. He removed the wadded cloth from the mouth of the glass and outstretched his arm towards the window, the tumbler held in his fingertips. He twisted his wrist, bending rays of evening sunshine through the glass so the light played on the bottles behind him. He placed it on the shelf beneath the bar top, edged it into position to join the orderly queue made by the others. Glancing around the room, he tucked the tail of his shirt back into his waistband and took up the seventh glass.

This was a time he had learned to savour: the small public bar of the Tayfillan Hotel quiet between afternoon and evening, the wood-lined room still and empty.

Donnie opened the till, took out a shilling and stowed it in the crook of his right elbow. Flexed both hands open, closed. Empty hands, see, he told imagined watching onlookers. Went to push up his sleeves. No cheating here. In rolling up his right sleeve he tweaked the coin from its hiding place. Rubbed his hands together, and the coin . . . was put quickly back into the till as he heard voices outside. Major Saltcoats strode into the room accompanied by two other men, hotel guests by the look of them. Donnie pulled his shoulders back as the hotel proprietor made straight for the bar, where he tapped the wood with a smart roll of his fingertips.

'Two glasses of the Marnay for our guests, MacArthur. Quick as you like.'

The cognac was within easy reach; Donnie could pluck it from the shelf behind him without the need to turn around while pinching the brandy glasses in his fingers and lining them up on the bar. He unstopped the bottle and poured out two measures. Saltcoats picked up the pair of glasses and inclined his head in a minute nod towards the bottle, which was Donnie's signal to pour a third snifter for Saltcoats himself. This one was picked up by Saltcoats' hooked pinkie finger before he returned to the fireside and his guests.

The light from the window was obscured by one bulky movement, and then another. Donnie could hear the sound of voices and a dog barking. He looked up. Through the glass he could see the bony hips of a cow swaying past outside. It was followed by another, and another.

At the other end of the room Major Saltcoats put down his drink, wiped his moustache and moved unhurriedly to the outside door, switching his monocle to his good eye. Beyond the window, Donnie could see some of the beasts on the hotel lawn, and Art McColl, the farmhand, striding towards them brandishing a crook.

'McColl!' the Major barked.

'The cows, sir,' McColl called back over his shoulder. 'One of those new girls was sent to bring them in. Not a sign of her. She'll maybe be up there still.' He whistled to his dog and set about driving the cattle on to the byre beyond the hotel.

Saltcoats withdrew his head from the doorway with a snort, turning back to his half-finished brandy. 'Well, MacArthur.' He drank and cocked his eye towards Donnie. 'Away up the hill with you. Go and see what's happened to this young lady, and bring her back to me for a word. I'll man the bar.'

Donnie turned from the window. 'Sir.'

It was humid outside, and quiet, the majority of the hotel guests not yet returned from their pleasure excursions. He could smell the cows, who were ambling back up beside the hotel, McColl's dog snaking and snapping around their legs. One of the younger heifers had her head buried in one of the hanging baskets. Donnie shunted his elbow into the animal's bony quarters to move her off. He raised a hand to his eyes; sun lit the gorse golden on the hill above the hotel. He couldn't see anyone up there.

Soon the bar would be busy, and then there would be the dinner service to begin and the errands to run in preparation for next morning; but not yet. Donnie had been awake since five and wouldn't get to his bed until after midnight, but so far the day had not caught up with him. Every movement felt clean, purposeful, practised.

He broke into a jog up the track, reaching the field that lay at the foot of the hill. He wasn't sure who he was looking for. An assortment of summer staff had arrived yesterday from Glasgow; he assumed this girl was among their number.

The field where the cows had come from was empty, the gate swinging open. Donnie looked around. 'Anyone up here?' he called, and a small voice answered him.

'Here. I'm here.'

Turning his head to the sound, he walked to the stone dyke and from there he could see the top of her head.

'You alright?' He went towards the ditch.

'Think so.'

He reached the edge and looked down at the girl half-sitting, half-crouching in the shallow trickle of mud and stones. She was thin, red-haired and freckle-faced, about his age. There was a stripe of mud on her blue dress, and mud in her hair also.

'What happened here?' he said.

'They were waiting just by the gate,' she said, 'and when I opened it they all went through a bit quick.' She levered herself up cautiously. 'Are they alright?' she asked.

'Aye, they're alright. What about yourself? You'd better be getting out of there.' Donnie bent and hesitated, uncertain as to where to put his hands. He settled on holding them out to her. She stretched out her arms and got a grip on his shirt. Her boots kicked at the earth as he pulled her up out of the ditch and then she leaned up against him for a second before letting out a yelp that made him jump.

'Think I've done something to my ankle.' She slid down to sit at the side of the track and tugged at the laces of her clumpy boots. She wasn't wearing any socks. She held the ankle in both hands and looked up at him. 'Och, I'm shamed to death,' she said. She didn't look it. Her voice went up and down and up again. 'That'll be me in disgrace, eh? And on my first day.' She was leaning forwards, trying to brush the dirt from her dress and her bare shins.

'Ah, well.' There was a gap he wasn't sure how to fill, so he said, 'McColl's taking care of it now. No harm done.'

She frowned. 'I'm not used to cows.'

'Aye.' He smiled. He thought her face looked a bit flushed; he hoped she wasn't about to start crying. Then she snorted and Donnie realised she was trying to stifle laughter. He cast an eye down the track: empty.

'Here.' He patted his pockets and withdrew the battered packet of cigarettes he'd been ekeing out all week, held it up to her. 'Do you want one of these?' He put two in his mouth and found matches and lit them, one after the other. He passed one to her. She touched it to her lips briefly and then held it between her thumb and first finger, which looked odd, furtive, and she smiled up at him through the light haze of smoke.

'Who am I thanking?'

'Donald,' he said. 'Donnie. Pleased to meet you.' He curled his toes up inside his shoes.

She flicked ash from the end of her cigarette into the ditch. 'Mary Rose.'

'Mary Rose,' he repeated. 'I've been sent to bring you down to Saltcoats.'

She nodded. 'Might be getting the sack already, Donald Donnie.' She didn't seem overly troubled by the prospect, turning her face up towards the sky. He sat down next to her.

'You're from around here?' she said.

'Aye. Up there, over the hill.'

She turned her head on one side to look at him and smiled, and he realised that he was waving his right arm around expansively as if conducting an orchestra.

There was silence for a minute, and then she said, 'I'm just up from Glasgow.'

He laughed and she squinted at him sideways, blowing a plume of smoke in the opposite direction. 'What's funny?'

He shrugged. 'I guessed so.'

'Oh, did you, now?'

'I did, aye.' He sucked down on his cigarette. 'I know Glasgow.'

'You've been there, have you?'

'Many times, Mary Rose,' he said. 'Well. Just the once. Partick. Some sights to see, eh?'

She shrugged. 'It's nicer up here. Working holiday.'

'Aye. You'll get yourself a nice sunburn.'

'To match yours?' She pointed at his arms where his sleeves were rolled up.

'Don't know about that, now.' He stretched out his arm, tugged at his cuff where his sun-darkened skin turned white. 'This is called a suntan.'

'My arse. That's sunburn, so it is.'

He laughed. Then he stood up. 'Look,' he said, 'I need to be getting back.' And then, when she did not stir, 'Have you met Saltcoats yet?'

87

'Not sure.'

'That means no, I reckon.' He began to walk down the path, looking at her over his shoulder, then remembered her ankle and turned back. 'C'mon now,' he said, 'or the sunburn will be all you have to remember this job by.' He helped her up and held her elbows and she hopped, experimentally. 'Can you walk on that?'

'Think so.'

He grinned. 'Was thinking I'd have to carry you there.'

She said nothing, and they walked slowly down the track, their shadows long in front of them. Just before they reached the yard gate she said to him, 'Promise you won't laugh if I tell you something?'

'What?'

'Promise first.'

He frowned. 'What?' he repeated.

'Something strange.'

He glanced at her sideways but she was looking at her feet. 'When I was walking up,' she said, 'it was like – ah, you will, you'll think I'm daft.' She smiled at him.

He took his hand off her elbow. 'Tell me,' he said, but he was looking down the hill now; he wanted to be back soon or he'd be catching it.

'It was like I was surrounded by – a crowd, a crowd of people. All walking beside me.'

'Right you are.' He moved off again.

'I know it sounds . . .' she said, and he shrugged. 'But that's what it felt like,' she went on. 'I had the feeling we were all walking in a big line up there, just heading up the hill together. And it was when I got to the gate, they were all pressing in at me. And I didn't have the space to open it. Swear to God. And I went into the ditch and I felt, well, footsteps going on ahead, over me. And then they were gone and everything was – normal again.'

'So.' He'd slowed to a stop. 'You saw a crowd of folk up on the hill?'

'No, I didn't see them. There was no one there.'

'Right. Heard them, then.'

'I think so. Kind of.' She turned to where he'd stopped on the track and swiped at his chest with her hand. 'You said you wouldn't laugh.'

'I'm not laughing,' he said.

'Aye but you nearly are. Look, I know it sounds daft.'

'Well.'

'Forget it,' she said. They had reached the yard now; all the cows had gone. Donnie wondered how long he had been away and who had seen them up there.

'I'd better get back to the bar,' he said. 'And Saltcoats wants a word with you.'

She looked him in the eye and smiled. There was a small gap between her two front teeth.

'I'll be seeing you,' he said.

But he did not, for days after that, although he'd managed to ask enough in a roundabout way to know she had not been sacked. Towards the end of that week, the humidity lifted and they had a fortnight of dry, fine weather. A fresh wave of visitors descended on the hotel and Donnie's duties increased tenfold. There were early mornings, stumbling home over the hill in the dawn to snatch a few hours of sleep at Crois na Coille before it was back to the hotel. If he had a morning off there were chores to be done for Bella. She would try to stuff his pockets with oatcakes as he left again in the afternoon. Sometimes if the guests stayed up late he would sleep at the hotel, unrolling a camp bed in the cupboard behind the tap room and slipping out as the kitchen staff arrived to start breakfast the next morning. He'd help McColl with the milking and then he'd feed and brush the horses, Tinto and Mannanan, before turning them out.

Tinto was a little piebald of about fourteen hands. Ursula Saltcoats liked to drive him in a trap for guests during the summer. He didn't do much work otherwise. He was elderly, quiet and calm, and Donnie could hop on to his back without a saddle or stirrups by standing on the drinking trough and swinging his leg over the pony's quarters. Sitting astride Tinto, he'd lead Mannanan, the handsome bay cob who belonged to the major. They'd plod out of the yard and down the track to the meadow that was their summer grazing. Early in the morning the mists would be still on the grass, each blade glistening and dew-webbed, white as lace. He'd unbuckle the horses' headcollars and watch them picking their way down to the rowan trees that bordered the burn, their noses low to the ground. Then it was back to the yard to muck out and polish the shooting brake that was used to pick up guests from the station. Check the van's oil. Many of these tasks were not among his official duties but there was extra money to be made, slipped into his pocket or his pay packet at the end of the week. The money from his wages mostly went to Bella, but he put a pound a week away in a jar. For the hazy and uncertain time that would come at the end of the summer. The future.

One morning, a week or so after their first meeting, he saw Mary Rose in the dining room, ready to begin serving breakfast. She looked very different from the girl he'd pulled from the ditch: dressed in black and white, with her bright hair pulled back from her face. Elegant. He turned away before she saw him, and felt foolish for doing so.

The next day he was unloading crates of beer from the van in the yard around the side of the kitchens when he heard his name called and turned around to find her in the kitchen doorway.

'Here. These are for you.' She was holding out a packet of Woodbines.

'Och no.' He straightened, shaking his head. 'Save them for yourself.'

'No, you will.' She stepped forward and tapped them into the breast pocket of his shirt, then turned before he had time to thank her and went back into the kitchens again.

'Who was that?' Bruce Langlands came around the corner as Donnie bent over the crates once more. He said nothing, continued unloading. 'Mary Rose,' said Bruce, and Donnie stopped, looked up.

'You know her?'

Bruce shrugged, grinned. 'Smasher, eh?'

Donnie straightened, feeling the crate heavy in his arms. 'She's alright.'

That Friday he was sent into Carrabhal to post an envelope of fishing licences. When he came out of the post office, Mary Rose was sitting on the wall outside. She hopped off the wall as if she had been waiting for him.

'You again,' she said. She gathered her hair in one hand and twisted it down her shoulder where it shone copper in the sun.

'Mary Rose.' He liked the way her name seesawed in his mouth. She fell into step with him and they walked the road back to the hotel together. He bought two strawberry Mivvies from the village shop and she told him about her family. Her father was Polish, and had stayed on after the war. Her mother was from County Wexford in Ireland. She described her brothers (three of them, all working at Fairfield shipyard in Govan) and her sisters, one of whom had married a welder and one who had gone out to Australia.

'How come you don't have a Polish name, then?' Donnie said.

'I do. Sikorska. Mam chose our first names, but she didn't think of the mouthful, did she?'

'Mary Rose Sikorska,' Donnie said. 'Sounds like a ballet dancer.'

'I always had to stand in for the man when we did dancing at school,' she said. 'And a Roman soldier in the school play. Every year. Tall, you see?'

Donnie laughed.

'I am.' She darted in front of him so he nearly bumped into her. 'See me, I come up to your nose and you must be over six foot.'

'You must be joking.'

'Here's one for you,' she said. 'Why did the foot laugh?'

'What's that?'

'A joke. Why did the foot laugh?' she repeated. He realised she was reading off the lolly stick. He'd long since thrown his away.

'Not a clue, Mary Rose,' he said, and kept walking. ''Cos it was tickled, or something.'

'Because it was toe happy!' she crowed.

'Very funny, aren't you?'

'I have my moments.'

'Shame that wasn't one of them.'

'You tell us a joke, then.'

'Never said mine were any better.' He tried to remember one that didn't involve an Irishman, a Scotsman and an Englishman. He landed on one he'd heard from Bruce, about a chicken that danced on a biscuit tin, but all he could remember was the punchline about blowing out the candle, and she was unimpressed.

'Well, that's your lot,' he said. 'That's the only clean one I know.'

'A dirty one will do.'

'I don't think so.'

'You think you'll shock me,' she said, and laughed.

'See now,' he said, 'why bother with jokes when I'm so naturally funny?'

'Dirty jokes are the only ones worth telling,' she said.

They walked on, and he made her laugh with his impressions of Saltcoats and McColl on the day the cows went wandering.

Thursday 19 March 1998

Anna

'*And thorns shall come in her palaces, nettles and brambles in the fortresses thereof: and it shall be a habitation of dragons, and a court for owls.*'

Fern settles her spectacles on to the bridge of her nose with a hooked finger and peers at me over the rims. 'Isaiah,' she says. 'Chapter thirty-four, verse thirteen.'

We are in her study in the middle of the morning. I am surreptitiously scraping dried jackdaw droppings off the back of the settee with a duster, listening to my great-aunt reciting scripture and pretending she doesn't have a hangover.

Fern's study is stacked with books and journals, four filing cabinets marking each corner of the room like turrets. Once, when I was only table-high, I was playing in here and knocked one of the reel-to-reel tape recorders on to the floor. It hit the ground with a crack, its mechanical insides spilling out. I heard my great-aunt galloping down the corridor in my direction, demanding to know what was going on. When she came into the room I had stared dumbly at her, convinced there would be hell to pay.

But Fern had bent down to my height, removing the conjoined tape reels from what was left of the damaged machine. Holding them like two fresh eggs, she'd sat down in her chair and placed them on the desk before her.

'These,' she had said, pointing to the reels, 'are precious. Not because of what they *are*, but because of what they *contain*. People's lives are in here, Anna. Their memories, their wisdom.

Their jokes, and – ' she flicked her fingers open like fireworks ' – their *spells*!'

I watch my great-aunt now as she closes the black Bible, a task that requires both hands. She carries it across the room, replacing it on its side in the alcove by the fire. Outside, the rain has eased and feeble sun rays are breaking through. The yellow hill is bathed in a storm-sick glow.

'Where people have lived, nettles will follow.' Fern plucks a half-smoked Regal from behind her right ear and points with it down the field beyond the window. 'Mina MacPherson's old house – there's a fortress of nettles, these days. I remember the night we could see the smoke and flames from where we lay in bed. Nodded off with one of these, like as not. It was Angus John went in for her, before the fire service arrived. Only just got her out in time.' She eyes the end of her cigarette. 'A house becomes ruined more quickly than one would imagine. They just come apart like an untied knot. And then, the nettles.'

I remember Mrs MacPherson's house. The walls had stood for some years after the fire. There were a few weeks one year when Jamie and I had taken to going there after school. Inside the house's shell, the twisted, darkened remains of a Rayburn Royal stove still stood against the back wall. Charred beams from the roof that had fallen in on the night of the fire lay on the ground. Someone had lined up empty jam jars on the wide stone lintel that still sat across the doorway.

By late spring you couldn't get near the house walls for nettles. When autumn came, we could see that there were good brambles to be had, but by then Mum had forbidden us from going up there. *The whole place could fall in on you*, she said, *and crush you to biscuit crumbs*.

'Mina MacPherson used to be a great one for the old place names,' Fern is saying, 'was she not?'

She is talking to Bella, who has appeared in the doorway, wiping floury hands on her pinny.

'He spent a good long time in Mina's house that summer, the professor,' Fern continues. 'I think our mother was jealous.'

Bella sniffs. 'She wasn't the only one, if I remember correctly.'

'What a summer that was,' says Fern.

'For you, maybe,' Bella says.

'Sorry, where is the professor?' I cut in.

'Och, he's off visiting down the road,' says Fern. 'He's taken his car. I will not forget,' she continues, 'how he came to the house that first time, on his bicycle. Our mother thought he was selling Bibles.'

'Yes,' says Bella. 'And her just after making black pudding, and her hands all covered in—'

Fern interrupts her, shaking with laughter. 'And he's standing there with his bicycle clips on, asking her about those old stories, right there on the doorstep.'

'There's our mother,' says Bella to me, 'all bloody to the elbows—'

'Diarmuid and Grainne, I think, was the tale he was on about,' says Fern. 'The lovers. Wasn't he killed by a gigantic boar?'

'He was.'

'Who was?' I ask, lost.

'Oh, that was Diarmuid, lovely Diarmuid of the old Fenian tales,' says Fern. 'There was a mark on his face; any woman who caught a glimpse of it would fall in love with him on the spot. Of course it all ended badly for him. The professor, now – well of course he wasn't the professor then, he was just a lad of twenty or so—'

'She did not know whether to make head nor tail of him,' says Bella.

'Neither did we, Bel,' says Fern.

'I mind you were awful soft on him.'

Fern doesn't reply immediately, rocking slowly back and forth on her heels, smiling, looking out of the window again.

'You were hardly able to speak for a week after he left.'

'Now that,' says Fern, 'I do not remember.' She gives me an unsettling wink. 'And he was married to a girl from London all that time,' she says, 'I do believe.'

'I'd say she had some weight of the sorrows on her,' tuts Bella. She turns back to me. 'Anna. I came to ask you. Young John Teelin was looking for a lift into town this afternoon. I thought you could take him.'

'No problem,' I say.

'They're working through by in the living room. I've made scones. They'll be getting hungry, no doubt. Would you be a pet and take them through for me?'

I follow Bella to the kitchen and lift the tray she has made up. Music drifts from the study; Fern has started to play the melodeon.

'That's an Irish song. "*An Buachaill Caol Dubh*", The slim dark boy,' Bella says. 'The professor taught her that tune all those years ago. And he always said, the song wasn't about a boy at all, but a glass of Guinness.' She tuts, her head on one side, listening. 'Aye,' she says, on one indrawn breath. 'And he would know.'

I make my way down the corridor to the living room, trying not to trip over the collies, and the English words to that song creep into my mind, as my mother used to sing it.

When I go to the market to make a purchase I grasp my earnest money within my hand

A dark slender boy still seeks and searches till he slips beside me, sedate and bland.

'Tis not long after, my senseless laughter will reach the rafters ...

*   *   *

'Tea break,' I announce, edging sideways to get the tray through the door. Erin and John Teelin are sitting on the settee behind a coffee table scattered with papers, maps and books. I hope I haven't interrupted some intimate moment. I haven't quite worked out what their relationship is.

Erin beams when she sees the tray. I wonder how anyone can have such perfectly white teeth. I smile back at her, hoping I can absolve my rudeness last night with offerings of other people's baking.

'I'll just put this on the floor,' I say. 'Save you moving everything.'

I lower the tray and Erin scoots off the sofa and plucks a scone from the pile. 'Come and join us,' she says to me, patting the carpet next to her.

My instinct is to politely refuse and leave them to it, but I find myself sitting down on the floor carefully, tucking my legs underneath me. I pour the tea. John Teelin takes his without milk. His cup is hotter than the sun and it wobbles in my hand, burning my fingers as I hold it out with the handle extended his way.

Erin bites into her scone and a stray bit of jam drops out on to the ledger John Teelin has just put down. 'We were talking to Fern about the professor's book this morning,' she says, her mouth full, 'and she showed us these early drafts. I just couldn't believe it.'

'What book's this?' I ask.

Her eyes widen above her mug. '*Tales from an Argyll Peninsula*,' she says.

I shrug, taking a sip of too-hot tea, feeling my tongue burn and fur.

Erin raises her eyebrows. 'Are you serious?'

'Why should she have heard of it?' John Teelin drawls. He opens the ledger again and flips through the pages, as if he expected nothing less.

'He wrote it back in the forties,' says Erin. 'It's a *seminal* text. Wait there.' She scrambles up and heads out of the room.

Silence falls. John Teelin doesn't look up. I pick a scone from the plate and balance it on my knee.

'Fine scones,' he says solemnly, at last. The way he says *scones* rhymes with *bones*. I didn't notice him eating one.

'Oh, Bella's a great baker,' I say.

'And here was me thinking you'd made them yourself, now.' Although his head is still bent, I can hear the smirk in his voice.

'God, no.' It comes out a bit more violently than I intended. 'This book, then?' I say.

He looks up briefly, then down again. 'Yeah,' he says. 'It's a book of tales collected from the people all around this area. Your great-grandmother's in it, I believe. Euphemia MacArthur.'

'Phamie,' I say. 'She was called Phamie.'

'Right,' he says. 'Well, there's contributions in it from Bella, too, and Janet MacArthur, your grandmother. If I'm right.' He leans on the *if* a little bit. He knows he is.

'Yes.' I say. 'Netta. She went to Canada.'

'Right, so.' He smiles tightly at me, closing the ledger with a snap and blowing his hair out of his eyes before settling back against the settee to drink his tea. I am starting to get the impression that he finds me awkward and vaguely amusing.

'Bella used to tell us stories,' I say. 'Tell them to us from her head, not read them from a book. All sorts of stories. Some she'd swear were true. A lot of them were funny, but we liked the spooky ones. In fact they scared us witless, a few of them, as kids. Some of those stories . . . they were really . . .' I look over to him, quickly, not expecting to catch his eye, but he's staring at me with disconcerting intensity. He listens for a living, I think. I hear my own words filling up the air.

Stop, I tell myself, and pick up the scone from my knee. *Stop talking so much*. 'Anyway,' I finish, lamely. 'She never needed a book.'

'Is that right?' Taking tobacco and papers out of his pocket, he begins to roll a cigarette. His long fingers are smudged with ink. When he dips his head to lick the seal of the paper I notice he has a small silvered scar, crescent-moon-shaped, on the bridge of his nose.

'Here,' he says, 'if it's no bother to you, Anna, I asked Bella this morning about getting a lift to the library.' He gets up to his feet, the cigarette held between his teeth, and starts patting his pockets for matches, obviously angling to leave.

'Yeah,' I say, 'I can take you. Whenever you like.' I wish I hadn't said that, as if I have nothing better to do.

'Thanks.' He goes over to the doorway and pauses, one hand holding it open. He moves with the casual grace of a sportsman: loose-limbed, assured. 'Ten minutes?' he says. 'That sound alright?'

'Twenty,' I say. 'I have to clear up this lot and there's a couple of other things to finish first.'

'Whatever suits you.' I think he's going to use my name again, but instead he says, 'Is it true you don't sing?'

'What?' I look up sharply at him. 'Yes, it's true.'

'I see.' He sings a snatch of the song I was humming before, on my way down the corridor. Only he sings it in Irish. '*Nuair théim ar aonach ag ceannach éadaigh, is bíonn an éirnis agam im' láimh.* Could have sworn I heard that, earlier.'

'Not me,' I say. 'Fern was playing it on the melodeon. And I don't speak Irish. And also, you forgot to put your finger in your ear.'

'My . . .?' He looks perplexed, then laughs. 'Well. That's true, at least.' He makes to leave, then turns to look back towards me. 'You know, it's not about a man, that song. It's in praise of Guinness.' He sticks his hands in his pockets, toes a worn patch in the carpet. 'The drink, you see?' His tone is patient, instructive.

'Yeah. I know what Guinness is.' I push things together on the tray. Things aren't fitting correctly; it's irritating.

'Right. And did you know they used to prescribe it to pregnant women? Doctors?'

I keep my head down, staring at the tray, hearing my pulse throbbing in my ears. There's no way. No way he could—

'And racehorses,' he is saying now. I breathe out. He means nothing by it. He's just talking. 'Arkle got through a couple of pints a day. Anyway. Twenty minutes, yeah?'

He walks away, whistling. I sit on the carpet for a minute, hunched over the tray. My tongue is still burning. I pull myself upright at the sound of footsteps on the stairs.

'Here.' Erin strides into the room and hands me a hardback book. *Tales from an Argyll Peninsula*, it says on the cover. *Collected from the Oral Tradition by William Croke*. The paper of the jacket feels slightly chalky and sticks to my fingers. The cover is a gaudy colour photograph; Crois na Coille is instantly recognisable beneath the hill.

'It's a first edition,' Erin breathes. 'Super-rare. Took me ages to get my hands on one. You don't even want to know what I paid for it. You've honestly never seen it before?'

I shake my head, flicking through the pages. Many of the stories I recognise immediately. 'The Girl Pursued by a Fairy Suitor', 'The Old Man of Lecknaban', 'Neil MacArthur's Snuff Mill'. I want to ask her how much it was, for these stories that my family told for free. But I keep quiet, turning to the middle section where there are three thick, shiny pages of photographs. There is a black and white picture of a group of people standing in the doorway of the house, captioned *The MacArthur Family*. Beneath the caption their names are given from left to right. John MacArthur, my great-grandfather, stands beside his wife Phamie. Her hand rests on the shoulder of a young boy with fair hair who is hugging a collie pup. Angus John. Beside him are the twins, recognisable even now. Bella is sturdy, blonde like her brother, while Fern is tall and thin. Twins in name only, Fern would sometimes remark.

The third girl is older, with dark hair. Netta MacArthur, my grandmother. She is gazing at the camera with an inscrutable expression.

'You can borrow it, if you like,' says Erin, and I realise I have lowered my face down only an inch or two away from the book.

I look up with a jolt, close the book and hold it out to her. 'Ah no, it's OK, thanks.' Accepting it would seem like some kind of an admission that she and John Teelin and the professor have knowledge of my family which is somehow closed to me, which makes me feel like an intruder.

'Are you sure?'

'Honestly.' I laugh uncomfortably. 'Knowing me, I'd probably spill something on it.'

'OK.' She takes the book from me, sits back on the sofa and picks up some papers from the coffee table. 'Where'd John get to?' she asks.

'Out for a smoke, I think.' I offer her some more tea but she declines, obviously keen to get back to her work, so I lift the tray and leave the room. There's no sign of John Teelin when I go through to the kitchen, but a thin plume of smoke gives away his presence in the back garden. I stop for a minute, pushing the tea tray between my hip and the sink, and without exactly looking I can picture the span of his shoulders in his white shirt, how his hair lifts in the breeze.

Shame he's a bit of a pillock.

I do the dishes and mop the floor, and then I take the keys for the Land Rover and go out into the yard. The petrol pump has to be primed before it will even consider starting; I pull the choke out before switching on the ignition and pressing the starter switch.

'Lovely wheels.' John Teelin is leaning against the barn door, watching me. His coat is slung across his shoulder and two of the collies sit at his feet, leaning against his legs and staring up at him so their bodies make perfect prism points. I lean over to open the Land Rover's passenger door and he hops in, depositing a satchel of files and papers in the footwell.

'Sooks,' I say to the dogs, who are now sidling around to the back of the vehicle, getting ready to chase or leap in the back, whichever opportunity presents itself first.

'This is like going back in time,' he says, looking around him. 'I've never been in one of these before.' He twists his head, considering the Land Rover's vintage innards. 'What is it, Series Two? Three?'

'Not a clue,' I say.

'Two, I reckon,' he says. He slides open the window, sticks his head out to survey the bashed bodywork and whistles at the collies, who stare mournfully back, whimpering. 'Dogs?' he enquires, turning back to me.

'We won't take them with us this time,' I say; 'they sound like the hounds of hell in the back with all the excitement of the big town.'

'Exactly how I feel myself,' he says.

I snigger. 'A trip to the library,' I say. 'Hold me back.'

He raises an eyebrow, grins. 'Don't knock it till you've tried it.'

'I've been to the bloody library before, John,' I say. There's an edge to my voice I didn't quite mean to be there.

'Of course,' he says. 'I was only kidding.'

'I know. Sorry.' I'm not a complete cow, I want to tell him. I concentrate on steering the Land Rover down the track to the road, skirting around potholes. He leans forward, his hands on his knees, staring out at the landscape around us, watching buzzards leaning into the wind above the rough grazing where it gives way to the planted forest.

'You know, she's not the way I thought she'd be – Bella,' he says suddenly.

'No?' You're not the way I thought you'd be either, I think.

'No. She's some woman, isn't she? I suppose I imagined her as a sort of Mother Goose character. Cuddly, you know? In fact, she's kind of severe.'

I have to laugh at the idea of Bella as cuddly, and after a moment he laughs too, as if relieved.

'Not that there's anything wrong with that,' he says. 'But Fern, though, she's lovely, isn't she? That room of hers – like an Aladdin's cave.' He shakes his head. 'How did Fern not make it into that book?'

I shrug. 'No use asking me. I didn't even know about that book until earlier, did I? But it was Bella their mother taught the stories to.' I feel the need to talk, to make up for earlier. 'Fern did teacher-training. She was in Glasgow during the war. Bella stayed behind and looked after their parents, and then she got married, to Archie. I think they maybe couldn't have children.' This is not something I have heard from Bella, of course, but Fern has hinted at it. 'Anyway, Bella brought up my dad as her own. Well, she and Archie both did, until he died. They had the tenancy of the farmland then, that used to be around Crois na Coille. It belonged to the Altnaglas estate. But Archie died when my dad was in his teens and the estate sold up to the Forestry Commission. A bit later Fern moved back up to Crois na Coille to live with Bella. And that's how they've been, since.'

I pause. It's happened again, me yakking on and on. 'So there you have it,' I say. 'A potted history of the recent MacArthur family, as far as I know it. You can put that in the book you're writing. Your research.'

Out of the corner of my eye I can see him shaking his head. 'It's not really that sort of book,' he says. 'It's more a biography, of the professor. His life and times. He's an extraordinary man. I wanted to start work on it while he was still alive, you know? Too many of these sorts of projects only get going once the person's dead and there's a hundred and one questions you wished you could have asked and of course it's too late.' He fiddles with the lever on the wiper motor. 'On the other side, of course, you don't have the safety and freedom of writing about someone who can't argue back. It's a bit of a balance. But he and I are close. He took some persuading, but he knows why I want to do it now. He might not have all that long.'

'Right,' I say. I wonder if I should have told him all those things about our family. He's probably mostly interested in how they fit in around the professor's life, not for their own sake. Just gathering data. I focus on the road, on the weaving dance of passing places, on avoiding the deep ditches at the side of the road. After about twenty minutes we pass the sign that reads, *You Are Now Entering Barnadine. Twinned with Eyebrow, Saskatchewan.* I resist the temptation to point out local landmarks as we pass them – the fountain where all the kids would gather on a Friday night, the parking spot by the graveyard, the Good Luck takeaway.

The library building is the kind you might mistake for a campsite toilet block, but John Teelin seems undaunted, descending from the Land Rover with his battered leather satchel dangling from his shoulder like an overgrown schoolboy. He pauses on the kerb, one hand tapping on the Land Rover roof. 'You're not – coming in, no?'

I shake my head. 'I've messages to get.' We agree to meet in an hour.

July 1960

Donnie

They began to seek each other out in the weeks that followed, Donnie and Mary Rose. He'd try to time his breaks for when she'd be on the back step outside the kitchens. If she wasn't there, he'd wait for her. The others started teasing him in the bar, whistling Michael Holliday's 'Starry Eyed', trying to make his ears turn red, succeeding. When he was working he'd find himself playing out conversations with her, saving up stories from his day, things to make her laugh.

Mary Rose, the other girls would holler through. *It's himself. Again.* They'd smirk at him until she appeared. He didn't care.

They didn't have much time off together, but on the odd evening when they were both free they'd walk out along the track, up towards the hill where they'd met that first day. Side by side. They had hardly touched since he'd pulled her out of that ditch. Sometimes their hands brushed as their arms swung, climbing the rocky track, before he opened the gate at the top field and they'd sit for a few minutes to catch their breath.

They talked all the time when they were together. They laughed at the same things. He found her clever and irreverent and far more outspoken than any girl he'd met before. In fact, he'd never met anyone like her, really. Certainly not the girls he'd palled about with in previous summers, not even Norma the butcher's daughter who didn't speak to him any more, not since Mary Rose had appeared to him from the ditch that day: Mary Rose of the mysterious visions and the laugh that set him sideways.

'Tell me your worst memory,' she said to him. They were sitting at the foot of the yellow hill beside the gate that led up on to the pass that crossed to the other side, to Donnie's home of Crois na Coille. Watching the horses standing nose to tail nibbling each other's backs, little and large. There was a smell of smoke on the air that made it feel almost autumnal although it was only July.

'My worst memory,' he said. 'Some question that is.'

'I'll tell you mine if you tell me yours.' She gathered her hair on top of her head.

'Oh, I'll tell you mine,' he said. 'Once I've decided what it is.'

He knew exactly what it was, no doubt about that. But he pushed it down, and tried to think of other things. The day that the garron sank in the bog and had to be shot. His Uncle Archie dying. He could fob her off with a thousand other fears, injuries, embarrassments. But finally he said, 'You know I was brought up by my Auntie Bella.'

'I do.'

'One time when I was very young,' he said, 'my mother came back. And they made me choose. Stay with Bella or go with her. I think that was the worst.'

She put her head sideways on her knees. He felt her eyes on him and he stared up at the hill as he told her.

When he finally looked at her, Mary Rose's eyes were wide. She squeezed his arm.

'Jeezo,' she said. 'You ever wonder if you should have gone with her?'

'Suppose I do, sometimes.'

'Bit much, when you were so wee and all, eh?' She paused, and then she said, 'Still. You were wanted. The pair of them were both wanting you.'

'I reckon.'

'It was the opposite with us. Too many kids. Knackered, my mam was. The three of us – we were the youngest, we sort of knew that we were the extras. Patrick and Frankie, that was different, they were the oldest two, the boys. And Bernadette, she was next. But me and John-Joe and Carm, nah. We were just Friday night weans, and we knew it.'

'Friday night?'

'Aye, just my dad when he got back from the pub. On he'd climb and there she'd be, knocked up with another one.' She laughed, pushed his shoulder suddenly. 'Do I shock you, Donnie MacArthur, do I?'

He caught her fingers in his hand and held them for a second, then dipped his head and brushed his lips to the underside of her wrist, where the needle-thin veins branched beneath skin so fine as to be nearly translucent. For a moment she cradled his cheek with her fingers, and then she took her hand away.

'Time to go,' she said. She stood up, brushing herself down, tugging at her skirt. 'I'll see you tomorrow.'

She started off down the track towards the hotel, and he watched her, thinking how purposefully she moved. Just before her head disappeared behind the lump in the road he jumped up and ran to catch her.

She swung round as he drew level with her, grinning and flicking her hair back.

'You never told me yours,' he said. 'Your worst memory.'

'Next time,' she said.

He fell into step beside her. 'I'll walk you down,' he said. 'There's strange folk around. You know.'

'Oh, I know,' she said.

He found a nest of kittens in the hay loft when feeding the horses one morning, huddled out of sight behind a beam. The mother was nowhere to be seen. He stirred the three tiny scraps of tabby fur gently with his finger, but they were unresponsive, stiff and cool to the touch. A shame, even if McColl would probably have drowned them in a sack had they been alive. Donnie turned away to heave a bale to the edge of the loft hatch, thinking to come back later and get rid of them, when a weak mew made him look back. A tiny black and white head was peeping out from between its dead siblings. It must have been underneath the others, staying warm. He scooped up the survivor, finding it to be pure white except for a heart-shaped splotch of black between its ears, like a little cap. Perhaps three weeks old, he reckoned. The kitten cried again and he tucked it into his shirt.

'Something for you,' he said to Mary Rose later that day.

He told her to close her eyes, but they flew open when he placed the small slip of life in her hands. She cradled the kitten, marvelling at its size, its blue eyes, its delicate paw pads as pink as her fingers. 'Is it a girl?' she asked, and he said he couldn't be sure but he thought it was a boy. She put the kitten down and walked her fingers across the floor, laughed as it attempted to bat at her hands. 'He's awful wee,' she said. 'Where's his mum?'

'No sign of her.' He didn't tell her about the others. The kitten mewed, a little wobbly on its feet still, its tiny mouth agape. 'It's hungry,' Donnie said. 'Will I show you how to feed it?'

She flicked an eyebrow at him. 'I know how to feed a cat, Donnie.'

'Aye, but it's different for a kitten this young. You've got to take care. Here.' He showed her how to get the kitten to take tiny bits of meat from the tip of a finger, how to clean it and rub its belly afterwards like the mother would.

'How do you know this?' she asked him.

He shrugged. 'Just do.' When Archie had farmed Crois na Coille while he was growing up, his uncle had seemed to be permanently saving or taking lives.

114

She stroked the tiny creature with the back of her finger as it fell asleep in her lap. 'He needs a name,' she said. 'What do you think?'

'Lucky,' said Donnie. 'But he's yours, Mary Rose. What do you want to call him?'

She ran her fingertip over the tiny dome of the cat's skull. 'Elvis.'

He laughed. 'What sort of a name is that for a cat?'

'Ssh. Don't wake the King.' She bent her head close to her lap, so its soft fur was against her cheek. 'He's beautiful. We were never allowed a pet at home. There were enough mouths to feed, so there were.' She looked up, grinned at him. 'Not like you, with your dogs and sheep and ducks and all that.' Then her face fell. 'I don't think I can keep him with me, though. What if Florrie found out I was keeping a wee cat?'

Florrie Stewart was the head of housekeeping at the hotel. She was kind enough but fierce and you crossed her at your peril. 'Ah, Florrie's that short-sighted, she'll never notice,' said Donnie.

Mary Rose made a face. 'Nearly lost my job with those cows, didn't I? Can't get the sack over a kitten.'

'Right enough,' said Donnie. 'Don't want you to get into trouble. I can ask Bella if we can take him to Crois na Coille for a while, just while he gets strong.' But it would be hers, he said. Mary Rose's. Perhaps she could visit him there, see how he grew.

Perhaps she would, she said.

Bella was on to him, of course. 'And who is she?' she asked, when Donnie came home that evening and introduced Elvis to the collies, watching carefully to be sure they didn't maul the wee scrap to death.

'It's a he,' Donnie said, his eyes on the kitten, and Bella said,

'You know that's not what I'm asking. When am I going to meet her?'

After some prodding from Bella, it was arranged that Mary Rose would visit for lunch the next week, when they both had the afternoon off. Donnie had never brought home someone she didn't know before, and Bella was polite but tense, on her guard.

'I'm sure she's a nice enough lassie,' she said afterwards, in the kitchen of Crois na Coille, 'but I just hope you're not losing your head, Donald. Mind it's not the same where she's from. The city.' She kept her back turned from him, hacking a knife through a cabbage, the blade thumping loudly on the board.

Donnie was bringing armfuls of firewood into the kitchen, stacking it beside the Rayburn. When he was finished he went up behind Bella and squeezed her shoulder and she put the knife down. Her hand came up and held his.

'And I dare say she's Catholic,' she said.

Donnie pretended he hadn't heard that. If Bella had her way he'd be at home forevermore. She said she wanted him to make his way in the world but he knew that she feared this too. She feared that 'the city', that nameless, many-tongued creature of vice and greed, would open its mouth and swallow him whole as soon as he turned his head towards it.

Thursday 19 March 1998

Anna

In the Co-op I trudge the aisles squinting at a list Bella gave me. My main mission is to complete this trip without seeing anyone I know, so as not to have to answer the inevitable questions about being back or, indeed, where I went. I am nearly successful, filling my basket quickly, paying for the items with the twenty pounds I took from Liam's jacket. It's that or shredding the money and dropping it into a bin. At least I'm not spending it on myself.

I dread to imagine how far overdrawn I must be by now. My student grant is long gone. I gave most of it to Liam, for reasons that seem so foolish and naïve now that my brain stutters over the memory. And I refused to take Bruce's offer of help, of course. His largesse stretched only so far as my mum could see it. We'd argued about that, Mum and I, and the argument had haemorrhaged into a fight, bleeding out in a surge of ugly recriminations that I don't like to think about either.

When I lived with Liam, there always seemed to be something rotten at the back of the fridge, something unidentifiable that didn't bear looking at too closely. Something that both of us silently refused to take responsibility for and throw out. And it's like that now, with me and Mum and Bruce. Even though we are back on speaking terms again, seeing each other is to open that door, if even just by a crack, and out leaks the stench of the unsayable.

I'll have to get a job. Perhaps they need shelf-stackers here. I could work night-times.

Head down and moving fast, I am making for the exit when I hear my name called and turn to see a girl with corkscrews of blonde hair pushing an overloaded trolley.

'Anna! It is you!' she is saying. 'Woah. You're in a hurry.'

'Hi, Leighanne.' I manage a weak smile. 'How are you?' Leighanne Leitch and I were in high school together. We'd both left after fourth year and worked at the Tayfillan Hotel that summer. She was kind, Leighanne. And fun. We used to have a laugh. We haven't spoken in two years at least.

'Is it nursing you're doing?' she is asking now. She is wearing eyeliner and lipliner and has definitely got blonder and slimmer. Her eyebrows seem to have disappeared altogether, but are beautifully pencilled in.

'Kind of,' I say. She nods and, bless her, doesn't ask more. 'What have you been up to yourself?' I ask, quickly.

'Ah, this and that. You know me, Anna.'

I don't really, I think. It's funny how we spent so much time together as teenagers, and how easily our lives have split now.

She is holding her left hand in front of my face now, wiggling her fingers.

'Oh, wow,' I say, registering the sparkling ring. 'Engaged. Wow. Ross?'

Her face screws up. 'Ross!' She throws back her head with a peal of laughter. 'Oh, my God. No. He went to Saudi. Can you believe it? He'll be looking like one of these now, so he will.' She plucks a packet of pink wafer biscuits from her trolley and brandishes it. 'I'm with Chris now.'

I do remember Ross as a bit of a peely-wally redhead. 'Chris,' I say, trying to remember. 'Chris Currie?' Ross's best friend.

'That's the one.'

'Congratulations.' Are you meant to say congratulations to the girl? I can never remember.

Chris Currie and Liam were mates and we are veering into dangerous territory; she is going to ask me in a minute if I'm with someone, and Liam's name is bound to come up. I ask her where she's working now and she launches into a complicated tale involving a lot of names I am evidently expected to know. I try to keep track but before long I am drifting, staring at a wee boy in the trolley opposite crushing savoury eggs into his mouth.

'I mean, I do know it's a bit out of the blue,' she is saying, and I realise that she has stopped speaking and is waiting for a reply.

'Sorry,' I say, 'what was that?'

'Just we're so stuck for staff at the hotel,' she says, 'and I've got a christening—'

'Which hotel?'

'I just said!' She giggles. 'Same old space cadet, eh, Anna? The Tayfillan. I'm still there, were you not hearing me? It's just wee Finlay, my sister's boy, he's being christened and that's in Helensburgh and I can't miss it, I mean I told them back when it was first arranged, but did he remember, no he didn't, and so now I'm stuck unless I can sort out cover, and . . . what do you think? You could stay in my room. If that makes a difference.'

A couple of shifts at the hotel. The money would certainly be handy, and it would buy me a little more time, to figure out what to do next. 'Yeah,' I say. 'I think it should be fine.'

She beams, clasps me briefly and tightly in a mini hug which takes me entirely by surprise. 'Honestly, Anna, you're a total star. Thank you.'

We say our goodbyes with her promising to sort it out with the hotel. I pull up the hood of my parka and go outside to the Land Rover, where I stow the bag of shopping and sit for a minute with my eyes closed. I keep feeling as if Liam is going to appear at any minute: swaggering around the corner, cruising down the road. I didn't tell him where I was going but it's not as if I've gone far. At least the hotel is not the sort of place he would just turn up.

I check my watch. I thought I'd have time to go to Boots but it's nearly an hour already since I left John Teelin at the library. I know too many people here to be waltzing around buying pregnancy tests in the middle of the day, anyway. Early morning, first thing. That would be the time. A couple of days and I might not even have to worry. It's not as if I haven't been late before.

And so I drive back to the library, where there are crows sitting on the handrails that line the steps and an old man with a bottle is nodding off on a bench outside. John Teelin isn't anywhere to be seen and I sit and chew my nails for a while, wondering if I should nip to the chemist's after all, or go in and find him. If he isn't ready I could book myself on to one of their computers, type out a CV. Or read a book, I suppose.

I used to love going into the library, when it was in the old building on Bank Street. I'd read my way through most of the children's section by the time I was eleven and as a teenager moved on to a list that Mr McCaig, my English teacher, gave me: classics and 'important twentieth-century works' that he recommended. He thought I was clever, or had the potential to be, I realise that now. He said I could get a place to study English anywhere I wanted, Glasgow or Edinburgh or even 'down south'. *Why not aim high, Anna? There are scholarships if you're prepared to work hard. You have the brains. You just have to put the work in.*

In the end, English was the only standard grade I managed to turn up for: Mum had been going through a bad relapse, the tremors so severe she couldn't drink or feed herself, let alone walk or use the toilet unaided. I disappointed Mr McCaig, I'm sure, dropping out of school at sixteen. I haven't seen him since; he may not still be alive.

It surprises me, I suppose, how no one asked, about me,

about Mum. But I took such care to be invisible, and Social Services never came near us; Mum had a morbid fear of social workers ever since Dad's death, when she'd managed to get us out of the caravan and into Beveridge Place. I scurried through my high school days like a hamster in a tube, focused on release. I was as unobtrusive as possible and unremarkable to both teachers and my fellow pupils, until I slipped silently out at the end of fourth year, and then it was as if I had never been at all. I try to remember the last book I read and find I can't remember. I finished *O Caledonia* the day Liam first came to our house. Perhaps that was it. Liam didn't have a single book in his flat except for a microwave cookbook his mum had given him. He didn't even have a microwave.

I'm absorbed in my own thoughts and get a shock when John Teelin opens up the Land Rover's passenger door, muttering apologies for being late.

'How did you get on?' I ask.

He doesn't reply, climbing into the cab and digging in his pocket for his tobacco, and I'm not sure if he's heard me. I wait for a bit, uncertain as to what to do. He looks distinctly untidier than when I left him, his shirt crumpled and his hair scruffy, standing on end in places as if he's been dragging his fingers through it.

'Are you OK?' I'm definitely not one to talk, it's true, but the words *hedge* and *backwards* come to mind. Perhaps he got caught up in a passionate clinch with one of the librarians. I smother a giggle at the thought and he sighs.

'Ah,' he says. 'Yeah. I'm fine. I'm just a bit disappointed. Let's just say it was not what I was hoping for.'

'It's just a wee local library. They try their best, but they don't have a great selection.'

He laughs, and then he looks over at me and stops. 'That's not the issue,' he says, but then he laughs again. 'It's – well, I've got a bit of a pet project, you might say.'

'Yeah?'

'I won't bore you with the details,' he says, 'but when my mother died, I found out – well.' He runs his hand across his forehead, speaking quickly. 'When she died, I found out she wasn't my real mam. I mean, she was my real mam, but – not my birth mother. I was adopted.'

'Oh.' This was not what I was expecting. 'That's hard.'

'Yeah.' He slides open the window. 'I mean, it's not uncommon. It's not uncommon where I'm from, anyway. Maybe not here either. But it turns out that it's harder than you'd think to find out about your family. Your real family.'

'I'm sure,' I say. I feel a mixture of awkwardness and tenderness, that he would tell me something so personal. 'So in the library, you were . . .'

'I've got her name, but not much else. And I'm just – I mean, I'm not obsessed with it, you know? I would just – anyway. Yeah.' He pushes splayed fingers round the back of his neck, tipping his head back and drawing breath. 'I found out a relation of mine was over here, in Argyll, during the forties. Bridget Halloran. She was a cousin of my mother's mother, I think. Anyway, she was over here during the war, for work, and, well, I really don't know how, whether it was an accident or what, but she died over here.'

I think it's the most I've ever heard him speak. He retrieves a folder from his bag and straightens again, shaking his head. 'This was the only thing I could come up with.' He lifts a photocopied piece of paper, pushes it in my direction. 'Have a look if you want.'

It is a copy of a newspaper clipping, a grainy black and white photograph of a group of girls in front of a barn. Some are in overalls or boiler suits. The caption beneath reads *Local Girls Welcome the 'Lumberjills' to Carrabhal.*

'Women's Timber Corps,' John Teelin says. 'She came here to work in the forests, during the war.'

'They look hardy,' I say. Two of the girls are holding a Clydesdale horse harnessed to a log. Others, presumably the 'local girls', are in spring dresses; some hold children by the hand or a baby in their arms. 'So which one was Bridget, then?'

'Well, this is it,' he says. 'I don't exactly know. The photo is of a welcome party when the Women's Timber Corps arrived: there's locals there, volunteers – some of them are dressed for work, obviously, but it's hard to be sure who's who.' He leans down and takes another photograph out of a folder. 'This is the only photo I've found of her so far,' he says.

The image looks as though it has been cut out and blown up from a larger print. Made up of black dots and white space, it could be any young woman really: light hair swept up at her temples and indistinct features.

'Not much to go on,' I agree. 'There might be folk around here, though, who could tell you more. I mean, Bella was around during the war, as I said. Fern was mostly away in Glasgow.'

'I suppose I could ask Bella,' John Teelin says. He slides the photographs back into his bag as I pull away from the kerb.

July 1960

Donnie

Major Saltcoats and his wife Ursula held a garden party at the hotel around midsummer each year. The hotel staff were expected to serve guests during the day, and were allowed their own party at night.

On the day of the party this year, Donnie started work just after five, helping McColl with the milking before joining a group of staff setting up the marquee on the hotel's lawn. Then, as the early morning mist lifted, he carried crates of glasses from the bar and emptied tins of fruit cocktail into tall jugs of Pimm's. The rest of the morning was taken up with any number of last-minute tasks demanded of him before he changed into a white jacket that had once belonged to Saltcoats ('in my rather slimmer youth'), ready to serve drinks to the arriving guests.

By the time the partygoers were mingling on the lawn it had turned into a beautiful day, one of the warmest of the year so far. Donnie stood behind a drinks table. He watched the quilled shimmer of starlings in the hedge that bordered the south side of the lawn. The guests were clustered in little groups of polite conversation. He wondered what on earth they found to talk about.

Mary Rose was one of the girls moving from group to group serving drinks and canapés. When she came to gather more glasses from the table he tried to catch her eye but she refused to take the bait, sailing off serenely without a glance as if she were one of the guests. He tried to see her with a stranger's eyes, floating about with her tray, her nose in the air. She turned round once, to wink at him when no one was looking, and he felt it like a small spark inside him.

At about four o'clock, there was a stir amid the guests with reports that a Rolls-Royce had pulled up outside the hotel. Saltcoats gripped Donnie's shoulder and steered him around to the front entrance. Donnie gaped at the car: a Silver Cloud as blue as the sky, the engine purring. A small, dapper man with hair combed slick to his scalp emerged from the interior.

'Jerome Mondegrene,' Saltcoats was saying. 'So good of you to drop in, old chap. Much obliged.'

'The pleasure, Salty, is all mine. All mine, no doubt. And it's Mondie, please.' The two men shook hands, grasping each other's elbows.

'This laddie here will park your car.' Saltcoats gestured to Donnie, who was loitering behind his employer.

It wasn't the first time Donnie had seen Jerome Mondegrene of Altnaglas. The man had a reputation for living a fairly reclusive existence but had made the odd appearance at church and charity teas and open days during his childhood. He had small, dark eyes and a prominent nose that jutted like the rudder of a boat. His skin, stretched tightly across the delicate bones of his face, had a slightly polished quality. He appeared both aged and childlike at the same time. 'Johnny in the Cradle', Donnie thought. It was one of Bella's stories, about a changeling fairy child who turned out to have great skill on the chanter and a predilection for whisky.

Saltcoats was crashing a hand down on Donnie's shoulder, saying, 'Young, I grant you, but competent behind the wheel. Isn't that right, MacArthur?'

'MacArthur . . .' Mondegrene's tone was soft and Donnie, not knowing where to look, fixed his eyes on the car. Mondegrene craned forward, looking at Donnie directly.

'Well,' he said. 'Just look at you.' One eye twitched, a tic that drew his eyelid down in a flutter, and then he rapped out, in a brisker tone, 'Hold yourself up, then, boy.' Donnie started involuntarily and Mondegrene lifted his hands skyward and sniffed, turning away with instructions to 'Give her a bit of a polish, will you.'

Saltcoats blustered his guest towards the garden with promises of a drink and acquaintances longing to meet him, and Donnie was left alone on the gravel beside the car.

He looked at his reflection in the car window, pulled his shoulders back, then opened the door and climbed gingerly into the cream interior. It smelt strongly of pipe smoke and aniseed. Donnie often ran guests to and from the station in the shooting brake, drove the Humber van for supplies and occasionally parked guests' cars, but he'd never set foot in a Rolls before.

Why the heck did he look at me like that? he wondered. He looked at his face in the rear-view mirror, smoothed down his hair. Then he inched the car cautiously across the gravel, parked around the side of the building, and fetched a chamois to polish it.

'Going up in the world, eh, Donnie-boy?'

It was his mate Bruce, with an older boy in tow whom Donnie didn't know. Bruce tended to come and go as he felt like it; he didn't officially have a job at the hotel but he often helped out with the fishing and the boats, when he wasn't working with his dad at the quarry. Now he was inspecting the car from all angles, whistling his admiration. The other lad stood back, saying nothing.

'This is Geordie,' Bruce said. 'Up for the week with his dad.'

'Alright?' Donnie nodded to Geordie, who nodded back, unsmiling. He was well built, with dark hair shorn close to his scalp and a pale, watchful face. Donnie realised he had seen him a few times, out with his father, a big burly man with a booming laugh. A policeman. His son slid along behind him as if he were his father's shadow. Bruce had taken them out a few times fishing.

'Thought you'd be in there pouring the champagne,' said Bruce, 'not playing the chauffeur.'

'Aye, I was.' Donnie twirled the car's key around his finger. 'I need to get back. You around later on?'

It would be later in the evening, much later, when the floor was cleared in the hotel's dining room and leftover food from the day was laid out on trestle tables. Last year there had even been a rather sober bowl of punch provided.

'I'll be there,' said Bruce. He turned to Geordie. 'You could come along too, if you've a mind,' he said. 'Be good craic.'

'Maybes,' Geordie replied. Donnie had the feeling he'd be asking his dad first.

The staff party that night played out as promised. There was dancing, and singing. One of the lads from Glasgow had brought his guitar. His party piece was 'Yakety Yak' and he played it about six times, his pal dancing around him pretending to play the sax, until Donnie thought his ears would burst in protest. They all ended up squashed into the public bar and Bruce, always surprisingly shy in company, was egging Donnie on to do his card and coin tricks. Donnie pretended to need persuading and then did a few, and a small crowd gathered round him. They asked him to do the tricks again and again, but he said the magic only worked a couple of times – too many and someone was sure to catch him out. Bruce was the perfect foil; Donnie made coins appear in his hands and his shoes and even underneath his shirt collar, and Bruce pretended to be stunned each time, big and blinking and game.

'This is like Christmas with my Uncle Paudie,' said a voice near his ear. 'Half-crowns up your nose.' Donnie looked round to Mary Rose who was standing close by his shoulder, her hair under the light shining the same bright copper as the coins in his hand. He flicked a penny high in the air, caught it, made it disappear in his fingers and reappear in her curls.

'Next you'll be pulling a rabbit from a hat,' she said.

'Ach, it's just done with a flick of the wrist.'

'I bet it is.' She smirked.

He laughed. Then he stood and made for the bar. Saltcoats had given him permission to open it on the proviso that he sold every drink and only poured what came out of the taps: no spirits. A few had brought bottles with them. There wasn't much money spent.

Mary Rose was reputed to have a lovely voice; they were all trying to get her to sing. It wasn't until Donnie went behind the bar and poured her a clandestine glass of sherry that she finally agreed, and then she waited until the room fell silent before she began. She leant on the bar in front of him with her gorgeous hair falling down her arms and she sang. Her voice was not loud but it carried. She did not close her eyes but looked up at the ceiling as if she was watching the song she sang unfold like a moving picture. It was the story of a mother singing to her baby as she drowned. It was possibly the saddest thing Donnie had ever heard. When it was finished there was silence; the song and the silence made everyone awkward. Some hid it by laughing and some asked her for something more cheerful. She smiled and sang 'The Spanish Lady' and the whole room joined in the chorus, the sound rising in a wave. Watching her as she sang, Donnie found himself think-ing of his mother Netta, and of the only possession he had which had belonged to her: an empty bottle of perfume, crys-tal-cut with a blue and gold label. *Shalimar*. He wondered where it was, if Bella had thrown it out. He couldn't ask her. It would upset her. Everything to do with his mother upset Bella. Donnie had learned that a long time ago.

When Mary Rose finished singing, he was done for. He thought of the time they'd spent together, of the things he'd told her. It was quite clear to him, in that moment, that she carried everything in the world he considered to be most precious, and yet he had never held on to her for more than a few seconds. He would have given anything to be alone with her, but he couldn't find the words before she'd smiled at him, hopped down from the bar stool and slipped away to the other side of the room.

He drew another pint. The barrel needed changing. He asked Bruce to take his place behind the bar while he went to the cellar. Bruce offered to go himself but Donnie said it was alright. He wanted the peace for a minute, some quiet away from the hot room and the voices. He saw Mary Rose raise her head as he flipped up the hinged bar top and left the room.

At the top of the cellar steps Donnie took the Tilley lamp off its hook and lit it. When the mantle glowed he pumped the plunger several times then walked down the steps. Eighteen steps; he counted them out of force of habit now, ever since he'd fallen his length last summer when he missed the last one. Having changed the barrel, he lingered for a moment to check the stock; Saltcoats would be asking questions come the morning.

It was as he started up the stairs once more that he heard a clunk and realised someone had shut the door at the top.

'Hey!' Donnie called. He heard voices on the other side, a scuffling sound and a thud. He stood still for a moment, listening, the darkness around him and the lamp hissing in his hand, and then he ran up the steps and put his shoulder to the door. He was braced to push as hard as he could but it opened easily and he stumbled into the narrow corridor.

There were two people against the opposite wall. He saw the end of a green skirt, and a man's leg pinning it down, and in the next second two things became clear to him: firstly, that the girl was Mary Rose, and secondly, that she was thrashing and trying to twist free against the man who was pressed against her, and who was now turning his head towards Donnie. His face had a livid scratch across one cheek and Donnie recognised Geordie Gilroy.

'Get out of there,' Donnie shouted. 'Get off her.'

Geordie released his grip on Mary Rose, who staggered forward against the opposite wall. Donnie put his hand on her shoulder. 'What's going on?' he said. He twisted his head to see Geordie already walking off smartly down the corridor.

Mary Rose leaned against the wall, wiping her face with the back of her arm. 'He was . . .' She was both angry and close to tears. 'He just –'

Ahead in the passageway Geordie did not stop or turn round, just carried on walking away. Donnie reached him before he made it round the corner, stretched and seized him by his shirt collar, pulling him around so hard he heard it rip. His other hand grabbed Geordie's neck, fingers digging in behind the Adam's apple. The impulse to squeeze and choke him surged through his muscles. Instead he pushed down hard and Geordie slumped towards the carpet on his knees.

'I saw you,' Donnie said.

Geordie's face was a blur below him. He said nothing.

Donnie shook him. 'I fucking well saw you,' he shouted.

Geordie's hands came up and took hold of Donnie's arms by the wrists. He pushed them away towards the floor, and Donnie took a step back. Geordie got to his feet slowly, purposefully, one leg at a time. He was taller than Donnie, and broader.

'You saw what?' he said. His face was impassive.

'I fucking saw you,' Donnie said again. He shoved Geordie hard and the boy stumbled sideways against the wall, his head knocking into a picture frame. 'If you lay a single finger on her again, I swear to God, I . . .'.

Geordie looked back at Donnie. His cheekbone was reddened and starting to swell; a lazy trickle of dark blood curled from his bottom lip like a stray hair. He said nothing. Didn't even blink.

Donnie took a deep breath. The urge to lash out reared up inside him. 'Is there something wrong with you?'

Again Geordie made no reply, just turned his head in the direction of the bar. He licked his bleeding lip and Donnie was sure there was a smirk on the boy's face as he started to walk away.

Mary Rose grabbed his arm. 'Leave him,' she said. 'The creep.' She spat towards Geordie's departing back.

The lights of the public bar crept beneath the door at the end of the dark corridor. The door's glass had newspapers tacked over it, and the light shone dimly through the printed pages. Now at a distance, Geordie turned around to face Mary Rose and Donnie. He put a hand up to his hair, smoothing it, then pulled the sleeves of his shirt down, one at a time. He looked at the lug of spit glistening on the carpet, then back towards them.

'Aye, on your way then,' shouted Donnie. 'Piss off.'

'Well,' Geordie said. 'I'm sure the pair of you will be very happy together.' His eyes locked on to Donnie's. 'I'll see you again,' he said, stabbing a finger towards him. Then he pulled the door open and light flooded into the corridor.

Mary Rose started off in the opposite direction. 'There's someone coming,' she said. Donnie followed her, feeling a bit sick. The way Geordie had just stood there, not even trying to fight back. It gave him a feeling of unease, a feeling that he wanted to wash his hands. If Saltcoats got even a sniff of this – and it was pretty likely he would – Donnie knew he would be out on his arse before breakfast tomorrow.

'Here,' he said, reaching her. 'This way.'

She followed him down the passageway that led to the kitchens. He opened a door to their right and they both ducked inside the full-length store cupboard. He listened, tried not to breathe. He heard muffled voices but couldn't make out any more.

'Ah, damn.' He realised he'd left the lamp standing on the floor. Still lit. 'Could burn the whole place down. I'll have to go and get it.'

'Wait,' she said. She was standing up straight next to him. He always forgot how tall she was. The store cupboard was cold. He could smell mothballs and onions and sacking. He could also smell the sweet scent of her hair. A hint of sherry. Their bodies were not touching but he could feel the fabric of her skirt against his hand. 'Wait a minute,' she said.

'Mary Rose,' he said quietly, 'what happened back there?'

She looked directly at him, her pupils large in the semi-darkness. She shook her head. 'I was – I was coming to find you,' she said. She looked down. 'He followed me. He's been mitching around me all week, actually. Just staring. I thought he was maybe not right or something. Then out there, there was someone behind me and I turned round and he pulled me back against the wall and I hit my head. Just here.'

She put a hand to her scalp and he put his hand on top of hers, just beneath the base of her skull where he could feel the soft weight of her hair. He was so close to her face he could see her lips were chapped.

'His hands were all over me,' she said. 'It was disgusting.'

'I'll kill him if he tries that again.' Gently, Donnie took his hand away from her head, opened the door a crack. The corridor was empty. He extinguished the lamp and hung it on its hook once more. In the bar he heard the wheeze of an accordion chord signalling the beginning of a dance.

'I just want to go,' she said.

'Aye. Let's get out of here. We'll go out the back of the kitchens.'

Somewhere between shutting the cupboard door behind them and the yard he felt her fingers twine around his. Together they walked down to the shore, where the dark water of the loch lapped against the bleached stones of the mooring, and the rowing boats knocked softly together in the gloom.

Thursday 19 March 1998

Anna

We stop in Carrabhal for petrol and it's only as I walk across the forecourt to pay that I see Maggie Gilmour, the Bleep, standing behind the counter. I hesitate for a moment, and then turn and motion to John Teelin to come into the shop.

The Bleep is always in her element when her local knowledge is called upon, but on this occasion she is stumped, peering at the photo and tutting.

'I'll have to ask the Oracle about that one,' she says, referring to her brother who sits through the back during the day. 'He was in the Forestry, round that time.'

She lifts the countertop and we follow her into the back of the shop. The air is so thick with cigarette smoke it takes me a second to locate the old man, who is almost subsumed within a squashy brown armchair in front of a TV. He is small and shrunken, yellowish-grey hair curling in an incongruous cowlick above his craggy face. A thin gold band glimmers in one ear.

'Lachie!' Maggie has to shout over the booming TV commentary. 'Couple of visitors for you. Wondering if they can pick your brains for a minute.'

For a few seconds Lachie gives no sign of having heard, and then he slowly raises the remote towards the telly and turns down the volume. He twists his head to survey the pair of us, moving with obvious effort.

'You're Donnie MacArthur's daughter, are you?' he says. I nod. He stubs out his cigarette in the dish that balances on his armchair and grins, revealing several gold teeth. His eyes have a glint in them like the sun on wet stones. 'Old Donnie-boy.' He lilts the words to the tune of 'Danny Boy'. 'Mine'll be a bottle of Macallan, eh?'

I look at him blankly.

'How's your mother keeping?' he asks me.

'She's doing OK, thanks.'

'Fine woman. Bloody shame, that was. Ah, Donnie-boy. What a shame.' He's talking more to himself than me. He looks at the TV, where racehorses are being led around the paddock. 'Gold Cup today,' he says. 'They'll be off in a minute. I'll give you a tip. See that there, that's Doran's Pride. You won't go far wrong there.' He is pointing to a beautiful chestnut horse with a big white blaze down its nose. 'No, won't go far wrong there,' he says again. 'Although if you're anything like your father you'll know the horses better than me.'

'I don't know anything about horses,' I say. It's true Dad loved them. He worked with them for a time, in the Forestry. He couldn't drive past a field of grazing horses without slowing or stopping. *Ah, look,* he'd say. *Horses.* If time allowed he'd be over the fence, clapping their thick necks, inspecting their teeth, murmuring to them as they huffed and prodded at his pockets, all rubbery lips and velveteen noses.

Lachie reaches for a packet of Benson & Hedges tucked down the side of his armchair. He offers the packet to me and I shake my head, but John Teelin takes one. Lachie strikes a match to light his own cigarette and then tosses the matchbox to John Teelin, who thanks him.

'Irish, are you?' Lachie says to him. He is back watching the telly. 'Doran's Pride is a Limerick lad himself.'

'Donegal,' John Teelin says. He puts the spent match in his pocket. I don't know how he can bear to breathe in any more smoke; the air in the back of the shop is practically blue. Now he looks around as if hoping for somewhere to sit, before going over to the old man's armchair and taking out the photo-copy from his bag, spreading it out on to the arm of the chair. The old man turns his head to look, blowing smoke from the corner of his mouth in the other direction.

'It's a bit of family research I'm doing,' says John Teelin. The cigarette wags as he speaks. 'And I was just wondering, would you be able to tell me the names of any of the girls in this picture?'

'The girls,' Lachie says, and he gives a laugh that turns into a hacking cough. 'The girls, eh, son? Bit old for you, no?'

John Teelin laughs dutifully. 'You're right there.' He seems at ease, in no hurry, the same as when he was tuning up his fiddle last night. I, on the other hand, am wondering how fast we can get out of here, so I can fill my lungs with lovely clean air.

The two men peer down at the paper for some time, and then Lachie clears his throat.

'That there,' he says, after about a minute, 'is Susan Carmichael.' He places a finger on one of the girls, then slides it along to her neighbour. 'And that was Daniel Lamont's daughter – can't mind her name. She was married to Tommy that had the shop in Kilchonnel. Think they went to Australia in the end.' He looks up at John Teelin. 'Irish, are you?' he says again. 'From whereabouts?'

John Teelin gives no indication that he's just answered this question. 'Donegal. Just outside of Ballintra.'

Lachie nods. 'These two were Irish, see,' he says, pointing to two girls sitting together in the front row. 'And look, this one here – ' he points to the girl sitting next to them ' – there's your sister, see?' And he stares right at me, nodding. 'Aye, your sister just there.'

'I don't—' I start, but then stop. 'Right,' I say. 'My sister.'

'Aye.' Lachie's gaze flicks up to the telly. 'Now then,' he says. 'We're nearly ready for the off.' He fumbles around for

143

the remote, which has slipped down among stacks of the *Racing Post*. John Teelin retrieves it for him and the booming commentary fills the small space again. The horses are milling around now behind the starter's tape; Doran's Pride is the favourite at nine to four. I can tell John Teelin would stay for the race given half a chance and I fight the urge to tug at his sleeve.

Mercifully, the Bleep appears again, hovering in the doorway, and I follow her out, John Teelin behind me. 'Thank you for your time,' he calls back to the armchair, but the old man is transfixed by the screen once again.

'Och, his memory's not getting any better.' The Bleep sighs as she closes the door behind her. 'And you won't get anything more out of him when the horses are running.'

I stand outside on the forecourt while John Teelin buys some Polo mints and a bottle of water. Back in the Land Rover I can still feel the pall of smoke clinging to my hair and skin. I slide open my window as far as it will go.

'I thought Crois na Coille was bad,' I say, 'with Fern puffing away on those Regals. But that was something else.' I glance across to John Teelin, who is back staring at the photocopy again.

'It's a terrible vice right enough,' he confirms. His eyes don't lift from the paper. He opens up the tube of mints and extracts one with his teeth. 'I liked the pair of them. Bet they could tell stories about this place till the cows came home.'

'You'd choke to death. You'd be as yellow as Lachie by the end.'

He proffers the mints. I take one.

'I guess one of those girls in the photo could be your . . .?' I trail off, trying to remember the family connection.

'If it is her, she was my grandmother's cousin, Bridget Halloran,' he says. 'But we'll see.' He puts the photocopy in his bag and looks over at me. 'And then there's your sister,' he says, and laughs.

'Yeah, I haven't got a clue what he meant by that. That picture must be at least fifty years old. A shame, him losing his memory like that.'

'Aye, well. Maybe there's something in it.'

Along the road there are daffodils in bloom. The tops of the hills are frosted with snow, but further down their slopes the gorse has come out.

'Is it spring yet, do you think?' I say. 'Or is it still winter?'

He looks up in that curiously attentive way of his. 'In the Irish alphabet, the letters are trees, and T is *teine*. Fire, the furze bush. And you could say that hill is ablaze with the furze, could you not?'

'Whin, it's called, here,' I say. '*When the whin is blooming, kissing's in season*. Bella likes to say that.'

'Does she now.' He glances at me, one eyebrow raised. 'It can bloom all year long, can't it?'

'I think that may be the point.'

'Do you think so, Anna?' He's turned away still, looking out of the window, but I can hear the smile in his voice. I remember hot days in summer when I was a child, running amok in the hills above the caravan with a fluid gaggle of other children. The urgent buzzing of bees, the blue and the yellow and the intense scent of the gorse which snagged clothes and scratched hands and cheeks. I try not to think about kissing.

'I'll have to tell Erin that saying,' he says. 'She collects all those proverbs and things like that in a wee notebook she has. She'll like that one.'

Of course she will, I think. Beautiful Erin, bonny and fragrant as gorse and a lot less prickly. I think of her dancing, of how his eyes were fixed on her every move as he played. I cast a glance in the mirror; there are cars building up behind us but nowhere yet to pull over to let them past and the Land Rover has never been known to go over fifty.

John Teelin takes out more papers and flicks through them as we drive, eating mints and tapping his pen against his teeth and making notes. I glance at him sideways, wondering if he's just doing all this on his own, or if he's got brothers and sisters. I try to imagine finding out what he told me about his mother, when she died. I think of my mum at the funeral, perched on that chair beside Bruce, the faraway look in her eyes. I will phone her. I will go to see her when Bruce isn't there. Soon.

I'm back at Angus John's house later that afternoon clearing out the contents of his kitchen. My great-uncle took a mini-malist approach to cookware and cutlery, but his store cupboard is jammed with all kinds of tins, most of them out of date. I clean and stack until my fingers sting red raw with the bleach.

It bothers me all afternoon. *Your sister*, Lachie said. What did he mean by that?

Back at Crois na Coille, I find Fern wearing rubber gloves, plucking nettles from behind the chicken coop and bundling them into an old feed sack. She refuses my offer of help.

'Won't be a minute,' she says. 'This is to rot down for ferti-liser.' She pulls at a clump and kicks the soil to loosen the plants, pulling up a clump by the long, sinuous roots. The colour reminds me of stained teeth.

'They smell a bit like death,' I say.

'Well, yes,' she says. 'Many stories have them growing over corpses.'

What a horrible idea. I remember something Jamie used to say when we were young. *Someone's died everywhere.*

'They're rife in graveyards,' Fern continues. 'And the sites of old houses. Like we were saying this morning. The nitrates, see. But it's not all doom and gloom. They used them for making cloth too, did you know that? And you can make a good soup. Nettle and adder soup, a speciality of our mother's.' She laughs and rubs her arm, where a stray nettle has swiped a stretch of white and red weals on her skin above the rubber glove. 'And now,' she says, binding the top of the sack, 'a cup of tea. Do you want one?'

We walk up to the house, Fern with the sack over her shoulder, me with the bag of tins clunking against my leg. Fern leaves the nettle sack at the front door and shoos a hen off the front step. 'They're all in there,' she whispers, nodding at the closed living room door. 'Recording with Bella.'

She goes into the kitchen and I make to follow her, tripping over a leather satchel that has been left in the hallway. John Teelin's bag. I stop for a minute, and then quickly, feeling furtive, I flip the top of the satchel open and take out the photograph we showed Lachie earlier. I close the bag and get to my feet.

'Fern,' I say, stepping into the kitchen, 'can I ask you something?'

'Of course.' She looks up from making tea.

'Have you seen this before?'

She leans forwards to look. 'I don't think so,' she says. She looks more closely. 'A picture of the lumberjills, is it?' She half turns away.

'Earlier on,' I say, 'John Teelin had this, from the library. And we showed it to Maggie the Bleep, and her brother. And her brother said to me, *There's your sister*. It was a bit weird. And then I thought, maybe he thought I was you, or Bella, or something.'

'That's funny. I'm not really sure if I would know.' Fern turns back and frowns, looking again at the photocopy I am holding. 'I don't think—' She stops, making a small exclamation of surprise. 'Do you know,' she says, 'I think that – that could be Netta.'

She points. Like the others, this girl's face is indistinct. Fern looks at me keenly. 'Where did you say you got this, Anna?'

I tell her about John Teelin and his search for his relative. 'The Bleep's brother, Lachie. He said these two might be Irish.' I tap the two girls.

'Now that rings a bell,' says Fern. 'Wait a minute, it'll come to me.' She picks up her tea, drinks. 'There was a summer there, when I was back . . . '41, '42 maybe, it was. We went to a few dances and Netta had made friends with two girls who had come over from Ireland. Lively girls. They were sisters, I think. For the life of me I can't remember their names. Flanahan . . . Houlaghan . . . no. Hmm.' She takes another sip of tea.

'Halloran?' I say.

'Yes!' Fern snaps her fingers. 'Did he say that was her name? Halloran. That was it. Bridget Halloran and . . . Josephine Halloran. Oh, lord. Our wee brother was forever ferrying them across the loch to those dances. The pet.'

'So they were sisters,' I say. 'Bridget, and – was it Josephine, did you just say?'

'Yes. Sisters.'

'Right. I see.' I pause, then say, 'If you wouldn't mind, Fern, not mentioning this to John? It's just that I took this out of his bag without asking.'

Fern tilts her head to one side, fixing me with a beady eye as I step into the hall corridor to tuck the photograph back into John Teelin's satchel. I dive back into the kitchen just as the living room door opens. Bella comes in and takes an apron from the hook in preparation for cooking, the professor close behind her, rubbing his hands.

'Fancy reliving the old glory days, Fern?' he is saying. 'Thought we might take a spin down Memory Lane, pop into the bar at the Tayfillan for a livener on the way back. John's volunteered to do the driving. What do you say?'

John Teelin is already outside with Erin. Telling him what Fern said about the Hallorans will have to wait.

'My coat's in the study,' Fern says. 'I'll just nip and get it.'

'Just be sure to get back in time for dinner,' Bella calls. 'I don't want all this food to go spare.'

Fern sighs, tipping her head back like a stubborn child. 'Don't worry, it won't,' she says to the ceiling.

Fern

In the study, Fern picks up her coat from the back of the chair. Then she stands before the fireplace and looks at the photograph of her, Bella and Netta as children that sits in the middle of the mantelpiece.

In the slipstream of the years, with flittings and floorboard cracks, cast-off cases and unopened boxes, this is one of the few pictures that remain from their childhood. It was taken in an Edinburgh department store, the only time they visited. A photographer had lights on poles and live exotic birds for customers to pose with inside the shop.

They had queued with their mother for nearly an hour. Wearing woollen coats with small sharp collars, they'd stood in front of a backdrop painted to look like a rainforest, a macaw on Bella's shoulder, a darkish feathery blur on Fern's bent wrist and a cockatoo in the crook of Netta's elbow.

We were all so beautiful then, thinks Fern, in the way that all young girls are beautiful, even the plain ones, like me – the loveliness of youth, uncalled for, like a sheen of sweat.

Netta appears to be laughing, or trying to stifle laughter, slightly bent forward with her eyes tightly shut. The cockatoo's head is turned away, hidden from view. It is pressing its beak to her hair, just above her ear, as if whispering secrets.

Fern feels again the nervous excitement of waiting, of watching the birds being taken to and from their cages as each group moved up the line. How quietly the beautiful creatures swayed on arms and hands, grasping with clawed toes, shifting a wing or plumping themselves in a shiver of feathers. The place had seemed like a portal to another world.

The summer of William Croke's visit, the last summer before the war, shimmers in Fern's memory like an enchantment. Remarkable how just a few months can be illuminated in such granular recollection, while years can gallop by unchecked.

She thinks of the night not long after he arrived, when people had gathered in the kitchen of Crois na Coille. The rustle of a bottle or two brought out from paper bags, the murmur of talk. A quiet anticipation rising with the pipe smoke, the smell of the yard coming off boots and shoes and the tang of the outdoors on their clothing.

Some that came were characters who would hardly be seen from one year's end to the next. Wild brothers from deep in the hills. A tough old woman, widowed in the war of the Boers, who smoked a pale clay pipe. People Angus John would be sent out to check on in the wake of a heavy snowstorm, or weeks of rain, and like as not they'd wonder what the fuss was about. Neillie Lamont would raise up his warbling voice. Mary Carmichael played with the fiddle on her knee, her eyes behind her round spectacles tightly closed with the effort. The windowpanes fogged over and streamed with wet. At such a time as suited him, Jimmy the Bus would place his cap solemnly on the table and step out to dance like thistledown on the tiled floor. Those who remembered the clefts in the mountain where the old stills once flowed sweet, the crossroad dances before the Great War, the old sets and steps, the stories behind the tunes. When he had come to the township, the collector William Croke had drawn them all out.

He is waiting for her now, looking up to the bend in the stairs. On the corner shelf rests a picture of Fern's father in military

151

uniform, the frame carrying the two mottos of his regiment: *Ne Obliviscaris; Sans Peur.*

'Dear Fern.' His voice from the corridor, half laughing. 'Are you ready? I'm not leaving without you.'

'*Never forget; Without fear,*' Fern murmurs. Out loud she says, 'I am always ready.'

In the hall she takes his arm, unsure who is leaning on whom.

1934–9

Netta

The summer I was fourteen I became fascinated by my own reflection. It wasn't so much vanity as curiosity. Myself as others saw me.

There were two mirrors in the house. One was dark-spotted with age and hung in the corridor by the front door. The second was a hand-held mirror, hexagonal in shape, with an enamel flower inlaid on the back. By arranging these two mirrors just so, I could see both the side of my face and the back of my head. When no one was watching I would pin my hair up and pinch my cheeks, turning this way and that to see myself in ways previously unknown to me.

If my father had seen me like this, he would have been horrified and ashamed. Vanity begot pride, and pride was the foremost of sins.

Each evening I would go up the hill to collect in our two cows who grazed on the high pasture during the long days of summer. There was a rough track that followed the path of a small burn. Fragments of those evenings lodged in my mind: the beat of my pulse at the crest of the hill, the dazzle of low evening sun.

One day in August I came over the ridge by the rocking stone and saw a movement up ahead in the river. I stopped. A man I did not recognise was wading in the part of the water where the burn flattened and widened as it ran into the loch. He held a long slim branch in one hand and was swirling his other arm slowly in the water, staring down as if he had lost something.

He lifted his head suddenly towards me and stopped still. The air rippled with the whistles of birds. I wanted to run but did not, and he straightened slowly, water slipping off his arms, and started wading towards me.

He didn't say a word but shook his wet hand and put it in his pocket, drawing out something in his fist. As he reached the shore where I was standing he stretched his arm out to me and I could see there was a pearl resting in his cupped palm. The skin of his hand was puffed and clean from the cold water but the nails on his curled fingers were black and broken. He closed his hand over and put it down by his side. I could see the crooked lines of dirt on his face when he smiled, and I could smell the river on him.

In the hour that followed I never learned his name. He taught me how to whistle to the song thrushes that sang all night on the hill in summer. How to plait and twist grass into rope, and how to make fire by striking a stone. When I made to leave he brought his face closer to mine than any stranger's had ever been before. His lips tasted of tobacco and his cheek was pressed to my nose. He smelt of grass and wood smoke and something else, half hidden to me, that brought with it an unrecognisable fear like a shape in fog.

Afterwards, I turned and walked down the hill without looking back. The cows picked their way ahead of me. I rehearsed tale after tale to explain my lateness, but when I arrived home I discovered a neighbour had been taken ill and my mother had gone to their house. No one asked me why I had taken so long on the hill.

When I went to undress that night I held the pearl he had given me in my fingers. A white nugget, little bigger than a peppercorn. I thought of it then as the beginning of everything, but by its nature it was something hard to define. Layer upon layer bound over time, an intruder prised from a split shell in a moment. I stared at its pale lustre glimmering in the evening's fading light.

At school we had learned to read books in English; at home my mother told us stories in Gaelic. Stories about the woman who saw death riding a bicycle, the man who had no tale to tell, and the girl who wove shirts from nettles. It was the search for tales such as these that brought William Croke to our door. He arrived from Dublin in the summer of 1939, young and handsome and persistent. He had been sent to Scotland by the Irish Folklore Commission to write down the stories of our peninsula: also songs, place names, sayings and local traditions. He visited our family frequently over the course of about a month. My father, almost bed-bound by then, enjoyed talking with him.

William Croke was particularly taken with my mother. Most unusual, he said to my father, for a woman to have such stories. The songs, yes, but the stories – something out of the ordinary, indeed.

Your own story is the hardest to tell, my mother would say.

She was raised by men, my father said. That's the reason her head is so full of those things.

My father's wartime experiences and the long years of ill health that had followed had not left a man to whom memories of the past were a comfort, but a man whose stern beliefs had hardened over time.

William Croke took my mother's tales down in notebooks. He would sit at the kitchen table writing as fast as he could, both in English and in Gaelic, whichever my mother was speaking. Like her, he could switch effortlessly between the two, and sometimes we would ask him to speak his native Irish and giggle at the strangeness of it. We could almost understand it, like speech heard underwater. When William Croke's notebooks ran out, Angus John tore him pages from his school jotter.

How she bloomed in those weeks, my mother, humming to herself as she worked, racking her memory for recollections she had believed lost or left behind. By the time William Croke left in August, promising to come back the next summer, he said that he had collected enough to publish a book. But we were at war within a month, and he did not come back.

I went to work at Altnaglas House a month after William Croke's departure, at the age of nineteen. I was not the first member of my family to do so: my father had worked on the estate since the Great War, when Altnaglas belonged to Sir Kenneth Mondegrene.

Much has been said about Sir Kenneth, but my father, who worked for him until sickness forced him to retire, maintained he was a good man. The two men were not friends, but shared a respect for duty and loyalty. Sir Kenneth's son Charlie had been killed on the Somme; my father had fought alongside him and tried to save him.

He only spoke about this as a much older man, when William Croke visited our house and they talked late into the evening. I sat at the top of the stairs out of sight and listened. Only with so little of it left could my father talk about his life, and then he spoke slowly, telling of how he had carried Charlie on his shoulder for over a mile back to the White City, as they called their trenches. Blood from the dying boy's burst lungs had run down my father's back as he carried him, and he himself had fallen and had come to in a shell hole, the chalk of the soil turning the puddled water white as milk.

How did I survive? he asked. No earthly mortal can give me an answer to that.

With Charlie's death, Altnaglas had lost its natural heir. When Sir Kenneth himself died in 1935, the estate was bequeathed to his stepson Jerome, the son of his second wife. In its time, this marriage caused many tongues to wag, because, as well as having a son, Caroline Morton was American and had been an actress in a former life.

Shortly after his ascension to the estate and the surname, Jerome Mondegrene had commissioned an audit of the entire estate. I overheard my father saying it appeared to be important to the young man that all now belonging to him was recognised as such.

The Big House, we all called it. There was no need for further definition. It crouched, massy and mysterious, on the other side of the hill from Crois na Coille. At its heart was a medieval tower, as Mondegrene would tell me later: the rambling wings were later additions, built and rebuilt following a number of fires over the years. The house was crowned with an enormous number of chimneys. There were gargoyles who clung precariously to their lofty stone nests and occasionally plummeted to the ground: it was advisable to stay well back from the walls in high winds.

The library was several centuries old. A catalogue of its contents would be required, and Jerome Mondegrene suggested to my father that I could do the work. I had been bound for secretarial college, but, with Europe beginning to stir into flames once more, my mother and father were keen that I should stay close to home, and so it was agreed.

On my first day, the housekeeper showed me into the library and left me alone before I had a chance to ask what I should do, or where to start. I stood in the centre of the room and stared around me, at the walls of books caged behind latticed shutters. It was peaceful, the incarcerated books orderly and silent, full of tales not told aloud. I liked to think of all that captive knowledge. At the far end of the library were two low bookcases in front of the bay windows. I crossed the room and knelt down to read the spines. I knew enough to know that the titles were in Latin, but was ignorant as to what they meant.

A small dry cough from behind me made me scramble to my feet. I had only ever seen Jerome Mondegrene at a distance before, in the fields with my father or passing in a motor car: never inside, and never when it was just the two of us. The first thing that struck me was that he was a small man: not much taller than me, and thin as a whittled stick. He backed up quietly against the library door to close it and then walked towards me, removing his pipe from his jacket pocket and tapping it gently in the palm of his other hand.

'She's arrived,' he said. He rocked forward on his toes as if to inspect my face.

'Sir,' I said, before I remembered that my mother had said not to address him until he told me what to call him.

'Mondie, please,' he said. 'That's what they call me. The question is, what shall I call you? My small bookkeeper, my inspector of all things printed and loose-leaved and bound.'

'Netta,' I said, and he gave a short laugh before pinching the small moustache above his top lip with his thumb and forefinger, as if to whip the laughter away.

'I know that very well,' he said. 'Janet MacArthur, as God is gracious. Sent here to be my reckoning.' He smoothed his hair, which gleamed slightly as if damp, and then gave a nod, striding over to a writing desk and picking up a large ledger. 'I've a great respect for books, you see,' he said. 'Words can kindle such a flame in one's soul. And, if not, they can make most useful firelighters.' He laughed when he saw my face. 'I am jesting, Netta, of course. Things haven't quite come to that. But, like anything, these things must earn their keep. And if there is buried treasure in this . . . leafy forest of mine, I want to know. I want to see the wood for the trees, Netta. Do you know what I mean?'

'Yes,' I said. 'You want to know what books you have, and if they're valuable.'

'Ha!' He slapped his pipe against his thigh and then put it in his mouth, tilting his head back and looking at me through half-closed eyes. 'She gets straight to the point,' he said. 'I hope you'll prove as meticulous as you are mercenary. *Caveat emptor*, dear Netta – let the buyer beware. Now take this.' He handed me the ledger, and started to explain how I was to work clockwise around the room, going through each case in turn, how to note the details of each book and pamphlet between the ledger's lines. 'Make sure you get the bloody spelling right,' he said. And with that, he turned and sat down in a baize chair by the fireplace.

'Well?' he enquired, his voice sharp. 'What's the delay? Off you go.' He watched me as I began to write; the pen sputtered and scratched on the first word.

'You are clever, of course you are,' he said, suddenly. 'Look at you, you're bursting with it.'

'I'll need some blotting paper,' I said. Mondegrene made no reply, but continued to watch me.

'*Corvus oculum corvi non eruit*,' he said. 'By the time you've finished here, you'll be able to tell me what that means. Or you'll have crow's feet from all that squinting at the print.' He shifted in his chair, crossing his feet at the ankles. I turned again to the shelf, my back to him. He was silent for a few minutes, and then, more quietly, he said, 'I get the impression you don't think very much of me, Netta.'

'I – we've hardly met, sir.'

'On the contrary, I remember you well when you were eight years old.' He laughed. 'You brought our shooting party bannocks and milk. I remember a little hatchling crow, glossy black and red-mouthed, fallen from its nest too soon and ravenous for the world. It takes one to know one.'

I could tell he was still looking at me and I didn't know what to do with my face or my body. Hoping to interrupt his line of sight, I crossed the room and picked up a pile of books that teetered on a low footstool. Children's books, I realised. They had bright dust jackets. 'Where should these go, sir?'

'Those,' he said, 'are my gift to you. Take them and read every damn one of them.' He jerked out of his chair and went to pour a drink from a table by the door. 'Out of the mouth of babes. Read them, damn it. Read all of them and you'll have read more than I ever have of this oppressive cacophony of so-called intellect.'

I put the books down and turned back to the ledger. Mondegrene went to the mantelpiece and lifted a picture frame from behind a paperweight shaped like a horse's hoof.

'Come here, Netta,' he said. 'I want to show you something.' And then, when I did not move, he made an impatient movement with his arm. 'For heaven's sake, come here, dammit. I'm not going to ravish you. Good God. Your honour will remain intact, I personally guarantee it.' He laughed. 'Here.'

I went over to him. He smelled of lemons and stale alcohol, like the bottom of an empty glass. He showed me the picture he had in his hand. 'Who do you think this is?' he said.

'Is it—'

'My mother,' he interjected.

'Yes, sir.'

'And do you know who she was?'

'Lady Mondegrene?'

He barked with laughter.

'I don't understand what you mean,' I said. 'Sir.' The paperweight ornament was a real horse's hoof; I could see the hide and black hair of the pastern merging neatly into a silver fetlock.

'What I mean, Netta,' he said, 'is do you know who she was, before she was *Lady Mondegrene*?'

I said I did not, although this was not quite true.

'But you've heard rumours, I'm sure,' he said.

I was silent. There was a tiny engraved plaque on the tip of the paperweight's toe. *The Bonnie Earl*, it read. I felt destabilised by the bizarreness of our conversation. My fingers itched to stroke the hoof's glossy surface.

'Answer me when I'm speaking to you, Netta. Tell me what people say.'

I looked at him then, full in the face. His eyes were black. 'I wouldn't know,' I said.

He laughed. 'Impossible, quite impossible. Why do you people pretend? I'll tell you who she was, my mother, I'll tell you. She was an actress. And do you know what people thought of actresses? Prostitutes. Whores. That's what you people think she was. And I was her pimp!' He laughed again. 'Me, eleven years old. That's what people thought of us, when we came here. Don't pretend otherwise, Netta; you must have heard the way people talk.'

'She was beautiful,' I said, which was true.

'Yes, yes,' he said, 'of course she was. She had talent too. And do you know what else she had, Netta?' He was enjoying himself now, I could tell. 'She had *me*,' he said, before I could conjure something to say. 'She had me,' he said again. 'And all of this, which came to me.' He swept an arm around his head, drained his drink. 'Sugar and slavery, that's how my stepfather's family made the money. Little did he think it would be passing to me. But what did he expect? He himself was the grandson of a usurper.' He looked down at me, smiling slyly. 'Do you know what that means?'

I stared at him. 'It means he – took something that wasn't his.'

'Of a sort, Netta,' he said. 'I knew you were clever. Altnaglas belonged to the Campbells, to Ebenezer Campbell, you see? Until Hector Mondegrene stole it when old Ebenezer was on his death bed. Hector – he was Sir Kenneth's grandfather – slipped a bumblebee into the corpse's mouth and used the

163

dead man's hand to sign the will – the will that bequeathed him this estate!' He tapped his empty glass against the wall. 'And did you know this house is haunted? By John Albany, the favourite son of old Ebenezer, who was done out of his inheritance. Oh, I feel for poor little John Albany, drifting around the house, and here's me, another bastard in this place! But there's no accounting for the wiles of the world, Netta.' He cocked his head on one side. 'Or is there, my little accountant? The higher one climbs, the harder it is to breathe.'

I cast around for a way to change the subject, looking down at the picture of Mondegrene's mother. 'Was she in Hollywood?' I asked.

'Ah, she should have been. Her *gross misfortune*, she called it. It was to have been her first film, *Folly of the Wise*, when her co-star was killed in a motorcar accident.'

'Oh, no,' I said.

'Oh, yes. His head was lopped clean off. And that was that. My mother never made it on to the silver screen. Her talent lay wasted.'

Mondegrene replaced the frame on the mantelpiece. He took a step back, staring at it.

'She was a coldblooded bitch anyway,' he said, swiping the photograph, the horse's hoof and a dozen other ornaments off the mantelpiece. They smashed loudly on the hearth and he stood still for a moment before bending forward to pick up the broken frame and its contents. I did not move, my body tense as a wire. As he straightened I could see that the shattered glass had made his fingers bleed.

He put his bleeding hand on my shoulder, squeezed it as if we were old friends. 'Excuse me,' he said. His voice was quiet. 'It is a Thursday, and on Thursdays I drink.'

He turned away and moved down the bookcases, calling out names of authors with accompanying comments. *All the words, too many words! Glorified claptrap! Lord, what a bore!*

Then he wheeled around, looking straight at me. 'Your eyes are most unusual,' he said. 'Tell me, have they always been like that?'

'Yes. They've always been like this, sir.'

'I had a little dog with eyes of different colours once,' he said. 'Unfortunately for him, I had to leave him back in Belgium.' He dropped the smashed frame to the floor again and went to pour himself another drink. 'I am giving you the rest of the day off, Netta,' he said to me with his back turned. 'The sun is well over the yard arm and it is now time for me to start drinking in earnest. *I will drink life to the lees.* Tennyson, that one. *Ulysses.* I'll read him to you, some time.'

I cleared my throat, the sound loud and rough in my head. 'What time tomorrow, sir?' My voice sounded small.

He looked round. 'Good God, child. You look as if you've seen the ghost of John Albany.' He sipped his drink, turning away again. 'Ten o'clock tomorrow. Now bugger off home, little crow.'

I walked home slowly over the hill. When I arrived back at Crois na Coille my mother was sitting at the table winding string that had come loose from a ball around her finger. She asked me why I was home so early.

I told her that I started properly tomorrow, and Mondegrene had just wanted to show me the library. My mother frowned. Her fingertip bulged and pinkened where the string dug in. 'Margaret Fair,' she said, naming the housekeeper. 'Was she there with you?'

'It was just him,' I said.

My mother sighed and shook her head. 'Well, I don't know,' she said. 'I just don't know.' She turned away to put the string back on the dresser. 'Don't tell your father,' she said, in low tones.

I said nothing. What, after all, was there to tell?

August 1960

Donnie

'Tell the ghillie I wish to go ashore.' Lady Wishart, perched imperiously in the prow of the boat, addressed her request to her husband the Colonel, who was faffing about with his fishing fly in the stern. God forbid you should make eye-contact with the staff, Donnie thought, much less speak to them directly. He pulled on the oars, digging his chin into his chest and pretending he hadn't heard.

There were four of them in the boat, one more than there should have been, for she was only ten foot – little more than a wooden dinghy. But Lady Wishart had announced at the last minute that her ashy-faced daughter (Binkie? Dinkie?) had expressed a wish to join them. All the larger boats had been taken by other hotel guests, and 'the girl's a slip of a thing, won't even know she's in there,' Lady Wishart had decreed.

Most of the lads seized the chance to get out on the water, but there was little pleasure in it for Donnie, especially when he was responsible for the boat. He was happiest on land. *A man can drown in an inch of water*, his uncle Angus John was fond of saying. Colonel Wishart was already three sheets to the wind, standing up, rocking about, sitting down again, leaning over the side.

Earlier that morning Donnie had asked Bruce to take the Wisharts out instead. But Bruce told him, with the hint of a grin, that he'd already had his orders and was to take out *the bobby and his boy* for the day.

So they were back, Geordie Gilroy and his father. Donnie

hadn't said a word about what had happened on their last visit back in July, and it seemed neither had the boy Geordie, because there'd been nothing, no words with Saltcoats. Yet.

He'd been out for over two hours now with the Wisharts and they had caught nothing. The weather conditions should have been perfect – a light rain was falling, but the fish weren't rising.

'Time for the ditty bag, MacArthur?' Colonel Wishart would suggest at frequent intervals, referring to the knapsack that held the refreshments: whisky and gin and a small flask of port. There was a cloud of midges around Wishart's head, and his poor daughter's ankles were red with bites.

Lady Wishart repeated her request to go ashore and the colonel batted at his left ear. 'Do you think we might – hum – make some sort of a landing, MacArthur? Ashore and what-not. I've had my orders from the powers that be, haha.'

'Sir.' Donnie cast about for the nearest island where they might set Lady Wishart down for a comfort break. He was tempted to aim for the one with the least number of trees and the sparsest ground cover. He edged the little boat into the wind. The prow lifted, and, when it slapped back down on the water, Binkie, or whatever her name was, gave a little screech and clutched on to a rowlock. Her knee touched Donnie's and she rocketed backwards as if stung. The boat pitched to one side and then the other as Lady Wishart moved astern and sat down heavily.

'She nearly turned over there!' chortled the colonel, as if this was a minor achievement. He reeled in his line again and chucked it back over the side.

There was a jolt and the boat jerked suddenly to one side and then the other and again nearly capsized. Wishart's line had snagged. He was hanging out over the back of the boat – he stretched out an arm – and the next moment he had toppled into the water. The tiny boat creaked and rocked at the rapid change in weight and Lady Wishart's daughter shrieked.

Ah, bloody hell, thought Donnie. He pushed on the oars, but with the unexpected movement the boat had already drifted away from where the colonel had gone in. Donnie called to him to take hold of the stern and Wishart grabbed once at the outboard which was propped out of the water before flapping and sinking again.

How the hell could he get the man back into the boat without the whole thing going over? Donnie had swum off a rowing boat a few times and had found it hard enough to get back in himself without help, let alone an overweight, inebriated man pushing sixty.

The boat gave another lurch – Lady Wishart, damn her, leaning over, trying to grab her husband's collar and very nearly capsizing the boat.

'Sit down!' roared Donnie, surprising himself. 'Please,' he added, as an afterthought. Amazingly, Lady Wishart obeyed. Donnie turned to the girl in front of him, grabbed both of her hands and put them on the oars. 'Move this one like this if we drift away,' he said. 'And this one if we go too far over that way. Can you? Please. Do it.'

She took the oars, shaking her head frantically. She had bitten her lip and there was a smear of blood at the side of her mouth. Everything was telling him to stay in the boat but – Wishart was still bobbing, not far off, sinking and rising, his face turned up to the sky.

Donnie took his jacket off, shook off his boots and slipped over the side.

He knew the sensation well, the freezing shock of the water that shrank your balls into your body and split your breath into short gasps. He managed to keep his head above water and grab at Wishart's soaking collar, gripping his shoulders, trying to remember what he'd once been taught – hook an arm around the man's neck, that was it, keep his face upright, and swim – but suddenly the colonel's arms latched around

171

his neck and Donnie found himself pushed below the water. He inhaled before he could stop himself, felt his lungs burning and then he was up again, gasping. He still had the tweed jacket in his hands and the man was clinging to him and they were both starting to sink.

A dark shape loomed and the next second a great bat to the side of Donnie's head sent him down again. When he surfaced this time the water in his eyes was searing and above him he could see the whey-faced girl flailing around. She'd smacked him on the head with an oar. She was now slicing and churning at the water, the boat swaying towards him.

Donnie pushed one last time, his legs pedalling. He got the man's head properly above the water, and they both took a ragged breath, the colonel still clawing and scrabbling around Donnie's neck. A wave of water went over them both and then Donnie heard shouts and the roar of an outboard so close to his head he was sure he was going to be hit. Suddenly a powerful force was sucking him out of the water: hands, pulling him up. He felt his ribs rasp against the ribs of the boat.

A great hand was crashing down on his back, slapping harder than was needed. The first thing he saw was a pair of green waders, planted square beside him, and filling the sky above was a big man with hair black and shiny as tarmacadam, flattened to one side of his head. He nudged Donnie with one massive booted foot.

'You'll do, lad, you'll do,' he boomed. 'Take your time there.'

'Where's—' He looked around. This wasn't the boat he'd come out of.

'We've got him.'

The ten-footer Donnie had left was alongside, Lady Wishart in the prow shouting and her daughter huddled over, crying. Colonel Wishart was crumpled in the stern. Bruce was standing over him, holding a bottle and a towel.

'Is he alright?' Donnie managed to ask.

The man above Donnie rumbled with laughter. 'Just a speck of water in the lungs, boy. Nothing for you to worry about. You sit yourself up there, now. Here, Langlands!' he shouted over to Bruce in the other boat, 'we'll be seeing you lochside, aye?'

Donnie felt the boat lift as the outboard gunned and they were away. He sat up slowly, manoeuvring himself on to one of the boat's benches. 'Thank you, sir,' he said.

It was then that he saw Geordie Gilroy, sitting hunched up in a big green coat, staring at Donnie without saying a word.

'No need for *sir*, boy. Name's Jim. Jim Gilroy. You've just been saved by the long arm of the law.' The man brought out a flask from his jacket and tipped it up to swallow, the gold of his signet ring flashing in the sun which had momentarily split through the clouds.

A silence fell as Jim Gilroy steered the boat around one of the small islands on the loch. *The burial island*, Bella called it. Centuries ago the MacArthurs had buried their dead there, she said, ensuring protection from wolves and grave-robbers. Nowadays all that remained were the ruins of an ancient chapel and headstones weathered to shapeless lumps. Donnie peered up at the tall pines that shrouded the island as they puttered past, saw a kestrel hovering above the trees, its head perfectly still, staring downwards. As they left the island behind, he looked to the shore, anticipating the swing of the boat towards the hotel's jetty, but Jim Gilroy's hand remained unmoving on the tiller and they kept going straight ahead. The throttle roared and the boat picked up speed like a horse tugging for its head, the prow rising and slamming down into slabs of black water. They were not going back. They were going around the headland.

'Here,' Donnie started, and Jim Gilroy looked round. His face was unsmiling now.

'Geordie, mind the tiller for me, eh?' he said, and at the tone of his voice Donnie felt his insides shrink a little. The big man moved lightly and fast, was standing over him now where he was sitting on the bench, and then the boat rocked slightly as he sat down opposite Donnie, eyes narrowed. At length he shook his head, made a tutting sound and then, before Donnie had even seen it move, his hand was around the back of Donnie's neck, squeezing.

'You are the lad,' he said, then turned his head. 'Eh? Geordie? This is him?'

Geordie nodded silently, looked away.

'Nah, son, I don't think so.' Jim reached out suddenly behind him and with his other arm struck Geordie a blow on the side of his head. 'You'll be watching this. You'll be watching, so you will.' He turned back to Donnie. 'I hear you and my boy had a run-in the other week,' he said. 'A scrap over some girl. Am I right?'

Donnie said nothing, forcing himself to look into the man's face without flinching. He could hear the lapping of water, and realised that the outboard's engine had been cut. 'The problem is,' Jim Gilroy continued, his voice almost pleasant, 'yon boy's not just any boy. That's my son, see? And it's up to me to show him how to hold himself. What to do about wee pricks like you. So we can't be having this. You see?' His hand tightened on Donnie's neck. 'You see?'

Donnie had just opened his mouth when the man punched him square on the jaw with such force that he was thrown back, hitting his head on the bench behind as he went down. Air and water seemed to spin; Donnie heard a kind of snuffling whimper as he lay in the wet at the bottom of the boat and it was a few seconds before he connected the sound to himself. His tongue was thick in his mouth and there was the taste of blood. He couldn't see straight, black and red pain clogging his face.

The rage he'd felt in the corridor that day rose in him again and he threw himself forward, only for the man to push him back as easily as closing a gate, twisting his arm up behind his back and pinning him down. 'You will fucking stay down till I've finished with you.'

Donnie felt a wet slap of spit land on the side of his cheek. Now the man's voice was quiet in his ear. 'I saved your life today,' he was saying, 'but there's every chance I'll change my mind. You hear me?'

Something hit his shoulder – a fist, a knee, Donnie wasn't sure, but he felt the pain all the way down to his hands.

'Must be water in your ears as well as your lungs.' Jim Gilroy gripped Donnie's jaw in his hand, twisting it towards him. The pain seared. 'I said, did you hear me?'

'Aye.' Donnie's voice barely made it out of his mouth.

'Good. That's good.' The man turned his head. 'Geordie?'

Geordie looked quickly at his father, his face expressionless. He stood and climbed clumsily over the bench in front of him, swaying slightly, holding on to the side of the boat. Then he swung his foot back and kicked his boot hard into Donnie's ribs. Donnie cried out, a wheezing sob. There was a singing in his ears. Somewhere above him Jim Gilroy was telling Geordie to stick it to him again, and Donnie was rolling over, the pain heavy in his body, great stripes of pain around his ribs that throbbed like a low engine. He was choking, sure he was going to be sick. The noise in his ears increased. It was the sound of another outboard engine and a voice he knew well was shouting across the water.

'Is everything quite in order?' Major Saltcoats was calling. He was standing in the prow of Bruce's boat.

Above Donnie, Jim Gilroy straightened. 'Absolutely, Salty,' he said. 'All fine here, near enough. Think we've worked up quite a thirst.' He chuckled, motioning towards the Tayfillan. Donnie got on to his hands and knees and vomited on to the duckboards. He looked up at the man above him, his vision swaying and swimming, and then over to Geordie. Geordie's eyes were fixed on his father. He was nodding in agreement.

'Very good.' Saltcoats nodded to Bruce, who started to turn his boat around.

Jim Gilroy ripped back the outboard's starter cord. The engine turned over, and the little boat rose up in the water as it too was pointed towards the shore.

Thursday 19 March 1998

Anna

Fern, the professor and Erin arrive back at Crois na Coille at twenty to eight. Their 'spin down Memory Lane' may have been more of a pub crawl, I think, as the professor and Fern totter in arm in arm, eyes bright and cheeks even brighter.

'Engine trouble,' says the professor, accounting for their lateness. 'John's doing something to my car. Oil or coolant or somesuch.' They bring with them the smell of fresh air and spirits and the professor brandishes a bottle of Drambuie at Bella, 'to apologise for our tardiness'.

Bella tuts, thanking him. 'Tell that lad to come in from the yard,' she says. 'I'll take a look at the car later.' Bella prides herself on her expertise in machinery. She has single-handedly maintained tractors, vans and the Land Rover over the years. My dad used to say he learned all he knew from her.

When John Teelin comes in there is oil on his shirt. He washes his hands at the sink and I fetch the shepherd's pie from the oven. The top is a bit burned and the mince is nearly liquid, slopping right up to the sides of the plates, but everyone eats with the appearance of enjoyment. When he is finished, Professor Croke sits back with a contented sigh.

'That was wonderful,' he says. 'A pie to end all pies, I would say. My compliments to the chef.' He's looking a bit pie-eyed himself, I think, but clearly means what he says.

The phone rings through in Fern's study.

'I'll get that.' I push my chair back from the table, gently pressing Fern back into her seat to finish the pool of mince on her plate.

In the study I lift the receiver.

'Anna,' says Bruce. 'That you?'

I mumble that it is.

'Good. Right. Two things. Number one. Your mother.'

Fear jags me in the gut. 'Is she OK?' I manage in a small voice, but he is already blustering onwards.

'She wants to see you, as do I. You can't be larking around down there forever. Dinner, at ours. Saturday.'

'I can't—' I begin, but Bruce is carrying on after a mere pause to draw breath.

'Number two,' he is saying. 'That runty boy Liam Bell came to the front door earlier to *harangue* your mother and me. He stood there bold as brass talking utter rubbish, and with a straight face claimed to be, and I quote, *worried* about you. I've no idea what he meant by that, but I'd think it wise for you to call the fellow and appease his paranoia. If he's mixed up in some kind of – *drugs thing* – then call the police. They're there to deal with that sort of issue, as far as I understand.'

I hold the phone slightly away from my ear, feeling a squeeze of nausea. Liam, looking for me at their house.

There is fuzz on the line, a dim mutter of voices. I think Bruce has put his hand over the mouthpiece. More rustling, and then, 'Ah,' he says, more clearly. 'Your mother, Anna. She'd like a word. Passing you over now.'

'Anna.' Mum's voice. 'How are you?'

'I'm fine,' I say. 'All fine. Why?' I should ask her how she is. I stare down at the white marks on my nails. If she talks about Liam too, I will scream.

'Well, I'd like to see you. We'd both really like to see you.'

I highly doubt the latter, but I keep my mouth shut.

'Saturday,' she is saying. 'We're going out for a meal. With Jamie and Lena. I'd really like you to be there too.'

'I'm working, Mum. At the hotel.' I'm in the middle of explaining to her about Leighanne and covering her shift when my eye falls on a curling poster of the signs of the Zodiac pinned above Fern's desk. My mum is Aries, the ram. Her birthday is on Saturday. My face heats with guilt. 'Lunch?' I offer weakly.

There is more rustling while she confers with Bruce. 'Lunch, yes,' she says. 'We can do that. Saturday, at ours. OK, Anna.' We agree on the time and I say goodbye before Bruce can take the phone again, placing the receiver softly back on to its cradle.

'Everything alright, Anna?' Bella and Fern turn concerned faces towards me as I resume my seat in the living room.

'Fine, thank you.' I force my face into a smile. 'Just Bruce, asking me round to lunch.'

The professor is still holding court, talking about the people from whom he has collected songs and stories over the years. *Informants*, he calls them, as if he were operating behind the Iron Curtain. It must be a strange life indeed, I think, lived in pursuit of other people's memories. 'Mina MacPherson,' he says. 'Is she still to the fore?'

'I do believe she's living yet,' Bella says.

The professor lets out a cry of triumph. 'I knew she would be,' he says. 'Born in a bow tent, tough as old tongs. That woman sang the finest version of "The Cruel Brother" I ever had the good fortune to hear.'

A shame that people don't conveniently disappear when you want them to. I thought I'd heard the last of Liam, but it would seem I was wrong.

'She's in the home,' Fern is saying.

'In body, at least,' says Bella. 'She did get a wee bit confused after the fire, it's true.'

There's no way I'm meeting up with him again, I think. He's sneaky like that. He'll try and wheedle his way back in. That's what he does. He makes you doubt yourself. Then you're stuck.

'Is the care home nearby?' the professor asks.

'Not too far,' says Bella. 'The Balsterrick.'

'We must pay her a visit,' the professor says to John Teelin and Erin.

Their conversation continues but I have stopped following and stare down at my plate. I suddenly feel alone, sitting at the crowded table. But isn't it not being alone that I'm afraid of? I put my hand on my stomach. No matter whether it's just me or I'm carrying the very beginning of a new life, I have to cut my ties with Liam, and that's all there is to it.

After the meal is finished, Erin and John Teelin cluster around the sink in the kitchen, murmuring to each other like an old couple – or a very new one. I can't work out whether they're flirting or just friends. I suppose I could ask, but I know I won't. Now he's teasing her about something and she's laughing, swiping the dishcloth at him, and I turn away, getting out the dustpan and brush to sweep the floor. It seems important to chase down the dwindling line of dirt at the edge of the dustpan over and over again.

'Earth to Anna,' Erin says, and I look up in surprise. Both she and John Teelin are looking at me expectantly. 'Bella said you were at college,' she says. 'Nursing, yeah?'

'Started nursing,' Bella said. 'Yet to finish.' She doesn't look up from where she is sitting by the stove, tapping a red pen on the puzzle page of the *Barnadine Star*.

'Yeah, that's right.' I get to my feet. The blood rushes to my toes and I close my eyes for a second as the world briefly goes grey and then spins back into full colour. I wipe the dresser top, manoeuvring the cloth carefully around the bottle of Drambuie. Then I go outside, shut up the hens and fill the

182

scuttle for the stove. Back in the kitchen, I take up the full bag from the dustbin and tour the kitchen surfaces looking for rubbish. An empty matchbox, a packet that recently contained biscuits. On the dresser there are a few creased Post-it notes and scraps of paper, which I scoop into the bag, followed by an empty dog food tin.

'Hey! Stop that.' John Teelin is across the room in two strides, holding out a hand. His face is hostile as he seizes the bin bag from me, wrenching it out of my hand before reaching in to pull out the papers and Post-it notes. 'I need these.' He pushes the bin bag back at me.

'Wow.' The abruptness of his movement makes my voice high and this angers me. 'Fine. Keep your hair on. What's so important?'

'What's so important?' he repeats. He glares at me for a second and then turns away, shaking his head.

Later that evening, we sit in the front room of Crois na Coille. The professor starts the tape recorder and says the date, time and place, like a police interview. Then he turns towards Bella, the *informant*, smiling at her to begin. There is an expectant lull in which I can hear the tape running like an indrawn breath, sucking in silence.

Bella begins to speak. From the first line I recognise the tale of the nettle spinner, which she told me and Jamie many times as kids. Erin sits in the corner, her slim legs folded into a knot which makes my joints ache just to look at her. She gazes at Bella with total concentration, her face a perfect study of reverence. I'm outside the circle, cradling a mug of hot lemon and honey. I resisted the temptation to top it up with whisky. I am trying to do the right thing.

John Teelin sits in front of me. As Bella talks, he writes continuously, his head bent, his hand speeding across the page. Shorthand, perhaps. I allow my eyes to rest on the hollow of lightly freckled skin at the back of his neck, where his dark hair dips like the tip of a paintbrush. I wonder what he thinks of this tale of sex, death and suffering – if he sees it only as an academic artefact, to be plucked and pressed in his notepad. To my surprise, I'd enjoyed spending the morning with him, started to think maybe I'd misjudged him as arrogant, superior. I should have known.

As Bella continues, scenes from the tale flit across her face. The laird arrives at the door, demanding that the girl visit him on the night before her wedding. The girl, cursing him, begins work on the shroud of nettles.

In front of me, John Teelin drops his pen. It lands near my toes. I could pick it up for him but then again, I could just leave it. I watch, lazy and slightly detached, as he feels about on the carpet behind him. He and Erin are definitely a couple, I decide. Or at least they have been at some point. The way she looks at him. I wonder if he's left a trail of broken hearts in his wake, or has had his own heart stoved in. Not that any of it matters to me. I don't give a shit. I have an abrupt memory of Liam, of a time when just to catch his eye was like looking into the sun: a dazzling, daring near-impossibility that would be seared on to the backs of my eyelids afterwards. I look down at the carpet and drink some more and wish I'd told John Teelin where to stick his bloody Post-it notes.

Bella's voice is low now, and slowing as she describes the laird growing sicker. He begins to look for the release of death, to beg the girl to finish the shroud so he can be at peace.

My left foot has gone to sleep. The collies lie in wait in the corridor. Moss has his front legs stretched out in front of him like a sphinx, his head up, amber eyes fixed on mine. I rest my head on my knees and close my eyes, slip under the coverlet of words, lulled by the rocking of Bella's foot which mimics the treadle of the spinning wheel. The girl's sweetheart has grown tired of waiting and has left her. She is alone with the

184

half-finished shroud woven of nettles, the cloth creeping from the loom underneath her red, swollen hands.

Bella is near to the end of her tale now, tugging on the loose ends to bring it to a close like a drawstring bag. The laird laid cold in his grave; her sweetheart returned. She finishes the story the same way as she finishes many of the ones that end happily: '*I danced at their wedding, and I got a silver cake sweeter than honey, but I was robbed on the way home and came back just as I left, and as I sit before you today.*'

She stops speaking. I open my eyes and see her settling back, smiling, drawing herself into the present once more. The professor breaks the silence, the tape machine still recording.

'That's marvellous, Bella,' he says. 'Superb. Just superb. And was that one of your mother's?'

Bella leans forward and plucks a bourbon biscuit off the plate on the low table in front of her. 'All the old ones, I learned from my mother.' She considers the biscuit in her hand. 'She taught me other things worth knowing too,' she says. 'How to skin a rabbit.' She looks up, and her eyes move from Erin in the corner, to John Teelin, still scribbling, and on to the professor. She reaches out to grasp Fern's hand. 'And how to catch a man!' As she laughs I see quite clearly the stouthearted, pretty young girl Bella once was.

I put the mug to my mouth again and drain it. 'Bella,' I say, 'do you remember the picture book we had as kids, about the man and the seal-wife? That was one of my favourites. I loved that.'

'Sounds like a selkie story,' says Erin. 'Doesn't it, John?'

'A plague,' drawls John Teelin in front of me. 'They're everywhere.'

Erin giggles, her hand over her mouth. Some kind of in-joke, I think.

'Oh. I'm so very sorry,' I say, and my voice sounds loud in the room. 'I shouldn't have said anything, should I? I must have

185

interrupted you. Go on, John, why don't you tell us a story? And another one after that, and another one after that. Go on.'

Fern starts to say something, as does Erin, and I catch sight of Bella's face, disapproving, ready to tear a strip off me for my rudeness as she would have done when I was much younger. But she only says, 'I don't remember it, Anna. It's not one of mine.'

I stand up feeling like a small child, knowing my face is red. I begin collecting cups and glasses.

John Teelin starts to say something, holding on to his empty cup for a moment, but I tug it from his grasp, refusing to meet his eye, and leave the room. In the kitchen I stand in the middle of the floor for a minute, rocking on my heels. I won't be telling him about the Hallorans any time soon. Let him find out for himself, if he can.

I swipe the bottle of Drambuie from the sideboard. It was an unwanted gift anyway. I climb the stairs to my room, leaving them to their fairytales.

Closing the bedroom door behind me, I climb into the gap between Erin's bed and mine. Then I remove the stopper from the bottle and put my teeth around the glass neck and drink it straight. The stuff is like syrup. I take another swig to be sure. I hear a burble of talk from downstairs, the clink of glasses. I think about putting my headphones on but my head is swirling with words, and images too: of the living room where I've just come from, or the *best room*, as it was then, when I was eight. Where they brought Dad before the funeral.

He was there for three days. We went on the third day. Someone brought us – not Mum; she had taken to her bed. The house was full of people smoking and eating sandwiches and there were glasses left in odd places, on windowsills and shelves, smudged with fingerprints and filled with tappings of cigarette ash.

186

Jamie and I were going to go in and see Dad, but at the last minute I found I couldn't, and then Jamie said he wouldn't go either. We waited in the kitchen where women were talking in low voices, washing up and putting bits of food on plates. Jamie and I got a fig roll and a cup of tea each and I spilled mine, the warm wetness seeping through the denim of my jeans.

What if it's not him? Jamie kept saying to me. We should check.

I told him to shut up and go in himself, then, and that made him cry a bit. Someone took him on their knee while I sat on my own with the teacup on my lap chattering in its saucer.

Jamie did go in eventually with Bella and afterwards I asked him but he didn't say much, just that Bella had kept saying *my beautiful boy*, and that Dad's hair was different. Like it had shrunk. Or something.

Hair can't shrink, I said.

I dunno, do I? Jamie was angry more than tearful this time. I went outside on my own and stood in the garden behind a sticky green bush. I looked down at the ground. If I couldn't cry I thought I would try being sick but I couldn't even manage that.

All day everyone had been talking about saying goodbye. It felt to me as though we were waiting, and that at some point my dad would walk around the corner, cheery and half-laughing at the fuss. And I would run into his arms and he would stoop to hold me, saying *hello you*, the way he always had. As I stood behind the bush I was beyond angry with myself for refusing to see him in the room, because beginning to sneak through my armour of disbelief was the awful recognition that I would never see him again.

Not long after the funeral, I broke my arm in two places. There were young trees growing on the steep banks where we played in the woods. If you ran down, grabbed the top of a

187

bent sapling and jumped, you could sometimes swing right over the tree itself and land on the other side.

It all ended badly, of course. At the hospital I needed a metal pin put in my arm. They thought I let go because I lost my grip but it was simply because I didn't hold on.

When Jamie and I went back to school after the summer holidays, no one knew what to say to us. No one signed my cast, which grew steadily greyer until it was time for it to be cut away. And then there was my arm again, much thinner than the other one.

I push up my sleeve and inspect the scars as they are today, a constellation of white dots and a faint thread of lines.

I still didn't cry, not once, in the weeks that followed Dad's death. I began to believe that, as truly as your own blood could be squeezed up when your skin broke, or you could hold your breath until the world went small, I was only on one side of the hill. On the other there was Dad and everything as it had been before.

And even still, sitting up here on my own, half-cut on the carpet in the room my father slept in as a boy, an existence of utter insignificance behind me and no clue as to what lies ahead, I realise I still can't quite treat myself as if I really exist.

Below me is the sound of talk and laughter and singing. I unzip my bag and find my Walkman, tug free the tangle of headphone wire and press play. The Associates' album *Sulk* fills my ears and I dial the volume up full so Billy Mackenzie's voice swoops over my senses.

Jamie

It was dark and he could hear the sounds of the night around him. Jamie climbed down from the cab saying a quiet prayer; the Hilux was really on its last legs now and just starting the engine had begun to feel less like an achievement and more like a miracle. He dropped the tailgate and began to gather his bits and pieces, feeling around for the head torch.

Once he could see what he was doing, he unpadlocked the caravan door. Setting down what he had brought with him in the doorway, he moved around the side and powered up the generator so he could switch on the bulb he'd strung up by a wire and put the kettle on for coffee. He rubbed his eyes as he waited for the water to boil.

Jamie had said goodbye to Lena after their dinner, and once she had left for work he'd sat on the sofa in their tiny living room studying the plan he'd been given by Geordie Gilroy. Last month he'd taken receipt of three fine blades from Duncan Robertson, one of which would be perfect for the plans he held in his hand: a core of Damascus steel, folded layers of iron and steel composite. Beautiful, functional, and high-quality.

He shovelled a spoonful of sugar into his coffee. It was a hell of a job to do in a week – he'd be lucky if the money he'd been given would cover materials. He told himself that if a thousand pounds was easily given, the rest would surely not be backwards in coming forwards. In fact, he had repeated this to himself God knew how many times in the past couple

189

of days. The sense of dread had not faded: *Not the sort to take up with lightly,* Bruce had said, and by now Bruce knew almost everyone in this town first-hand. But he got me the commission in the first place, Jamie thought. He sighed out loud, the sigh turning into a groan. Just a job. That was all. A job to put money in the bank.

The coffee was rank, but Jamie tossed it back and made another. He had a long night ahead of him.

August 1960

Donnie

At the Tayfillan, Colonel Wishart was seen by the doctor and taken off down to the District Hospital in Barnadine. Donnie got to take the night off, which was just as well. His face throbbed, his shoulder was turning purple and who knew what had happened to his ribs, but worse was the great bruised ache inside him, like being winded. He thought it was pretty obvious, looking in the mirror on lifting his head from a basin of cold water in the gents', that he'd been punched in the face, but the doctor just said that Donnie must have taken a bit of a dunt from the oar hitting him on the head, guessed it wasn't the last injury he'd have from a woman at the helm, hahaha, and that he'd better take it easy for the next few days.

Bruce knew fine well what had happened. You should go to the police, he said, which was ironic if nothing else. He only said it once. Donnie wasn't sure where to go, only that he couldn't face home yet: Bella and her questions. She'd be on the warpath if she found out. When Bruce went home, Donnie took himself down to the jetty and smoked a cigarette that stung his swollen face as he stared out across the calm loch. He thought of the weight of the water that had pressed in on him earlier. And then he knew what he wanted to do.

It was quiet around the back of the kitchens where Mary Rose had first handed him those cigarettes, all those weeks before. He waited. He could hear the sounds from the back of the bar across the courtyard. The kitchen doors banged and Mina Nicholson came out, arm in arm with a girl in a checked smock. 'Been in the wars, Donnie?' she said to him when she saw him, and he shook his head, trying to smile, but his face was too stiff.

It was a few minutes before Mary Rose appeared through the kitchen doors, her glorious hair whipping around her shoulders. 'My God, Donnie, your face!' she said, and looked as if she was about to burst into tears. She was wearing the blue dress he remembered from the day they'd met on the hill.

'I'm fine,' he said. 'Fine.' He pushed himself off the wall, with a bit of an effort.

'I feel scared just to see you,' she said. 'They were saying the man fell out of the boat and you jumped in and nearly died yourself and that big policeman pulled you out and saved the pair of you.'

'Aye, well. Something like that.' What else was he going to say: that he'd got himself kicked around like a football by Geordie Gilroy and his old man? Donnie reached out and grasped her around the waist and pulled her tight up against him. The wave of pain as she pressed against his bruised ribs was cruelly sweet. He bent to put his lips to her ear. 'Mary Rose,' he said. 'I love you.'

She twisted a bit in his arms, touched his face and he winced.

'I love you,' he said again.

'I'd say you do.' She was smiling.

'I want us to be married,' he said.

She stopped smiling. 'Donnie,' she said.

He put his face to her neck and kissed her. 'Mary Rose Sikorska,' he said, 'will you marry me?'

'Donnie,' she said again. 'Stop now.' Her arms came up and she put them on his chest and pushed him gently back. 'Let's go for a walk.'

'Is that your answer?'

'Come for a walk with me or you won't get an answer at all,' she said.

So they went for a walk, up the hill, hand in hand. And when they reached the ditch where he'd found her at the beginning of the summer she sat down so her legs hung over the edge of the ditch and when he sat down next to her she took his shirt collar in her hands and pulled his face to hers and they kissed for a long time. He slid down into the ditch so he was on his knees before her, their mouths pressed together, his face burning and throbbing. Then she slipped down beside him, until finally they lay full-length together, entwined, him with the earth and stones of the ditch to his back and her weight pressing down on top of him.

She kissed his cheeks and his neck and undid his shirt and laid her lips to the bruised skin of his chest and his stomach until he thought the longing would crush him. He tried to say her name but her tongue was in his mouth and her hands were sliding up his legs and he held her hips and stroked the hot, smooth skin of her stomach, his hands nearly spanning her waist underneath the dress. Her legs wound around him, her fingers splayed in his hair, and when she kissed his neck he felt her teeth. She had his belt unbuckled and they rolled over so she was smiling up at him with her hair all spread on the dark peat of the ditch and he said, 'You are the most beautiful.' And then she was pulling him down and inside and she was closing in on him, her head tipped back to the earth as she arched against him and he held her and was undone, undone, undone, his breath short, drowning for the second time that day, the end at the beginning, the circle and the flame.

'Putting on a green gown,' she said, afterwards. 'That's what they call it, doing that outside.' She lay on the grassy bank with her hands underneath her head, staring up at the sky, the uneven gap of blue framed with golden gorse.

Next to her, Donnie was trying not to let in the nagging voice saying what if someone had seen them, or missed them?

He was trying not to tell her again that he loved her. He hurt just about everywhere, was hoping he wasn't bleeding to death somewhere inside. He turned his head to kiss her cheek.

'Do you want a smoke?' he said.

'You owe those men your life,' Bella said to Donnie, when she heard about the incident on the loch involving the Wisharts. He had kept quiet about what had happened with Jim Gilroy afterwards. She said it several times. *You owe them your life.*

To *owe* was to be indebted, Donnie thought. He wondered if it was the kind of debt that got called in.

Two days later they climbed the yellow hill again, he and Mary Rose, following the path of the burn. His bruises were starting to fade. Battle scars, she said. The hero of the hour. Which was one way of seeing it. The bobby and his boy had departed the day after the loch incident and Donnie hoped there would be no return visit before the summer was over.

They walked the pass and he showed her the cup- and ring-marked stones and the entrance to the bone caves up by the ridge. When they reached the loch, he told her there were pearls to be found in the mussels that lay on the riverbed, if you were willing to take the time to look.

She shrugged, looking unconvinced.

'You don't believe me?' he said. 'It's true. Like I say. If you look long enough, they're here to be found.' He took off his boots, rolled his trouser legs up and waded into the shallow river. 'It's the old ones you're looking for,' he said. 'The big, gnarly ones have the biggest, most beautiful pearls.'

He looked back over his shoulder. She had sat down on the coarse grass of the bank, smiling and shaking her head.

'If I find one, Mary Rose, you'll have it,' he said.

The night before, lying in his bed at Crois na Coille, he'd opened the drawer beside his bed. It was still there, the river pearl nestled in a twist of paper, as it had been ever since he could remember. It could do better than stay hidden in a drawer, gathering dust.

Now, being careful she couldn't see, he slipped the pearl out of his pocket and waded upstream a little further, holding it tightly in his hand. He bent to the water, pretending to sift through the slimy stones with his hands before straightening, suddenly. 'I don't believe it.'

'What is it?' She got up quickly, despite herself, and drew level with him, standing above him on the bank.

He opened his hand and held the pearl up to her.

'I don't believe it either.' Mary Rose took the pearl and sat down on the riverbank with a thump.

'Will you marry me now, Mary Rose?'

She was laughing, pushing her hair from her face and staring at what she held in her hand. 'Oh, Donnie,' she said at last. 'We're just too young.'

'Don't say that,' he said. 'Just tell me if you don't want to.' He watched her rolling the pearl between her fingers. Held his breath.

'I do want to,' she said. 'I do. But it's not enough, Donnie, just wanting.'

'How do you mean, not enough?'

She stood up again. 'I won't be like my ma,' she said. 'Worn to a shim, and my da without a pot to piss in.' She looked him full in the face. 'You'll need more than a pearl in your pocket, Donnie.'

He looked down at the water, feeling foolish.

'Some money to go with your big plans,' she said. 'That's what you need. Then it'll be fine. Do you hear me? It'll be fine. We just need a bit of money first, and then we'll see.' She kissed his nose, pressing her cheek against his, and he put his arms around her.

But later, as he walked home to Crois na Coille in the after-glow of the sunset, he felt that something heavy had settled inside of him. He found for the first time that he could almost make himself believe he disliked her.

It had taken him by surprise, he told himself. All of this. He'd let himself like her too much, Mary Rose, and it was an almost painful thing, like parched thirst in the moment before drinking.

'You're too stuck on her, I reckon,' Bruce said to him. They were fishing the lochan above Crois na Coille in September, sitting on rocks by the shoreline. The Glasgow workers had gone home two weeks ago, Mary Rose among them. Donnie had her address and had promised to write to her until they could see each other again soon. 'She'll have someone else before the winter's out,' Bruce carried on. 'Just saying. And you might change your mind when she's three weeks away.'

'I won't be changing my mind.' Donnie didn't know why Bruce kept talking about her. His mind was set on something else, not unrelated. Money. What did he have to offer her, Mary Rose? Fuck all. After she'd left, Donnie had looked round at the place he'd grown up and asked himself questions that he'd never given much thought to before.

Money. It wasn't a thing that was ever exactly plentiful, but Archie, when he'd been alive, hadn't seemed to lack it. Money was only for some things – sale days at the mart, rent day. Just about everything else was swapped or bartered. But then the Forestry had bought up the land on which Archie had held the tenancy, and the sheep were sold, the cows too. Archie had put the money from the livestock into a newly opened bank account and died the next month: taken a heart attack and keeled over in one of the steep fields on the hill that would shortly be sown by trees. What money was left was Bella's now and she got by on little enough. He could never ask her for money, and he never would. Now he could see he needed a plan.

A week later, with wide-legged trousers and pockets that

jangled, a few of the tunnellers from the new hydro scheme nearby rolled into the public bar at the hotel. They were celebrating the completion of the dam at Culdarroch and nearly drank the place dry. As the evening unfolded, the tunnellers bought drinks for everyone and talked about the next job they were moving on to, way up north in Sutherland. Donnie kept his ears and his eyes open. At the end of the night it fell to Donnie to peel one of them off the bar. Shouldering one of the drunk man's outflung arms, he was able to find some answers to his questions from the man's slightly less stewed pal.

The following evening, he unrolled an Ordnance Survey map on the kitchen table at Crois na Coille.

'Here's the thing,' he said to Bruce. He leant on his elbows over the map and told Bruce about the men he'd met the previous night. 'Flash wasn't even the word for them. Spending money at the bar hand over fist. They were down from the dam and they're heading to a new job just starting up north, in Sutherland. Inchsuardal, is the name of the place. Way up in the hills. They were telling me they're yet to get all the boys they need up there.'

Bruce raised his eyebrows.

'You know yourself there's a pile of money to be made,' Donnie said. 'I think we should get ourselves up there. I'll tell you this. I'm buggered if I'm going to be mucking around here for much longer.'

Bruce said nothing. He had his mouth full eating his way through Bella's oatcakes, the butter on them as thick as the cheese.

'We'll need money to get us on the train to Dingwall,' Donnie pressed on. 'And from there the lads last night were telling me there's a bus runs up to the site.'

Bruce nodded slowly.

'What do you reckon?' Donnie pushed. He knew what he was asking – for Bruce to put his hand in his pocket, to get themselves all the way up to the back of beyond on spec and see if they might get some work. Bruce already had a few bob and it wasn't exactly the offer of a lifetime, but Donnie wasn't keen on turning up among a load of hammer-throwers on his own. At least if Bruce was with him they'd be getting two for one.

'It's funny, you know,' Bruce said. 'I've cousins up there, myself. Well, *a* cousin, any road. They're making money at these schemes, half of them standing around doing bugger all.' He grinned suddenly, his freckles wide across his nose, and Donnie grinned back at him. He'd known it.

'You're on for it, then?' he said.

Bruce reached for another oatcake. 'I'm on for it, Donnie-boy.'

Telling Bella was the part Donnie had worried about, but she was alright: proud he had a plan. She thought he'd be safe enough with Bruce. He handed in his notice at the hotel the following week and he and Bruce booked their tickets on the train.

When the day came, Donnie said goodbye to Bella, who surprised him with the parting gift of a split-new jacket. He was so touched he kissed her on the cheek, not something he often did, and then he was off.

As the train left Carrabhal, Donnie pressed his face to the window as they slid past the churchyard where his uncle Archie lay. I hope there's a better life awaiting me than running about after a tangle of sheep all your days, he said silently to the deceased. The yellow hill was bathed in late summer sunlight, and he shivered suddenly, looking up.

Friday 20 March 1998

Anna

It begins, as always, with the fizz of a match, with the swing of an arm, with the opening of a hand. The spark sails through the dark, sending flames gobbling up the glistening trail of fuel. I can feel, rather than smell, the petrol in the air. It lifts the tiny hairs on my skin. It tips my head back until my shoulders pinch my spine tight, tighter than the hot skin on my face. My fingertips stretch down to the ground, then rise like sun rays to the sky. As the first tentative flames start to lap the caravan's walls I am gathering in the breath to shriek with the sheer crackling thrill of it.

Then comes the shove in my back that pitches me forward, and we're running up the hill together, Jamie and I. The sleeve of his jacket is clutched in my hand, and we're swarming through the bracken, scrambling up grassy tussocks. With every gasp I taste the smoke at the back of my throat. When we reach the lip of the old quarry we slither down its rocky face, grazing our knuckles and knees, kicking stones that roll and bounce all the way down to the moonscape ground beneath. Once on the level we tear towards Jamie's pickup, rip the doors open, dive into the cab.

We roar away, down the track. In front of us the sky is sunfall-red in the gathering dusk. I pull down the sun visor, meeting my own bloodshot eyes in the mirror. Behind us, smoke is rising in a dark plume from the burning caravan like a malevolent genie released from a lamp. By the time we hit the road, the fire has the appearance of something solid and the caravan is barely a memory inside sheets of red flame. I'm laughing. Jamie's got his foot to the floor and the pine trees on either side of the road are a blur. My

hands are pointing towards the sky again and I am rising up, up.
Perhaps I will soar through the roof while everything else falls to
the earth, in a scatter of feathery ash.

Erin is still sleeping. I didn't even hear her come into the room last night. I know, as I wake, that I have had the dream again.

My eyelids are sticky and my tongue feels like a pork scratching. Gingerly, I reach under the bed and feel for the bottle neck of the Drambuie, holding it up to my bleary eyes. Over half of it gone. The smell of it makes me seriously consider the possibility of throwing up.

It's early and the house is quiet. I retrieve my jeans and t-shirt from where I dumped them beside the bed last night and pull them on under the blankets. Then I slump down the stairs and into the kitchen in the direction of tea and toast. The kettle is hot. Odd.

'It's just after boiling,' says a voice from the corner, and I wheel round. John Teelin sits tucked in between the corner of the kitchen table and the wall, papers spread out before him.

'Tea?' I mutter, waving a teabag in his direction.

He shakes his head. 'No, you're grand.' He's thumbing through a sheaf of papers, looking horribly fresh with his dark hair gleaming in the sunlight and lighting up the faint freckles on the side of his face. 'How's the form today, then,' he asks, without looking up.

'Alright,' I mumble. 'Yourself?'

'You kind of slipped off early last night, eh?' He lifts his head, shading his eyes with his fingers.

I squash the teabag forcefully against the side of the mug, watching the hot water turn amber under the spoon. 'Look—'

He interrupts me. 'Anna. I have a feeling I owe you a bit of an apology. About last night. I'm thinking maybe I was being an eejit. I get a bit hung up on my work. I'm sorry.'

I sip the scalding tea with my back to him. "S'OK, I suppose,' I say. I'm a sucker for an apology. 'I had some bad news.' This sounds a bit overdramatic, just for hearing that my ex was looking for me.

'Yeah?' he says, and waits, but I'm not falling for that again.

'Yeah,' I confirm. Holding the tea firmly in front of me like a shield, I make for the kitchen door.

'Ah,' he says. 'Too bad.'

The back of my neck pricks, and I stop despite myself. 'What?'

'It's just, well, you'll remember that photograph I showed you. I'm after thinking if I wasn't a bit hasty.'

I am eyeing the toaster, wondering if there's any bread left. 'I asked Fern about the photocopy you showed me,' I say in a rush. 'You know, my grandmother Netta is just sitting beside her. Beside – your relation. Bridget.'

'The photograph?' He pauses. 'The one in my bag, you mean?'

'Well, yeah, the photocopy of the Forestry girls. I didn't mean – I wasn't going through your things or anything, it was just, Fern was there and . . .' I trail off.

'OK.' He raises an eyebrow, grins irritatingly at me.

'The one we showed to Lachie, you know?' I plough on. 'In the petrol station yesterday. *There's your sister.* I think it was Netta he was meaning when he said that to me. My grandmother – Dad's mum. Fern and Bella's sister.'

John Teelin roots around in the pile of papers in front of him and finds the photocopy. I move over to his side.

'That's her,' I say, putting my finger on the girl Fern identified as Netta.

He dips his head to look. 'This small world,' he mutters, 'never ceases to surprise me.'

I tap the photocopy once more. 'Fern told me that this is Netta, and this is Josephine Halloran.'

'Josephine?' He swivels to look up at me, a shaft of light falling into his face. 'You mean Bridget.'

'No,' I say. I point again to the picture. 'That's Bridget there. That's Josephine next to her, and that's Netta beside her.'

'Josephine.' He frowns.

'Josephine and Bridget Halloran were sisters,' I say. 'Fern remembers them. My grandmother Netta was friends with the two of them during the war. Mind what Lachie said? The *two* of them, Irish. They were sisters.'

There's a short silence. 'I never heard of Bridget having a sister,' he says. He turns back to stare at the photo. 'Hm. Would you know what time the library opens?'

'Early, I think. People come in for the papers or to use a computer before work.'

I can feel his foot start to jog up and down under the table.

'I'll stick a jumper on and take you down just now, if you like,' I say.

'Ah,' he says, a little quickly, 'are you sure, now? I don't want to keep you from – well – but that would be great, Anna.' He meets my eye and grins happily, like a wee boy. 'Just great.'

'Two minutes.' I take my tea upstairs, catching a glimpse of myself in the mirror. Jesus. I might need more than two minutes.

Quarter of an hour later I'm back downstairs with clean clothes and freshly washed hair. John Teelin is nowhere to be seen – smoking out the back, no doubt – but on the table there is a piece of buttered toast cut into quarters.

We bump down the track in the Land Rover with Moss the collie perched on the middle seat between us, his tongue lolling with excitement. I'm not sure how he got out of the byre but collies are a law unto themselves, as Bella says. Without a job to do they become self-employed.

'He'll only bark and wake everyone up if we leave him,' John

Teelin points out. His hand twirls in the dog's coat, absent-mindedly unpicking tangles. 'What happened to Josephine, I wonder? I've never heard of her at all. She might even still be alive. It's not often I come across someone who could still be in the land of the living.' He says nothing for a minute, looking out of the window. 'Then there's your grandmother,' he says.

My mouth is still full of cold toast; I chew, swallow. 'How do you mean?'

'Well. She's another one who disappeared, isn't she?'

'Well,' I frown, 'not exactly *disappeared*. She moved to Canada. I don't know the details. I think they all lost touch. I've always had the impression there might have been a bit of a falling out. But I don't know, really.'

'I think you look like her.'

I glance across at him quickly, slightly startled. The picture from the paper could be almost anyone. 'How would you know?'

'Last night Fern showed me a photo of herself and her sisters,' he says. 'You'll have seen it. The one where they're all holding those fancy birds. You look like Netta, I think.'

'Oh, hardly.' I feel pathetically pleased. 'They're just kids in that photo. Netta was beautiful. I mean, really striking. Like Jackie Kennedy, that's what Fern says.' I feel myself blushing. I sound exactly as if I'm fishing for compliments.

'Ah, well,' he says vaguely. 'It must be the hair or something.'

I touch my wayward, permatangled curls. 'I've been thinking about cutting mine off,' I say. 'Donating it to charity.' This is not strictly true and I regret saying it.

He is looking out of the window. 'Anna,' he says, not turning, 'you seemed a bit pissed off at me, last night. Not just about the papers. When I said the stuff about the selkies. I'm sorry. I wasn't thinking.' He doesn't give me time to respond. 'The thing is, it's a bit of a running joke. Between me and

Erin. You probably just thought I was being a dick. I'm sorry. It probably meant something to you, that story.'

I nod.

'It's just, whenever Erin or I pick up a book *inspired by myth and lore*, there's almost always a selkie or a kelpie skulking around in it somewhere. You know. In a puddle out the back or something.'

'Or in the bath upstairs,' I add.

'Well, exactly. You can bet your granny on it.'

'I wouldn't bet my granny on anything.' I say, then, 'I suppose it was just one of those things I loved when I was a child. I shouldn't have been so prickly about it, maybe.'

'Sure, everyone has their sharp edges,' he says.

'It was a bit of a sad story. That's what I remember.'

'It seems to have a pull on the imagination, the seal people, right enough. The Connellys in Ireland are said to be descended from seals. I think it's a bit – overdone, that's all. But I didn't mean to offend you. I'm sorry about that.'

'It's OK.' I pull into a passing place to let the post van past. To our left the river is in spate, full of melted mountain snow.

"So," he says, "Netta. What do you think she would be doing with herself out there, these days? Have you any idea whereabouts in Canada she ended up?"

"I really don't know very much about her," I say. "She left for Newfoundland just after the war, I think. But like I say, I really don't know. They lost touch with her, way before I was born."

"Fern said last night it was 1947, when they last saw her." John Teelin says. "And of course she left your dad behind. That's sad, isn't it?" He breaks off, scratching his ear. "I mean, obviously. I don't know if you want to talk about this or whatever."

'I don't mind.' I shake my head. 'It's one of those things. Bella brought him up. She never really talks of it. I mean, my dad knew Bella was his auntie, not his mother.'

'So it's a bit of a mystery.'

'It's just one of those things,' I say again. 'I suppose we might have heard if she'd passed away over there, but maybe not. Or perhaps Fern and Bella do know.'

'It's the same back home,' he says. 'Not much talked of. Still, I think I'd want to know.'

'Yeah.' I find myself smiling. 'But that's you. You're nosy for a living.'

He laughs. 'No, I'll have to correct you there, Anna. I make a living being nosy. You've got to keep asking questions, you see?'

'Even the ones with no answers?'

'Oh, there'll be answers, for sure,' he says. 'They might just be, I don't know, *missing in action*.'

'But you might not like what you find when you start poking about.'

'Those who cannot remember the past are condemned to repeat it.'

'Did Winston Churchill say that?'

He huffs in indignation. 'That old bugger? No, he did not. This was a Spanish fellow. George someone.'

'Still,' I say, 'it's not an excuse to live in the past, is it? I mean, sometimes people forget things for a reason.'

'Like it or not, the past lives in you,' he says. 'In us all. And yeah – ' he leans back, half closes his eyes ' – it's not all rosy, that's for sure. I'm just ... ah, I'm just trying to ask better questions. Trying to learn from the answers.'

'You're braver than me,' I say, 'talking about Netta in front of Bella. I wouldn't say it's a family secret exactly, but she never speaks about her.'

I don't know why I can't seem to stop talking when I am around John Teelin. It isn't like me.

'Oh,' he says. 'Like I said, I asked Fern. When Bella was out of the room. So I can't claim any credit for courage, that's for sure.'

I pull up opposite the library. Moss bounces forward, forelegs either side of the unwieldy gearstick, and I get a slaver of drool down the left side of my face. 'So do you think you'll find much today?' I ask.

'Suppose I'm going to be looking for this Josephine,' he says. 'See what I can find.'

He can hardly wait until the Land Rover has stopped before he gets out. A girl waiting at the bus stop with a swish of shiny red hair turns to look at him, blatantly giving him the eye as he paces across the road to the library.

I wouldn't bother, I tell her silently. It would seem that being long dead, or at least mysteriously absent, is the best way to be of interest to John Teelin.

It's now or never, no ifs, no buts. In Boots I buy a pregnancy test. In fact, I buy two. I've rehearsed what I'm going to say, but in the end I just go to the pharmacy counter and check it's no one I know.

On returning to the Land Rover I find Moss has eaten his way through the remainder of my toast and put some tooth marks in the steering wheel for good measure.

'Brat,' I tell him. I'll be back for John Teelin at three, so I drive down to Angus John's to put in a final shift clearing the house. I promised I'd get through the last of it today, before everyone leaves tomorrow and I decamp to the hotel to cover Leighanne's shifts over the weekend.

The house is nearly empty now and it doesn't feel like anyone's any more. The floors and walls are an out-of-date map of what once was. All that's left in the living room is the hi-fi on the table, and the cases that hold Angus John's record collection. I am about to get the tests out of my bag when I hear the creak of the garden gate and see the top of Fern's head from the window, bobbing up the path. I stuff them back in my bag as Moss launches himself towards the front door in delight.

Fern says there's something she'd like to show me, if it's still there. She sits with me on the floor as we sort through the records one by one, making two piles. I ask her what she is searching for, but she doesn't reply, thumbing through the three cases with a mysterious little smile. When she reaches the third case she gives a cluck of triumph and holds up a small, shabby-looking cover. 'Now! He did keep it!' She nudges me. 'What do you see here?'

I shuffle over to look. The record has a scarlet centre, the word *VICTOR* written in gold letters under the picture of the dog listening to the gramophone. *Kashmiri Song*, it reads, beneath. *John McCormack, Tenor.*

I look at Fern. She is still smiling. 'See the cover?' she says. Along the top there is a blue sloping scrawl which reads,

> *To Angus John, our 'Gallant Ferry-Man'*
> *with many thanks!*
> *A little something to tide you over*
> *until you can join us across the water.*
> *with love and gratitude from J, B, N.*

'There you go,' Fern says. 'You were asking about them, and that's it.'

'J, B, N.' I say. 'Is that—'

'Josephine, Bridget, Netta. As I said, he was forever ferrying them across the loch, to the dances and all sorts.'

'He must have been quite young.'

'Oh, fourteen, fifteen. This was an old song, even back then, my mother loved it. It was one of their favourites I think, the two Irish girls and Netta.' Fern sends her voice up high, a falsetto. '*Pale hands I loved beside the Shalimar.*'

I trace the message's faded ink. 'What do they mean, *across the water*?'

'Well, Canada, of course,' she says. She pauses. 'I suppose there's no reason you should know this. I know Bella wouldn't have told you.'

'Know what?'

'Your grandmother Netta didn't leave for Canada on a whim. She went because of Vincent. A lovely man. He was a serviceman from Newfoundland. They were engaged, you see? But he died in the war. Netta was never the same after. And then she had Donnie – your father, just a little baby, her on her own – and she wasn't well.'

'Was Vincent the father, then?' I ask. 'Dad's father?'

Fern is quiet for some time, looking down. Then she says, 'I don't think so, Anna. The dates . . . Vincent died too long before your dad was born. I'm sorry, I don't know. She would never say. Not to any of us.' She sighs, tugs the sleeves of her cardigan down her arms. 'You have to remember, Anna: back then, to have a baby out of wedlock, as it was called – well, it was seen as a terrible, shameful thing for a young woman. A sin. Some families would turn you out. They were sent away, to homes for unmarried mothers, and then the babies were adopted. It might have been that way for Netta if our father had still been alive, but he passed away shortly before all this happened. You heard of women throwing themselves downstairs, or using knitting needles . . . well. I'm sure you know of this, Anna. Things are different now, thank God. Not perfect, but better.'

'Yes,' I manage. My throat is tight and I keep my eyes on the record, the inked writing. I feel sick to my stomach. Fern has never talked about this to me before. I wonder why she is telling me now.

'Netta refused to say who the father was,' she continues. 'And I think that made people think the worst. You know, there were so many stories at the time, local women going with all these servicemen who were over here, all this moralistic hand-wringing.' Fern laughs wryly. 'You can see why I wanted to get away. We all dreamt of leaving at one point or another. But Netta was determined, despite everything. It turned out in the end that she could get passage on a ship to Canada. It was the Canadian government who set it up. War brides, they called them. You had to go to London, to get all the paperwork sorted out. Netta could start a new life in Newfoundland, living with Vincent's family.'

She breaks off and puts the record gently down on the carpet. 'When they say *join us across the water*, they mean join us in Canada. They all had a plan to go: Bridget, Josephine, Netta, and Angus John too, when he was old enough. But Bridget died.'

'She died,' I repeat. I remember John Teelin telling me this in the car.

'Yes,' says Fern. 'While they were still here. She had some sort of accident, I think. I would have been away in Glasgow at the time, and I don't know what happened to Josephine after that. And, as you know, Angus John travelled the world before settling back here, on his own doorstep. Such a very long time ago, Anna. Fifty years,' she says softly. 'Those of us who have that long to look back on will tell you it feels like no time at all, until you consider all that has happened in between. Such is the elasticity of our memories.'

She looks at her hands, one thumb drawing circles in her other palm. 'It was very difficult. For Netta, obviously, but for Bella too. Archie was a good deal older than her, and I know she longed for children, but she lost so many before they were born. So perhaps it was unsurprising that she took it hard, very hard, Netta expecting. I know she's not proud of that now. But who can honestly say they've always acted impeccably? I know she still finds it painful. And with everything that came after. You'd think now we're older it wouldn't be, but if you don't talk about things for so long, it becomes almost impossible.'

I fight a great urge to confess myself, to tell her about my situation, but I only say, 'I see.' I wish I could say something substantial and meaningful, but settle with taking Fern's worn fingers in mine. My hands look as though they are made of different material from hers, yet her grip is strong, cool and comforting as it ever was.

'We had no address for her,' says Fern. 'And we thought she would come back. After Donnie . . . after your father passed, we tried, Angus John and I.' She sighs. 'I suppose we were cowards after that. Well, I was. I thought she might have got in touch with Angus John. They were close, the pair of them. And just recently . . .' Fern draws in her breath suddenly. 'But sometimes you have to accept, Anna, that some folk find new lives, new families, and they don't want the old ones to come knocking. And now,' she says, pressing my fingers in hers, 'would you be a gem and give me a hand up?'

I stand and help her to her feet; she weighs so little. Bones like a bird. 'I'll come with you,' I say. 'Back to the house.'

As we are walking down the path arm in arm, Fern turns her head to look at me and I catch her eye for a second.

'Fern,' I say, 'I – can I tell you something?'

I study the ground as we walk, and I think of Netta on her own with the baby, the baby who became my father. She must have been about my age when she had him. The thought of it terrifies me, and calms me in a way I don't quite understand. There are still the two pregnancy tests in my bag, sitting on the living room floor in Angus John's house.

I realise Fern is waiting for me to go on. I let out an awkward half-laugh. 'It's nothing, sorry,' I say. I squeeze her arm. 'It doesn't matter just now.'

June 1942

Angus John

They were singing as he rowed, Netta and Bridget at the stern with Effie Gillies squeezed in between them. Josephine was sitting in the prow, pretending to be a figurehead with her hand screening her face from the dark horizon, throwing out lines from a song into the night.

Netta and Bridget were swaying and joining in and Effie was ticking them off; they were squashing her, she said, shushing them. Sound carried too well on the water; they'd be heard.

Josephine just laughed. 'Ah, Effie, would you stop?' She twisted to address Angus John at the oars. 'The boatman doesn't mind, does he? Not a bother on him.' She flung her arm in his direction, the pitch of her voice dropping theatrically. 'Once more across the water, MacArthur!'

Angus John kept his head down so she wouldn't see him smiling, and because once he was looking at her it was hard to do anything else. He focused on the dip and pull of the oars, sending the wee boat flashing through the water. There was barely enough light to see by, just Josephine holding the lamp which was dipping every which way as she started up her singing again. But that hardly mattered to Angus John. He knew his way on the water as he knew his way around the house, and tonight the loch was still and perfect, just their rowing boat abroad on the smooth black circle which filled the cleft of the hills that rose up all around them.

He was full, in that instant, with the rightness of things, as if his whole life had been saving up for this journey: boatman to

Effie, the beautiful Halloran sisters and Netta, whom he loved more than anyone. Josephine was of an age with Netta, years older than him, but he was sure that he loved her, too, or at least something like that.

I wish this were forever, he thought. I wish we could always be like this. But all too soon the crossing he could have rowed in his sleep was over, and he was shipping the oars and letting the boat drift in slowly to nudge up against the jetty of Altnaglas.

'I'll go,' Netta said, a hand on his shoulder as she stepped past him to hop ashore with the painter. As they got out of the boat, one after the other, each girl kissed his forehead, as if he were a child, and thanked him. Then they scrambled up the bank to the path that wound back through the grounds up to Altnaglas House. When they reached the broad curve of the driveway, they said their goodnights, and the Hallorans and Netta set off towards the big house where they stayed. Effie and Angus John walked onwards together, down the tarmacked road.

The hill pass would be quicker to Crois na Coille, but Effie lived along the road, so Angus John walked with her, the long way round. He knew he was just a wee scrap of a boy to Effie, who was nippy as a terrier, but she seemed happy enough to talk away to him when it was just them, giving him the rundown of the dance they had just been to: who had been at the drink and who was carrying on with whom. So he just walked at her side, carrying the sugar and the matches that a friend of his mother's had given him to take home. There were rock cakes in the bundle, too, and he ate some as they walked along, offering one to Effie. She said to put them away out of her sight, she couldn't be doing with the temptation.

A bat flicked past above their heads and Effie squealed, a hand to her curls. Why did people always think they would tangle in their hair, thought Angus John, when it was clear bats could navigate in the dark better than anyone? He turned his head back and saw Altnaglas House bathed in moonlight, its dark windows glistening.

'Bonny, isn't it, under the moon?' said Effie. 'Like the pictures.'

'It is.'

Effie moved off again and Angus John was about to follow when his eye was caught by movement to the side of the house. He narrowed his eyes, sure he could make out two figures walking up the long field that ran to the east of the gardens. One dark-haired, the other light. He saw, for a second, a glimmer of Netta's white scarf and heard the faintest shade of laughter, and he watched until they disappeared up the pass that led over the hill.

Angus John turned back to the road, puzzled. He couldn't think why it was just the two of them, or why they would be going over the pass at this time of night. He thought about saying something to Effie, but she had stopped in the road, standing on one leg shaking her foot, complaining of a blister on her heel and a pebble in her shoe.

He thought, but couldn't be sure, that they were holding hands, his sister and Bridget Halloran, as they climbed the hill.

He was to ferry the girls across the loch many times during that summer, before everything that happened. Yet in years to come he found it was that glance behind that had made the imprint onto the innermost chamber of his mind. There was a way about it, he would think: the house lit by the moon careening through the night like a pallid horseman, and the press of everything he did not understand within the world he had thought so familiar.

To this he would return, time after time, silently moving through the memory of that small journey. How lightly the dark had lain, in that long field.

Netta

My work in the library at Altnaglas had continued all through the winter and into the spring of 1940. By then the Canadian troops had arrived at the training centre that had been established at Barnadine, on the shores of Loch Leck.

I was courted by Vincent Randall from Saint Bride's, Newfoundland. *My jewel*, Vince would call me. *My best girl.* I'd tell him that if he puffed me up any more I'd burst. He'd laugh and say that he only spoke the truth.

When war was declared, Mondegrene had become involved in the establishment of the Local Defence Volunteer Company. Childhood polio, plus injuries incurred during the mysterious Belgian years, about which he only hinted, had rendered him unfit for active service. Mondegrene liked to tease me about Vince. 'I should marry you, Netta,' he said, once.

Vince generated joy as a fuel that carried him through life, a fuel that burned and drew people towards him. He had a way of telling jokes, deliberately, willing you to laugh, leaning forward with his hand resting on his knee. His arms were bear-strong; he could lift all three of us, Fern and Bella and me, spin us round until up was sideways. And when we were alone he would hold me and kiss me most seriously and most tenderly, so I would feel the blood coursing through the core of my body in a triangle of lust and longing – and love, I was sure. I didn't know if I'd be able to wait until we were married, and I wasn't at all sure I wanted to.

But Vince, who could steer a boat with one hand and roll

me a cigarette with the other, who always asked tenderly after my family's health, who promised me a life in Newfoundland after the war, who was hero-worshipped by his men and who had somehow, inexplicably, picked me as his companion, was found dead in his bed early on the morning of the second of July 1941. His heart had stopped in his sleep, and his body, perfect in every way and only missing that vital spark, was shipped home to his sisters where they lived on Route 1, Saint Bride's, Newfoundland. A heart murmur, the doctors said. Undetectable, rare. He was twenty-six.

I could hardly speak of my grief, for Vince was only one of many, and he had died cradled in warm sheets, his body whole, not blown apart, shot, or drowned. It felt like a cruel joke, not at all like the sort Vince would tell.

The rest of the summer was hot. Flies rose in clouds around the rhododendrons in front of Altnaglas House, and Margaret Fair the housekeeper had cleg bites the size of pennies along her leg. I realised that it was true, after all: that I was going to die myself, one day, and that this was an immovable, unarguable fact that had previously only seemed to apply to others.

After Vince's death Mondegrene started to ask me to sit with him in the evenings, as he drank. He didn't joke any more about marrying me. Instead he started talking to me affection-ately. The way he looked at me was sentimental, the same as when he stared into the liquid brown eyes of Tip, his pointer bitch, and rubbed her ears. Sometimes he would put a hand on my shoulder or curl a lock of my hair around his fingers, always with the same preoccupied expression, as if his hand was acting in a way entirely unknown to his mind.

I would keep still until he moved away.

At home, my father's health was worsening, his lungs labour-ing, his heart failing. My mother's health was also suffering, and Bella and I started to fall into our relative roles, with Bella keeping the house and caring for our parents, and my work at Atlnaglas providing a welcome addition to my father's war pension. The pair of us had never been close. I did not have Bella's patience or strength, and hated seeing my parents this way. With Fern away in Glasgow, I was shamefully keen to leave Crois na Coille, and towards the end of the summer I moved into the servants' quarters at Altnaglas, all alone, at the other end of the house from Mondegrene's rooms.

By now the legions of staff the Mondegrenes had employed before the first war had dwindled. There was now only me and the redoubtable Margaret Fair, who was in her sixties. She was always threatening to leave and go to her sister's in Helensburgh. The house was falling to pieces around her ears, she said: a poor shadow of what it had been when she had come here as a young woman. She carried out her duties for Mondegrene with a surly deference that seemed to amuse rather than anger him.

At Altnaglas I had my first room of my own, wood-clad and white-painted, at the top of the house. I lay in bed on my side at nights, my knees tucked to my chin. I would listen to the creaks and groans of the great house, settling on its old bones like a dragon on its hoard. I imagined walking up the yellow hill, tearing my hair and wailing. By the time winter turned I was thin and poor-looking, but I was – against the odds, as it seemed to me – still living.

And then, in the spring of 1942, when I should have been a bride, the land girls arrived.

I watched them disembark from the station at Barnadine. The local press was there to take pictures of the arrival of the 'lumberjills,' as they dubbed them. Girls from all over, from the cities and towns, schoolteachers and factory workers and debutantes, fresh from a training camp in Angus on the other side of the country. They were put up in the servants' wing of Altnaglas along with me; the place was transformed overnight by girls' voices rattling up and down the stairs. The next day they went out to work in the woods, and at the end of the first week there was a dance on the other side of the loch, to welcome them all. I forget who persuaded me to go.

From Altnaglas we were rowed across the loch to the dance by my brother Angus John. How his ears flamed. He had never been in the company of so many women. The small boat was full. I was crammed up next to two Irish girls, one fair and the other dark. They were sisters, they told me, Josephine and Bridget Halloran. Their mother had died of the Spanish flu, and they had been all over, wherever their father could get work. From Belfast to Brighton and all seven ways around the ship, in Josephine's words.

'The Emergency', Bridget called it, this war that had brought them to Altnaglas to fell and plant trees. I understood about as much of Ireland as I did of the war that was raging across Europe, which was to say, very little indeed.

The Halloran sisters were not like anyone I had known before. They were only two years older than me, it turned out, but were so much more worldly-wise. Josephine was dark-haired, Bridget fair, and both were startlingly blue-eyed. Josephine was the more outgoing of the pair. She could have gone on stage; in fact, if you believed all her stories, you would have thought she had. In a certain light we used to say she looked like Hedy Lamarr.

Bridget was a little quieter, more thoughtful, with a dry sense of humour. They were a double act really, the sisters, playing off each other with perfect timing, the one setting up the joke or story and the other saying something quick and so clever they'd have you doubled over.

In the hall that first evening there were about six girls to every man, and not a drink to be had except for lemonade, but *we'll dance with ourselves, anyhow*, said Josephine, and she did.

Bridget asked me if I would partner her in the second half.

'I'll be the man,' she said. Her arm fitted snugly around my waist. Her hand felt small in mine, compared to a man's.

'It's as blistered as any man's, though,' she said, when I told her this. My father used always to spit on his hands before work and my brother did the same; I suggested maybe she should try that.

Most of the girls danced as if conscious of being looked upon, but not Bridget. She moved without show or fuss, guiding me swiftly and determinedly around the room, one corner of her bottom lip drawn into her mouth in concentration. I could feel the muscles flexed in her arms, a strength in her body I did not possess.

The hall was narrow and I could feel the floor moving up and down beneath my feet. Bridget was saying something but it was hard to make out the words. I had to lean in so close to her mouth that her lips brushed my ear.

'The band are very good,' she was saying. 'Are they from around here?'

I looked up to the makeshift stage, where three elderly men played accordions, shoulders lifting with the lilt of the music. I nodded. Josephine had in fact managed to find a man to dance with – well, of course she had – Eddie Barry from the bar at Portdonan. And good luck to her, muttered Bridget ominously.

We went outside for air, the pair of us. Bridget pulled out her little compact and I watched her putting on her lipstick. 'Do you want to try some?' she asked. I had no make-up; my father would never have stood for it.

Bridget made me stand still, and then leant her hand on my chin to paint my mouth. There was something thrilling about her touching the skin of my face. Afterwards I looked in the mirror of the compact she held out. The lines of my lips were very distinct, as if they had been finely sculpted. I held the tiny mirror at arm's length so both of us were reflected in the glass.

'Only your eyes, Netta,' Bridget said, 'they're that unusual. Have they always been that way?'

The lipstick had a thick, cloying scent. My lips felt heavy, my mouth moving in an exaggerated way when I talked. I told her yes, as far as I knew, ever since I was a baby, when one stayed blue and one went dark.

'Back home they might say you had the second sight,' Bridget said. 'One for this world and one for the next.'

We went back in again and danced and danced, two-steps and waltzes and some country set dances that I showed her how to do. By the end of the night I thought I'd never tire of dancing with Bridget Halloran. She'd spoil you for dancing with a man, so light on her feet and never treading on your toes.

When the evening was over we stood outside the hall and someone came round with the bread and butter pieces that were left over from the break in the middle. After a while one of the girls said, 'It's getting on, isn't the shebang turning up?'

Even though it was spring, the midges were out in force and we were slapping them from our skin and itching.

'I'm not standing around to be eaten alive, girls,' Josephine announced. 'Who's for a run?'

If anyone else had said it I was sure she would have been shouted down, but because it was Josephine, and she already had her shoes in her hands, we all jogged down the road under the cool sky, with the black loch licking at the stones where the road fell away. I was watching out for motor cars – they would not have their lights on – but no one passed us. Running through the dark in that group brought with it an excitement, an elation even, and before too long we were nearly sprinting, calling to each other and laughing at nothing at all. The girls seemed entirely unaffected by the exercise but after ten minutes I struggled to keep up, feeling the breath rasping in

225

my throat. I stayed behind for a minute, coughing. Bridget slapped me on the back and laughed, waiting with me while I drew my breath.

'And here's me thinking you'd be fit as a hoot,' she said, 'you're that skinny. It's all the ciggies.'

'Nonsense,' I said. 'They're menthol.'

It was Mondegrene who had given me the cigarettes. You could hardly buy them here for love nor money now, yet he always seemed to have a ready supply. I gave her a puff but she peched and gasped and said she'd never tried something so disgusting in her life.

She was shivering. I took my scarf off from around my neck and wrapped it around hers. Her skin was petal-fine. It gleamed in the moonlight. I wanted to tell her how beautiful I thought she was, but I could not quite say it.

When we began to walk to join the others she asked me if I had a man and I told her about Vincent, and what had happened to him. She was quiet for a while. Then she said, 'I believe in the quality of the life you're given, Netta, not the length of it. It sounds as though he had a good life. And now it's complete.'

'I feel I hate him sometimes for it,' I said. 'For going.' I never thought I would say that to anyone, but she just nodded and as if in reply, a great screech came from the pine woods high above. Bridget shrieked and grabbed my arm with fingers like pincers.

'It's only an owl,' I said. I laughed, wiped my eyes on my sleeve. '*Cailleach oidhche* – old woman of the night.'

Bridget snorted and said, 'Our word in Irish is *sgreachog*. Jesus Mary, what an unholy sound, screeching away.'

'My *seanair* used to nail them to the barn door,' I said. 'To ward off lightning.'

'Nasty old thing,' Bridget said, and from her tone I wasn't sure whether she meant my grandfather or the owl. We walked back to the others, her small, rough hand in mine.

I did not think I could have laboured as the land girls did: hard, dangerous work. One of the girls was buried under a fall of timber while loading in the third week and it was sheer luck that she was pulled out alive, though she lost all her teeth. In the weeks that followed we went dancing nearly every week-end and even if there were plenty of men, we only danced together, myself and Bridget Halloran.

Friday 20 March 1998

Anna

John Teelin is waiting for me outside the library, pacing up and down the pavement, smoking a cigarette. He looks up briefly as I pull in and nods tersely before grinding the butt beneath his foot and climbing into the cab.

'How did you get on?' I ask. 'Any joy?'

He shakes his head. He's swapped the cigarette for a plastic biro, chewing on the end as he thumbs through his notebook. His cheeriness of earlier appears to have evaporated. I think of the dinner I'm meant to be cooking this evening, of the pregnancy tests in my bag back at Angus John's. I'm not going to sit here like a bloody chauffeur.

'Hey. John.' I sound the horn twice in quick succession and he starts.

'Jesus!'

'No, it's me, Anna. I was asking you, did you find anything? In the library?'

'Yeah. Sorry. This.' He passes me a piece of paper, barely looking up. 'Women's Institute newsletter, October 1942.'

Funds raised towards local ambulance service, I read. I scan the text quickly.

The sale, which raised over £12 for the local ambulance service, was organised by WTC member Miss Josephine Halloran, in memory of her sister Bridget, whose sudden death was deeply felt by all who knew her. Mr John Campbell of the hospital trust was quoted as saying …

*　　*　　*

The picture shows a striking dark-haired woman shaking hands with a stout man in a suit. She is slim and elegant-looking. I look up at him. 'You did find her, then. And Bridget's mentioned there too.'

He shakes his head. 'Yeah. But the whole thing's a bit of a frustration, to be honest.' He slaps the notebook closed and leans his head back, shutting his eyes tightly. 'It's dispiriting. Every time I lift a stone, there's another underneath. And another, and another. I'm running out of road.'

What exactly are you hoping to find, I wonder. 'You know,' I say, 'I've something to show you, back at Crois na Coille.'

'Yeah?' He opens one eye cautiously.

'Ah, you'll need to wait and see,' I grin. I don't want to describe the LP before showing it to him. He raises an eyebrow and I realise this has come out slightly more provocatively than I meant it to. 'Look,' I hurry on, 'you might think you're getting nowhere when you're sitting in the library going through stacks of dusty papers. But we're here. Where they were. I know this place like the back of my hand. Where is Bridget buried?'

He rubs his forehead with his knuckles. 'I don't know. I haven't been able to find a record. I looked for her last time I was back in Donegal, but I couldn't find anything.'

'Well, what about here? This is where she died, you said. There's only one cemetary in Carrabhal. If we find her, who knows where that'll lead you? We could go there now.'

He turns to look at me. 'Is there a Catholic church here?'

'Er, yes. But there's no graveyard there, to my knowledge. The cemetery holds everyone. I think it's . . . compartmental-ised.' I'm sure that's not the right word. 'My great-uncle Angus John is there.'

He looks at me properly for the first time since getting into the Land Rover. 'No. Don't worry yourself, Anna. You need to get on, I'm sure. This has taken up enough of your time.'

'Belt up.' I resist the urge to lean across and click his seat-belt into place. 'We're going.' I crane my head out of the open window, checking for cars coming up behind me before pulling out into the road. Beside me John Teelin stretches his limbs, sighs. I change gear with a crunch.

'Did you find out how Bridget died?' I ask. 'Fern said she had an accident but seemed hazy on the details.'

'No. There's very little about her at all. Just the record of her death, and a few words in the paper.' He drums his fingers on his knee, and we crawl down the long ribbon of the main street without a further word between us.

I park outside the cemetery. Angus John's headstone isn't up yet; if I'd known earlier that we'd be coming, I'd have brought some flowers to put on his grave. We divide the area up, John Teelin taking one side and me the other, and he strides off, ducking his head to read each stone in turn.

We spend almost an hour walking slowly amid the stones, staring at the ones it's possible to read. The grass is green here; the trees are in bud. It is as if spring has sneaked in while I was looking the other way. There are doves in the trees above, rabbits scurrying between the stones when disturbed. I try not to think of their burrows, enmeshed with the remains of the other inhabitants of the soil.

I have no luck finding Bridget Halloran's grave on my side, and when John Teelin joins me again he shakes his head. 'No sign.'

'Me neither,' I say. 'Sorry.'

'Anna, there's no need for sorry.'

'I know. I just wanted to help.'

'I appreciate it.' He gives me a rueful smile and puts his hands in his pockets, taps the ground with the toe of his shoe. 'I'm the one who's sorry, really. You were right. I had a word with myself, back there. Digging around in the past, trying to find out about people of my blood I never knew. It's a sort of addiction. I suppose.' He pulls his tobacco from his pocket. 'Where there's pleasure, there's pain. At some point you decide you need it in your life.' He glances at me. 'Perhaps you know this yourself.'

I don't know how to reply and say nothing until we're back at the Land Rover again.

'You know what?' I stop before getting into the cab. 'There is one more place we could try.'

'Yeah?' He rubs the dented bonnet of the Land Rover absent-mindedly with his sleeve. 'Where's that, then?'

'There's a wee burial ground at Altnaglas. The chapel is on the estate.'

'Altnaglas,' he says. 'That's where they were working, the land girls. On the Altnaglas estate and all around that part of the woods.'

I nod. It's also near where we scattered our dad's ashes up on the hill. 'It's on the way back, anyway,' I say. 'Just near the care home where I used to work.'

'If you're sure.'

'I'm sure.'

Up ahead the road is closed. I swing down a side street and wind through the housing estate, making for the road out of town.

'I used to live here,' I say, indicating with my thumb. 'Beveridge Place, just up there. Me and my mum. Before she married again.'

He nods. 'And then you did nursing, is that right?'

'Kind of,' I mutter. 'I was caring for Mum, before. She's got multiple sclerosis. It's relapsing-remitting. In good spells you wouldn't know there was anything the matter with her, but at the worst times she needs a wheelchair. I looked after her. And then she got married to Bruce, and I went to the city for a while. But it didn't work out. So I'm back here.' My voice sounds falsely bright, even to me. 'Just planning my next step, you know? The next move.'

'Well, good for you,' he says.

I wait for the regret of talking about this to roll in, but it doesn't. 'It sounds pathetic, doesn't it?' I say. I try to imagine his life at university, his independence, his purpose. 'I bet it sounds pathetic to you.'

'No,' he says, quietly. 'It doesn't.' After a moment he says, 'You know, you're fairly harsh on yourself, Anna.' His voice is gentle, and there is something about his saying my name that seems to thicken the air I'm breathing.

'I'm not so sure. I literally never talk about this stuff.' I try to laugh to puncture the tension, but it doesn't come out quite right. 'Maybe I just need to get over myself.'

We drive on in silence for a while, and then he says, 'I looked after my mam. Before she passed. I wouldn't have wanted anyone else to do it but it isn't something I'd wish on anyone.'

'No.' I have to squeeze the word out. I can hardly bear the feeling that he would be sorry for me.

He doesn't speak again until we leave the town, and then he clears his throat.

'I should tell you something, Anna,' he says. 'I did actually find something else. In the library. It was a newspaper report about your dad.'

'Oh.'

'I don't really know what to say. I didn't realise. I'm sorry, Anna. I wasn't looking for it. In case you think . . . it was just, you know. The girl helping me, she mentioned it when I said the name MacArthur and I – well. I guess I wondered. Perhaps I shouldn't have done. I'm sorry, Anna,' he repeats. 'A terrible thing to happen to you at that age.'

I want to tell him he has nothing to apologise for but I don't trust myself to speak, so I say nothing.

The Altnaglas cemetery sits a little way up the yellow hill, a hundred yards or so past the entrance to the estate itself. We park by the road and climb the hill to where the cemetary's low stone wall is surrounded by imposing rhododendrons. John Teelin opens the small iron gate, tugging it free from the undergrowth that has ensnared its lowest bars. I go in first and we walk up the sunken stone path into the graveyard.

It is a quiet place, still and small. The light falls in slices through the trees, illuminating grave slabs and stones which now have the appearance of being scattered, haphazard. To the west, the remains of the medieval chapel is sunk in grass and dead bracken. John Teelin peels off to explore the side closest to the chapel. On my right is a half-collapsed stone table, a relief carving of a long, straight sword and a skull just visible beneath the moss. Sir Kenneth Mondegrene's grave is here, next to his two wives. His first wife has a large angel with sweeping wings.

I glance over at John Teelin, and see he has dropped down on one knee before a stone on the other side of the cemetery from where I am standing. His arm is stretched out, his knuckles resting on top of a small, plain stone. He is quite still.

I find myself trying to move quietly as I approach. He is smiling slightly, looking at the stone.

'There you are,' I hear him saying, under his breath.

'You've found it?'

He looks up, still smiling, and nods. The stone is no higher than my knee, bare granite. The inscription is plain, in small letters. *In Loving Memory of Bridget Mary Halloran, RIP. 1918–1942.*

'Just twenty-three or twenty-four, she was,' he says. 'Younger than me.'

We stand together, looking down. 'It's a lovely spot to rest in,' I say.

John Teelin takes a photograph and we walk back to the Land Rover. There is a collection of stones arranged in a small patch of green outwith the main wall; he asks me what they are and I tell him it's where the Mondegrene family buried their dogs. He shakes his head.

In the Land Rover we sit for a moment. The only sound is birdsong. The key is in my hand but I don't start the engine yet. My senses seem hyper-alert, drawn tight as a violin string, high and delicate. I am meticulously aware of my body; its edges where it meets the space between us. I listen to my breathing as if it is the sound of someone else. I feel suddenly, mortifyingly close to tears.

John Teelin says nothing beside me, and it is beautiful, this quiet broken only by blackbirds. I think, but cannot be sure, that I hear a cuckoo, the first one of the year, the lilt of its two-note call. I know if he says anything to me, anything kind, anything quiet, I will cry. I feel sick and hungry at the same time.

It dawns on me that of course this is Fern and Bella's Land Rover, and they always keep emergency supplies in here.

I open the door and jump to the ground. The air is muggy. Opening up the back, I find the canvas bag stowed in the spare wheel, and amid the blankets and spare socks there is a bar of Kendal mint cake.

'Anna?' John Teelin has also got out and is standing on the passenger side of the Land Rover when I emerge. 'You OK?'

'Yes.' I smile at him, tear open the wrapper and break off a piece of mint cake. It gleams like a tiny iceberg. 'Do you want some?' I extend the wrapper towards him, but he shakes his head, turning to stare around at the landscape before us.

'It's beautiful up here, isn't it?' He points down to the shimmer of water stretching around the toe of the peninsula. 'Is that the sea?'

'Yeah. Next stop Ireland.'

'Dál Riata,' he says. 'It was the one kingdom, there and here, over a thousand years ago. All of the western seaboard here, in Argyll, and what's part of Antrim now. The sea was a link, not a barrier.' He grins at me. 'Not Donegal though. We were doing our own thing, in the west.'

237

'I get the feeling you always do your own thing.'

He shrugs. 'Hardly. Much as I'd like to. Perhaps when I find out who I am, that's when I'll be free. I'm sure that's a quote from somewhere. Not Churchill, either.' He glances over to me. 'You're quiet, Anna. Something on your mind?

'My dad was found not far from here.'

'Oh.' After a pause he says, 'I'm sorry. Do you want to go?'

I shake my head. We stand in silence for a few seconds, but I find I want to explain, to tell him what happened. 'He just fell,' I say. 'The other side of the road, it's quite a steep drop, down to the loch shore. That's why they have those barriers there. The trees weren't so big then. He'd been drinking. We were on our way to Glasgow, in the car.'

The sweetness of the mint cake is making my teeth ache. I scrunch the wrapper around what is left of the bar. 'It had been planned for a while. We were going to go to the zoo. And Dad rocked up drunk; he'd totally forgotten about the trip. They were fighting, and Mum threw him out of the car. They were fighting a lot, then. He was probably walking back to the caravan, or maybe he was just trying to get down to the water. I don't know. He just fell, and he died here.'

John Teelin shakes his head. 'I'm so sorry, Anna,' he says.

'Yeah. It was a long time ago now.'

'Your mum, does she –'

'She can't – we don't talk about it. We've never really talked about it.'

'I'm sorry,' he says again. He shifts his balance, and I think for a second that he is going to hug me, but he just touches my shoulder as if he has said something else. He steps away and we stand side by side as a tractor rattles by on the road. When it has passed I watch a cloud of tiny insects rising from the bracken beyond the barrier on the other side, flickering in a shaft of sunlight.

*   *   *

My mum was driving that night, her jaw clenched tight and her shoulders shaking. My dad was beside her.

Jamie and I were tucked under a scratchy blanket in the back. He was sleeping; I held his hand. In my head I was telling myself a story I can still remember. It was one I told myself all the time. In the story we lived in a wooden hut, all four of us, and there was condensed milk for breakfast. In the hut there was a chest containing a silver city and a golden city and a bronze city. If we needed something, we could simply climb into the chest and find it and money never changed hands.

I heard Mum's voice from the front seat, low and tense. The indicator ticked, and the car pulled in, stopped. Mum said quietly, in the tone she used for arguing in front of us, 'Are you trying to humiliate me, Donnie?'

My dad said no, he wasn't. He was calling her *Rosie*. Just keep going, keep driving, he was saying, he wouldn't—

'Enough.' Mum's whispered words hissed out like steam. Words like *last chance. You've blown it now.*

I think my dad was reaching for her but his movements were clumsy and she pulled away, turned her head. 'Keep your damned voice down. I won't have you waking the kids.'

It was too late for that. In the back, Jamie and I looked noiselessly into each other's eyes. Jamie's were glinting with tears but he did not make a sound.

My dad was angry then, telling her to just drive, put her fucking foot down, and my mum, as if she had waited for him to lose it, said, 'And so I will, God help me, but you'll get out and walk. You know this bloody road better than your own family; it'll take you home.' She leant over and opened the passenger door. 'Go on and get out.'

He sat there looking at her for a minute, and then he said, 'If that's what you want.'

'It is.' She turned her head away.

'Then I'm fucking gone.'

'Good.'

Dad turned to us in the back. 'Your mum's a bitch,' he said. Then he reeled from the seat and was out of the car, slamming the door shut behind him. I twisted around as much as the seatbelt would allow, pressing my face against the window. Mum pulled away and it was just Dad standing there, up on the verge, illuminated in the dull pink glow of the brake lights. His hands were upturned, his arms open. He was gazing at me and I looked back until we rounded the bend.

Jamie watched, his eyes brimming over as I twisted and scrambled to my knees to see—

Mum was saying my name, still with that deadly chill inside it. 'Sit down,' she said. 'Now. And do your seatbelt up. Good girl.' A dim shining on her cheek as she checked the rear mirror and turned her eyes back to the road ahead. 'We'll see him tomorrow. Now settle down, both of you, and go back to sleep. We'll be there before long.'

'But how will he –'

'He'll be here when we get back.'

But he wasn't.

A search party found him two days later, face-down in boggy water at the bottom of the wooded gully that sloped steeply from the road to the loch.

Death by misadventure, the Procurator Fiscal concluded.

All that he left was the caravan, surrounded by his carrion cars, the innards plucked out, and the empty foundations of the house whose walls had never grown, and now never would.

All his best-laid schemes, just outlines on the earth.

July 1942

Netta

At Altnaglas, my strange librarian life continued.

'There is a war on,' Margaret Fair would sniff, while I arranged all Scott's works alphabetically and talked quietly to Alacrity, Mondegrene's deerhound. When July came there was endless rain; I thought of my brother and wondered how he was, working out on the hill. He was too young to enlist.

I thought also of Bridget's mouth, and the dried, crusted blood on the skin beneath her swollen nose one evening. She had been struck by the end of a chain that slithered off a log. I felt as if my whole being was centred on Friday, when I would see her again.

'Couldn't we all be sisters,' Bridget said to me once. 'You and Josephine, you're like two peas.'

'You're more like me than my own sisters,' I told her. 'They're not like me at all.'

I had taken to wearing my hair brushed up, the way the Hallorans did. We shared scrapings of lipstick, powder, scent. Mondegrene had given me a bottle of his mother's perfume, Guerlain's Shalimar, a quarter of it still left. 'She wore this every day of her life,' he said. 'Even to the grave. I insist you have it.'

Couldn't we all be sisters. Bridget's face would come to me very clearly as I worked among the library shelves, her face framed by her hair, featherweight, honey-smelling. She was small and lithe but not thin, her belly a little rounded, a slight bulge around the waist belt she always wore, a hint of heaviness in her calves and ankles. The utter certainty with which she carried herself made you almost envy those things. *I am absolutely this way,* her body seemed to say. I admired her so very much. I loved her rootedness in the wide world, when I felt so uncertain of everything.

When there was no dancing, the girls arranged other things to do on their permitted days off. Some of the locals said, with some suspicion, that they seemed very set on enjoying themselves.

Angus John turned up at Altnaglas one morning, and with his ears pink as foxgloves, his cap held awkwardly behind his back, he managed to stutter out an offer to take Bridget and Josephine fishing.

'Not without me you won't,' I said, and smiled at the look on his face, caught between gratitude and resentment.

Josephine said they'd love to go, if he didn't mind teaching a pair of amateurs.

'Sure she's only ever fished for compliments,' Bridget said.

We showed them how to cast a fly in an open field so as not to get the line tangled, and then we walked up the hill to the lochan of the small corrie, which was a tiny loch in a deep crevice of the yellow hill. It was a secret place for us, the only fresh water we were allowed to fish, where brown trout could be found. There was an agreement between Mondegrene and my father that we could keep whatever we caught from there.

Where the mouth of the river widened and flowed into the lochan, the fish could sometimes be seen, almost stock still, just their fins rippling almost imperceptibly in the rills of the current. In the peaty water their bellies shone a deep gold, and their backs were stippled with dark spots. It was as if they held within them both the day and the night.

There was too much sun to be a good day for a catch, said my brother. It was warm, although ripples of wind stirred the water. Certainly we caught nothing at all that morning. Josephine and Bridget started to pretend that they were an elderly, bungling couple of their own devising styled Lord and Lady Bumfop-Droop, in search of the Salmon of Knowledge. They were turning over stones and splashing in pools and poking sticks into rabbit holes until we were laughing so much we could barely breathe.

Angus John suggested we move around the lochan to where the trees were thicker and the water was more shaded. Josephine said she'd join him, but Bridget and I decided to stay in the sun. Angus John whistled to his dog and set off with Josephine, the two rods he'd brought slung over his shoulder, his jacket hanging loosely from his hand, and I saw how my little brother had grown, was nearly a man. Bridget and I sat down at the edge of the lochan to sun our faces.

My feet felt swollen and hot after the walk. I took my shoes off. There were dragonflies swooping and sparkling over the water. The yellow hill craned above us, steep and forbidding.

Bridget lay back on the shore, closed her eyes. Her hair was golden at the tips. The sun fell on her closed eyelids, showing them to be as delicately veined as leaves. Her nose was sunburned.

I stood up, and she opened her eyes as she felt my shadow fall across her face.

'Will we take a dip?' I said.

She raised her head without moving the rest of her body. 'You go ahead.'

'Come on.'

'I would if I could swim,' she said. She laid her head back down.

'I'll learn you.' There was a restlessness in the heat. I couldn't stand still. 'Come on.' I felt the strongest urge to shed my clothes, to slough off the layers that hung on my body like a constricting skin.

She sat up unhurriedly, clasping an arm about her knees, the other hand pulling tiny pink flowers of moss campion from the ground. 'I'll paddle, so. Just to please you.' She looked me up and down, smiled slowly. 'You're not really dressed for a swim, Netta.'

'It's more usual to *un*dress, I think.'

One eyebrow raised. She tipped her head back and laughed up at me, pushing her hair off her forehead with her fingers. 'Go on, then,' she said. 'Dare you.'

I said nothing, just turned around and walked a few feet back from the loch, to a raised grassy bank. I took off my blouse, hung it on a gorse bush. I took off my stockings and my skirt so I was standing in my slip. Although the sun was warm, there was a cool breeze that raised goose flesh on my arms and legs. I felt as if I had drunk something that had gone straight to my head.

On the shore, Bridget had shed her shoes and stockings and was standing bare-legged, her skirt hitched over her knees, dipping her foot into the water before recoiling.

'It's colder than bloody death, anyway,' she said. She turned around, looking for me. 'Where have you got to, Netta?'

I stepped down from the bank and started to run, racing to the shore of the lochan. My feet slid and bruised on the stones. I didn't stop when I got to the water, stumbling forward, splashing and churning, and when I felt the cold up to my knees I flung myself forward. It was icy, enveloping, and then it was only cold. I swam a few strokes and pulled my head up, gasping, my hair streaming wet into my eyes, and I heard Bridget laughing behind me.

'Come on,' I called. 'It's not deep. You can put your feet down any time.'

'If they haven't frozen solid,' she said.

I looked around, about to call out to her again, and stopped. She was standing in the shallows taking off her clothes. All her clothes. She bent, splashing herself and emitting tiny squeals. Her curved body was pale as milk. Then she sank down into the water, her hands over her breasts. She was short of breath and her teeth were chattering; she wiped her nose with the back of her hand. 'Holy Mother of God. I can't even breathe. How in the—'

I swam towards her, telling her to take a deep breath, to fill her lungs with air, to float. She would manage it for a second, only to thrash and let water up her nose, and then she would sneeze and sink. I grabbed her without thinking, before remembering her nakedness, and felt the twist of her body in my hands as she turned in the water. Her skin was soft and cold and there seemed to be no end to it. I felt her hands on my shoulders, her strong, tense fingers digging into the muscle. I fought the impulse to press myself against her, against the entirety of her body.

We held on to each other for a minute, her wet face against my chest, her sopping hair in my mouth as she struggled to find her footing, and then she pushed off and swam strongly away, as elegant as a porpoise.

'Thought you couldn't swim!' I called.

Bridget stopped and stood and turned around. She was laughing, her golden hair turned amber in streaks down her cheeks. I stood up, threw my slip in a bunched ball to the shore and sank down again, bare to the weight of the water all around me.

She dived down. I saw her pale watery shape beneath the surface. She circled round behind me and tried to pull me backwards. Her fingers were rough and clutching. I wanted to cover her, to wrap my arms and my legs around her waist between her ribs and her hips, where her body was soft. On her face I saw what I was feeling: excitement, uncertainty. The sense that neither of us knew what we were doing nor were quite in control of doing it.

She pulled me towards her and put her lips to my collar-bone. We sank down together until only our eyes remained above the water; we watched each other again. Beneath the water our arms reached out. Our legs tangled. I'd never touched another person like this. Her body felt so familiar to me. It was as if we were trying to find where one of us ended and the other began. She ducked her head under the water and I felt her lips on my stomach, below my navel, somewhere between a lick and a bite. When her face broke the water again I linked my fingers around the back of her head and brought her mouth to mine and kissed it. For a second her mouth opened and I felt her tongue touch my own, so warm and soft amid all that cold.

Above us the mountains: silent, megalithic onlookers. I could hear the lapping of the water on the shore, the birds, and the wind soughing through the swaying birches at the edge of the lochan. All else was silent. My body was tingling, as if each muscle and nerve were aglow. I felt I could have struck out for the pine-dark island in the middle of the lochan and swum all the way back again, without needing to take a breath.

We made our way back to the shore and waded up on to the stones. I picked up my soaking slip where it washed in and out on minute breakers at the edge of the water. I found where the rest of my clothes had fallen beneath the gorse and pulled them on. They scratched and clung to my wet skin, my hair dampening the collar of my blouse. Some distance away from me, Bridget did the same.

When we were dressed we walked along the shore, gathering driftwood and dry bracken. We built a fire and sat close beside it as it smouldered, watching the wood as it charred white and fell, blue smoke curling into our faces and hair. There was hardly a word spoken between us, until first Josephine and then Angus John arrived back, Josephine holding a small trout by its tail.

For the rest of the afternoon, as we sat around the fire, I looked at Bridget and sometimes I saw her and sometimes I saw only the sun in her face. I thought of the caves in the mountain, the tiny opening through which I'd been told the sun's rays crept on midsummer to flood the dark rock with golden light, illuminating a secret space carved with spirals, and I knew that nothing would ever be the same.

Friday 20 March 1998

Anna

I turn the Land Rover up the track to Crois na Coille. I think of this place as Bella's domain: sturdy and resilient, as she is. Fern is birdlike, unbound to one place.

My mum is hard on the great-aunts. I am sure Bella was not kind to her in the wake of my dad's death, in her own grief. She was always on the outside of things in the MacArthur family, my mother: peripheral, while Jamie and I were taken into the heart of the house.

When I saw John Teelin kneeling in front of that headstone, it dawned on me that there is a geology to family with its generational layers, the pressures that bond it together or split it apart. Netta was only a few years older than me when she left here. Her story is slipping away, not enough of it left to really tell. To leave and return is one thing, but to leave your son and never come back is another. I have thought of my family's history at Crois na Coille as something familiar, but Netta feels so unknown to me.

Back in the yard of Crois na Coille I step on the brake and the Land Rover lurches to a halt with an offended creak. 'Come on,' I say to John Teelin. 'You need to see this.' I jog the gearstick into neutral, open the door and jump down, landing in a puddle. He follows me across the yard, heading towards the house.

Inside, it is quiet. I pull off my wet shoes and find Erin on her own in the living room, reading a book. She looks up briefly, pulling an earphone off to tell me that Professor Croke,

Fern and Bella have gone to pay a visit to Mrs MacPherson in the care home.

I dart from the living room into the hallway. The stack of records Fern and I went through at Angus John's house is sitting beside the stairs. It takes me a few minutes to find *Kashmiri Song*.

On the kitchen table, John Teelin has laid out his photocopies from the library and is leaning over them, arms folded across the back of a chair. I slide the LP on to the table, showing him the handwriting on the cover.

'This is a record that Bridget and Josephine gave to my great-uncle Angus John,' I say. 'He knew them too, he would row them across the loch to the dances and back, with Netta. See the initials? Their names are all here. Fern told me all this earlier for the first time. They were really close, apparently – they spent a lot of time together. Angus John was too young, but Fern told me that the three of them had a plan to move away to Canada, together, and for him to join them.'

He stares at me for a moment, his eyes slightly narrowed, and I can't tell what he's thinking.

'What do you think?' I say. 'Maybe I should have mentioned this earlier?'

'I think this is great.' He lifts the record to look at it more closely, runs his finger under the handwriting on the cover. 'Is that what they mean here: *across the water*?'

'Yeah, I think so. To Canada.'

He pushes his hair out of his eyes. 'I mean, it could explain why I've found nothing in the UK or Ireland about Josephine,' he says. 'If she moved to Canada, all those years ago. She could still be alive over there. Netta went after the war, didn't she?'

'Yes, she was a war bride. Well, sort of. Her fiancé was a Canadian soldier but he died. She had a baby, too – my father, Donnie. But she left him behind, here. Fern says . . .' I pause.

'Fern says Netta wasn't well, after having my dad. In the head, I think she meant.'

'Right,' he says slowly. 'So.' He picks up his pen, taps it on the table as he speaks. 'Bridget arrives here with her sister Josephine, in . . .' he casts an eye over his notes '. . . spring 1942. They work as lumberjills, and they stay at Altnaglas House. And at some point something happens to poor Bridget. And . . .' he looks up at me, smiles '. . . thanks to you, we know she's buried in the graveyard at Altnaglas. There's no sign of Josephine, but it's possible she emigrated to Canada at the same time as Netta. Just the two of them.' He takes a step towards the door. 'Erin,' he calls through, 'can I trouble you for a minute?'

When Erin comes into the kitchen, John Teelin tells her what we discovered in the graveyard that afternoon and shows her the record.

'Oh, my,' she says. Her finger traces the ink of the names.

'How could I find out about a person who emigrated to Canada after the war?' John Teelin asks.

'Josephine? That shouldn't be too hard,' Erin says. 'There'd be a landing pass, documents. If she married a serviceman, there'd be records from the Canadian Wives' Bureau, no doubt. The war brides – it's quite a story, back home.'

I try not to feel a bit pissed off that Erin seems to know all about John Teelin's family already and is so willing to be helpful. I realise I'd started to think about it as something just shared between the two of us.

'I have a friend who works at the National Archives of Canada in Ottawa,' she is saying. 'That's where all those kinds of records are kept. I'm sure he'd be able to look for you.'

'That would be great.' John Teelin's voice is quiet; he is looking down at the photocopies. 'Thanks,' he says. 'Thanks so much, Erin. That would be fantastic.'

'It'll be expensive, to make the call,' she says. 'I'll wait till we're back in the department, and I can maybe clear it with them

– research costs. But we're talking a couple of days, at least, till they'd get back to us. They can fax through whatever they find.'

There is the rumble of a car engine at the end of the track; the others have returned from the care home. There's a pot of peeled potatoes sitting in a pan of water in the sink and a steak pie on the counter, pushed back out of the dogs' reach. Erin fetches coal from outside and John Teelin feeds the Rayburn, prodding the embers into life with a poker. I watch his hands, his fingers scuffed with coal dust.

'I hope you find her,' I say. 'I hope you find Josephine.'

'Oh. Sure, I'll let you know what we find, Anna. Either way.' He puts down the poker, straightens. 'If you'd like to know.'

'Yes,' I say. 'I would like to know.'

Later, the final evening of their visit has drawn in around us. Fern, Bella and the professor have been back for a few hours and the fire has been lit in the living room. It is a feeling I remember from childhood stays here, the darkness creeping up the field to the house, the feeling of warmth and safety within Crois na Coille's thick walls.

'The days have a fair stretch to them now,' Bella says, looking out of the kitchen window to the hill beyond. 'Spring won't be long in making herself known.'

The back door stands ajar; outside, the collies are eating from metal bowls with quick, urgent bites. Fern and the professor are sitting together on the sofa listening to Angus John's records, meandering through the music.

We all gather by the fire before we eat. The professor produces a bottle of wine for the occasion and everyone has a glass except for me. I've picked up my bag from Angus John's but there is so little privacy here. There isn't even a lock on the bathroom door. As soon as I get to the hotel I'm going to do a pregnancy test and put paid to this havering, not knowing one way or the other. Until then, no more drinking.

256

The professor proposes a toast to Angus John. 'A great man for the music,' he says, lifting his glass. Bella doles out wedges of pie and when everyone has a plate, the professor raises his fork aloft and insists on reciting 'The Song of Wandering Aengus'. Fern dabs a little at her eyes. It was thoughtful of him to pick a short one, I think, because everyone else is clearly ravenous.

After dinner, the house lapses into quiet conviviality. Erin curls up on a chair by the fire and John Teelin takes up the fiddle, the professor occasionally breaking into snatches of song when he recognises the tune.

'Ah, he makes that instrument sing like a skylark,' says Fern. The pair of them sit arm in arm, swaying in time to the music. What is between them is a mystery to me. Perhaps it is to them too. As I watch, Fern turns a little towards the professor as if to lean into him. She looks at his arm where it touches hers, but he is only immersed in the music. John Teelin goes into another tune and the professor half lifts his glass and leans forward, away from Fern, who is left unbalanced. She re-centres her weight alone. She's held a flame for him so long, and he seems so unaware of her. I know what it's like to circle in orbit around someone whose attention is elsewhere. I wonder if this is the last time Fern will see him. I wonder if this will be enough.

The professor curls Fern's hand in his and asks John Teelin for '*An Buachaill Caol Dubh*'.

It is a slow tune, the melody lovely in its mournfulness. I watch John Teelin play, his eyes closed. What was it he said earlier? *Where there's pleasure, there's pain.* When he is playing he seems a different person altogether; entirely within himself, unreachable. The notes from the dusty wood beneath the bow are drawn to the surface, darkly shining like water in a well pail. *Slow air* is right, I think: a music that slows the breathing, that makes space in the unyielding pace of time.

I might never see John Teelin again after tomorrow either. I try to imagine him ageing, the skin of his face coarsened, his hair leached of its rich colour, the planes and angles of his frame filled out and blurred with the stuffing of advancing years.

When he has finished playing, he rests the fiddle on his knee and leans over to the table to reach for his glass. For a moment our eyes meet and I wonder who I might become, the skins I will slip in and out of as the years go by. I get up and finish clearing the table, gathering the glasses, sliding unused cutlery back into its ancient presentation box. Who knows if it will come out again.

In the kitchen Bella starts the washing-up. She's been so much in the spotlight the past few days, the centre of attention. It seems much more natural to me, somehow, to find her on her own. I have never been as close to Bella as I am to Fern; Bella has always been self-contained, her kindness enclosed in provision and care rather than affection. I wonder if she will miss their company when the three visitors are gone.

I take up a tea towel and join her. 'What have you been finding out, then?' she asks, with her typical directness. She doesn't look up from the sink.

'Oh.' I pause in the middle of drying. 'He's been researching his family tree, John. Two girls who came over from Ireland during the war.'

Bella sniffs. 'Right you are.'

I am about to ask her if she knew them when she says, 'Well, they'll be off tomorrow, any road, and it's probably for the best. But what about you, Anna? Where are you off to?'

I tell her about Leighanne, about my plans to work at the Tayfillan Hotel for a few days.

She waves that away. 'And after that? Will you stay with your brother? Or will you be taking up your nursing course again?'

'Jamie and Lena are just so – well, busy,' I say, 'what with the baby arriving and everything. And I could stay with Mum, only . . .'

Bella turns to face me, her hands dripping with suds. 'Ah, you should make peace with your mother, Anna.'

I think about saying that I'm going to lunch with her tomorrow, but decide I'll sound defensive.

Bella turns back to the water. 'Jamie's going great guns with the jobs, I hear.'

I tell her that his last job was for Jerome Mondegrene of Altnaglas.

'Mondegrene,' she repeats. She slots a plate into the drying rack. 'He'll be glad to have that behind him.' She's in a strange mood tonight, restless yet resigned. A record starts up next door and I see her shoulders relax. She smiles. 'It's quite the thing to hear these old songs again,' she says.

I take a deep breath. 'Have you ever heard the 'Kashmiri Song' – Pale Hands I Loved . . .?' I venture.

She turns around. 'Has Netta been singing that one to you?'

This startles me. I honestly think it's the first time I've ever heard Bella say Netta's name aloud.

'I mean – Fern, of course. Fern,' she says. 'They sang it, all the time, when we were young.' She turns back to the sink with an air of finality that I take as a cue not to ask any more questions.

I make my sixth cup of tea of the day and return to the living room. It is later than I thought; the professor has dozed off in his chair and no one has the heart to wake him. Bella and Fern take themselves off to bed not long after that, and then it's only me and John Teelin and Erin. Perhaps it is the alcohol or the fact it is their final night, but there is a companionable ease between us tonight and I relax into our conversation. We stay up well past midnight, Erin and I sitting at the kitchen table beside the open window with a candle burning in a dish. Erin talks about Canada and where she grew up: their holiday cottage in Muskoka Lakes, their golden retrievers, the colours in the fall. John Teelin reclines in the low chair by the stove, rolling cigarettes for himself and Erin, blowing smoke out into the dark. He doesn't say very much and finally goes silent altogether. When I look over I see he has fallen asleep in his chair, his head resting on his hand.

'We must have been boring him,' I giggle.

Erin is drinking ginger ale and whisky, and I can't tell if she's exactly drunk, but she is certainly on her way. 'Would you look at him,' she says, looking over with a soft smile on her face.

If I don't ask now, I think, I'll never know.

'Is there a story with you two?' I say. 'Are you together?'

'Together?' She raises an eyebrow, brushing ash from her lap. She takes her time replying, as if considering. 'You know, back when we were undergrads, in college,' she says, 'it was always the two of us, vying for the top of the year. Who would get this award – it was a cash prize, a bequest, for the highest marks in the department. He won it twice, me once. People think I'm dumb because I look like Little Bo Peep, but I'm not. And I work hard.' She grins at me. 'The only person I didn't mind losing to was him. Not that I'd tell him that.' She laughs, then lowers her voice. 'I guess, apart from the winning of it, with my family, it didn't make much difference. But with him ... well. It was maybe more important. Financially, I mean. He's had to work for every single thing. Take every chance going. But he never makes a big deal of it. I admire that about him.'

'You two are close, then,' I say.

'Yeah. I used to call him a dark horse but he's just ... quiet. Kind of old-fashioned, I suppose. He only really speaks when he's got something to say. And then you can't get him to shut up.' She laughs. 'But your question. He did ask me to dinner once, in our first year. That alone should give you an idea of how clueless he is sometimes.'

'How do you mean?'

She laughs, turning her face upwards to the ceiling, then shakes her head. 'What do you think?'

'I'm not following.'

'Right. Well, OK. I guess you could say, Anna, that I'm not that interested in men. Not even – ' she nods over at him ' – that man, although he's a good one, I'll give you that.' She raises her eyebrows at me. 'If you follow me now.'

'Oh,' I say. 'Right.' I feel about twelve. 'Sorry. I'm an idiot.'

'There's no sorry about it,' she says, and laughs. I feel suddenly fond of her.

'Anyway. Enough about me.' She grins and leans forward. 'You should tell him,' she says. 'Tell him you like him.'

I am seized with the desire to deny it, as if we were teenagers. But what's the use of that? 'Is it . . . really obvious?'

Erin's smile widens. She shrugs.

I scrunch my eyes shut. 'Ah.'

'I don't want to say join the queue.' She laughs. 'But when we were doing fieldwork in Kerry, there was this girl – well, woman, really – who used to cycle for, like, a couple of *hours* to see him every day,' she says. 'She knitted him socks and everything. And, the thing is . . .' She taps ash into the candle dish. 'I honestly don't think he even cottoned on how much she fancied him. Or, if he did, he wouldn't admit to it. He's kind of obtuse that way. So. Are you going to tell him, or what?'

'No! Definitely not.'

'Why not?'

I shake my head. 'He isn't . . . I don't think he would be – I don't know, interested in someone like me.'

Erin frowns, shrugs. 'I don't even know what people mean when they say that.'

'And I can't knit. Not even a scarf. Definitely not socks.'

Erin laughs and I rub my face, feeling self-conscious, thinking about going to bed. Instead, somehow, I find myself telling Erin about falling out with Bruce, and all about Liam, everything back from when we were in school, right up to the night I left Killearn Street nearly a week ago. My suspicions about being pregnant.

'Oh, my God,' she says. 'You wasted that much time on an asshole like that?'

'Yeah, I know,' I say.

'He sounds like a real piece of shit.'

I say nothing.

'But you do have to do that test, don't you?' she says. 'It's not the end of the world either way, but you have to know.'

I nod, not looking at her. 'I reckon part of the reason I'm scared is because I think I'd want to keep it.'

'Well. That wouldn't be so bad, would it?' she says, briskly.

'It's the fact it might be . . . connecting me to him like that. Forever.'

She stubs out her cigarette, sits back in her chair. 'Do the test, Anna. Once you know, you'll make the right decision.'

I look over at John Teelin. *Do you think he likes me?* I want to ask, but it sounds pathetic, so I don't.

Erin gets up. 'Well, it's past my bedtime. I'm just going to tuck in Sleeping Beauty here.' She drapes John Teelin with a blanket while I clear ashtrays and glasses from the table trying not to make a sound, and then we creep upstairs to our beds and lie awake for a spell under the eaves, whispering and giggling like teenagers. This is like the sleepovers I never had, I feel like telling her, but she's fallen asleep.

Wednesday 2 September 1942

Mondegrene

He had been walking for perhaps an hour in the woods. His heart beat against the bars of his ribs. But his breathing was slow, and deep. A pause between inhalation and exhalation in which he heard the sound of starlings.

He'd come down this morning, as he often did, to visit his mother's tree. It was a giant sequoia, a century old at least. He knew exactly the spot on the trunk where their entwined initials were cut into the bark, but the letters were misshapen and unreadable now. He and his mother had carved them not long after they arrived at Altnaglas, when they would go walking together. It had been the one part of his new life he had treasured, back then.

The boxing tree, his stepfather had used to call it. Its bark was spongy; you could drive a fist into it without injury. He did that now.

As a young man he'd made these woods his own. The winding coral-coloured paths of fallen pine needles between the trees, the calls of the animals and birds became familiar to him. He'd found out early on that he was an excellent shot. But he wasn't so interested in the shooting parties or in the stalking of deer on the hill with his stepfather. He liked to be alone, just his dog and his gun, looking and listening for movement in the trees.

Now the woods were truly his own, by law, and he found himself coming out less. There were plans for the forest to be felled; the lumberjills, the girls who had arrived a few months ago, would begin to cut it down before the year was over.

265

He would tell them to take down the sequoia first, he thought.

He heard voices and stepped closer to the trunk, whistled Tip to heel. Whoever it was would not see him. As he gazed down the wooded slope he heard a laugh, and another, and he knew it was Netta MacArthur.

Sure enough, she emerged from the path that ran under the footbridge, arm in arm with another woman, a blonde. Their faces were close. They did not see him.

His wrist flared sharply with pain. He swore softly and flicked away the wasp that had stung him as he rested his hand against the tree trunk. He stood, breathing hard. The pair did not stop or turn but quickened their pace. He heard Netta laugh again. He said her name under his breath as together she and her companion passed into the thicket of trees where the path led down towards the loch.

He lowered himself slowly to sit beneath the spread of the great tree. Sitting on the ground returned him to childhood. Putting his fingers in the earth, he closed his eyes and tried to collect himself, to think of her face, but he could see it only in parts. The light eye and the dark eye, the irregularity which both captivated and unbalanced him entirely. A pinkness of ear through a curl of hair. The quick slick dart of her tongue wetting her lip, her hair that glinted in the sun like oil spreading on water.

When he opened his eyes again his head was resting against the soft bark. He did not think he had slept but he was disorientated, a blur of half-dreams chasing themselves in his mind and leaving him unsure of how much time had passed. Tip crouched on her belly, panting, watching him.

There was someone coming on the path; he heard the crunch of quick footsteps. It was Netta again, returning on the loch path, but this time she was walking fast, her head down, and she was alone. He watched her until she rounded the bend and disappeared amid the trees, and then he got slowly to his feet. To follow her or to walk down to the loch? He considered for a few seconds, and then Tip whimpered and he followed his dog. Let the animal decide.

Saturday 21 March 1998

Anna

Professor Croke, John Teelin and Erin leave the following morning. They offer me a lift to the hotel, but I say I'll walk, and get the bus into town. 'Mum's birthday,' I explain, and Bella nods.

'Good,' she says. 'That's good.'

The professor hugs Fern and Bella and I awkwardly shake hands with everyone. Erin gives me a hug. She looks fresh and glowing in spite of the late night. We promise to keep in touch but I wonder if we will. When she turns away to help the professor into the car, I realise that John Teelin is standing next to me. The wind blows my hair into his face and suddenly he is reaching out, lifting it away. I stand very still.

'Here.' He tucks it back behind my ear.

'Thanks,' I say. But now he is talking about the weather, about what kind of day it is and what kind of day it might become, and he's not really looking at me but instead is looking down the road, as if he's already away. I resist the impulse to put my fingers to my neck where he touched my skin. I want to say something memorable to him, or at least something about some other time, somewhere else, but before the words reach my lips he has said goodbye and turned away, taking the keys from his pocket and opening the driver's door of the old Volvo.

Fern and Bella and I line up in a row to watch them go, their hands waving out of rolled-down windows. The two younger collies chase the car all the way down the track, old Bree loping behind them for a few paces before stopping and looking on forlornly with a low swish of her tail. The horn sounds twice before the car disappears around the final bend of the track that winds down to the main road.

I don't want to hang about after they've gone. I collect my things and say goodbye to my great-aunts, odd and lovely as they are. In the house up the road, Angus John's possessions are stacked neatly in cardboard boxes to be taken to the Salvation Army. Fern is meeting someone from the estate agent's next week, to see if the house is worth anything: the plot if nothing else.

Bereft of its contents, Angus John's house looks shabbier than ever. Crois na Coille, its thick stone walls over a foot deep in places, seems reassuringly solid and lasting by comparison. I touch the lumpy wall on my way out of the door and I hug Fern and Bella each in turn and thank them for having me to stay, promising to return soon. And then I walk the thirty minutes down to the bus stop, in the sunshine.

I pass Mina MacPherson's old house on my way, or what is left of it. The nettles have come up again after the winter, carpeting the inside where the roofless walls are open to the sky, filling the hole of the fireplace at the gable end.

He only wanted to talk to me about the weather, I think.

Wednesday 2 September 1942

Netta

We had been walking for half an hour. Over the past months we had grown used to moving together, setting the same pace, side by side. We never had to stop for the other to catch up. Now we walked as we danced, in rhythm. We would grasp one another's hands lightly, a curving brush of fingertips. I was coming to know Bridget's hands as well as I knew my own.

The afternoon light fell dappled through the trees. It was September, the end of the summer no longer in doubt. In the news, we heard that the Germans had reached Stalingrad.

So many shades of green in the woods. I could feel the steady pound of my heart as we moved down the path, the sound of birds above us in the branches and gulls, further off. The distant putter of motors. We told each other of our childhoods, and of stories with three wishes.

It had become an unspoken rule between us that we took these walks alone, just the pair of us. *Your constitutionals*, Josephine would tease us, but she had no interest in joining and did not seem jealous at the increasing amount of time Bridget and I spent together. Josephine liked to spend her time off reading magazines with some of the other girls, or making trips into Barnadine to keep up to date with the latest arrivals at the training centre.

Sometimes, when Bridget and I were together, I would try to feel the passing of time as a physical sensation, each minute a door of sleepy seconds which could be hinged open slowly. With practice, I could open this door at will, step inside the room of our being together where time could be squeezed out of shape, no longer my master.

I knew the path well: a circle, through the trees that ran down to the loch, along the shore and up to the road. For once, I had needed to persuade Bridget to come with me this morning: she hadn't felt well, she'd said. I told her I would take us down to where the mouth of the wide river entered the loch. Just a short while, I said, and she had agreed. We never needed much persuading to spend time in each other's company.

The path narrowed and I went ahead, listening to Bridget's voice as she picked her way over tree roots. I pointed to the loch, glimmering through the trees below.

'We climb down this way,' I told her.

At the shore of the loch we fell quiet. The light was dazzling; sparks skimming on the water. I could feel the sun on our skin, the breeze that moved the hair around Bridget's face. We sat side by side, four knees in a row and our arms wrapped around our legs. Bridget stretched her hand out and put it on my knee. I was about to put mine on top of hers, when she leant down on it and stood up.

I stood too, and paddled out into the loch a few feet from the shore. My feet on the pebbles were an unstructured white in the peaty water. I turned and saw her at the edge of the water, leaning back slightly, and when I picked my way back to her she was standing a few inches above me, on the ridge of rough grass that ran along the shore.

I reached forward to take her hand, low by her waist. Her face in the sunlight just above me was golden, impassive. I could see the faintest lustre of sweat on her neck. I lifted my head to hers, just for a moment, to kiss her cheek, but she turned as I moved. My lips brushed her skin and I kissed her mouth. She was looking down, her face drawn into itself.

She let go of my hand. 'I'm late,' she said.

I thought she meant she had to be getting back. I put my arm around her waist and kissed her on the cheek. Then I stepped back, the water now lapping at my ankles, still half smiling, my arm reaching out again – but Bridget moved away from me, shaking her head. Her face was sad, and she was beyond me. I heard my laughter dry to a crackle of sound.

'I'm late, Netta,' she said. 'I think I'm expecting. I think I'm pregnant.'

I shook my head in confusion and must have said something, for she repeated it. And then she said, 'I'm not sure how.'

I stared at her. She was speaking again, I was sure: her lips were moving. But I had lost my hearing. All that remained was a pitch like the wind, roaring to its own echo. I felt as if I would fall to the ground, seep into the stones, downwards into the earth. But I did not. The two of us stood facing each other like partners about to join at the beginning of a dance. Bridget curved suddenly to one side, turning. I followed blindly, shadowing the shape of her movement.

This is death, I thought, all over again, and in that moment I realised that she was my bright, golden centre and I had grown around her, in all the time that had been allowed to us in the past few months, and that there was no part of me that was not encircling her, now we were pearled together. And yet she was leaving me.

I'm not sure how, she had said. Her back was turned to me and she was walking away, along the edge of the loch. The brightness of the water sliced my eyes. I felt the space open between us like a wound. The high, dull sound rang in my ears and my neck pulsed, thick and choking. I took my collar in my fist and tugged until the seam tore. And then, stumbling forward, my eyes blurring, I reached out to her, to stop her, to hold her fast. My fingers grasped her upper arm but she didn't stop and I tightened my grip, trying to pull her back to me.

Bridget was still for a second, and then she wrenched herself away sharply. Her body twisted, she flung one arm out in front of her, and then she crumpled to the ground.

I stood in the water, looking up into the woods where the moss was a soft and supernaturally bright green. I could not hear a sound. Bridget was moving, writhing at my feet at the edge of the loch, her hands scraping on the pebbles, and I saw her mouth open, her wrist with blood on it. Some part of me knew I should bend down, help her, but I could not hear her.

Be still, I thought. Be quiet.

I waited until we were both still, and quiet.

Above the forest, a cloud of starlings, swaying and swirling around the trees that lined the loch. I looked up at them for some time. When I looked down again, I knew I would walk past her, and go through the wood, to rejoin the road.

Saturday 21 March 1998

Anna

On the bus I keep my headphones in my ears and turn up the volume loud enough to drown out any thoughts of where I'm going next. I get off a stop early from Bruce's bungalow and buy flowers, a five-pound book token and chocolates shaped like seashells. I linger over the birthday cards. Mum is famed for her schmaltzy card choices: fuzzy teddy bears, kittens in heart-shaped boxes and sentimental rhyming messages. It used to be a sort of joke between us. But that was then. I choose one with balloons on the front and a simple message, and scrawl my name inside it.

The bungalow is stuffy. Mum is sitting in the conservatory at the back, a crossword on her lap. Bruce is in the kitchen listening to Steely Dan. He is wearing a pink shirt and smells of Joop!. He fusses around pouring us fizzy grape juice and Mum thanks him in that silly, affected way they speak to each other sometimes. I perch on the edge of a wicker chair while Bruce goes to find something to 'stick these flowers in'.

On the glass table in front of me there is a plate of sandwiches. Bruce is proud of his sandwiches. His fillings of choice are spread neatly and evenly from crust to crust and are those manufactured specially for the purpose – Sandwich Spread, a concoction of anonymous vegetable specks bound in gloop, or beige pastes which come in small glass jars labelled chicken, beef, or salmon, if he's feeling fancy.

'Thanks for coming, Anna,' Mum is saying. She puts down her puzzle and lifts her glass to me. Her face has a funny twist to it, as if she has folded something away beneath it. She wears a new watch: it circles her wrist with delicately glimmering links of gold and silver, a crystal crust around the face. It gives her slim arm a purposeful elegance. When we were growing up, Mum used to navigate her way through the day with the help of a battered Casio that had quite possibly belonged to Dad.

'Happy birthday,' I say. I dig in my rucksack and find the card, slightly crumpled, the book token inside. I hand it over, wishing I had spent more on the book token. I wonder if she still reads. The bungalow is noticeably devoid of books. When we lived in Beveridge Place Mum often watched TV with a thick, shiny-covered paperback by Jackie Collins or Penny Vincenzi on her lap.

Bruce is back. He makes for the sandwiches. Always garnished with a clutch of cress on top. The tit. I start to reach for a sandwich before he has a chance to scoop up the plate and offer it around. It's always been a dead cert way to piss him off, refusing to adhere to his fussy rules and ways of doing things.

This time, though, something in Mum's expression stops me. She is leaning forward, looking closely at my face, and I know that this means she has something to say, something which is not good, and my heart begins to beat quickly. Her MS. A relapse. Cancer. I take a sandwich absent-mindedly when it's offered to me and hear myself saying *thank you* to Bruce, who looks chuffed with himself, exchanges a look with Mum and exits the room.

'Mum?' I say. My voice is anxious.

She smiles at me. There are creases at the corners of her eyes, deeper than I remember. 'I've been looking through some things,' she says. 'For the new baby coming.' She is unfolding something from her lap: velvety folds of cloth which, as she holds it up, assumes the form of a minute

282

babygro with an embroidered monkey's face on the front. She lays it flat on her knee, stroking the plush material the right way, holding up a tiny, empty foot for a second, and then she leans to the side and takes a little box off the table beside her. I remember seeing that box on her dressing table. It is light brown leather in the shape of a heart. I never knew what it contained.

Not quite looking at me, she says, 'He would have been thirty-five today.'

She looks down, passes the box from one hand to the other. 'Michael,' she says. 'Did you know that he was born on my birthday?'

'Oh, Mum,' I say. 'Of course. I'm sorry. I wasn't thinking.'

Mum doesn't mention Michael often. We'd known about him our whole lives, Jamie and I, the baby boy who was still-born before we came along, but he was hardly spoken of, as if Mum found it too painful to imagine all of us together.

We sit in the conservatory, Steely Dan still playing and Bruce banging pots in the kitchen. She tells me things she remembers from when Jamie and I were small, and then she talks to me about Michael.

October 1960

Donnie

It was the furthest north they'd ever been.

'Wasteland,' Bruce said, looking out over the low grey hills, the pale flat moor. A meagre sunset was turning the loch beneath them to white gold. The pair of them were standing outside the caravan, blowing on mugs of tea the colour of orange juice.

Donnie nodded but he wasn't really bothered about scenery; his mind was set on the job. From the camp you could just see the tip of scaffolding sticking up above the hill where the dam was being built. Just a job, he was telling himself, but thinking of the stories he'd heard: the height, and the graft. It was daunting.

He decided against sharing his thoughts with Bruce. '*There's gold in them thar hills*,' he drawled, opting for his best American accent.

'What the heck was that?' Bruce said. 'Better not do that in front of the lads here or they'll think there's something wrong with you.'

'Wrong with me?' said Donnie. 'Not if they see you first.'

It was Saturday night and the camp was quiet. When they'd got here, there had been a crowd of men waiting to get into the van and then it had driven straight off again, jammed full and heading for the nearest hotel.

No one had suggested Donnie and Bruce come along. But that was all to the good: they had precisely no spending money, not even the price of a half-pint between them. An old man with a bald head and one eye like a chipped marble had shown them the two-berth caravan they would bunk in until they knew whether or not they'd be taken on. He'd told them to report to the site office at seven on Monday morning. Nothing doing on a Sunday, he told them.

Bruce threw the rest of his tea on the ground and smirked at Donnie. 'Sure if there's gold in that concrete you'll find it.' He circled his shoulders like a boxer going into the ring. Donnie laughed at the pair of them then, two wallies strutting about in front of a shoddy caravan, the kings of sod-all. They'd made it this far, at least.

Standing outside for the last minutes of the evening, they listened to the wheezing of a melodeon from somewhere further down the line of huts and caravans, out of sight.

They'd got the train to Inverness together and then on to Dingwall and met the van that took them up to the site at Inchsuardal. There were a couple of others going on up to Sutherland too; men who smelt of grease and sweat and had done a couple of sites already. They didn't say much. When the driver asked how Donnie and Bruce had got on the job, Bruce mentioned his cousin's name. The mood had lightened a bit after that and on the way Donnie learned two new swear words and a three-card trick.

'In the money soon,' Bruce had said in a low voice, nudging Donnie as the pair of them swung down from the van and saw the site for the first time.

'If we don't get our cards the first day and get thrown off the bloody job,' muttered Donnie. He'd heard stories about that.

They had gumboots and caps, half a carton of cigarettes, a few biscuits and a packet of Trebor mints between them. Bruce's old man had given him a scraping of cash to get kitted out and they'd gone to a second-hand outfitter in Inverness.

Bruce had at first insisted that they would each get something but Donnie said no. He had his present from Bella and didn't want to owe anyone.

'Your man in there said it was a donkey jacket.' Bruce tipped the collar up on his new purchase.

'If the cap fits, eh?'

Bruce had looked a bit put out then and Donnie had said, 'Ah, come on, now, you look the business.' His pal could be a wee bit sensitive.

On Monday morning it was raining. They filed into the hot cabin where the office was and waited. Donnie sniffed and thought he detected the warm reek of stale piss.

'It's your jacket,' he said to Bruce.

'Fuck off,' said Bruce, out of the corner of his mouth, but five minutes later Donnie was watching his friend trying to sniff his sleeve while pretending to wipe his nose.

The men were a motley crew: Irish, Polish, Scottish, all ages. Some of them couldn't write, Donnie saw; they just put an X next to their names on the list. Their cards were all filed away and then they went and stood outside, awaiting the van that would take them up the hill.

'You look like a day-tripper,' Bruce whispered to Donnie with a snigger. Trying to cover up the nerves.

'Least I'm not reeking of piss,' Donnie said.

'Is this us in, then, do you think?'

'We'll see soon enough, won't we.'

They got up to the dam to find they had been banded with an Irish crew, all massive men a good few years older than the two of them. The crew watched the van arrive, all sitting on the ground, turning as one as Donnie and Bruce got out. The van drove away and the new recruits formed an awkward clump and waited to be told what to do.

Donnie took it upon himself to walk over to the crew, his hand stuck out, just to see what happened. A small, stocky man stood up as he approached. Donnie introduced himself, trying to make his voice as deep and gruff as it would go.

The man said nothing at first, just sucked on his cigarette. There were flecks of tobacco on his chin and his skin was like sandpaper. He raised his eyebrows.

'We've got ourselves a right pretty wee charmer now, lads,' he said, to the men behind him. 'Eh? Has he not got lovely manners on him? Hands soft as muck too, I don't doubt.'

There were a few laughs. Donnie stood his ground, planted there with his hand out.

'Well, Donnybrook Fair,' the man said. 'I'm McGill, and it's a true pleasure to meet you, no doubt. But this here – ' he jerked his thumb ' – is a great fucking pipe we need shifted. And I'm needing lads to help me shift it, you hear me, and it's just the one kind of a pipe that gets shifted by fine fucking manners, eh, sham?'

The men behind McGill laughed again.

'We're ready,' said Donnie.

There followed twenty minutes of grunting, slipping and sliding in the mud until McGill stopped them with a roar. 'Fuck's sake, ladies,' he said. 'I'm needing a team of men to get this thing up the hill. If you're just here to look on, buy a fucking paper.'

By the time McGill was satisfied, Donnie was surprised that his arms were still attached to his shoulders.

'Donnybrook,' hollered McGill, from further up the line. 'Whereabouts are you?'

Donnie stood up, feeling as if his back would snap in two.

'Now then,' said McGill. 'I'll shake your hand now there's a bit of dirt on it. And where are you from?'

Donnie opened his mouth but McGill laughed and stopped him. 'No matter. We leave where we're from for the sake of peace, eh, lads? We do that here. The question is, are you here with us?'

He offered Donnie his hand and they shook. 'I am,' he said.

'Good man yourself,' said McGill.

In the weeks that followed, Bruce got himself into the tunnels with the drill, but Donnie, more often than not, found himself stuck outside with the grease gun. It was boring as hell and the pay was no use. Work, eat, sleep, repeat. Come Saturdays the bus took the men down to the one pub that would serve them in Lairg.

Donnie had yet to even get on the bus to the pub but, again, he'd heard stories. The foreman here had taken the oath, back in his teens, didn't touch a drop and was a stickler for Sundays, but Saturday nights were big business before the clock turned. Donnie still had bugger-all to pay for drink. Bruce was doing better now he was a tunneller.

They were in the canteen one evening, the cook hacking slabs of beige flesh and gristle from enormous trays and slapping them on to the passing plates. Bruce scoffed what was left of his meat and potatoes and got up, wiping his face with the sleeve of his shirt, looking for pudding.

'Donnybrook Fair,' said an unmistakable voice above Donnie's head. The next moment McGill had sat himself down in Bruce's empty chair, making the whole table shake. 'Tell me this now,' said McGill. 'Can you drive?'

Donnie nodded, swallowed. 'I can.'

'There's a wee job needs doing. Fella I know works in Glasgow. Runs up with a case now and then for the lads. Would you be able to give us a lift?'

Donnie nodded.

'Right so,' said McGill. 'And here, Donnybrook.' A finger as broad as a Wall's sausage poked his chest. 'Don't be running your mouth off about this.'

Donnie nodded again. 'I won't,' he said.

McGill gripped his shoulder and pushed off towards the door, weaving between the tables slow as a basking shark. Donnie looked around the canteen, wondered why he'd been singled out from so many of the other men on site. Then again, why wouldn't he be? Most of these thick bastards were going nowhere. He picked up his fork again. Maybe his luck was about to change.

It was a brother-in-law of McGill's who had the racket going, a van making its way up to the site by Inchsuardal every other week. The Rhino, as he was known. Cases for the boys, he would say to Donnie, who would sling them in the back of a borrowed van. Then they'd drive back to the drill in silence, McGill and Donnie, smoking Woodbines until the air was thick as velvet.

Bruce was against the whole business. In fact, the boy seemed to have become lost up his own arse, and he wasn't going to trouble himself giving Donnie a hand up behind him. 'I can't ask for you to be given a go in the tunnels just cause you're my pal, can I?' he'd say. 'I had to work my way up, you know, prove that I could do it. It's dangerous in there, you know.'

'Aye,' said Donnie, 'I know that fine. But it's a chance to prove myself I'm looking for, too.'

'Not my decision, is it,' Bruce said. 'Anyway, chances are you'll be moving up on your own. You just keep on greasing those derricks. You know it won't be long before you get a chance to drive the crane yourself.'

It was easy for Bruce to say. His rise through the ranks seemed to have been a doddle, with his cousin's connections. Donnie had a feeling he would be stuck as a sodding grease monkey until he got sacked or quit, and he was fed up. He was ready to give up a good night's sleep to do a job for a bit of *cash in claw*, as McGill called it. Every couple of weeks they'd barrel down the road on half a tank of diesel pinched from the site, heading for a disused training camp at Loch Eilish where the Rhino would be waiting.

One Saturday night after such a run Donnie found himself in the borrowed van taking a load of the boys into Lairg. They were served in the public bar of a hotel with a sign in the window that read *No Irish*, but inside there was only a skelf of a girl serving, who poured their drinks and took their money alright.

Donnie asked her what time she stopped serving, it being a Saturday night, and she blew her lank fringe from her eyes and gave him a baleful, *who wants to know* stare.

'You're happy enough to serve on a Sunday morning, then,' he said, and she shrugged.

'If they want to drink on a Sunday,' she said, 'we'll take their money. They're near drinking us dry as it is. I could fill them glasses from the drip tray and they wouldn't notice.'

The next week Donnie was there again, and this time someone else drove the van. He stayed on until the wee small hours of the morning when she locked up the bar and told him he could come up for a nightcap, if he wanted to. Donnie found he didn't *not* want to; it was easy, all too easy, to follow her up the stairs of the empty hotel. He thought of Mary Rose. He told himself she was still making her own mind up, one way or another.

On the landing the girl turned around to face him, unsmiling, opened the door behind her and pulled him roughly into one of the large bedrooms that smelt of damp and furniture polish. She was pushing him up against the wall with surprising strength and undoing his shirt from the bottom up, muttering in his ear that they wouldn't be doing this again, just this one time. He realised he didn't even know her name, but it didn't seem like the time to ask.

There was no sign of her when he woke early the next morning, and he lay on the unmade bed for a couple of seconds wondering where the hell he was before he remembered. His throat was dry, and The Fear had him firmly in its grip. From downstairs came the sound of a man's voice shouting and swearing, of things being banged around. Donnie got up and pulled on his clothes, shivering, went to the window and saw a man stalking out of the hotel's front door towards the Ford Consul parked opposite.

He heard the car pull away as he went down the stairs, cautiously, his muscles condensed and tender. The girl was hunched at the bar, the rank smell of last night's spilled drink, sweat and cigarettes in the air. She was holding her face in her hand, and there was blood on her fingers.

'What the hell was that,' said Donnie.

'Mr Simpson,' she said without looking up.

'And who's he?'

'He says the stocktaking is all shot and I've lost him money.' She turned her eyes on him; she wasn't crying but she looked as if she might be about to.

'Did he do that to you?' he asked, indicating the cut on her face.

She didn't answer his question. 'I've to make it up out of my wages,' she said. 'He'd have sacked me there and then, but no one else wants to work the Saturday shift since the hydro boys started.'

'Here,' said Donnie. He dampened a rag in the sink, held it to her cheek. Her eyes swelled with tears. 'Ah, come on, now,' he said, 'it's not so bad. Listen. I might be able to sort you something out. If I could get you a wee bit, till your numbers are up? Give you a bit of time to balance the books.'

She sniffed, staring at him. 'And where would you be getting that from?'

'Well, that's for me to worry about. What do you say to it?'

'Maybe. I'm not looking to get into any more trouble.'

'It'll be no trouble at all,' Donnie said.

*   *   *

294

McGill huffed and puffed at first, but Donnie managed to convince him without too much bother. He was better with figures than he was with the grease gun, he realised.

'Since you've told me something,' McGill said to him, 'I'll tell you something. It's not just the stout that we've got going there.'

'Is it not?' Donnie said. I knew it, he thought.

'Might have a wee amber spring going as well,' said McGill. 'Think that might be part of your grand plan, eh?'

'How much are we talking?'

'Ten barrels, six bottles of whisky, that was the script a couple of months back.'

'Right,' said Donnie. 'I reckon double the bottles.'

The double order went down so fast at the hotel that they were back to pub stock after a few days. McGill upped the order to half again. By the end of the month Donnie had done two more runs and they were starting to make a bit of money, he and McGill.

'We'll be going half extra again, eh? The van's big enough. Think you could shift that?'

That evening Bruce dropped the news that he was planning to move on to a new job. There was good work to be had down in Perthshire, he said, and for better pay. Did Donnie fancy it?

'You're alright,' Donnie said. It didn't come as much of a surprise. Bruce was moving up in the world, or so he thought. 'I think I'll stay where I am.'

'If you're sure, then,' said Bruce. There was a pause. 'Be seeing you back home.'

'Thanks for asking all the same,' said Donnie. 'Good luck.'

'Aye,' Bruce said. He left the next morning.

Donnie wrote to Bella each week without fail when he received his pay packet, folding money into the envelope, sending his love. He missed home, he realised, with something like surprise.

He also wrote to Mary Rose. Postcards in envelopes, more like. First he would write that he was getting on well with his work and saving money. Then that he missed her. Both she and the summer they'd spent together seemed very far away. He could remember her laugh, the silk of her skin as he ran his hands up her back. But her face was a little like a mirage, shimmering just out of focus and indistinct, and, when he did manage to glimpse it, he thought she looked disappointed in him.

In turn, the letters she wrote to him were also brief. She had very neat handwriting. She had got a job in a dog food factory. She never wrote that she loved him but she drew hearts, all around her signature. It was something, at least, to hold on to.

The day after his conversation with McGill, Donnie borrowed a tape and measured the back of the van. As he'd thought, there was no way all that drink would fit. Truth be told, they were making far more money from the whisky.

He found McGill and outlined his suggestion: halve the barrels but take double the whisky.

'You think you're telling me what to do now, Donnybrook?' McGill was in a mood; he had a great bruise down the left side of his face, red and purple. Donnie had heard they'd taken a conman to task the previous night, a Gentleman Jim type who had turned up with a Crown and Anchor board packed in a case, fleecing those susceptible to taking a chance with their wages. 'We'll take the extra bottles, right enough, but you'd better know what you're doing.' McGill's breath hung heavy in the air between them. 'Because if not, there'll be a lot of trouble in it for all of us.'

The night of the pick-up was cold, the dark early now the clocks had gone back. Donnie sat in the van and shivered and smoked, waiting for McGill to come out of his caravan, but there was no show. Instead, another one of the crew came out to tell Donnie that McGill had been taken to hospital, suspected appendicitis.

'Roaring like a pig all evening, he was,' the man said, and Donnie thought but did not say, some coincidence that is. He went back to the van. He sat down in the driver's seat and cleared his throat and spat out of the door and slammed it shut. Half an hour he'd wasted there. He'd have to drive like the clappers to meet the Rhino.

The road was icy in places and the van's tyres bald as a monkey's palm. He drove as fast as he dared, hunched over the wheel, blowing on the windscreen and clearing it with his hand, and when he finally arrived – thank Christ – the man was still there. 'Some fucking time this is,' he was griping. 'Just on your own, are you?'

Donnie explained about McGill. The Rhino shook his head. 'Fuck's sake,' he said. 'I wanted to see the look on his face. Still. You can see for yourself.'

He opened up the back and Donnie found himself staring down at more than fifty bottles of Macallan single malt. 'You tell McGill our friend has thrown in twenty more bottles on top of the thirty-six he asked for.'

Donnie whistled. 'And what am I supposed to do with all this?'

'Och, calm yourself,' said the Rhino. 'You'll take these up the road, and you'll do as you've done, and we'll all split the money from the extra as usual.' He tapped the enormous pockmarked nose that had given him his nickname.

When they'd loaded the whisky and the Rhino had left, Donnie sat in his van and lit a cigarette, wondering if he'd taken leave of his senses. There was nearly twice as much whisky in the back as he'd imagined; he'd even had to stack some on the seat next to him, packed in straw.

He thought about the cash. He reckoned there was six weeks' wages in the extra whisky. He thought about knocking on Mary Rose's door with all that in his pocket.

He drove on a bit, his lights dipped. He lit another cigarette and slid the window open a crack to let a blast of freezing air into the cab. He thought about going back to McGill to give him the full story, but the truth was he'd already decided what he was going to do.

He'd take a few of the extra bottles the Rhino had given him straight to the hotel and get them into the optics as fast as he could. He'd take the drink McGill was expecting back to camp, and do whatever he was told with it – leave it in the van, throw it under a tarp, whatever. He reckoned McGill might be out of action for a while, if all was as it seemed, possibly not back on the drink for a few days at least. By then, Donnie would be away with his share. Skim the cream off the top. McGill would probably do the same, given half a chance, and so Donnie told himself it wasn't exactly unfair.

He put his foot to the floor and the van's engine rose to an urgent whine.

A mile from Strathconordan he was pulled over by a police car. What were the fucking chances? Not a soul for miles around. Donnie sat in the driver's seat as a big man approached the window, leaned down.

'Well, well. MacArthur.'

Donnie looked up with a jerk. A big slab of a face, dark hair.

'Geordie Gilroy,' the man was saying. 'Sutherland Constabulary.' He leaned down further. 'Remember me, do you, MacArthur?'

Donnie stared at him. 'You're police now?' he managed, in the end.

'Passed out last month. Chip off the old block, you could say.'

'Right.'

Donnie could not equate the wedge of a man standing beside the car with the pathetic lump he'd encountered back in the summer. The young man's whole demeanour was different, standing with his arms crossed, officious, staring unsmilingly into the car. Donnie could almost feel the slug of saliva on his cheek again, as if he were slumped once more on the boards of the rowing boat with Geordie's father standing over him laughing.

'How's the old man?' he said.

It was the wrong thing to say. Gilroy's eyes narrowed. He brought a hand down heavily on the window frame of the van. 'I'll have to stop you there, MacArthur. Do you know you were driving well over the speed limit on this road?'

A wisp of straw from the passenger seat blew out through the open window. Donnie felt a bit of a twist in his guts. 'Och,' he said. 'You know, I'm sorry. A friend of mine has just gone into hospital with appendicitis.'

Gilroy's torch swept over Donnie's face, alighting on the box in the front seat. He chuckled, softly. 'I suppose it's better than a punnet of grapes. Is all that for him, aye?'

Donnie nodded wordlessly. Some part of his mind was wondering, vaguely, if he could get the jail for this. He imagined writing to Mary Rose and telling her he was inside. Fat chance he'd have then.

'I see.' Gilroy took a step back, still craning in through the window. 'Where are you really heading for?'

'Back to the site up by the dam.' Perhaps honesty would be the best policy.

Gilroy straightened, spat on the ground. 'What's in the back?'

Donnie shrugged.

'You can tell me, or I can have a look myself.'

'More of the same.'

'How much more?'

'Enough to keep the boys happy for a couple of days at least.'

Gilroy laughed. 'Look, I know fine well where you've been.

And I know where this is from, what's been going on; even the trees talk here. I know McGill fine.'

Donnie said nothing.

'I'll tell you, Donnie-boy,' said Gilroy, 'what's going to happen. I'll be taking that wee hamper in the front seat home with me, and you'll be on your way to wherever you're going. I'm sure I'll be seeing you soon. It's a great job those lads are doing, and you just let them know that Geordie Gilroy isn't going to stand in the way of a few nips at the end of a hard slog. Eh? Eh?' He laughed, and Donnie had a clear memory of Gilroy's father at the tiller that day. Just a speck of water in the lungs, boy.

'But you tell them this,' Gilroy continued. 'If I ever catch wind of this in the trees again, and it hasn't come straight to me first, I'll have this wee racket shut down quicker than you can say *one for the road*, and the whole lot of you down the station for good measure. Is that understood, MacArthur? You make sure and tell them that.'

And with that, Gilroy opened the passenger door, lifted out one of the crates of whisky, straw and all, and walked off into the night, humming 'Lilliburlero' through the torch in his teeth.

Saturday 21 March 1998

Anna

It is late afternoon and looking like rain when I leave the bungalow. I am planning to walk out along the road to the hotel.

'It's at least three miles, Anna,' Bruce says.

'It's OK,' I say. I watch him as he puts away the crockery from our lunch, taking the plates and mugs from the rack and stacking them neatly in the cupboards. He flicks the kettle on to make tea for my mum, who still sits in the darkening conservatory, lost in thought.

'In the rain?' Bruce sighs. 'That road's not to be trusted when it's fine. It's just daft to go worrying your mother like that, certainly not today. I'll drive you.' He lines up her pill box and a rich tea biscuit on a tray beside her favourite mug, and then he looks at me, his head on one side. He looks tired. Slightly grey beneath the ruddy skin.

'I'll take that through to her,' I say, indicating the tray, and I can tell he is about to refuse, but stops himself, and nods instead. 'Actually,' I say quickly, 'if you do it, I'll finish putting these away. And I will take you up on that lift. Thank you.'

He looks slightly surprised, slightly pleased, and lifts the tray, which looks faintly odd in his large hands.

'Right you are, Anna,' he says. 'Right you are.'

I wonder what Bruce's life is like, looking after Mum these days. I want to say to him that we were coping, before, that we didn't need rescuing. But perhaps that wasn't true, at least not for the pair of us. Perhaps I've only thought of myself, these past years. Perhaps that is what Jamie means when he calls me petty. Perhaps he is right. The thought is not a comfortable one. I try to put away the rest of the dishes as quietly and as quickly as I can, opening unfamiliar cupboards and drawers to find out where they go, and when Bruce comes back through I gather my bag and go through to say goodbye to Mum. She squeezes my hand and I almost tell her that I love her, but not quite.

Leighanne has left me her key for the staff accommodation as promised. It's a simple single room with a washbasin, and she's left it tidy. I close the door, dump my bag on the newly made up bed and get out the two pregnancy tests. Moving quickly, before I can put it off any longer, I drink one glass of water from the tap, and then another. Then I rip open one of the test boxes and go into the tiny bathroom.

Once its done, I close the lid of the toilet and sit back down, staring at the stick in my hand as I wait for the result to emerge. I read the text on the box again. *A positive test result is almost certainly correct. However, a negative result is less reliable.*

'Children are a beautiful blessing,' my mother said earlier. 'Jamie will know that soon. I want you to remember that.' We'd sat in the conservatory and I'd thought about what she'd told me and what I haven't told her, but might have to, soon.

It started with Liam the summer Jamie left school. Jamie and some mates were upstairs getting ready to go out for the evening. I was putting on the tea for Mum and me. Liam Bell came down the stairs without the others.

Mum was in the living room watching *Telly Addicts*. Liam sat down at the kitchen table with his elbows making a square in front of him. 'What's for tea, then?' he said.

I up-ended a jar of pasta sauce in the pan. He was not watching me, but tapping his feet and glancing periodically up the stairs. I could smell his aftershave and I was thinking about the girls I'd seen him with, sharp and lipglossy and hair-tossy, and how I was more or less in my jammies, hair scraped back from the spots on my forehead.

'You going out this weekend?' Liam was saying. Just filling the silence.

'Don't think so.'

I'd heard Nicola Beaton discussing Liam: *Swear to God*, she'd said, *I'd give a kidney*.

'You should come out with us some time,' he was saying now. I wanted to laugh at the idea of me wedged in the back of a car between Neil and Stuart Shand doing donuts in the Somerfield car park.

'Bookworm, are you?' he said, which seemed to be an entirely random observation, until I turned round and saw he had my library copy of *O Caledonia* in his hands.

'Yep.'

'Looks like a weird one,' he said, and told me the only book he'd ever read was *Charlie and the Chocolate Factory*, because he'd had to, back in primary seven. 'And that was weird too. Fucking Oompa-Loompas, what's the craic with that? The bloke who wrote it must have been tripping off his nut, no?'

I shook my head and did actually laugh then, although his remark wasn't that funny, and started to scoop pasta on to two plates. I was wondering if I should offer him some, thought there really wasn't enough and that would mean he would stay even longer, when he came over and took one, saying quietly, 'This one for your mum, aye? I'll take it through.'

Space invader, his scuffed hand next to mine. There were white marks in his thumbnail. I could sense where the reddish-brown skin of his neck turned pale just beyond the edge of his collar, and the fine links of a gold chain disappeared beneath his shirt. I stood in the kitchen and looked at my reflection, my face just a little pool of white in the dark window, and then I heard him in the living room, laughing with my mum.

It was September before I saw him again, parked across the street from the high school in a car with loud music blasting. I was nearly past before I realised it was him, when my friend Leighanne said, 'Oh, my God, don't look now but Liam Bell is pure *staring* at you.'

I felt tight and swollen all over, as if the whole of me had just ballooned out like a shirt on a clothesline. But I didn't look and then we were past and Leighanne was gawking at me, saying, 'What's going on with you two, then?'

'Nothing,' I said, truthfully. 'There's nothing.'

The next week Jamie said he and some mates were going into town and did I want to come along? I'd nearly said yes before I remembered I couldn't. It was just after I had helped Mum in her bath and she was asleep. When the doorbell rang I opened it and nearly shut it again, I was that surprised to see Liam standing there.

He asked if my brother was about and I said he wasn't. Liam said could he come in for a bit, and then he was in the house, his shoulders in a black jacket nearly spanning the breadth of our tiny hallway. I could smell alcohol on him but he didn't seem drunk.

I said did he want a drink, or something like that, and went to turn towards the kitchen but he said no, wait. Then he reached out and wrapped his arms about my shoulders, and we were kissing before I'd even had time to take a breath. His hands climbed my backbone and his fingers slid beneath the catch on my bra, and all the time his mouth roved from my neck and my ears and back to my lips as if searching for something. My arms remained straight by my sides, and after a while I opened my eyes a crack to see his were closed. I started to feel as if I was not quite in my own body, but lurking somewhere above us, perhaps at the top of the stairs, staring down.

This made me think of Mum, and that made me take a step back and we stood there for perhaps one second before I said, 'You might find Jamie in the Royal; that's where he drinks most nights anyways.'

Liam said, 'Right you are, then.'

'Wait a minute,' I said, 'you never said hello to my mum.'

He goggled at me.

'Joke,' I clarified. 'J-o-k-e.'

He shook his head, then laughed. 'You,' he said, 'are some cracker.' And he wiped his mouth with the flat of his hand and left.

When he'd gone, I sat on the stairs for a while with my fingertips to my bruised lips and a pounding in the base of my belly, and then I went slowly up the stairs, into the bathroom, and looked in the toothpaste-flecked mirror above the sink. There was a faint red shadow all around my mouth, up to my nose and down to my chin, where his stubble had grazed my skin.

After that, my world shrank down, dividing itself between two people, inside and outside. Inside, taking care of Mum, and outside, Liam Bell, our secret stretched between us.

His body beneath my hands was solid. We'd go driving in his car, way out along the beach road, by the old boat sheds, no one around, headlights off, radio on low. The Stone Roses, quiet. I'd tell myself right up until the last minute that I might not, this time, before he leant over, bent his head to mine.

It makes me shudder, thinking about it now. The shame that I let it happen. I make up excuses for my younger self but it only makes it worse – my eagerness to please, when things were pretty desperate with Mum. With Jamie away, I was fending for myself.

Liam never acknowledged me as his girlfriend, not even when we were in Glasgow and I was living with him in the flat his dad had bought. Seeing him with some other girl: that was what it had taken, in the end. Not that I truly believe she was the first. I clearly had some other kind of classification in his mind.

And to think of him being a father, the feckless waster.

I look down and finally, the answer has emerged. One dark line. Negative: not pregnant. I take an enormous breath. I can't quite relax until I've done the second test. I wait.

Still negative.

I thought I'd want to cry, or shout with relief, but I settle for stretching up, high as I can, to touch the low bathroom ceiling with my fingertips. I acknowledge the tiniest thread of sorrow amid the relief. Not everyone gets away with their youth.

September 1942

Netta

My father told us there were caves up on the yellow hill which held the bones of animals, some long extinct: wolves, bears, reindeer. Animals of a colder, wilder time. My father would say that when ice covered the earth, they gathered in the caves for shelter, and died.

My mother, of course, had another explanation: that the bone caves had been home to a race of giants and the bones were the remains of their hunting and feasting. The hill is hollow, she said. Some of those caves would take you down into the centre of the earth.

It was Josephine who found her, who carried Bridget in her arms, all the way into the stableyard at Altnaglas.

'She needs a doctor,' she was screaming, 'and the priest, where's the priest?'

I watched them from the window of my room. Then I went and lay in my bed as still as a stone, the roar still rising and falling in my ears. I heard later that Father Michael arrived and began to perform the last rites before the ambulance came and took her away.

'The doctor says she maybe had a seizure,' Josephine told me later. She stood in the doorway of my room, pale and desperate-looking. Her voice sounded choked and was the quietest I'd ever heard it. She was wearing the white scarf I had given Bridget the first night we had danced together. I closed my eyes.

'Or a bleed in her brain. She's never been sick a day in her life, my sister.' She started to sob. 'She was going to have a baby, did you know that?' she was saying. 'My God, how did I not know that?'

I turned over in bed to look at her, but I did not get up. I did not think I would be able to stand.

'At least three months gone,' she was saying. 'Why in God's name did she not tell me? What was she doing, down there by the loch, with no one to help her? Does no one know anything?'

The white scarf wound around her throat like a bandage. I turned over again and looked at the uneven lines the brush had left in the paint on the wall.

'Perhaps she didn't know herself,' I said.

The next week brought the news that my father had gone into a sharp decline and was not expected to have many days left. Mondegrene gave me leave and I walked back to Crois na Coille, out over the high pass in my summer shoes, and remembered another story my mother told, in which a girl had disappeared on the hill. Years later, her sister, herding cattle on the mountain, heard a voice, singing:

There are seven iron locks
Between me and my home
And the man of the dark mantle
Who stole me away.

I thought about the caves often. I thought of climbing the hill, and of going down inside, deeper and deeper.

When I returned to Altnaglas after my father died, Mondegrene started to have officers up from the training centre at Barnadine to drink at the house. I stayed out of the way and carried on as before. The cataloguing was almost complete. One evening I was finishing my work for the day when I realised he was standing in the doorway watching me.

'How is your mother keeping, Netta?' he asked me.

I was compiling all the copies of *Blackwood's Magazine*, checking them off against an inventory I had found.

'She's been better,' I said.

'A damn shame,' said Mondegrene. 'Please tell her that if there is anything I can do, she needs only to ask.'

'Thank you, sir,' I said.

Number fifteen was missing. Number twelve, the next periodical I picked up, had the remains of a squashed bluebottle on the cover. I slid it into the pile. Sunlight fell through the window and dust caught in the light.

'I'm grateful to you,' I found myself saying. 'My family are all very grateful to you.'

There was silence from the corner. I turned my face down towards the piles of books. After about five minutes, he said, 'Your father was a fine man. One of nature's true gentlemen, my own stepfather used to say.'

'My mother took good care of him,' I said.

'Your mother, yes,' he said. 'Wonderful woman.' He was silent for some time, watching me. 'Netta,' he said, at length, 'would you be so good as to hand me Tennyson's *Poems*. On the mantel.'

I crossed the room and brought it over to him. It was a dark green book, heavier than I would have expected. 'My thanks,' he said, taking it from me. '*Immortal age beside immortal youth, and all I was, in ashes.*'

I didn't know what he meant by that. I assumed it was a quote from one of the poems. He was fond of quotes, although I was rarely able to recognise them. He stood there looking at me, lint all over his jacket, tobacco on his pullover. The smell of old whisky on him.

'Do you think we change very much, Netta, from young to old?' he said.

313

'Yes.'

'And yet I can still see you as a child, if I narrow my eyes.'

'Then I'd prefer you didn't narrow your eyes.'

'Is that so, Netta?' His tone was startled; for a second I thought he was angry. His rages were rare but acute. But then he laughed instead. 'I can't think which I like best,' he said. 'The clever child or the angry young woman.' He weighed the book in his hand.

I turned my head away. 'I should be getting on, sir,' I said. 'I'm nearly finished.'

'I don't see the hurry,' he said. 'Can you imagine there must have once been a time when it was possible to read every book in existence? Most books are ten a penny, nowadays. But this one—' He raised Tennyson's *Poems*, 'This one is a little different. I am going to show you what's inside, Netta. Something from my youth that made me a man.'

He lowered the book, and opened it, and when I saw what was inside I stepped back. Most of the pages had been cut out, and in the hollowed-out space there lay a pistol.

He laughed and snapped the book shut. 'So tell me, what did you see?' he said.

'You keep a gun in there, sir.'

'A Luger, to be precise,' he said. 'My most prized possession.'

'I see.'

'I'll tell you what you see, Netta. You see a loaded gun that came damn close to killing me, once. Or rather, the German holding it did. In a stinking Belgian cellar. August the twenty-fifth, 1914, the city of Leuven. Not just me, but my mother also. I was just a child. A damn close shave. But . . .' He put the book behind his back, held out his left hand with one finger pointing at the ceiling. 'But. The tables turned. I turned them, and it's the sole reason I am here today at all. For what came for me – to end my life – saved it. Do you see now?'

'I believe I do,' I said. I crossed to the window, raised the sash and breathed the chill air from the garden. The smell of the cold earth. Did the drink bring out who he really was, I asked myself, or simply reflect yet another posture in an endless chain of mirrors? I had once been clever, I thought, although I had known nothing, and now I knew too much, and it had stupefied me.

He went over to the drinks tray, poured out a clean glass of sherry. 'We'll drink to close shaves and steady hands, Netta,' he said, extending the glass to me.

'Thank you, sir,' I said, 'but I won't.'

'You will,' he said. 'You will.'

When I had finished the first glass he insisted I drank another.

'You were very friendly with those two Irish girls,' he said to me when I had finished the second glass.

My heart lurched but I made no reply. Mondegrene eyed me over the top of his own glass before turning on his heel and walking to the gramophone. 'I would like to play you something,' he said.

There was a crackle and opening bars of piano, before a high female voice started singing.

Pale hands I loved beside the Shalimar
Where are you now? Who lies beneath your spell?

It was a different version from the one I knew. It sounded older. When the song finished, he lifted the needle and placed it back at the start, still eyeing me.

'This was my mother's favourite song,' he said. 'Of course she sang it better than Maggie Teyte. Much better.' He swallowed his drink, listening, and when the music finished he put the record on again for a third time. When he turned to me, his eyes looked a little glassy. 'Dance with me, Netta,' he said.

'Oh. I can't,' I said. 'I was never taught how.'

'I'll teach you. Dance with me.'

'Honestly,' I said. 'I'm not being modest, I really can't.'

He laughed then, threw his head back suddenly. 'So you'll dance with a pikey Irish lassie who can't even read or write, but you'll turn me down? You come here.'

I placed my drink down, shaking my head. He grinned and strode over to me. The music went on playing.

'Now don't be absurd,' he was saying in a gentle voice. 'I learned in Paris. I'll teach you. Like this.'

I moved my feet slowly, uncomfortably, and he sighed.

'My shoulder,' he said, 'put your hand on my shoulder,' and I felt his fingers grasp delicately at my waist.

We danced. He was hardly a head taller than me, and light and agile on his feet. His arms around me were wiry. He could certainly dance. We floated slowly around the Indian rug on the library floor and then he said, craning his head back, 'You see? This is fine, isn't it?'

I said nothing. I closed my eyes.

Whom do you lead on Rapture's roadway, far,
Before you agonise them in farewell?

I could cry, perhaps. I imagined how it would feel, my face pressed into the wool of his jacket.

'You know,' he was saying, above my head, 'they were saying some bloody odd things about you, Netta, the lads at camp. Some bloody odd things.' We continued to dance; he continued to hold me. 'That men aren't enough for you.' He carried on speaking as if musing to himself. 'That you think you're too good for us. All perfectly true, no doubt. You are too good for us, Netta. You are too good for me.' His grip tightened. 'Do you think that, hmm?'

'I don't think I'm good,' I said.

316

He ran a finger down the side of my face, pushing it in under my cheekbone to turn my face to his. 'And yet you are a fine one, Netta,' he said. His breath in my face smelled slightly of aniseed. 'Always thought so myself. Always.' He was suddenly very still. Then he said softly, 'So what is it that's wrong with me, Netta? Am I too much of a man, or not man enough? I believe you think of me as barely human. Christ. You slinking around with that little bogtrotter. She was a sly one. You know sometimes I think . . . you should know.' He laughed. 'She knew what side her bread was buttered on, that one. I'll tell you something. She came to me one night, she was waiting, downstairs, when I came in. Like this – ' he put his hands on my shoulders ' – as bold as brass. The little minx.'

I stepped back. 'I should be going,' I said.

'But I didn't, Netta,' he carried on soothingly, as if I hadn't spoken. 'I did not. I have more honour than that. Women throw themselves at me, did you know? They do. It's the truth. But not you. So what is it? What is it that's wrong with me?'

'I don't think about it like that, sir.'

'But this is the interesting thing.' His tone was thoughtful, preoccupied. 'I saw you. I saw the pair of you. You and Bridget Halloran. In the woods that day.'

I tried to turn away, but I was too close to him and his grip was too tight. We were locked together, still in the pose of dancing. 'That's right,' he carried on. 'I saw you, going down to the loch. And here's the thing.' He rested his chin on the top of my head for a moment and intoned in a singsong voice, '*Two little ducks went out one day, over the hills and far away. Mother duck said quack quack quack, but only one little duck came back.*'

'You saw nothing,' I said.

'Sometimes the heart sees what's invisible to the eye,' he said. 'But you never cared for Tennyson, did you?'

'Please let me go.'

317

'Oh, Netta.' He was shaking his head, regarding me almost sorrowfully. 'What have you done? What on earth happened to you?'

Pale hands, pink tipped, like Lotus buds that float
On those cool waters where we used to dwell ...

I tried to step back again but he held on to me. His hands went to my waist. He slid his fingers beneath my blouse and I closed my eyes, set my teeth.

'You think you're too good for me.' His hands were sliding up my back and then down again. I stood still as stone. 'You like that, though, don't you?' he was saying. 'You like that.' He dipped his head and put his face between my breasts. I could feel his chin digging into the top of my ribs. His hair under the light of the chandelier was the colour of sherry. When he raised his head again, the skin on his face was flushed.

'Say something.' His voice still soft, beguiling. Like oil, spreading in liquid. 'Say you will, for me. Netta. Please. Just once. Just once, for me.'

He kept repeating it.

I thought of Vincent, whirling me in his arms, and I thought of Bridget, dancing with Bridget, the absorption on her face, of being held in her hands. What does it matter, in the end, I thought, if it comes to nothing after all? What, in the end, does any of it matter? It could almost be felt as freedom, this emptiness, this ability to let be. When I closed my eyes I could see only light on the water, shattering my vision like glass.

Mondegrene moaned and moved me gently over to the settee, and I felt the cushions in the small of my back, his hands on the insides of my knees. When he leant over me I turned my face on its side so my cheek pressed into the red brocade. I looked at the spines of the books, which were shuddering in a rainbow of colours and textures before my eyes. I blinked, but my vision would not clear. My body would no longer respond to my commands. I had stepped from my skin and without it I was shivering, I was wading up to my waist in glittering water that froze me to my bones, and all the while the music played.

I would have rather felt you round my throat,
Crushing out life, than waving me farewell!
Pale hands I loved beside the Shalimar,
Where are you now? Who lies beneath your spell?

Sunday 22 March 1998

Anna

We saw the Northern Lights once, Jamie and I. It was the twenty-fifth of January. I know this because I'd spent the night transporting trifurcated plates of haggis, neeps and tatties from the kitchen to the dining room of the Tayfillan, serving a bunch of kilted businessmen. One of them had discreetly thrown up under the table during the Toast to the Lassies.

It was at first a flaring, and then a flickering of light. It slid over the horizon between the town and the sea.

The aliens have finally landed in Barnadine, Jamie said.

They won't be short of company here, I replied, and when he stopped the car we both stared at the edge of the sky, as it billowed pink and green.

Na Fir-Chlis, my father called them: the nimble men, whose dances and skirmishes light up the sky on a few special evenings each year. You might go your whole life and never see them, he would tell us, so be thankful if you do – even if it's just a glimpse, and over before you know it.

'I don't know your name, but I know you're Donnie's daughter.'

It's a man I don't recognise leaning on the bar, his face folded like an origami crane. I tell him that I am. I'm nearing the end of my afternoon shift at the hotel. I haven't eaten and feel dizzy from so much standing up.

'God rest him, Donnie MacArthur,' says the man. His breath could knock out a small dog. 'You pour me a glass of

Macallan, and I'll tell you a story about your dad that not many know. Every time I think about old Donnie-boy, may his soul rest in peace, I think about him and that whisky.'

I serve him as a few men join him at the bar, the drinking-all-day types. The man sits askew on a bar stool and tells a confused story I have not heard before, from when my dad was working on the hydro dams and got himself involved with what sounds like a dodgy booze scam. I don't really take it all in. The men at the bar are roaring with laughter; they love the idea of my dad rushing around in a wee van stuffed to the gunnels with Scotch, trying to steer clear of the police.

'Some man for one man,' they say. 'Some craic altogether.' They toast him, and for the first time in a long time when hearing about my dad, I feel obstinately proud.

I'm working a split shift and I'm done by three. One of the boys in the kitchen has made me a cheese toastie, and I eat half of it in two bites as I walk outside to sit on one of the picnic benches. It is sunny and I'm thinking I might go for a walk before my evening shift starts.

The manager comes outside and heads towards me.

'There's a lad been calling for you,' he says, as he draws nearer. 'He's on the phone now – here.'

He thrusts the cordless telephone into my hand before I can say anything, and on the end of the line I hear Liam's voice.

'Finally,' he is saying down the line. 'What the fuck, Anna? I got your wee note. What the fuck are you pl—?'

'You can stop right there,' I cut him off. Take a deep breath. 'I've heard enough of your shit to last me a lifetime, Liam. I told you everything I had to say in that letter, and I told you not to get in touch with me.'

The manager is walking away slowly, blatantly listening in. I fight the impulse to raise my voice, lowering it instead. 'You've turned up at Bruce and Mum's door and now you're

324

calling me. Are you honestly telling me you've got nothing better to do than bother me for the rest of your life?'

There's silence on the other end and I can hear him breathing. 'You are fucking kidding me,' he says. He laughs. 'All you've got is me. All you've got.'

'You've tried to tell me that so many times that you believe it yourself,' I say. I sound like someone else. I find I only have to open my mouth, and the words keep rolling out. 'There is no you and me. Never has been. You made sure of that, didn't you?'

'You'd better be telling me that this is a joke,' he says. 'You're a fucking joke, anyway.'

'We never had the same sense of humour, it's true,' I say. 'In fact, we don't have anything in common at all, do we?'

His voice changes to a whine. 'I don't get it,' he says. 'All I've done for you.'

I hold the receiver a little further away from me, so as not to have his voice directly in my ear. 'You're not exactly a bad man, Liam,' I say, speaking slowly and clearly as if he were very old or very young. 'You're just not a good one. We're not kids any more. Whatever it was, it's over. I'd suggest you start looking elsewhere. In fact, I know you already have.'

He is quiet for a minute, then he laughs. When he speaks again, his voice has thinned to a hiss. 'You think you're something now, do you, Anna MacArthur?' he says. 'Think you're someone? Well, I'm telling you, you're fucking *nothing*. Fucking pathetic is what you are. Listen to yourself. Fuck's sake. Think you'll get better than me, do you? Think anyone else'll go near you and your bloody car crash of a family? Wednesday fucking Addams, that's what they used to call you in school. I took a fucking chance on you, put myself out, and this is the thanks I get? The state of you. Psycho bitch.'

He pauses for a second and I know from the way his breath snags as he inhales that the crying will come next.

325

'Enough,' I cut in, before the pleading can begin. My voice is steady: sublimely serene. 'It was enough a long time ago. Goodbye, Liam. Don't call me ever again.'

I hang up the phone. I've never enjoyed the second half of a toastie more.

1943–1946

Netta

It was Bella who delivered my baby when he came.

My sister and her husband Archie were living at Crois na Coille because Bella was looking after our mother. Following our father's death, our mother's mind seemed to become a jumbled and cloudy place, pierced only by the scandal and shame of her eldest daughter's return from Altnaglas not as one, but two. Bella had been married two years and her desire for a child of her own and subsequent anguish from lost pregnancies became matched only by her loathing of me for my casual, unwanted conception of that which she most desired.

She would not ask who the father was, although the question squeezed itself into every silence she adopted whenever we were together. I could not tell her. To speak of it would snare the reality of something I could hardly believe was the truth, although I could feel it, the quickening, the movement of tiny arms and legs inside my treacherous body.

I wouldn't say, and she wouldn't ask, and when my labour pains came on months later I crawled on my hands and knees to bar the bedroom door with a chair as she hammered and shouted. I hunched on the floor, wishing to die, but she had the door off its hinges with a single shove – she had always been powerfully built, even as a teenager – and tended to me with the same blend of rough urgency and pragmatism I had seen her exercise while helping my brother with the calving.

'Perhaps you don't even know,' she hissed, as she turned me over and I twisted, blood-sodden, on sheets that seemed to scald my skin. 'Perhaps there were that many officers you just can't tell which one.'

At the end, just before I lost consciousness, she stood above me, cradling the baby in a blanket. The cord still bound him to me, yet she held him close to her chest. 'A boy,' I think she said, and for the first time in months it was not hatred but loving triumph that was written on her face as she stared down at the bundle she held.

I heard voices and footsteps on the stairs and the edges of the room started to go black and fuzzy, clouding my view of Bella and the baby above me. I tried to reach out my arms but seemed to have forgotten how to.

'You were calling out someone's name,' Bella was saying. 'Why on earth were you asking for Bridget?' But the world was spinning and shrinking fast, until it became just a thread of light so thin it could slip through the eye of a needle.

When I woke up it was hours later. The doctor said that my sister had saved my life, that I had nearly bled to death and it was a wonder I survived. Was I not grateful for my sister, her care, her unflappable calm, her cool-headed practicality?

'I want to see him,' I said. 'Please let me see him.' But my sister was taking care of him now, the doctor said, and it would be best to keep it that way until I recovered.

Not long afterwards, I leaned over the edge of despair and looked down, breathing the draught that came upwards in the darkness, pulling it in and out of my lungs. I wanted to fall. There were miles to go, downwards, and I knew I had only to shift my balance.

One day, I tried to give him away. But Joan and her daughter Chrissie, who would come to our door selling goods from a basket, would not take the baby from me.

How I envied those two, walking out over the hills in that summer of 1944, just the two of them on the edge of everything, while the world beyond them tore like a ripped seam, and I sat and mourned afresh at home, a strange changeling child who would not be easy in my arms, but shrieked and bawled, great choking gulps that would make him sick unless Bella took him and soothed him.

As the pair left I saw Joan tug the little girl's shawl up over the back of her head, but Chrissie slipped out from underneath her outstretched arm, turning to look back, once. Joan did not look back. I buried my face in the baby's blanket and wept while he screamed and screamed, until Bella appeared in the doorway behind me and lifted him away.

'You do not deserve one hair on his head,' she said to me as she left the room, and part of me was glad that at last someone had said it out loud.

Not long after that, Mondegrene came to our house in his car. I stayed upstairs while he spoke with my mother, my arms around my ribs, my forehead to the window frame. What was he telling them, I wondered. Outside, the wind rippled the grassy slope of the yellow hill like a tidal sea. If I closed my eyes I could feel it, the wind whipping my skin, my limbs growing lighter as I left everything below me and climbed into the thinner air. *The higher you climb,* I remembered him telling me, *the harder it is to breathe.*

'You're to come downstairs.' Bella came into the room behind me, putting down a case that had belonged to our father. It had been packed for several weeks, I knew. I heard the baby crying downstairs, my mother hushing him. Was it not what I wanted: to leave? I followed Bella downstairs and she held my arm as she walked me out to the car, closing the door and stowing the case. It would just be for a short while, my mother said. Her face bore traces of recent tears, but she was not crying now. Of the baby there was no sign.

I could not look at them, or at Mondegrene; if I looked at him I would be lost altogether. In the passenger seat I turned my face away to watch the rain weeping down the glass window. We passed my brother, out in the fields with a neighbour. It was weaning time and they were separating the lambs from the ewes. The frantic bleating from both sides made me want to put my hands over my ears. I sank down a little in the seat so he would not see me. At our father's funeral, Angus John had read a passage from Jeremiah, where God spoke through the prophet about the city of Babylon: words by father was fond of reciting by heart. *My people have been lost sheep; their shepherds have led them astray and caused them to roam on the mountains. They wandered over mountain and hill and forgot their own resting place.*

Mondegrene drove me some distance, to a grey house surrounded by tall trees. 'A peaceful place, Netta,' he said, 'where you'll be cared for. They say a change is as good as a rest.'

So this was to be my resting place.

I remember little about that time. I saw few people. I saw the seasons change outside my window and yet weeks and months became almost indistinguishable from nights and days. A woman with a cleft lip took care of me. She said prayers with me. There were perhaps two Christmases. Maybe more. I ate plain food. My bed was made of iron and the sheets were starched. Above the bed was a sampler which read *Enter ye in at the strait gate.*

Mondegrene visited me often. Sometimes he would bring me an apple, which he would halve as he sat in the visitor's chair, his legs crossed at the ankles, a small penknife in his hand with which he would pare out the core. He would place the two pieces on my bedside table before taking his leave, and the apple's pale flesh would turn brown in the dank air. He took me out for drives. And then, one day, without warning, he drove me home again to Crois na Coille. I was not what I had once been, he told me. I would not wander again.

332

There was no place for me at home with Bella and Archie, so I returned to my room at Altnaglas, although not to my previous employment. It was Bella, of course, who had taken care of Donald while I was away. And I found that my change-ling child had bloomed into a lovely, smiley wee lad.

All I could think of was how to get him back. *For they who have sown the wind will reap the whirlwind,* my father would proclaim of the misdeeds of others. It was my only consola-tion, that he had not lived long enough to sit in judgement of the sins of his eldest daughter.

My brother Angus John had joined the merchant navy. Home on leave, he came to be my only comfort in those weeks that followed my return. The bright-haired boy I remembered was becoming sea-worn and storm-bleached, the roll of the waves in his walk. He called round most evenings to see me. I had no other visitors, but Mondegrene would allow Angus John to sit in the snug with me in the evenings. We would drink together; spirits from bottles that he brought. I swallowed the liquor down like water and he would tell me stories of the places he had been: of great whales swimming in vast oceans, of the colours and smells and languages of far-off ports. I would close my eyes and see it all before me: the rise and fall of molten suns, the mighty, sail-tearing storms. Angus John made light of the dangers – torpedoes and fires and drown-ings – and I did not ask for more, just topped up his glass. I feared for him, but he was free in a way I was not, and I envied that.

He brought music that we would listen to together. He had become fond of jazz. *Jump Blues,* he called it. My favourite record was 'A Night in Tunisia'. It had an unknowable, ruth-less liberty to it that I found both painful and calming. But one evening he put on 'Kashmiri Song'.

We had once loved that song – all of us – but I could find no sweetness there now, no beguiling murmur but a roar borne

333

on a shrill shriek – sinking and rising, awash, dragged on currents hither and yon. I bent my head to my lap and rocked and could not tell my brother why.

After that evening Mondegrene said that he felt that my brother's visits might be proving a hindrance rather than a help, and it would be best if he did not visit the next time he was home. A precautionary measure, as my health was still somewhat frail.

But it was after that evening I started to formulate my plan. I read the message on the sleeve of that record as if it were a religious tract. *Across the water.* Canada. A chance to shed the layers imprisoning the person I once was within the person I had become. I began to make enquiries.

October 1960–August 1985

Donnie

A right rags-to-riches story it had been at the beginning. He'd driven through the night to Glasgow where he'd sold the rest of the whisky to a stallholder at the Barras: not as much money as he could have made, but the thick wad of notes was more than Donnie had ever held before. Then he drove out east to one of the new estates. It took him a good hour of driving up and down streets that all looked the same before he arrived at her door.

He knocked, squinting at his reflection in the tiny square of glass on the front door and smoothing his hair. Then the door was opening and, like a miracle, Mary Rose was standing in front of him, her bright hair pinned high on her head and her skirt shorter than any dream.

'Oh, my God,' she said.

'I've done what you asked,' Donnie said. 'Look.' He pulled the notes from his pocket; her eyes widened.

'Donnie!' She pushed his hand holding the money down to his side, her eyes darting down the street. 'Are you forgetting where you are?'

'You told me I would need enough money,' he said. 'So here I am.'

'Where did you get that?' she said.

'What do you mean? I worked for it, Mary Rose. So will you?'

She cast a look behind her, then stepped forwards, softly closing the door at her back. 'Will I what?' she asked, her voice low.

He took a deep breath. 'Will—'

'Donnie.' She cut him off, kissing him firmly on the cheek. She took hold of his hand, folding her fingers around his, around the money. 'It's awful nice to see you,' she said. 'Come in and meet my mam.'

They married the following spring, and by the summer he was working for the Forestry, and Mary Rose was back full-time at the Tayfillan. It had seemed as if things were falling into place. Jerome Mondegrene had all but given them a quarter-acre of land to build on, and Donnie had brought home a static caravan from the mart, 'to see us through the house-build'. Bella had offered for them to stay at Crois na Coille but Donnie didn't think that Mary Rose would stick the constant hints about babies, and having their own space was as novel as it was exciting for both of them.

The first few months of living together had been the best of Donnie's life, no doubt about it. Although they were working all hours in the week, they tried to eat together in the evenings, and then they would sit up listening to music: he loved Johnny Cash, she loved Patsy Cline. And then to bed, where he'd never known so much pleasure.

By autumn, they'd saved enough to buy a third-hand, two-door Morris Minor that Donnie spent hours working on until it ran more or less good as new. Weekends they would often get in the car and go for drives and long walks with sand-wiches and a flask. Before that, Donnie had only ever climbed hills when helping his uncle gather the sheep. Returning home at night, they drank sweetheart stout outside the caravan in the darkness and tried to name all the stars they could see. They laughed all the time. They often spoke of the future, but to live in the present was rich enough.

When Mary Rose eventually became pregnant, they were overjoyed. They talked about the house they would build, the trips they would take as a family: fishing, to the islands, and how they would have more children and visit the castle in Edinburgh and chew sticks of rock on the promenade. When their baby was born, the baby they called Michael, he was perfect in every way. He was born on Mary Rose's birthday. The best birthday gift in the world, people might have said. But people did not say that, because Michael was born without a cry. He never saw a glimpse of daylight. Mary Rose and Donnie never got to take him home. The umbilical cord had slipped and been squeezed by the baby's own weight, cutting off his blood supply.

For months afterwards Donnie could not shake the feeling that he was to blame in some way. If he had been more alert to the things that could go wrong . . . If he had driven her to the hospital earlier . . . Worse, he worried that Mary Rose blamed herself, although she denied this and would not talk to him about it further. She would not mention Michael's name. Now there was something that they never spoke about.

Money was tight. The house-build had to be put off for a while. In the Forestry Donnie worked the last four Clydesdale horses in the area, hauling newly cut timber. He liked the work, but even at the start he knew his new job was an old one, soon to become obsolete. All over the country the Forestry were replacing the big horses with new machines. Feller-bunchers, forwarders, excavators and cherry-pickers were coming in to make light work of all the jobs: felling, clearing, chipping, transplanting, hauling. New boys fresh from college were taking up the jobs. At first Donnie was often called upon to fix the machines when they failed, but soon there were specialists for that who turned up in company cars, wearing overalls branded with names like Fobro, Kockums, Bruunett. When the horses were retired, he left the Forestry and got work at the local garage, where business was fairly good. He thought maybe he could go out on his own in a few years. Once the house was built.

After Michael, Mary Rose didn't go back to the Tayfillan. She did a correspondence course in bookkeeping, learned how to cut hair. She learned fast. Some new holiday lodges were built on the west side of the loch, styled as log cabins. They proved popular. Tourists' cars began to throng the single-track roads in summer. Mary Rose took a job cleaning the lodges. She cut people's hair in their own homes. She kept the books for Bruce Langlands, who had recently taken over from his dad at the quarry. Bruce was now talking about expanding, getting into this new fish-farming venture with a Norwegian business partner. You've always been a cold fish, Donnie said to him. He could tell Bruce didn't think it was funny.

Life was rammed to the gunnels, making ends meet. Some weeks he and Mary Rose hardly saw each other in daylight. It was almost laughable to remember the freedom of those early days. And then, suddenly, when they had almost accepted that it wasn't going to happen again, Mary Rose found she was pregnant once more.

The next nine months were tense, with none of the naïve joy of her previous pregnancy. Donnie worked three jobs so Mary Rose could ease back on hers. He took on more hours at the garage, still dreaming of having his own business one day. Those dreams seemed far off. He ghillied for the Altnaglas estate, dug graves in the local cemetery for a time. Keeps me fit, he said down the pub. Keeps me on the right side of the turf. Hollow laughter. He smoked more. Found himself in the bar most nights. Told himself he was working hard. Told himself he was doing it for her. Told himself he was happy enough.

Jamie arrived safely the following summer, a small baby with a big scream. Donnie had been terrified the night he arrived. Rarely had he felt so useless, barely moving from the hospital chair until the midwife came for him, smiling. A second chance. A second life. A love that grew with each passing day.

Back at the caravan Mary Rose boiled endless kettles and bathed Jamie in the kitchen sink. Sometimes, while she slept, Donnie sat on the caravan's steps under the stars, his son in his arms. Thinking about his own mother, and the father he'd never known. Swearing that he would do better.

No more babies until we build the house, Mary Rose said. But before too long she was expecting again and along came Anna, a wild scrap of energy and independence. She came quickly, taking everyone by surprise, and when Donnie laid eyes on her for the first time he was brought to tears. A baby girl too. We are the luckiest pair in the world, he said quietly to Mary Rose, and she brushed her hand against first his and then the new baby's cheek.

There was no way Donnie could describe what he felt for his family. It was not what he had expected. He would have done anything. Anything to keep them safe. Anything to make sure they got what he knew they deserved. He would graft until his fingers bled. But it was never quite enough.

Mary Rose said he spread himself too thin. If he could just get the start he needed, to go up in the world. If someone would give him a chance. A proper chance, not a wink and a few quid in cash with the promise of more later down the line. But the memory of what she had said to him, that day by the river when he'd fished out the pearl, was never far away. That she needed more. He had not given her that, yet.

At the end of the summer, the year after Anna was born, Donnie was invited to the end-of-season party at Altnaglas estate. Mary Rose was triumphant. See, she said. I told you, if you kept up the brown-nosing long enough. It wasn't quite how Donnie saw himself, but he hired a suit for the occasion which cost him the best part of a fortnight's wages. She smiled when she saw him and asked if anyone had seen her man recently, who was this handsome stranger? When she laughed, he saw the deep caves under her eyes. She leaned up against him, kissed him as if they were teenagers again. Make the most of it, she said. He told her he would. He told her he loved her. He thought he hadn't told her that in a long time. Too long. He did love her.

To his surprise, he was greeted at the entrance of Altnaglas House by Jerome Mondegrene himself. A drink was put in his hand with a murmur of welcome. Inside there were small cigars and brandies doing the rounds. Help yourself, help yourself, Mondegrene purred. Donnie hovered over a small table in front of an ornate mirror and withdrew a cigarette from a silver case, picked up the lighter that was lying next to it. A nice silver lighter, heavy in the hand, the sort Bogart used in *The Maltese Falcon*. He'd always wanted one of those.

In the mirror he caught sight of Mondegrene behind him, staring. Their eyes met in the glass's reflection for an instant, before Mondegrene gave a tiny nod and walked elegantly away.

More drinks, more brandies, and then, after midnight, a hand was placed on Donnie's shoulder. A big hand, a golden signet ring set with a black stone on the pinkie finger.

Geordie Gilroy, whom Donnie hadn't seen since that night up near Inchsuardal. He greeted Donnie like a long-lost brother, and guided him sleekly outside, full of bonhomie, hail-fellow-well-met. Had Donnie not heard he was in Mondegrene's employ these days? Thought the news would have travelled down the pipeline by now. He'd left the police force by the time he was forty, he told Donnie. Done my time by then. He laughed. You'd be the same yourself by now.

No doubt, said Donnie. Not a clue, really, what the man meant by that. I suppose you're right, aye.

Gilroy offered Donnie the job as a driver right there and then. Donnie thought the man was taking the mick at first, that it was some kind of joke. He almost laughed before he realised that Gilroy was being serious, as he outlined what the job entailed: trips to the cash-and-carry, ferrying guests to and from the corporate parties he was setting up at Altnaglas. Gilroy named the wage Donnie would be paid and stood back a fraction, waiting for an answer.

When Donnie took the suit off in the caravan that night, something heavy fell out of the trouser pocket and thudded to the floor. He bent down and picked up the Dupont lighter. No memory of putting it in his pocket.

He meant to return it; he really did. Just never got round to it.

Things moved fast after that. The driving job paid decently enough and at first Donnie couldn't believe how easy it was. Wine and supplies for the parties at Altnaglas. The odd chauffeuring job for Mondegrene.

But then it turned into bringing girls from Glasgow. Girls who can spot a good time a mile off, Gilroy called them. And the guests.

The guests. Donnie had known before that these people existed, but he found it hard to believe that some of these men were real. Perhaps that was the point. Their titles and names were vague. *In the property game*, one of them had said, when Donnie had asked; quickly, he learned not to ask anything at all. Everything seemed to be a game. Even the instructions he was given, on those journeys to the city to pick up the pinstriped partygoers, had a certain air of intrigue to them, like undercover assignations. These, too, it was best not to ask too much about.

It was the best job he'd ever had, that was one way of looking at it. Or it was the worst thing he'd ever done. He had two bosses now: it was like working on two decks of a ship. Some days he'd be taking Mondegrene down to the Sports and

Models shop and passing comment on the old man's choice of fishing flies. The same week, he would be doing runs to the city for Gilroy, saying as little as possible. Not just collecting guests, by now, but goods that came in tightly compressed polythene packages. Times were changing.

The people around the estate changed, too. No longer the plummy-voiced, plum-faced sort who had flocked to the estate for shooting and fishing when he was a lad. Nowadays, there were always suits around the place, cocktails, parties with loud music that played on all night, all week. Few of the guests would come back; they came for a one-off bender. Occasionally Donnie would think he recognised someone, maybe off the telly or a sportsman, but, again, it was certainly best not to ask; best to not even look too closely.

Most evenings, he would be going to the train station or driving to the city to pick up the *overnighters*, as they were referred to. Nearly always girls from here or there, who'd stay for a night or two. Sometimes not only girls, but boys too, and some, Donnie thought, who looked far too young to be there.

The children were at school now. Jamie was quick with numbers, good with his hands. Anna was reading everything in sight. Their thirst for knowledge, their curiosity and wonder at the world seemed endless. He taught them what he had learned as a child. The names of plants and how to recognise the calls of birds. How to light a fire, make bracken spears and tie a fishing fly. To whistle with two fingers and call to the owls at night by blowing into cupped hands.

At school they were learning about the world. Things were different since Donnie had attended the same school, belted in front of the class for answering the teacher in Gaelic. Soon they'd know far more than he ever would.

You're away too much, Mary Rose would say to him. So late. Every night. When was the last time you kissed the kids goodnight? The hours you're working. It's too much.

That was what she always said. Too much for too little. She knew so little of the way things were. She knew so little of what he actually did. He had made sure of that, as it had to be that way, but it made things harder.

You'll have to speak to that Jerome Mondegrene, she'd say. What have you got to show for the hours you spend in those bloody cars, driving the toffs up, down and all around? Not exactly on the up and up, are we?

If I don't do it, there's plenty of others ready to take my place, he'd say. And then where would we be?

Maybe we wouldn't be in this sorry state, she'd say. Still in this bloody caravan. You could go offshore. My pal Diane, her man's gone on the rigs now, so he has, and he—

And see my family even less, Donnie would say. I won't be doing that.

They argued about it for a while. And then, somewhere along the line, they just about stopped arguing. Now it wasn't unusual for days to pass without them speaking properly to each other.

But he was doing it for her. He was doing it for them.

Late summer, the middle of the eighties. Nights like this found Donnie outside Altnaglas House in the car ready to drive, listening to the news on the radio. A three-year-old boy from Dublin had just become the youngest person to ever receive a heart and lung transplant. A guest flicked a fifty-pound note Donnie's way as he swaggered up the driveway to the house; Donnie was evidently expected to scrabble around for it on his hands and knees as it blew under the car. When he emerged with the note, Geordie Gilroy was standing above him.

'Some people have no respect,' Gilroy said. 'Makes me sick.'

Donnie got to his feet, shaking his head. 'No matter. What can you do, eh?'

Gilroy made a strange sort of sucking noise with his mouth; his lips were wet. He was watching the man weaving unsteadily up to the house.

'I'll show you what I can do,' he said quietly. 'You wait here.'

As if Donnie was doing anything else. He sometimes got a chilled feeling in his stomach just before something bad happened. He had it now.

'There's some say respect has to be earned,' said Gilroy. 'And then there's some say it should be surrendered.' He laughed suddenly, a violent bark. 'Which camp do you fall into, MacArthur?' And without waiting for a reply he set off, stalking up the drive in pursuit of the inebriated guest, overtaking him and knocking him to the ground with a flick of his arm.

Donnie turned away. He didn't want to see. He thought about the road home. He could walk away and never come back. He would make it in time for the kids' bedtime. Mary Rose would be surprised to see him. He would take her to dinner. He would take her to bed. He would hand in his notice here tomorrow. He'd find work elsewhere. Far away if needs be. He'd take them to New Zealand if he had to. Canada.

He got back into the car. He sat with his head in his hands until a sharp tap on the windscreen made him look up once more. Gilroy again, his tie slightly askew, rearranging his jacket.

Slowly, so slowly, Donnie wound down the window, and Gilroy leaned in, breathing heavily. There were three glossy beads of blood above his right eyebrow. His eyes were glittering and darting this way and that. Donnie wondered if he'd been sampling more than the drinks on offer.

'It would seem, MacArthur, that we have a space on our guest list tonight,' he said. He flicked his head towards the house. 'Come and join us.'

'I'm fine here,' said Donnie. 'I've my job to do.'

'And as your employer,' Gilroy said, 'I'm telling you what your duties are tonight.' He reached into the car in a quick movement and tapped Donnie on the cheek with two fingers. 'I said, come and join the fucking party.'

Donnie got out of the car. He closed the door and followed Gilroy up the drive. There were big lights throwing up their beams from the lawns in front of the house. Gilroy's figure cast a huge shadow; Donnie walked behind him. They passed a suit jacket balled up on the grass like a discarded napkin. Blood on the gravel. He walked in Geordie Gilroy's wake, towards the entrance of Altnaglas where light was spilling out on to the stone steps and music throbbed inside.

'How's your man?' he said to Gilroy.

Gilroy cleared his throat. 'He's no better than he should be.' He quickened his pace. His boots crunched on the stones. 'A wonder what a bit of a hiding can do for a lad. Something I learned from my father. He'll be a new man tomorrow. And if he isn't, you can stick him out with the bins in the morning, eh, MacArthur?' Gilroy's laugh was a single note. He took the steps up to the entrance hall in two strides. He flung his arms wide as he walked through the doors.

Fucking screw loose there, Donnie thought as he stepped inside the house.

Monday 23 March 1998

Jamie

Jamie woke early to the sound of birds and gusting winds that rocked the caravan. This was becoming a habit. He dug down deeper in his sleeping bag, shut his eyes and tried to give himself a minute longer. Another second and he had snaked out a hand to check the new sword was still there on the floor beside him.

All that was left to do was the engraving, and then some finishing touches: grinding the edge to its final sharpness, binding the handle with calf leather and polishing the whole thing to within an inch of its life. All things that he could easily achieve in the next couple of days, he thought, turning on to his back and rubbing his face.

The first problem was that despite repeated trips to the phone box down the road, the number he'd been given by this Geordie Gilroy kept ringing out. The second problem was the pickup. When Jamie had finally been ready to leave the caravan last night, it had flat-out refused to start. He had tried all the tricks, but even jump leads hitched to the generator had failed to get that heap of junk moving. He worried that the old wreck was barely worth pushing to the scrapyard, but he'd call Davie this morning and see what price he could get for it, and figure out what to do.

Bloody hell, he muttered aloud. Squeezed from all sides like a lemon. He rolled over on to his side and the whole caravan creaked.

It had always been a strange sort of sanctuary to him, this place, despite everything. Jamie dreamed, sometimes, about doing what his dad had never managed: of building on the site, if he could ever get the money together. He'd made enquiries, but it was clear from the get-go that the whole process would be far beyond his means. And in any case, although the plot had been gifted to his dad by Jerome Mondegrene, it seemed nothing was in writing.

The quarter-acre on which the caravan sat was overgrown, wild, belonging to no one but the dead. *Property is theft,* Anna had been fond of saying, the summer he'd left home. Going through an anarchic phase, when in reality she was becoming too timid to live in the wider world beyond the house. He always felt guilty thinking about that time. Should have done more to help his mum. But, as Lena would have said were she here now, *you cannot ride a bicycle backwards and steer straight ahead.* I'll try Gilroy again today, Jamie thought, but if I can't get hold of him I'll have to pay him a visit in person, when the sword's ready.

He needed the rest of the money pronto, there were no two ways about it. The death of the pickup made everything more urgent. He had visions of Lena going into labour, stranded: an ambulance that didn't arrive, a taxi he couldn't afford. Awful. That cannot happen, he told himself. If he didn't get the money it was all going to go to shite. He scrunched his eyes shut and listened to the branches scratching on the roof of the caravan like gigantic claws.

In his mind he rehearsed the drive up to Kilchroan Lodge to see Geordie Gilroy. If he still couldn't get hold of the man on the phone in the next day or two, he'd just have to get himself up there somehow. It dawned on him that he'd probably have to borrow his mum's Fiesta. Nothing like arriving in style.

Anna

Davie the scrappie is triangular in shape, his arms permanently held out from his sides like an action figure. 'Who's this little lady, then?' were his opening words to me, addressed over my head to Jamie.

Jamie and I arrived at the scrapyard in separate cars, me having borrowed mum's Fiesta again and Jamie steering his now-condemned pickup, towed here by the yard's recovery truck. Jamie's edgy as hell. He's dodged all my small talk about how he's doing, how Lena is. I'm flat out, is all he'll say, and he won't tell me what with. We don't usually keep anything from each other.

Leaving Davie and Jamie to haggle over the pickup, I go for a mooch around the scrapyard, willing Jamie to get on with it so I can get back to the hotel. I've given up my lunch break so I could come here to drop off the pickup and give Jamie a lift back, and am now starting to regret it, as neither Davie nor my brother seem in any hurry to conclude the deal.

Watching the mesmeric progress of the mechanical grabber on a crane delving down into junk piles, I am reminded of my first and only gambling addiction, back when I was a kid and the shows used to come to Barnadine. I would spend as long as I could beside the glass case filled with soft toys, jiggling the controls of the pincers that never quite managed to hold on to the teddy of my choice, plugging the last of my hard-earned coppers obsessively into the slot.

When I finally go back, Jamie and Davie have abandoned the pickup and are peering under the bonnet of a Vauxhall Cavalier the colour of snot. 'Belter of a family car for you, lad,' Davie is saying to Jamie, who is nodding and going, *nice, could be, aye,* all sweaty and distracted. I'll give him five minutes before stepping in and telling him we have to go.

To fill the time, I take a turn down one side of the yard's corrugated iron shed, walking past warped trolleys, prams and pipes. There are numberplates slung up on the wall, and I look at them for a while, scrambling and unscrambling the letters to make words, imagining the vehicles they came from. It's a raw day and my fingers have gone dead. I dig my hands deep into the pockets of my coat and my right hand closes on a crumpled can: the one I took from the caravan, the day of Angus John's funeral. The one with the photograph of Dad and that woman torn up inside. There's a dustbin overflowing with oil tins beside the office door and it's just as I am dropping the can into the bin that I see it, nailed askew up there.

It's an old-fashioned plate, white on black. *ZOO 222*.

I stare at it. I know those letters, those numbers.

'Excuse me,' I say, hurrying over to where Davie and Jamie are finally unloading the pickup. My voice sounds panicked; my throat is tight. 'Excuse me. Where did that numberplate come from?' I point back inside the shed.

'Eh?' Davie's gaze follows my arm. His eyes scrunch to slits. 'Och, that one.' He shakes his head. 'Been around a while. Came off a junker a good few years back now. Had to keep that plate – it's a bloody zoo around here – hey – Carl! Carl!' he shouts back towards the office. 'Put that bastard biscuit tin down, would you – I can hear you in there!' He turns back to my brother, shaking his head. 'Bloody pig, that boy. On work experience from school. Just sits there scoffing all day. Anyways. You know the score, Jamie—' He breaks off, scratching his arse, turns around to look at the numberplate again.

'You know,' he says, 'speaking of pigs – it used to belong to a bobby round here, the car that numberplate came off. Och, what's his name – George something. Galbraith, was it, Gordon . . . nah . . .' He trails off.

Carl appears in the door of the office, chewing. He's skinny and grinning, his face a riot of ferocious pimples.

Davie shakes his head. 'Sorry, it's gone.'

I look up at the numberplate again, heart pounding, my body dense with adrenaline as if I'm about to run a race. Jamie and Davie are undoing the straps securing the pickup when Davie snaps his fingers and turns around.

'Gilroy,' he says. 'It's come back to me now. Geordie Gilroy, that was his name. Jesus, that was it. Not the type you'd want to meet on a dark night, your man.'

The name doesn't mean anything to me. Beside me, Jamie drops the end of the strap he is holding and the ratchet hits the floor with a clang. 'Geordie Gilroy?' he says. 'You know him?'

Davie takes a sodden tissue out of his pocket and wipes his forehead. 'Ach, no. Not well. He was . . . well. Best not speak ill of the dead and all, and he's probably dead by now.'

Jamie drives me back to the hotel in Mum's Fiesta. He's still not saying much. I can't get the image of the numberplate out of my head, the monochrome, cryptic code. *ZOO 222*.

We're nearly at the hotel when he turns to me. 'Why were you asking all those questions in there, about that plate?'

I shake my head. 'I just thought . . . I'm sure I've seen it before. That's all.'

'Aye?' He's hunched over the wheel of the Fiesta like a bird over its prey. 'You sounded a bit, I dunno, freaked out about it. It was kind of weird, to be honest.'

'It got me thinking about that night. Driving to Glasgow. You know. The night that Dad . . .'

'Jesus.' He frowns. 'Really?'

'I don't know.' I sigh, staring out of the window. 'Maybe I'm just . . . do you remember Mum was planning to take us to the zoo on that trip?'

'What are you on about?' He shakes his head, looking baffled. 'We weren't going to the zoo. We were just going to get school stuff, weren't we, and see Nan and that. That was it.'

I swallow. 'No, we were definitely going to the zoo. I've remembered it ever since.'

'First I've heard of it, Anna. I think you've maybe made that bit up.' He tries to bend round to see my face. 'You doing OK?'

'Yeah.' I keep looking out of the window. 'Fine. You?'

'That guy Davie was on about,' he says, ignoring the question, 'he's still around, you know. Gilroy.'

'What?'

'Aye. He's not dead. Far from it.'

'How do you know?'

'Because I'm doing a bit of work for him.' Jamie flips the indicator before drawing in to the hotel car park. 'He's commissioned a sword from me. A claymore. The thing's nearly ready, actually, and I need it gone and paid for, except I'm having trouble getting hold of him.'

'Right,' I say. 'The way Davie spoke about him, he sounded like a bit of a nutter.'

'Yeah?' Jamie rolls his eyes. 'Let me tell you, you get used to nutters, making swords for a living. All my clients are nutters in one way or another. He was perfectly sound to me, straightforward.'

He parks outside the hotel and I get out of the car, lean back in. 'Take care of yourself, will you?' I say.

'Always, little sis.' He grins at me, goes to mess my hair, and I duck away.

356

'I mean it. And give my love to Lena. Any day now!' I step back and close the Fiesta's door. I'm running late for my afternoon shift.

It's later, when I'm finished, that I sit on the edge of the bed in my room and close my eyes and make myself think back to that night. The back seat of the car, the darkness. All my memories begin and end with seeing Dad's face in the lights as we drive away. But that number plate. *ZOO 222.* Did I see it that night? I try to reach back, to hold the memory steady in my mind, but those pale numbers and letters elude me like shapes in dark water, revealed for an instant before submerging once more. It brings with it a sickening tremor in the core of my body.

I need to speak to Jamie again. I gather some coins and go downstairs to use the payphone in the foyer to call his flat. When he answers, I tell him to stay away from Geordie Gilroy.

'Are you mental?' he says, when he's heard me out. 'Are you actually off your rocker? What do you even think he's done? I don't think you get it, Anna. The sword's made. I need the money. I'm going to deliver it as soon as I can.'

'You could just keep it,' I say. 'Give him his money back. Sell it on.'

'It's fuck-all! Just a numberplate hanging on a wall,' he says, as if I haven't spoken. 'Do you even understand the pressure I'm under right now? Jesus. I really don't need this.' I hear him draw a long breath before his voice comes down the line once more. 'Anna.' His tone a tad more gentle. 'Are you doing OK? Are you alright?'

'I'm not sure.' The sound of my voice is small.

He's quiet for a minute. 'Do you want me to come and see you? When I'm finished up here, we could go for a spin. Like we used to.'

'No, it's OK,' I say. 'But I think I know what I need to do.'

357

'And what's that?'

I hear the pips on the line, signalling I am rapidly running out of money. I look down at the change in my hand.

'Jamie,' I say, 'I love y—'

But the call has ended. Slowly, I replace the receiver back on its hook. I count the coins in my hand, rocking to and fro on my toes. I line up the coins on the edge of the ledge in front of me, and then I take a quick look around the reception area. Empty. I stick a fifty pence into the slot and dial. This isn't how I imagined having this conversation, but I can't worry about that now.

I need to speak to my mum.

'Langlands 667.' It's Bruce, of course. I'd forgotten that he answers the phone as if it were still the 1950s. It sounds as if he has his mouth full.

'Hello, Bruce,' I say. 'It's Anna.'

There's a pause, in which I hear him chewing, then swallowing.

'I'd like to speak to Mum, please,' I say.

'Excuse me.' He burps discreetly. 'Just finishing my beef paste sandwich.' There is a slightly confidential air to his tone. 'Very good.' Another pause. He clears his throat. 'Hang on a tick. I'll fetch your mother.'

I wait, prodding the change in front of me into numerical order. Beside the phone booth is a stand holding leaflets. I flick the paper edges with my fingers, leaning a little further between the two wings of the telephone booth, and then Mum's voice is at the end of the line.

'Anna,' she is saying. 'Anna. Is everything alright?'

When I finish speaking to my mum I replace the phone very quietly and find my way back to Leighanne's room. Up the stairs, past the picture of my father as a boy, so softly, with my head down and keeping close to the wall so I am not part of anything that is happening around me.

I close the door behind me and lock it and then I cry for a short while. The crying is not as bad as I'd feared. I should have done it years ago.

Later I fall asleep, and dream of fire.

August 1985

Donnie

His head was reeling and he tipped it back until it touched the wall behind him. He brought both hands to his face, pressing his eyes and cheeks. Touching his own skin felt strange, prickly, as if he were full of static electricity.

There was something on his chest. It took an effort to drag his eyes open. Pink painted fingernails. A blonde girl was snuggling into his neck and it was easiest to let his head rest on hers. Her perfume was dense in his nostrils, faintly nauseating. He felt her hand snaking around his waist and pulling him sideways towards her. Her body was tight against his; the buttons on his shirt crushed against his breastbone.

A piercing screech made him pull away, and the room careened about him. One of the dancers had fallen off the table – no, the table had fallen, taking her down with it, and she was getting to her feet amid the wreckage of glasses and bottles, laughing, blood on her elbows, purple glitter and a wet stain all down her satiny dress.

Someone was calling his name. He looked around and was nearly blinded by a camera flash. Purple and green lights swam in front of his eyes and when his vision cleared he saw a man backing away with a camera still half raised, wagging a finger. Bruce fucking Langlands. Whatever he was doing here. Donnie opened his mouth to say his friend's name but all that came out was a slurred clutter of sounds.

There was opera music playing, glossy vowels shimmying up high. In the middle of the room women were standing on chairs, weaving about unsteadily, one hanging halfway over a man's back. On the settee opposite him, a writhing of white arms and legs, hairy nipples, breasts encased in a black bra, a gloved hand holding a cigarette. Donnie detached the blonde girl from his waist, shaking his head and holding up his left hand to show his wedding ring. She slumped back, giggling. He staggered to his feet. The heat in here was deadly.

He was turned round by the shoulder, a tall man looming over him. 'There you are.' Geordie Gilroy took his cigar out of his mouth, peered beyond Donnie into the gloom. 'You're a fast mover, MacArthur,' he said, 'I'll give you that.'

Donnie ducked his head, found himself staring at Gilroy's black leather boots and gulped down a wave of nausea.

'What's the matter with you, man?' Gilroy steered him by the arm towards the doors that opened out on to the balcony. Donnie felt as if his feet were hardly touching the floor. A couple in a clinch were already out there. When they saw Gilroy they moved away inside. Donnie rested his head against the wall, pressing his forehead against the cool stone. He fought the urge to get down on to his knees at the feet of one of the stone dogs that flanked the balcony railings.

Gilroy's arm coiled around Donnie's shoulders and he was pulled up straight again. The world spun. Christ. He'd never been like this on the drink before. How he'd got so hammered was beyond him.

Gilroy was booming above his head. 'Surprised to see you in such a state, MacArthur. Thought you of all people would be able to hold your whisky.' Another one of those laughs that seemed to ricochet off the walls of the house behind them, and then Gilroy strode back inside. Donnie sank down with the stone at his back.

Below him, music was playing, not the thud of the speakers inside, but a band playing outside. Through the bars of the balcony he could see a figure standing alone, looking up at the

364

house. A small, delicate man in a pale suit beneath a wisp of smoke, graceful. A glass in his hand. Beyond all the clutter, Jerome Mondegrene was surveying the scene, one hand moving in time to the music. The light from the outdoor lamps danced in the glass he held. A minute passed. Donnie closed his eyes and let the music drift into a spiralling haze.

He awoke with no sense of place or time and a pounding headache. His throat ached and his entire skin felt bruised. He hunched on the balcony shivering like a dog. There was light breaking in the distance. He must have been out here for some time. Steadying himself against the wall, he got slowly to his feet.

There were sounds coming from the room inside. He stood still to look in. The door on the other side of the room was closing with a gentle swish and a click. He was about to step inside, thinking it was empty, when he saw the shape on the carpet.

It was the blonde girl from last night. He had a blurry memory of the camera flash, recognised her by her pink top, her painted nails. She was lying on the floor on her side; he could see blood on her face and she was making a dreadful sound, a low, soft wail that hardly sounded human. He took a step back on to the balcony, swallowing a swell of sickness. Standing there in the half-light, he hunched forward, pressing his hands into his thighs, and then he went into the room.

It was dim and smelt of smoke, something sweet and disgusting beneath it. He bent down by the girl's head. She was breathing but barely conscious, one eye swollen shut, the other rolled up under her eyelid so only the white was exposed. There was blood on her face and mouth and arms, her skin slick-looking and wet. She made no sign of knowing he was there.

He picked her up as gently as he could and her head lolled back against his arm. There was white froth on her lips, running from the corner of her mouth. Fucking hell. He carried her from the room and went down the stairs, every muscle protesting.

He was halfway down the corridor when he heard his name. He stopped before turning around slowly, the girl heavy in his arms. Gilroy was standing at the end of the corridor, smoking a cigar. He didn't look at the girl. He was looking at Donnie.

'What the hell happened here?' Donnie said. His voice came out cracked. He licked his dry lips.

Gilroy said nothing for a moment, just stood and smoked as though he were standing outside a board meeting. 'Like Sodom and Gomorrah here last night,' he said. 'Like beasts. Worse than beasts. I see so little I like in the worst of people.'

'We have to get her to hospital,' Donnie said.

'Oh, I wouldn't know about that.' Gilroy turned, stubbed out his cigar in a discarded drinks tray. 'It's hard to sympathise with those who don't know their limits. Plenty of space here for a daft lassie who's overindulged to sleep it off. Let's just leave it at that.' Gilroy leant in, and Donnie realised that what the man had just said was for anyone who might have been listening, but not for him. 'Here's the thing, MacArthur.' Gilroy's voice was quiet, precise. 'We all have problems. It's the cost of doing business; it's the cost of having friends. You'll come to know this, but I'll spell it out for you now.' He jabbed a finger into Donnie's arm so forcefully it felt as if it could go straight through the muscle and stick in his side. 'She was your problem last night, and she's your fucking problem today.'

Gilroy stepped back, stretching out his wrist and shaking his watch out from under the sleeve of his jacket. 'Would you look at that,' he said, in his familiar, declamatory style. 'I'm fishing with the Gilberts across the loch today. Time waits for no man, does it?'

366

Donnie turned away from him and staggered down the corridor, out to the car. You bastard, he thought. Whatever this is, it's certainly none of my doing.

He stopped in the ambulance bay outside the hospital's double doors and got out of the car, leaving the engine running. Moving as fast as he dared, he yanked open the passenger door, leaning in to gather the girl up in his arms. He put his hand behind her head and she made a noise as if she was trying to speak, her eyes opening a crack to look at him. He couldn't hear her and bent his head down more closely. Her mouth was all bloodied. She was definitely saying something but he couldn't make it out.

'I'm sorry,' he said. He moved her as carefully as he could out of the car. The only other thought in his mind was that he couldn't be seen. The heels of her bare feet caught on the uneven concrete as he half carried her through the hospital doors. He left her just inside in the warmth, on a bench a few feet from the empty reception desk. 'I'm sorry,' he said again. Her head was sunk on to her chest. He turned around and walked back out to the car without looking round.

Two minutes out of Barnadine he pulled off the road on to a Forestry track and stopped the car. His hands were shaking; he thought he was going to vomit. He sat in the car and stared at himself in the rear-view mirror, struggling to find a thought. He pressed his forehead with his fingers. He couldn't calm himself. He couldn't focus.

'Are you kidding me, Donnie? Were you there?'

Somehow he had made it home, slipping into the caravan without waking the kids. It was just past six in the morning; Mary Rose was awake but still in bed. He'd told her that someone at the house had been taken to hospital. He'd tried to avoid telling her it was one of the girls, at first, but she'd got it out of him before long.

'What was wrong with her?' she'd asked. 'Too much to drink, was it? Why didn't they just call an ambulance?'

'There was no time,' he said. He turned away. 'It's sorted now.'

'Jeezo,' she said. 'You're white as any sheet, Donnie. I know when you're lying to me. What was going on up there?'

He shook his head and sat down on the edge of the bed, leaned down to take his shoes off.

'Where was Geordie Gilroy when all this was happening, anyway?' she went on. 'Are you just his bellboy now, is that it? You tell me all the time that you don't work for him, that you work for Mondegrene.'

'Can you just leave it, Mary Rose?'

She jerked upright in the bed. 'I will not leave it, so help me,' she said. 'What kind of a man is out all night, driving around with God knows who, doing God knows what, and his wife and children at home? You're that kind now, are you? You turn up, stinking of drink – and is that blood on your shirt? Swear to God, Donnie.'

He turned round, looked her in the eye. 'The lassie had been battered to within an inch of her life,' he said. 'If I'd left her where she was, she'd be dead by now. I had to take her. There wasn't time.'

Mary Rose was silent, staring at him with her eyes wide.

'I didn't ask that bastard Gilroy for anything,' he said, 'because I know fine it was him that did it. OK? I think he'd been at her and then he left her covered in blood, the eyes rolling in the back of her head. What was I supposed to do? You tell me, Mary Rose.'

'You should've called the police,' she was saying. 'You should call them now.'

'No.' Donnie held his hand up in front of her face. He tried

368

not to shout. 'No. That's the last thing we'll do. You don't know what it's like up there. We can't get drawn into all that.'

'For crying out loud. Call the police.' It was an instruction she kept on repeating.

'I don't know what to do,' he said.

'I've told you.' She turned and got out of bed. 'And finding a backbone, first off, that would be a bloody start.' She stood looking down at him for a second, shaking her head, her eyes narrowed. 'I have to get the kids up,' she said. 'Get everything washed and packed.'

'Packed?'

Her tongue clicked in irritation. 'Glasgow,' she said. 'Tonight. We're going to Glasgow tonight. The kids haven't seen their nan all summer holidays, and they're back to school next week. We talked about all this; you know we did.' And then, when he did not reply, 'You forgot, did you? Jesus, Donnie, get your head screwed on. Don't you dare be coming in late tonight, not again. If you're not back with the car in time, I swear to God.'

He was standing in the shower when he started shaking. He thought he might be crying. She was half-dead, at least, he told himself, and he didn't even flinch, Gilroy. He didn't even look. Gone fishing. It was sick. He took a deep breath, letting the water pour over his face. I should have seen this coming, he thought. I should have known I'd pay the price for looking the other way, the wee gofer who keeps his mouth shut and his wallet open.

There was one thing Mary Rose was right about: he couldn't stand for this. But he was damned if he was going to the police. It was Mondegrene he'd speak to first.

'MacArthur,' Jerome Mondegrene said. 'Running late?'

Donnie had driven back up to Altnaglas House wearing a clean white shirt with a stiff collar, and had parked around the

369

back of the house. All the other cars seemed to have gone. Good. He had to speak to Mondegrene on his own.

Mondegrene was standing at the top of the steps by the house's main entrance, his two pointers at his feet. A blue silk handkerchief in his jacket pocket, today. When he saw Donnie he lifted a hand to his eyes as if squinting into the sun.

'I need to talk to you, sir,' Donnie said. 'I'm sorry to ask.'

Mondegrene took him into the library and stood by the fireplace leaning on a stick while Donnie told him what he had come for.

'Quite the allegation, MacArthur,' he said, when Donnie had finished speaking. 'And you saw this with your own eyes, yes?'

'I didn't – I didn't see him do it, sir. But it's what he said to me.' The way he'd said it, he thought. 'I found her lying on the floor. She'd been beaten. Badly. And he knew, Gilroy. He wasn't shocked, or surprised.'

'Very well, MacArthur,' said Mondegrene. 'I will speak to Mr Gilroy, and get to the bottom of this.' He shook his head slowly, gazing into the empty grate. 'One must respect a man with principles, although they can be such a rod for our backs, can they not?' Mondegrene inclined his head, waved his fingers gently in the direction of the door. 'Be careful, MacArthur,' he said, and Donnie knew he was dismissed.

Gilroy

Good morning, everybody, he murmured under his breath. He'd parked just off the road, a little way up a forestry track. The trees kept his car from view but he could see the caravan on the hill clearly enough, and he could see who came and went more clearly still: the woman, the two children running in and out of the open door. He inched the car window down a touch; it was important to listen. His index finger was cut; he ran his thumbnail along it.

He waited.

He had been there long enough to see Donnie MacArthur come and go. No prizes for guessing where he was going – to tell tales to Mondegrene – and where he'd almost certainly go after that: straight to the bar to drown his sorrows. Gilroy was reminded of a phrase an old friend in the force had been fond of. *This,* his colleague would say, *will come to fuck-all.*

The problem with so many men, he thought: their lack of stamina.

The question he kept playing with was – what would be best?

He waited.

By the time he was drawing the last drag from his last cigarette, the evening was drawing in. The woman had been out earlier to hang washing on the line. He'd watched her take it in again and stop to look down the road. The two children seemed to be allowed to run more or less wild, playing out of sight on the other side of the caravan.

He waited.

It was dark when MacArthur returned. Gilroy heard the car clip the strainer post as it turned up the track. He wondered how a man could leave the founds of his own house rotting in the ground for so long.

Now MacArthur was getting out of the car, the door left open behind him, the dull interior light aglow. He watched the man weave his way up to the caravan door. He was certain he'd been correct in his assumption regarding the two desti-nations: Altnaglas, followed by the bar of the Royal. MacArthur was a predictable drunk: slow, limited, useful up to a point, like the rook in a game of chess.

He heard the expected domestic fireworks erupt from indoors. The woman's voice raised, crying him all the bastards, before the caravan door was slung open once more and there she stood, with bags in her hands.

She was making for the car now, loose red hair swinging like some cheap harlot. She looked over her shoulder, calling to her children to follow on, which they did, the boy and the girl in mismatched clothing, straggling in her wake like dishev-elled ducklings. The girl was turning round, perhaps looking for her father. You would imagine both children were likely to become him in one way or another.

He watched MacArthur hurry out of the caravan after them and haul himself into the passenger seat of the car. It was as laughable as it was tragic to think how that man had once fancied himself as some kind of Highland hero back when they were younger, and now look at him. Her driving him around in that tin can. The Ford Fiesta began to hurtle down the track from the caravan to the main road, one headlight out.

The radio came on softly. Bay City Rollers, 'Give a Little Love'. Something likeable about the tune, Gilroy thought. A teenage dream, indeed. He tapped his fingers gently on the steering wheel as he followed on.

Tuesday 24 March 1998

Anna

The manager comes in as I am finishing up my shift the next afternoon, vacuuming the carpet in the lounge bar before the evening gets under way.

'There's a guy at the door for you,' he shouts over the hum of the vacuum cleaner. 'Shall I ask him never to call you ever again?'

I shut off the vacuum cleaner with a stamp of my foot and stalk through to the reception, dusting my hands, leaving him and his suppressed snigger behind. I knew he was listening in the other day. If Liam Bell is in reception I'm just going to kick him square in the bollocks and send him packing. The cheek of him, turning up here.

I stride into reception, and stop. It is not Liam. It is John Teelin, leaning up against the reception desk.

'Afternoon,' he says casually, as though we'd arranged this. 'Fern said I'd find you here. Can we have a word? Or I can come back later. I know you're working.'

He's had a haircut, short up the sides. Same lopsided lazy grin. I feel as if I've been knocked in the ribs.

'I'm just finishing.' I clear my throat. 'Have you driven all this way up from . . .?'

'Glasgow, yeah. Just this morning. I wanted to come and tell you myself. I've got some news. I heard back from—'

'Hang on a sec,' I interrupt him. We're standing in the middle of the floor and behind him Fiona on reception is twirling a pencil around her fringe and making googly, what-have-we-here eyes at me. I've left the vacuum abandoned in the bar. 'I'll just finish up here,' I say, 'and then I'm done. Do you want a drink while you're waiting? Something to eat?'

He buys two lemonades from the bar. I tidy the vacuum away, wheedle a plate of chips from the kitchen and take them outside to where he is sitting.

'It's – nice to see you again,' I say to him, and he nods but says nothing. He has that intent, preoccupied look that I recognise from those trips to the library. I put down the plate, shunt an overflowing ashtray out of the way. I was fiercely hungry before his unexpected arrival but now eating seems significantly less important. 'How was your drive?'

He nods tersely. 'It was no bother, yeah. But here, listen. Erin phoned me last night. It turns out Josephine did manage to make her way to Canada after all.'

'Wow,' I say. 'You found her.'

'Yeah,' he says. 'By all accounts she's spent the past fifty years living in Newfoundland. Looks like she's had a pretty good life there. She was married, with a family, worked at the same place for almost forty years. But do you know this, she only died two weeks ago. Isn't that the strangest thing? I only just missed her. By a couple of weeks.'

'Oh, John. That's a real shame. I'm so sorry.'

'I know. Imagine if I could have spoken with her. All that life she'd have had. It would have been something, wouldn't it?' He pauses for a second and I see his face change, light up for a moment at the thought of talking to this distant relation. It is some cherished sense of kinship, I think, that drives him to seek out these people from beyond his own past, his family. Perhaps a kind of love.

'The important thing is to have tracked her down,' he is saying now. 'At least I know something about what happened to her. I mean, I didn't even know she existed before. I still wouldn't, if it weren't for you.'

I realise I have been staring at his lips while he talks and look down, chasing flecks of salt around the plate with my finger. I put another chip in my mouth in case any of the other thoughts my mind keeps throwing in the way should inadvertently make themselves heard.

'But that's not the main reason I'm here,' he says. 'There's something else I have to tell you.'

He draws a deep breath. I hold mine.

'How do I put this,' he says. He glances up at the ceiling, back down again. 'I found out some more about Netta, too.'

'Oh. Right.' *Fucking pathetic*, I can hear Liam sneering. *Wednesday fucking Addams*. It had seemed almost funny at the time, but not so funny now. 'What is it?'

He looks unaccountably anxious. 'It's sort of hard to say, to be honest. Let me think . . . probably best to start at the beginning. So there's a ticket for Netta MacArthur, leaving for Canada and arriving in Halifax in Nova Scotia in January 1947, that's true enough. But after that, there's not one single sign of her. No record of any kind. No mention of her anywhere.'

'How do you mean?'

'Well, this is the thing.' He starts speaking quickly, leaning forward on his elbows, staring at me in that direct, disconcerting way of his. 'It's hard to imagine someone starting a new life in a new country, living there for as long as Netta is supposed to have done, and not leaving a single trace. No voter register, provincial records, property registration – you name it. Not one mention of Netta MacArthur anywhere. And so I wonder if she changed her name when she reached Canada, or . . .' He stops to take a breath. 'The thing is, Anna, I thought about it, all the time I was driving up here in the car. And I think there is one explanation, but it might be difficult to hear.'

'OK,' I say. 'Just tell me. Don't worry.'

377

'With Josephine,' he says, 'there was something strange as well. No ticket for her leaving for Canada – no proof of her leaving Scotland, or in fact any records of any part of her journey. No travel documents, no landing form, no nothing. Now with Netta, the *only* record we have of her are her travel documents, her landing form. When you put these two things together, you have Janet MacArthur on the RMS *Aquitania* arriving in Halifax, and then she vanishes, never to be seen or heard of again. Then, the day after Netta supposedly arrives in the country, Josephine Halloran appears, already in Canada, to start her new life.'

'OK,' I say again.

'What I'm starting to think,' he says, 'is that maybe Josephine travelled out to Canada using Netta's ticket, under Netta's name, and that Netta never went at all. She never left.' He tips his head on one side, taps a chip absent-mindedly against the side of the plate. 'Anna? What do you think?'

'God, I have no idea,' I say. 'I mean, if Netta never left for Canada, the obvious question is where on earth did she go? What happened to her? Do you think Josephine stole the ticket from her?' I shake my head. 'Where is she now?'

'Yeah, that's the question,' he says. 'Assuming I'm right, of course. There might well be a pretty simple explanation, I suppose. I just don't know. It's like I said, isn't it? Turn over one stone and there's another one underneath.'

'Is it even possible, to do that, to just head off to another country and pretend to be someone else?' In the following silence I can hear dishes being scraped and the purr of the air-conditioning at the back of the kitchens. 'I asked Fern if she ever heard from Netta,' I say. 'She pretty much said no. She thought Angus John might have done, though. I don't know about Bella'

He says nothing, just drains his lemonade and sets the can back on the table, flicking the ring pull absent-mindedly.

378

'I know what you're going to say,' I tell him.

He looks up. 'What am I going to say?'

'Ask better questions.'

He grins. 'Always.'

We drive over to Crois na Coille in John Teelin's Golf with Rod Stewart on the tape player. 'I'd offer to change the cassette,' he says, 'but it's been stuck in there for over a year.'

I giggle. It cracks me up, the thought of him driving around listening to 'Maggie May' on a loop. 'My mum loves Rod Stewart,' I say. 'It's not what I would have expected of you.'

'Ah, you just don't know me that well yet,' he says. He laughs as he says it. Then he says, 'It belonged to – someone else, in fact. But then it got wedged in there and – well.'

Join the queue, I remember Erin saying.

Fern is clearly surprised to see me when we arrive at Crois na Coille; even more surprised to see the pair of us. She keeps making eyes at me and funny smiling faces; really quite embarrassing. We drink tea in the kitchen and I croon nonsense to the collies until I've nearly talked us out of the door again and realise I'm just going to have to come out with it.

'Fern,' I say, 'can I ask you something?'

'Of course, pet.' She's engrossed in trying to pop the top off a biscuit tin. 'Anything at all.'

This is encouraging. I wait for her to sit back down at the table with three Blue Ribands on a plate.

'When we were in Angus John's house,' I say, 'you said that you thought Angus John might have kept in touch with Netta.'

'I did,' she says.

'Do you know if that's true?' I press on. 'You said you tried to get in touch with her after Dad died. Have you ever heard from her, Fern, since she left? Do you know if Angus John did? Or Bella?'

379

Fern looks down at her plate. I let the silence run, not liking myself very much. I don't dare look at John Teelin beside me. He takes a sip of his tea and unwraps a biscuit from the plate.

'Have you never heard from her?' I say gently, and Fern looks at me, and smiles. She shakes her head, sighing.

'Until last week, Anna,' I would have had to say no. I believe none of us had, since the day she left. But last week, I think she sent us something. A parcel. Just before Angus John's funeral. I'll show you if you'd like.'

Not for the first time today, I feel completely at a loss. We follow Fern into the living room, shutting the dogs in the kitchen. John Teelin and I sit on the sofa behind the coffee table and I hold a faded cushion on my lap.

'Let me just go and fetch it,' Fern says.

John Teelin and I look at one another when she's gone. I raise my eyebrows at him.

'We'll just see, will we?' he says.

I don't quite know what I expect to come back through the door, but I didn't anticipate the cardboard box that Fern returns with. As she places it on the coffee table I can see that it's covered in Sellotape, yellowing and peeling like tree bark, and that its tidemarked surface is covered in small stickers like a vintage suitcase.

From the box Fern takes out a small pile of photographs, which she spreads on the coffee table. There is an element of ceremony to her movements. She goes back into the box and lifts out a white scarf, placing it next to the photographs. Then she moves the box to the floor and hands me a piece of paper.

'She sent a message to Angus John,' she says, 'after all this time,' and I hear the depth of sadness in her voice.

I look down. *Dearest Angus John,* I read. *I thought you might like to see these. I'd always hoped to return, and tell you about my 'new' life, as it was then. But it would seem that time is against me, and this may be the only way I can. As we used to say – Once more across the water, MacArthur!*

The letter is signed with a kiss and a scribble of a rowing boat. Beside me, John Teelin waits politely. I look over at Fern, feeling I should ask her permission before passing it his way. She waves her hand in his direction.

He scans the lines quickly. '*Once more across the water, MacArthur!*' he mutters, and looks at Fern. 'Canada,' he says.

'That's right.' Fern sits down in an armchair, holding the scarf in her lap and running it through her hands like a rosary. 'Is there a particular reason you're asking me this now?'

I open my mouth to reply when I hear the front door and Bella's voice, speaking to the dogs. The next moment, the door is open and the room is awash with collies, all noses and waving tails that sweep some of the photos from the table. I see Bella stand in the hallway for a moment, looking through to Fern. Then she puts her head around the door and greets me and John Teelin.

'Ach, stay where you are,' she says, already backing out again. 'I'll put the kettle on. Will you stay for your tea?' Not waiting for an answer, she heads back down the corridor to the kitchen.

I bend to scoop fallen photographs from the floor and John Teelin stands up, holding the folder that contains his family research. He bends down by Fern's armchair and starts to explain, quietly yet concisely, what little we have come to learn over the last week. As he speaks, he puts the photocopies he made in the library on to the coffee table. 'This all came together for the first time last night, you see,' he says, 'and that's why I came back. I didn't know if I should, you know?'

'No, John,' says Fern, 'It's nice to see you.' She pauses. Then, 'But where else would Netta have gone?' Her voice is low, thoughtful.

I've been looking out of the window while John Teelin speaks to Fern. Listening to him explain for a second time, I try to reimagine what he is saying as if I were someone else. I'm still holding the photographs I picked up from the floor, and I lean forward to put them back on the table, placing them next to John Teelin's photocopies. The picture of Josephine Halloran that he found in the library is on top; I pick it up and hold it next to one of the photographs from the box, which shows a dark-haired woman of around fifty or so lowering a birthday cake down at the head of a table. At first I don't see it, but the more I look, the more I am convinced that these photographs show the same person. I think John Teelin is right.

'Can you have a look at this, both of you?' I say, and he leans forward, Fern beside him.

'You see, I do think these women are one and the same.' I point to the handsome, dark-haired woman. 'Josephine Halloran. Don't you think?'

'May I?' John Teelin takes the two images from me, placing one on each knee. He holds his head in his hands as he inspects them. 'Yes,' he says at length. 'I'd say you could be right, Anna. Even through the years, they look the same.' He looks at Fern. 'Could it be Josephine who sent this box to your brother?'

'Josephine?' Fern fusses with her spectacles. 'I can hardly remember Josephine. But it's true they were thick as thieves, she and Angus John, despite their difference in age. I remember Netta teasing him about it.' She sounds distressed, sucking on the leg of her glasses. 'Photographs aren't really true, are they? They're just a . . . counterfoil. Of a living moment.' She squeezes her eyes closed. 'It's how people hold themselves, speak, laugh. I can't imagine Netta as a fixed image.'

When she opens her eyes again I think there are tears in them. I reach out for her hand and hold it in her lap. She looks down at our enfolded fingers as she goes on.

382

'She wasn't well in her mind, Netta. After she had Donnie, she was away for some time. It was a sort of hospital, I believe. I wish I had done more, known more, but I was caught up in my own freedom, I suppose. Being away myself, and a whole world outside, just opening up. My own name, Anna, on a payslip! I was busy. Being busy is a terrible excuse for inattention.' She sighs. 'We knew she was planning to go to Canada. And then she was – just gone. I don't even know who saw her off.' Fern sits down in her chair once more. 'It was the RMS *Aquitania*,' she says. 'I will remember that name till the day I die. But I can't, I can't tell – she never even came to say goodbye, properly. Not even to say goodbye,' she repeats, slowly. 'And she never came back.'

There is a faint clinking of china teacups and Bella is in the doorway, standing very straight, holding a wicker tray. When she speaks, she looks only at Fern.

'But she did, Fern,' she says. 'She did come back.'

We all watch her as she moves into the room and over to the table, where she clears a small space for cups and a teapot amid the photographs. It's gone very quiet; outside, I can hear the chatter of starlings. They are gathering to roost in the trees that line the edge of the slope of the yellow hill. I try and remember what the name for it is, that swooping congregation of starlings.

Bella sits down and folds her hands into a neat envelope on her lap. 'She did come back,' she says again. 'Once. For Donnie. Before she sailed.'

'For Donnie?' Fern looks confused.

'She wanted to take Donnie away.' Bella tilts her chin in minute defiance to the room at large, not making eye-contact with any of us. 'I couldn't let that happen,' she says, her voice quietening a little. 'I couldn't let her take that beautiful boy. It was Jerome Mondegrene who brought her to the house. And it was him who took her to the station.' She looks

383

again to Fern, reaches a hand over to touch her sister's fingers as they grip the chair's armrest. 'I'm sorry, Fern. It wasn't that I wanted to keep it from you. I just didn't know how tell you.'

Murmuration, I think. The word is *murmuration*.

Wednesday 29 January 1947

Donnie

Netta is standing by the kitchen door. Her face is white and her mouth is a red line. Donnie is sitting at the kitchen table on his high stool. His toy blocks, each stamped with a letter, are spread in front of him, but he is not playing any more.

His Auntie Bella is beside him. Her hands are folded in her lap and she is staring at him the way she does when he has done something wrong and it begins to frighten him.

'You're happy here, aren't you, Donnie?' she says. It is not Gaelic she is speaking but English, the language of school, the language Bella speaks to strangers. 'You love playing outside and you love the animals.'

He means to nod but blinks instead.

'Everyone you know,' Bella carries on, 'is here, aren't they?' She looks across the room to Netta, who is standing very still with her arms wrapped around her body. 'Your mother, this lady here, she's going to Canada. It's a place far away across the ocean. A long way from here. She wants to take you away with her, Donnie.'

Netta steps over to him suddenly, going down on her knees before him at the table. She smells sharp, strange. She takes both of his hands in hers. 'My boy,' she is saying to him. 'Just you and me, Donald. An adventure. In Canada.' She picks a letter block from the table and begins to spell it out with him. *C for cat*. He repeats it back to her. *A for apple, N for nest* – and Bella stops them, suddenly.

'You have to be a big boy now, Donnie,' she says. 'You have to decide what you want to do. Do you want to stay here with me, with everyone you know, with all the animals, or do you want to go away, far away, with your mother? With Netta?'

Both women's gazes are glassy and wet-looking and they are fixed on Donnie.

'Everything you know,' repeats Bella, 'is here.'

Netta squeezes his hands. 'I'm sorry I had to be away for so long,' she says. 'But I'm better now.' There is a tear running down her nose and he puts his finger out to stop it. 'Please, my love. With me. Your mum. Will you?'

Donnie looks down at Netta. He nods.

'You will?' It is as if someone has switched a light on beneath Netta's skin. He nods again.

There is a screech of wood on the tiles as Bella pushes her chair back from the table. She sobs, one hand over her face.

'Auntie Bel,' Donnie calls to her, scared, but she won't look at him and makes for the door.

'No!' Donnie is crying too, wrenching his hands from Netta's and sliding from his stool. He stumbles across the room to Bella. He just catches her before she opens the kitchen door, flinging his arms about her legs, burying his head in her skirt. The sobs are coming up in his chest as if he's been winded.

He feels her stoop down and sweep him off the ground and he is tight in her arms now. He feels her cheek wet on his forehead as she holds him.

'You, Auntie Bel,' he is sobbing. 'I want to stay with you.'

'There now,' she is saying. 'There now. Of course you're staying here.' Her fingers dry his tears, smooth his hair from his face. He feels her chin resting on the top of his head. 'That's enough,' she says to Netta. 'He's made his decision.'

Bella carries him upstairs and puts him to bed. She tells him he'll be staying here forever.

Donnie slowly stops crying. Why is she going? He keeps asking. Why can't we all stay together?

Bella strokes his forehead, tells him to stay in bed. She whistles to Bran and lifts the dog right into the bed beside him. Bran lays his broad head on Donnie's chest and closes his eyes with a sigh. Bella tells him a story about a witch who could control the weather by making knots in a piece of wool and who would put to sea in an eggshell.

He's tired. Lulled by the dog's warmth, he falls asleep.

In the morning the world is white with snow, and his mother is gone.

Sunday 25 August 1985

Donnie

'Go on and get out,' she said. She opened the car door, turned her head away.

He put a hand on her arm and Mary Rose twitched him off like a horsefly.

'If that's what you want,' he said.

'It is.' She wouldn't look at him.

He sat there looking at her for a minute, and then he said, 'Then I'm fucking gone.'

'Good.'

He was seized by fury, something he'd sworn he wouldn't give in to. He turned around in his seat. 'Your mum's a bitch,' he snarled at the kids in the back. Jamie's eyes were full of tears; Anna's were dark and staring. The words felt good in his mouth but sounded awful out in the sealed space of the car. Then he was outside and the night air was cold and damp on his face.

The car lurched forward, tyres grating, and vividly he saw his daughter's face pressed to the back window, her palms suckered to the glass, her mouth crumpling. He straightened and shouted, swearing, and when the hill knocked the sound straight back at him he kicked the ground.

He paced, crossed his arms over his chest. Then he dug his hand into his jeans and found the lighter, the one he'd taken from that first party at Altnaglas all those years ago. You stupid bugger, he thought. One cigarette left in his shirt pocket. He lit it, perched on the crash barrier and the two fingers holding

393

the tip to his lips forced him to breathe steadily. He inhaled and stared up at the dark sky and felt the smirr of rain on his face.

'Stupid bugger,' he said out loud. Inhaled again and felt the flush in his veins. 'Go west,' he said, and laughed at himself. In times of trouble, head north, head west. He closed his eyes. He'd always been west. He'd never gone anywhere. All he'd ever wanted was—

'You stupid fucking bugger,' he said again into the darkness, and laughed till tears stung in the corners of his eyes. Then he stood and flicked the cigarette butt into the woods. Forestry signs be damned. *CARELESSNESS causes fire*. Be a miracle if anything caught in this mush.

His shadow loomed before him, his legs nearly as long as eternity. The glimpse of a story Bella told him, the boy who had cut his shadow from his feet and—

His shadow.

His shadow.

He was standing suddenly in a pool of light; there was a car behind him. He twisted to see over his left shoulder. The light dimmed and he recognised the numberplate, the ringed hand on the wheel.

He'd jumped the barrier and was halfway down the bank by the time he could hear the soft grind of tyres on gravel. The car creeping forward, the engine silent, just the sidelights on. Dark, and shining.

Tuesday 24 March 1998

Anna

We're back at the hotel, in Leighanne's room. I've finished the evening shift. John Teelin has booked one of the guest rooms for the night. I'm perched on the bed and he's sitting on the floor beside the kettle, squeezing two teabags into cups with his bare hands.

'I'm supposing that this Mondegrene fella is the one we need to speak to next,' John Teelin says.

'What would we ask him?'

He shakes his fingers dry, leans forward to hand me the tea. 'I think it's less about what we ask and more about seeing what he has to say. Have you met him before?'

'He's a very old man now,' I say. 'He's been in the Balsterrick Care Home for a good few years. I don't know how long. I did a work placement there about three years ago. That's the only time I met him. But my dad used to work for him. Well, for the estate. Loads of people did around here.' I shake my head, my thoughts crowded with all we have learned in the past few days. Netta, Bella, my father as a child.

John Teelin nods but says nothing for a bit, rolling a cigarette. I find myself staring at his lean fingers, the veins cording the backs of his hands, his bony knuckles. There is a tiny sway inside me, like the first glance down before losing balance. I think about telling him he can't light up in here, decide not to. I take a sip of tea. Out in the corridor someone walks past. There is a squeak of trolley wheels. The door of the room next to us opens and closes.

'Something strange happened yesterday,' I say, and he looks up at me with what I now recognise as his listening posture. He listens with his entire being. I still find it slightly unnerving. I wonder if it is a physical impulse, this telling him things the thinking part of me doesn't necessarily want him to hear.

'You know when I told you about my dad, the night he died,' I say. 'You know I said we were going to the zoo? Maybe you don't remember.'

'I remember.' His long legs are stretched out before him on the floor; mine are doubled up beneath me and I can tell if I move I'm going to be swamped with pins and needles.

'Well. Yesterday, I was at this scrapyard with my brother – don't ask. And anyway, I was talking to him about that night, and I'd always thought we were going to go to the zoo. I was sure of it, in myself, that it was the whole point of the trip in the first place. But when I asked Jamie about it, he nearly – well, he had no idea what I was on about.'

I realise I've started in the middle. 'I don't know how to talk about this, really.' I shift on the mattress and flex my toes. 'I just think I remember it, but I can't be sure. Do you know what I mean?'

'Go on.'

'In the scrapyard there was this numberplate. *ZOO 222.* And I'm sure I've seen it before.' I draw a deep breath. I know what I think but I can't bring myself to say it. I know what I can see but I can't bring myself to look. My face is hot, but the rest of my body feels cold, as if I might start trembling.

'Where did you see it before?' John Teelin asks.

I lie down flat on the bed and the pins and needles surge through my legs. I stare straight up at the ceiling as I speak, quickly. 'I saw it that night. I saw that numberplate out of the back window of Mum's car as we pulled away and left Dad by the side of the road.' I shut my eyes. 'I think I've had these two things mixed up, like I've remembered them wrong. The zoo.

The numberplate. And I think Jamie was right. We weren't going to the zoo. But I saw that numberplate. *ZOO 222.* Clear as day.'

He says nothing but I know he's still listening.

'Davie – the guy who has the yard – he told me that the numberplate belonged to a man called George Gilroy,' I say. 'No, Geordie. Geordie Gilroy. And if I'm right – and John, I'd swear it was the same numberplate – then maybe that man met my dad, after he was chucked out of the car that night. Maybe he was the last one to see him. I just don't know. But the thing is, my brother Jamie is working for him now, this man Gilroy. And I'm worried about him. Seeing that thing yesterday. I just felt – dread.' I sigh, rub my eyes with the flat of my palm. 'But I don't know what all this means. If it means anything at all.'

John Teelin is quiet for a minute, tapping his unlit cigarette on his knee. 'Doubt,' he says. 'It plagues us all.' He looks up at me, looks away. 'You know, the professor said something to me once about doubt. When you don't know what to think, he said, go deeper, not broader.'

'Right.' I look up at the ceiling.

'So, let's try this,' he goes on. 'What do you know about this Geordie Gilroy?'

'Hardly anything. Just that Jamie's working for him right now, making some kind of sword. Don't know what it's for or why he asked Jamie to get involved either.'

'OK,' he says. 'And how does Jamie know him?'

'I'm not sure.' I think of the spirals in the rocks on the yellow hill. Of the snake eating its tail. 'I think it might have been through Jerome Mondegrene,' I say. 'Jamie just made a dirk for him, a week or so ago.'

'Ah,' he says. 'There you go. Mondegrene, again. He's our next port of call for sure.' He gets to his feet, stretching, then pulls the curtain aside and opens the window on to the hotel courtyard.

'I think I need to speak to Jamie first,' I say. 'If I can get a hold of him.'

John Teelin leans out over the windowsill, sparking a lighter held to the tip of his cigarette. I watch him in profile, the tiny flare of flame throwing shadow into the hollow of his cheek. 'We'll go and see Mondegrene tomorrow.' His voice drifts in from the outside.

Against my better judgement, I like the way he says this, as if it is normal to assume that we'll go together. Maybe he'll stay up here for a while, and – stop, I tell myself, just stop. He's leaving tomorrow. This is nothing; he's just being kind.

The night air creeps into the room, fresh and chill, laced with smoke. A moth drawn inside flutters frantically around the ceiling light. John Teelin looks back over his shoulder, to the clock on the wall whose hands stand at a quarter to midnight. 'It's getting on,' he says. 'I'm keeping you up. I'll finish this and get out of your way.'

'Have you ever given up?' I say. 'Smoking.'

'I have. Sure, it's not hard. I'm after doing it a thousand times.'

I laugh and he turns his head, smirking. 'It's a bad habit,' he says. 'Abysmal, in fact. But it keeps me in good humour.' He flicks the butt from his fingers in a tiny, sparking arc to the courtyard outside, then withdraws his head, steps back to close the window. 'Right,' he says. 'I'll be on my way.'

I watch the flex of muscle in his arms as he draws down the sash and there is a pang in the pit of my belly like a shot of raw spirit.

'Or,' I say, in a voice that sounds not quite like mine, 'you could stay.'

He says nothing for a second, his back to me. He is very still, his head bowed. My toes curl in mortification. I can hardly believe I just said that. Perhaps he didn't hear.

But then he places his lighter down on the window ledge and turns towards me, his eyebrows slightly raised as if he, too, is surprised. He steps forward to where I am sitting on the bed and leans down, propping his arms either side of my waist.

I am frozen with the simple, sudden intensity of his body nearly but not quite touching mine. The warm beauty of it like sunshine. He smells of the outdoors, of smoke. His face is inconceivably close, blurring the tiny scar on his nose, and his eyes are fixed intently on mine, grey as the shallow sea. We stay like that for a moment that seems to stretch, pull itself taut. If I move my head a fraction my lips will meet his, and I want this more than anything, and then there is a loud rap on the door and I twist out from beneath his arms and off the bed in shock.

It's late; the thought occurs to me that it might be the manager. I smooth my clothes, trying to tamp down the pulse that started to beat right through me a short moment ago.

But it isn't the manager. It's Lena, practically in her night-clothes and a big jacket, her hair spilling loose around her shoulders.

My heart rises in my throat. 'Jamie?' I say.

'Have you seen him? He has come here?'

I shake my head, moving aside to let her in, but she stands on the threshold, twisting her hands.

'He went out late yesterday and was not home last night,' she says. 'Working, always working. We had hospital appointment today and where was he? Working in caravan. Sunday night too he stays away. I tell him he wants to be here for me, he has to show up. I go to hospital on my own today. Martin gives me a lift. And now they will induce me next Thursday. I will have our baby next Thursday, Anna.'

'Oh, my God, Lena, I'm sorry,' I say. 'But I haven't seen him since yesterday morning when we were at the scrapyard.

His pickup broke down; he's borrowed Mum's car. I know he went back to the flat for a bit, after that – I called him there – but maybe you were at work. I haven't spoken to him today.'

She makes a little hissing sound between her teeth. 'You know, I am just sick of this. The not being where he says he will be. How can I rely on man who does not come back when he says?' She is looking at me fiercely as if I'm hiding my brother in my room somewhere, and then her eyes flick behind me to fall on John Teelin. She sighs, and seems to deflate slightly. She puts a hand on her belly. 'Sorry, Anna, coming here. It is not your fault. I interrupt. You are busy, hmm?'

'Nope,' I say quickly. 'Not busy at all. How are you getting home?'

'Oh, just Martin brings me,' she says. 'He waits.' She looks at John Teelin again, grins at me.

'I don't have a car now,' I say. 'But tomorrow I should be able to go up to the caravan if it's helpful. Give Jamie a rocket. I know he's really stressed about this new commission. He is thinking of you, I know that. But it's like he just gets on to a narrow track with his work and that consumes everything. He thinks he's doing his best for you but he can't see the wood for the trees.' I stop, feeling that I'm making excuses for my brother.

'Wood for the . . .?' Lena shakes her head. 'No matter. Maybe I go to the caravan now,' she says. 'Give him a – how do you say? A rocket. I interrupt,' she says again. 'Sorry.'

'No, you don't interrupt,' I say, laughing. I hug her, or at least an approximation of it in her rotund state, kissing her on the cheek. 'He loves you,' I promise her. 'He loves you both. He just gets lost up his own arse sometimes.'

She looks at me for a minute, as if deciphering my words, then throws back her head. 'Ha! Lost up his own – yes. Is good. Yes. Goodnight, Anna,' she says.

I watch her walk down the corridor. I would never say 'waddle' about Lena, she is too swan-like for that, but even swans are ungainly on land.

John Teelin is behind me. 'I think I'll say goodnight too, Anna,' he says.

'OK,' I say. I can't say anything else. I can't quite look at his face. 'I'll see you in the morning.'

When he's gone, I turn back to my empty room. I pick up his unfinished tea from the floor and drink it, tarry and sweet and stone cold now, and I sit on my own on the edge of the bed.

Sunday 25 August 1985

Gilroy

He opened the car door and got out and walked to the side of the road where it curved around the bend. He placed both hands on the metal barrier and leant over and looked down into the darkness. The moving wood, the denseness of the trees as if nothing was there at all. Then he went back to the car and killed the sidelights and got the Maglite from the glove box. He switched it on, pointing it down at the ground. He went back to the barrier and flooded the place with light so the branches lit up bronze and the dark became webbed with white fog. The beam caught on something else, too: a glimmer of silver near his boot. He bent and picked up a lighter, damp in his fingertips. Tossed it in his palm, put it into his pocket. Then he stepped over the barrier and climbed down the bank, boots sinking in moss, holding on to the slim tree trunks of the growing forest with his left hand, panning the torch slowly with his right. The woods simmered with muffled noise. Below him, the loch. He wiped wet from his face with his sleeve.

He walked side-on to the hill for a time. Then he dropped down and moved along the bank of the loch, above the shingle, sweeping the torch up into the trees. Slowly. Still no car had come past on the road above when he found him. He damn near tripped over the form that measured its length on the shoreline, below a sapling snapped in two. The legs on the shingle and the white shirt up on the bank in a boggy puddle of water. He took a step back and looked. Donnie MacArthur lay belly-down with arms and one leg bent as if trying to climb the ground. Head turned to one side, blood in the hair and nose. Still breathing. Out cold.

Gilroy extended the toe of his boot, rested it gently on the upturned cheek and rocked it face-down into the shallow pool of water. Then he switched off the torch and climbed back up to the car, the way he'd come.

Wednesday 25 March 1998

Anna

I wake early the next morning and for some time I lie with my eyes closed, remembering where I am. The dream plays out like a film I've seen before. I remember last night, the expression on John Teelin's face, inches from mine. Hard to believe that wasn't a dream as well.

I turn on my side. I think then of my mum, our phone call. The conversation we'd never had, all the years we lived together, all the years I cared for her. All the years I never asked.

The Things My Mother Said

She said, *I miss him every day. Every single day.*
I felt he was pushing me away, but he was the one who fell.
I have to live with that.
I think I have nearly learned to live with that.
I read a book. It told me to tell him, I forgive you. I believe I
*   have forgiven him now. For leaving us.*
I think I am a selfish person. I thought I had to be.
You never cried for him, Anna. You never cried for your dad.
If I say I'm sorry is that enough? It's not enough. I know.
It was the guilt I felt. I was scared of driving you away, Anna.
I know I drove away from him.
I thought he was strong. But I was stronger than him.
I should have carried him when he was weak. I know that now.
I know how you feel about Bruce. But he is trying, in his own
*   way.*

*He cares for me. He would care for you too, only I know you
    don't need him to.*
I know that hasn't come out quite right.
*I told you we lost a child, your father and I. He never had a
    breath of life, Michael.*
We could never quite come back from that.
*He had so much life in him, your father. I spent those years in
    the caravan feeling like a ghost. I couldn't forgive him for it.*
I know we should have talked about this years ago.
*But do words help, I don't know. This isn't a book. Words
    cannot mend a life lost.*
She said, *When I let go of loss, the anger, the guilt, I found that
    it was only love that remained.*
She said, *I loved him. How I loved him. And I love him still.*

And I said that I understood. I said that I loved her.

My alarm clock beeps. If I don't hurry I'm going to be late.
I swing my legs over the side of the bed and hurriedly dress.
I'm on the breakfast shift this morning.

John Teelin walks into the dining room as I'm clearing up after
the departed guests.

'We've just stopped serving,' I say, 'but if you'd like
something . . .'

He waves his hand. 'Ah, no, no. I'll just have a coffee. If
that's alright.' He turns away to pick up a cup from the table
and I catch a glimpse of the manager, who is lurking around
outside the door, raising his eyebrows at me and tapping his
watch. I go back to loading plates on to the trolley beside me.

'Here. I'll give you a hand.' John Teelin downs his coffee in
one, puts his cup on the tray and starts piling them up.

I clear my throat, struggling to meet his eye. 'Do you think
you – could we go to the caravan when I'm finished here? Try

and catch Jamie before we head up to the home to see Mondegrene.'

He nods, scooping up plates and saucers. 'Not a bother. I'll see you when you're ready. I'll just wait by the car.'

'Some time this week would be appreciated, Anna,' the manager calls through the door in an exasperated tone. He will be glad when Leighanne returns, that's for sure.

'Sorry,' I shout. 'Going as fast as I can.'

'Here,' John Teelin says, 'I think he likes you.'

I cast him a surreptitious glance, smothering laughter.

We drive down the peninsula in John Teelin's Golf. It's raining and foggy. The last time I took this road was just over a week ago, before Angus John's funeral, although it feels far longer. John Teelin is quiet at the wheel. I'm tired after the early start and the morning's work. I don't know when I got to sleep last night, and I wonder when he did.

'Anna.' He straightens in his seat, casts a quick glance in the rear-view mirror. Our eyes meet in the glass. 'Just thinking about something. Forgive me if this comes out in the wrong way.'

I wait.

He clears his throat. 'Why do you think they never tried to find Netta, get in touch again?'

'Oh.' This was not what I was expecting him to say. 'I couldn't tell you exactly. In their own ways it's as if the day she left was the day she stepped out of their lives. Bella hardly talks about her. If she does, it's as though Netta's part of the past, like any of the other stories she tells. And Fern – well, Fern's more open, she talks about Netta more often, but it's almost as if she's imaginary, or a kind of distant image, like a film star. I wonder what Fern thinks now, after what Bella said.'

I break off, watching the fields flitting past outside. Some childlike part of my mind imagining galloping and jumping a

413

horse over the fences and walls. 'I can't imagine what it's like to believe one thing for so long that's so important, let alone to find out in the end that someone close to you has kept you in the dark, has lied to you.' I fall silent, feeling self-conscious.

'But maybe, after fifty years, when you've known each other so well, lived together for so long, maybe you would understand why someone would do that, even if it pains you.' John Teelin's voice is quiet and considered. He glances briefly over to me.

"If you slow down here,' I say, 'the caravan's just up on the left after this bend.'

We turn up the track and I want to tell him the site's more run-down now than when we lived here, but I don't say anything.

The padlock is on the door, and the place is empty. We peer through the windows. Jamie has been here, as I thought. There's a green sleeping bag curled on the floor like a maggot, some cans and some loose change on the table.

'Ah, he's away,' I say. 'Stupid bugger.'

We walk back to the car together. The rain has stopped but it's still misty and close; I swat midges from my face. 'I have this sort of recurring dream about setting fire to this place,' I tell John Teelin. 'It was a kind of game we used to play as teenagers, Jamie and I. Pretending that we'd burn it down, build the house Dad never built. I don't know why it keeps coming back to me.'

'Does it worry you?' he says, and I laugh, because he never says quite what I expect him to.

'No. Not really. It's calming, in a way. I know that sounds weird.'

He shrugs. 'Maybe in the end you will tear it down, and one of you will build a home up here. Someone should. Look at that view.'

I smile. He's right. Every time I come up here I think of the caravan like an old shrine, dishevelled and sacred, and yet it's true. It is beautiful up here.

'Maybe one day I will,' I say.

'What time do you have to be back at the hotel?'

'My shift starts at eight.'

'OK,' he says. 'Shall we go and pay Jerome Mondegrene this visit, then?'

'I suppose so.' I'm not looking forward to it, but at least I won't have to go on my own. 'It's not far from here.'

'He's our spider in the web,' John Teelin says.

I shudder at the thought of it.

Jamie

Jamie heard Lena's key in the front door and star-jumped into the hall. He'd been bombing around the flat ever since he got back, wiping surfaces and vacuuming. His latest gastronomic creation was simmering on the hob, a simple red pasta sauce, and he'd had the foresight to buy flowers from the supermarket. Tomatoes, garlic, some oregano and one pound fifty on the flowers had taken him into the outer reaches of his overdraft.

'Surprise!' he called, as she stepped over the threshold.

Lena's mouth opened in shock as she took in the flowers on the table, the gleaming kitchen worktop and the bubbling pot on the hob.

'I didn't forget, see? Your last day at work. Something to celebrate, eh?' He kissed her. She didn't kiss him back. He took her coat as she sank down on the sofa, shaking her head all the while.

'I am very angry with you,' she said. 'Where were you? Sunday night, Monday night, last night. Three days you are away. I was very worried. I—'

'I'm really sorry, Lena,' he said. 'Really sorry. I should have called. I had to work at the caravan to get the sword finished and this morning I had to go and see a lad about a new car. For us. I wanted to surprise you.'

'You did surprise me,' she said. 'You forget?'

She keeps staring at him until he remembers. 'Oh, God,' he said. 'Oh, shit, Lena, the hospital appointment. I'm so, so sorry. The pickup died, I had to scrap it, and . . . did you go? Is everything OK? God, I'm so sorry.'

'I am sorry also. Sorry is not helping.'

'I—'

'And you did not leave a message,' she said. 'You just disappear.'

'Lena,' he said, 'I'm grovelling here. The sword is finished. I'll deliver it tonight. And then I'm done. It won't happen again. I promise. Please tell me how the scan went?'

'They want to start things off next Thursday,' she said. 'Because of the – amniotic fluid, is not enough around baby. So I go in a week tomorrow. Induction.'

'Oh, my God,' he said. 'Right. Sorry. Sorry sorry. OK.' He took a deep breath. 'But the baby is OK? They're happy with everything else?'

He was going to be a dad next Thursday. She wasn't officially due for another two weeks.

'Yes, baby is OK,' she said. 'But you had better be there, to take me.'

'I will, Lena. It'll be all sorted by then. I have another car lined up, just need to . . . look, I've got loads to tell you. Loads. I've made dinner. We'll have a proper chat about this, make a plan for next week. You'll need to pack and everything. It will be fine. I promise.'

'I have had bag packed for two weeks already,' she said, unimpressed. Her cheeks puffed out, and then she blew out the air and gave him a small hint of a smile. 'The flat is looking . . . better. You did all of this?' She was gazing around. 'Well.' Her smile broadened slightly as she looked him up and down. 'You, not so much.'

'Ah, yeah.' He hadn't quite had time to shower before she'd arrived and was still wearing paint-stained shorts and his favourite Scotland shirt from 1982. He went to the hob and stirred the pot on the stove, pulled garlic bread from the oven and poured her a glass of squash.

'You get started with that,' he said, bringing the glass over to where she still sat on the sofa, 'and I'll jump in the shower. Won't be long. When we've eaten I've got to go and deliver the sword, tonight. And then ... *we're in the money, we're in the money.*'

Crass, yes, and he didn't know the rest of the song, but who cared? His good mood was unassailable. In the bathroom he turned on the shower, and then off again. He strode back into the kitchen and knelt on the threadbare carpet in front of Lena.

'I am sorry,' he said to her. 'I'm trying to work hard but I'm not always doing that well. Soon the three of us will have more money and a new car and we'll be able to enjoy ourselves a little bit more.' He held her hand, squeezed it tightly. 'I love you, Lena,' he said. 'I really love you.'

'I love you also.' She stroked the back of his neck. He kissed her forehead and got up to go back to the shower. On his way past the hi-fi he pressed her favourite *Ultimate Chill-Out* CD into the player. 'Nearly forgot – Whale Song. Just don't nod off before you've had your tea.'

Back in the shower, he shut his eyes against the lather of shampoo and cranked up the water as hot as it would go, steaming every speck of dirt that had gathered over the past few days from his pores. When he turned off the shower he heard Lena on the phone next door.

'Yes,' she was saying. 'Yes, he has made flat like show home. Very nice. I might have to forgive him.'

It was nearly all fine. It had definitely been the right decision, coming back here first. Waking up this morning in the caravan had been the worst. In the Fiesta, driving up to meet the lad about the pickup, he'd blasted the radiator and caught the scent coming off his own skin – old sweat and smoke and diesel. Bloody disgrace.

The pickup he viewed was only five years old, and in decent enough nick. The guy had seemed alright and was happy to hold on to it until later this evening. With that done, he'd pulled over into a lay-by just before the opening to the gates of the Altnaglas estate. The sword was held within a leather scabbard and he'd put a sheet over it, in the back seat. He had been up half the night polishing it and it was as ready as it would ever be.

The heat in the car and the sound of the radio had lulled him off to sleep. He had been awoken by a bang on the window, and jerked awake to see a thin man in brightly coloured walking gear staring at him. Jamie wound down the window.

'Are you OK?' The man was German, a woman with a droopy sun hat behind him.

'Aye, aye, fine, dead on, thanks.' Winding up the window again, he started the car and drove on up the track. He passed the big house of Altnaglas and carried on, further up the glen, right up to the gates of Kilchroan Lodge, the address Geordie Gilroy had given him. There was a steel-grey Range Rover parked in the wide gravel turning circle at the front of the house, and a handful of other swanky cars.

The house itself was unrecognisable from the last time Jamie had been up there, as a boy. Then it had been a dilapidated Victorian hunting lodge, the exterior shabby with peeling paint, rusty dog kennels and a stable block with a sagging roof. Now there was no sign of the outbuildings or kennels, but the house itself looked about three times the size, gleaming white as a wedding cake with two winged extensions built on either end and an immaculate expanse of velvety lawn at the front. The place had evidently undergone a bit of an upgrade.

There was no sign of life until he heard a whirring, whining sound and saw a dark green Argocat with a covered roof and extra seats bucketing down from the hill. There was a dead deer strapped to the back and three or four big men in the seats. Jamie recognised the man driving; the slicked silver hair, the dark suit now swapped for camouflage hunting gear. Geordie Gilroy, the prize stag himself.

He'd looked down at his stale, stained clothes. His teeth felt furry, his mouth a midden. He wasn't going to present anything to anyone in that state. He'd turned the Fiesta around for the journey back down the hill. He'd go home, surprise Lena, and he'd be back, later.

Now he came out of the shower and put on a white shirt and suit trousers. He dithered for a while about a tie; decided against it.

'So handsome,' Lena exclaimed, when she saw him. She dished up the pasta and he ate as speedily as he dared, trying not to spill sauce on the shirt. Before he left she made him wear the tie after all, fastening it with the little silver pin in the shape of a stag that had been the first present she'd ever given him.

The sun was just beginning to go down when he arrived back at Kilchroan Lodge, and he felt a prickle of nervous energy as he drew up. The other cars had gone; the grey Range Rover was now the only vehicle parked by the house. By the time Jamie stood on the step, holding the sword in his arms, he felt far more jumpy than he had anticipated.

He lifted the iron knocker on the front door and rapped it several times, but no one answered. He waited, and waited, but still no one came to the door.

Anna

Jerome Mondegrene is hunched in his chair, glowering out of the window. This is a man who knew my great-grandfather, whom my grandmother Netta and my dad worked for, who gave Dad the land that I grew up on. When I last met him three years ago or so, I didn't know how enmeshed he was in the history of my family, his shadow-shifter's shape. And yet in this shrivelled shell there seems to be so little.

I look over at John Teelin, asking him mutely to say something. His eyes meet mine and he gives me a small nod. Then he introduces himself to Mondegrene, shaking his hand, and sits down opposite him.

'A fine day we're having,' he says. He gestures to the rain-washed window, clasping his hands in his lap. Mondegrene makes no reply. His eyes are moving across the back wall of the room behind us.

'I have a photograph I'd like to show you,' John Teelin continues. Still Mondegrene says nothing as John Teelin leans forward, and takes a copy of *Tales from an Argyll Peninsula* out of his bag. He turns to the centre page, where the MacArthur family are assembled in front of Crois na Coille. He extends the open book to Mondegrene. 'Netta MacArthur,' he says, pointing. 'I believe she worked for you, at one time. Do you remember her, I wonder?'

He might as well not have spoken. Mondegrene looks past him with eyes like jellied eels. John Teelin closes the book with a thud, and only then does Mondegrene turn his head.

'Oh, do go on, dear boy,' he says. His voice is thin, reedy, but still heavy with sarcasm.

John Teelin opens the book once more and repeats his question, but although Mondegrene continues to stare at him as he talks, he makes no reply.

'Alright so.' John Teelin puts the book down and straightens, a hand resting on his knee. His voice when he speaks again has an edge of frustration to it.

'We'll try this another way. We know you took Netta MacArthur to the station the night she left here on her way to Canada. We just want to know what happened after that. Did she get the boat in the end? Or go somewhere else? What do you know about that?'

Mondegrene is still glaring mutely at John Teelin when one of the carers bustles up to his chair with a bowl of soup and a paper bib. As she fixes the bib on his front, Mondegrene turns to fix me with his watery stare.

'I've learnt in my life,' he says, his voice quavering, 'that you can't even trust the staff to look after themselves, let alone to look after you. You should know that, Anna MacArthur.'

You're a liar, I think. A liar.

We leave and sit in the car outside.

'Well,' John Teelin says. 'That was interesting.'

'That's one way of putting it,' I say. I feel strangely shaky. I ask for a draw of his cigarette and he passes it to me. 'He said nothing to you on purpose.' I inhale the bitter smoke and try not to cough. 'He was trying to play you like a fiddle.'

'You're right, of course. He's not going to tell us anything.'

I sit quietly, seething with frustration.

John Teelin smiles, and I see the glimmer of the little crescent-shaped scar on the bridge of his nose. 'Bollocks to him, then.' He says. 'People like that, they aren't worth the time of day, no matter what they know.'

We look at each other for a couple of seconds. I can't tell what he is thinking. I pass him the cigarette and pull the passenger door of the Golf closed.

He looks up to the sky through the open car window. 'You know,' he says, 'I feel like I've been round here a while, but I've hardly seen anything of the place.'

'The sights,' I say.

'That's it exactly. The sights.'

'And what did you have in mind?'

'As I'm saying, I have no idea. I thought I could draw upon some local knowledge.'

'What do you want to know?'

'I'd like to see the sea,' he says.

'It's over there.' I point. 'You know, between the land and the sky.'

He actually turns to look and I can't help but laugh.

'Very witty, MacArthur.'

'It's Anna to you.'

'Anna,' he says. It is ridiculous, how much I like him saying my name.

'If it's water you want,' I say, 'you can get down to the loch not far from here. There's the path. It's a circle, down and back through those trees. If you want to go.'

'I do want to go.'

'Come on, then,' I say. 'I'll show you.'

'It's past one. Is there a pub or something where we can get a bite to eat first?'

I grin. 'I'm sure there's somewhere that will do us a nice bowl of soup.'

An hour or so later we leave the car beside the opening of the path that leads down through the trees. We walk down to the shore side by side. I feel like breaking into a run, jumping to try and catch overhanging branches like a child. There is the press of energy inside me: power, even, pushing at my sides so I walk taller and take up more space. I feel like I might say anything, do as I please, and it would be alright.

I tell him that he should watch out for tree roots.

'Forget the hotel,' he says, 'you should do this for a living. Guided tours. You could go on the buses with one of those tightly knotted scarves and a small headset.'

'You're a visionary. Just one of the many career paths I've never considered.'

'Ah, there's still time.'

'Apparently,' I say. 'I'm younger than you, anyway.'

'You are. And look at me. Eternal student. Lived off the state since I was eighteen.'

'Have you?'

'Well. Spent a good few summers pulling pints. And one changing tyres in a garage. I auditioned for Riverdance back then, too.'

'No.' I burst out laughing, before reining myself in. 'Sorry. Did you really?'

'Yeah, really. Couldn't have done it anyway. It was when my mam was sick.'

'Oh.'

'Not really up my street to be honest.'

'The women are very beautiful.'

'They are, of course.' He grins wickedly at me. 'And the men are very handsome. I thought I'd be perfect.'

I'm trying to think of a suitably arch reply when I trip, nearly measuring my length on the path, and he grabs me by the arm, hauls me upright. 'Steady. Mind those roots, will you? Can't have the tour guide cracking her skull.'

I laugh, and he does too, and the sound snags in my ears. The handful of times I've been high, it felt like this. Below us I can see the loch through the trees, silvery calm.

'How's your mum keeping?' he asks.

424

'Yeah, she's OK. She's in one of her good phases. We had a proper conversation the other day.'

'Yeah?'

'We talked about my dad.'

'That's good.' When I don't reply he looks at me sideways. 'Is it good?'

'Yes,' I say. 'It was good. It was.'

I can't tell whether he squeezes my arm or takes an uneven step.

'You must think my family is totally dysfunctional,' I say.

'No more than the usual. Not that I have much of a family to judge it by.' He shrugs. 'It's the lineage of these things anyway, isn't it? How things have come to be the way they are. I mean, the causes of our actions aren't the same as the reasons we act.'

'You know, if I'm going to be a tour guide, maybe you can find a job making up cryptic crossword clues.'

'Well, OK.' He opens his free hand, considering it, then clicks his fingers. 'Here's an example. It was the news about Josephine, finding out what happened to her, that caused me to come back.'

'Right.'

'But if I'm being honest, that's not the reason I'm still here.'

'I see.' We have come to a standstill by the shore of the loch. The rain has lifted but there is a white fog lying low on the water. It is as if the colour has been leached out of the world entirely, the whole scene black and grey and white.

'So why are you still here?' I ask him.

'Would you look at that, now,' John Teelin says. 'Beautiful.' He tips his head back, staring at the sky, shading his eyes with his fingers. He is wearing the dark wool jacket I remember from the first day I saw him at Crois na Coille. I want, very much, to put my arms around him.

'There, look,' he says. 'Heron.'

I follow his hand, to the bird clanking across the sky, mechanical in flight.

I take a deep breath. 'Last night,' I say. 'I—' but he breaks in.

'Do you have another fella?'

'No,' I say, in surprise. My heart lifts, with the truth of it. 'I don't.'

He crouches down, ducking his head. He is picking up stones and inspecting them, discarding them.

'Do you?' I ask, thinking of what Erin said. My voice sounds rough. 'I mean, do you have someone?'

I'm fully expecting him to say no, but he doesn't. Instead he nods, without lifting his head. 'There is someone I'm fond of, right enough.'

'Oh.' The word comes out of me involuntarily, like the sudden twinge in my wrists, the diving sensation in my belly. I stand still, watching him.

He stands up, a stone in his hand. He holds it up to the light with narrowed eyes, inspecting its edges, then turns away from me to skim it on the loch's leaden surface.

'I haven't known her very long,' he says.

'Right.' I feel slightly sick.

'When I first met her, she made it pretty clear she didn't think much of me.'

'Right,' I repeat. This seems to be the only word I'm capable of.

'Yeah. She told me where to get off, alright.' He skims another stone, in six perfect leaps. 'Prickly. We had a bit of a set-to about the selkies,' he says.

I look up sharply. He is still not looking my way, but I see his lips curving.

I pick up a small pebble and throw it at him.

He ducks, and laughs. 'Her aim isn't up to much either, in fairness,' he says. 'Sure, I shouldn't be thinking of her at all. I

426

think I—' He stops laughing, his eyes meeting mine. 'I can't seem to not think about her,' he says, quietly. 'All the time, if I'm honest.'

I can't move from the spot I'm standing on, or say anything at all.

'It was all that was on my mind that last day,' he is saying, now. 'In the yard, when I left. When I'd come back. How to see you again.' He's looking at me as if he's asked me a question to which he's not sure he wants the answer. I've never seen him look so uncertain.

'You could have said,' I manage at last.

'I couldn't. But I am now. Saying.'

We stand facing each other; I'm not sure who takes the first step forward, but the distance between us is somehow closed. I stand, tentatively, on my toes and slip my hands under his coat. There is delight in pressing my palms to his back, in feeling the warmth and the solidity of his body through his shirt as he folds me tightly in his arms.

'You know, I wasn't at all sure this would happen,' I say into his neck, and I feel him smiling.

'Were you not.' His lips are soft against my ear.

'Were you?'

'Well.' He gives a tiny murmur, like a laugh cut short, and touches my cheek with his thumb. His hands are warm, his fingertips slightly rough. 'I had my hopes.'

I could reply to this, but I just smile and turn my head a little, leaning so my mouth brushes his, and then he is kissing me and it is wonderful.

Jamie

He knocked again and waited, before walking around the side of Kilchroan Lodge, unsure of what to do. The grounds, like the house itself, were pristine: not a weed in the gravel, not a blade of grass out of place. Around the back of the house, he tried a door and found it unlocked. He leaned his head inside.

'Hello?' His voice fell into the empty space, returning in a faint echo, and Jamie hesitated a moment. 'Screw it,' he muttered, and slipped inside, finding himself in a shadowy tiled room which smelt of wax jackets and leather.

There was light coming from under the door in front of him and he opened it to find himself in a long corridor, low-ceilinged. The corridor was lit by electric lights shaped to look like flaming torches on the walls, and paintings of every size and description. Modern art with garish colours and abstract patterns were crammed up against dark oil paintings of fruit and hunting scenes. Nudes sprawled on untidy sheets abutted portraits of haughty-looking characters in grey wigs and frilly clothing. There were paintings of gleaming, muscular horses, solemn children who looked as if they'd never been young, piles of dead birds. It was weirdly quiet.

Jamie caught sight of himself in a great gilded mirror as he walked down the corridor. He looked furtive and vaguely ridiculous in his smart clothes, carrying the enormous sword encased in leather. At the end of the corridor he opened a thickly studded door on to a small snug room. There was yet another door on the opposite wall, next to the hearth in which a log fire was burning. Two squat leather armchairs with studs in the arms were pulled up close to the flames on either side of a low table. Near the fireside there was a stuffed wildcat, its mouth stretched in a dried-up snarl.

Jamie looked around the walls, and his breath caught suddenly in his throat. On the other side of the room, opposite the fireplace, there hung an elegant basket-hilted sword. Swirls and hearts etched on the blade. He would have recognised it anywhere – it was the other sword from the pair Angus John had found on the hill. And hanging beside that – the Mondegrene Dirk. Not the replica he himself had made for Jerome Mondegrene; he knew that at once. The original, then? The one that Bruce had told him was lost?

Jesus, Jamie thought. What were these doing here? He stepped closer, feeling the heat of the fire prickle his back as he stared upwards. The firelight played off the burnished steel, the perfectly graceful taper of the dirk's blade. It was the original alright. He'd studied enough photos while making the replica.

He was straining upwards on the balls of his feet to read the engraved inscription, *of kerns and gallowglasses is supplied,* when a shadow fell across the white wall in front of him.

'MacArthur,' said a voice. 'I see you've come dressed as the birthday boy.'

Jamie spun round; the sword he was carrying caught on the tartan carpet and nearly sent him sprawling. 'Mr Gilroy,' he said. His voice sounded more confident than he felt. His heart had started to pound. He'd rehearsed what he was going to say, before, but that didn't really seem to apply any more.

Geordie Gilroy moved into the room, closing the door next to the fire silently behind him. 'Sit.' He motioned to the leather armchairs and sat down in one himself. Jamie followed suit, remembering the bizarre, menacing waltz when they had first met outside the pub. The fire crackled and spat a tiny spark into the room. Jamie set the sword across the arms of the chair he was sitting in, so it lay in front of him like the bar on a rollercoaster.

'Let yourself in, did you?' Gilroy's eyes flicked to the swords on the wall and then back to Jamie.

'Well, you see, I tried—' Jamie began, but Gilroy cut him off mid-sentence.

'Tell me,' he said, 'have you seen this place before?'

Jamie nodded. 'Yeah. Not for years, though. It was about half the size back then. And really run-down.'

'I see.'

'I mean, it's incredible now. I've never seen somewhere so immaculate and . . . grand.' Jamie watched Gilroy's face as he spoke, trying to find guidance about what to say.

'You were giving these close inspection.' Gilroy pointed up to the sword and the dirk on the wall opposite the fire.

'I suppose I was, aye.' Jamie twisted around to look at them. 'I was surprised to see the dirk, if I'm honest. When Bruce asked me to make the replica, he said the original had been lost.'

Gilroy's eyes never left Jamie's face. 'Yes,' he said. 'And I found it.'

Jamie nodded uncomfortably, unsure whether or not this was meant to be a joke, and Gilroy made a grunt that might have been a laugh, his expression between smiling and snarling before his face flattened once again. He leaned forward and said, 'Are you going to show me what you've made me?'

'Of course.' Jamie looked down at the sword in his lap and began to prattle. 'It's been a huge challenge in size and in scale. One of my best jobs ever – I can't thank you enough for the opportunity. Here.' He offered the sword up to Gilroy.

Gilroy stood up wordlessly and lifted the sword from his hands. Standing above Jamie and holding the sword vertically, he rested the point of the weapon in its scabbard on the ground and unsheathed the blade in one quick movement. The blade slid from the scabbard like a salmon leaping upstream, silver flashing in the firelight, and Gilroy stretched his arm above his head before lowering the sword, holding it out in front of him and looking straight down the edge of the steel blade. He turned his wrist to inspect the other side, his head back, one eye half-closed.

Jamie got up from his chair. Gilroy was over a foot taller than him, and there was something intimidating about standing shoulder to shoulder with a man that size now brandishing a three-and-a-half-foot-long sword with ease.

'As you can see,' he said, 'crafted exactly to your specifications. At forty-two inches I'd say it's the biggest piece I've made yet.' He moved round to Gilroy's other side. 'I have to congratulate you on your taste, sir. And if I could get you to hold it – like this, see, you'll feel the weight of it, perfect in the balance. Such a simple design, but I think beauty's always to be found in simplicity. It certainly has its own challenge.'

Gilroy turned his head and looked at Jamie square in the eye at point-blank range. His jaw was hanging slightly ajar.

'How long did it take you to make this in the end?' he asked.

It was not the question Jamie had expected. Before he could answer, Gilroy raised his right hand, the sword held tight in his grip. The blade flashed again as he drew his arm back and then Gilroy threw the sword like a javelin across the room, where it ricocheted off the stone wall before landing on the floor with a thud.

Jamie stood rooted to the spot, staring at where it had hit the ground. He had been too shocked to even step back. Gilroy was right in his face now. 'However long it took you, son,' he was saying, 'it was too long.' He stabbed a finger towards the chair. 'Sit,' he said again, and Jamie sat.

'It's taken me twenty years to build what you see around you now.' Gilroy's voice was not loud, but every word seemed to have its own weight. 'My first twenty years of work were pissed away in the police. So take it from me, I know the difference between a day wasted and a day put to use.' He unfastened the button at the bottom of his suit jacket and sat down once more, folding his hands in front of him in a triangle. 'You and that pretty little girlfriend of yours, you've a baby on the way, haven't you? Time to start taking your craft seriously. There's real money to be made, you hear me? Real money.'

Jamie said nothing. Beside him, Gilroy kept speaking. 'Yes, I took the Mondegrene Dirk from Altnaglas House. And I took that sword there, too.' He pointed to where the pair hung on the wall. 'It took me many years to get the full measure of Jerome Mondegrene but I saw through him quickly enough. The public schooling, the theatrics. He was weak. A weak man crippled by his own good fortune. You see, MacArthur, I've taken everything I've got from someone else, ripped it from their hands, but I've never taken more from anyone than Jerome Mondegrene. And the best of it, the worst of it, is that I've always known he wants me to.' Gilroy laughed, his head tilted to one side. 'When Bruce told me he knew of someone who could make a copy of that dirk, I was interested. Usual story. Old Mondie, misty-eyed about something he barely remembered, asking questions, going on about it. I wasn't going to give him this one.' He pointed to the dirk on the wall. 'This one is mine now. But to think there was a man somewhere who'd pour blood and sweat and time into replicating another man's work. I had to meet a man like that. You have an eye for detail, MacArthur. As a forger does. You can focus. And I can see you're strong. Work-strong, just like your father was. Just a pity the mind didn't follow suit, in his case. Every day, you see, I put to good use. And you're going to start doing the same. You're going to come and work for me. We'll find an excellent market for your big toys. I know of it already. One where the eye sees plenty and the heart doesn't grieve over it. An excellent market.'

Gilroy propped himself back in his chair, stretching out his legs in front of him. 'You see, ' he went on, 'we've a friend in common. Your stepfather Bruce and I met not long before I met young Donnie MacArthur, all those years ago. Did he ever tell you of the day he was half drowned in the loch, your father?' Gilroy laughed. 'I'd bet money he never told you about that.' He made a cutting gesture with his hand. 'But to continue. I spent ten years working my way up here, laughing at old Mondie's shit jokes, listening to him talking endlessly about himself.'

Gilroy paused. The room was deadly quiet except for the hissing of a log in the grate. He nudged it with the toe of his boot so it fell to ashes, releasing a shower of sparks. 'The old house of Altnaglas used to be grand,' he said. 'Used to be an impressive place, the whole estate. But Jerome Mondegrene, he sat in there, in that great house, like a rat in a hole. I was his only visitor for the better part of ten years. No one has lived there since he was moved out to that care home, no next of kin, nothing.' He settled back in his chair, his hands mapping out his words as he spoke. 'So I will be taking on Altnaglas myself, when that old bastard's dead and buried. A business venture. And I'm not minded to pay serious money for something I could near enough get for nothing. So while the place has been empty, I've had a few boys up there, quietly, discreetly taking the artworks off the wall, silverware out of the drawers, radiators off the walls, pulling the fireplaces out, all tucked away for later. It's got to look worthless, you understand. When I buy the estate for a song I'll bring the place back to life. A revival. The art will go back on the walls, the original fireplaces back in place, all marble and gold and teak, and I'll have made a fortune before I've even started. The place'll be mine. The situation is progressing, you see. Things are

433

ramping up now.' Gilroy leaned in. 'Old Mondie's not got long left, and I'm still shifting all the shite that's left down there. Keep the best, burn the rest.' He settled himself back for a moment, looking at Jamie as if he expected a reply.

'OK,' Jamie said. A nutter, Anna had said. Well, she hadn't been far wrong.

Gilroy folded his arms. 'No doubt you'll be wondering, MacArthur, why I'm telling you this. Well, we all have our parts to play in this old world we find ourselves in, and here's yours. What you're going to do is this. You're going to drive a van for me down to Glasgow, as and when, to meet a friend of mine. Give him whatever's in the back, just the stuff that's not worth my while keeping, and you'll be paid in cash when you get back. Your first run'll be tonight.'

Gilroy reached inside his jacket and withdrew a thick envelope. He nodded towards the claymore, lying where it had fallen on the ground, and lobbed the envelope on to the table. 'Here's the money you're due,' he said. 'Mind there's more where that came from. In the meantime, I'll find a few – collectors, shall we say, desperate for original pieces, infamous dirks or mythical swords.' He laughed. 'And I'll pay you to make whatever old shit they're after. Give the people what they want, eh? They'll never be able to tell the difference, and a few extra quid should keep you and that foreign lassie of yours together. A looker, isn't she? You stick with me, MacArthur, and I'll keep you right.' He stood up. 'And if you're anything like your father, you'll need all the help you can get.'

Gilroy slapped Jamie on the side of his arm and grinned like a wild dog. 'You wait there. I'll be back.' And with that, he made for the door.

Jamie was shaking, furious. He could hardly bear to leave the claymore on the floor any longer. Working on it for the week, he'd barely slept. It was the best thing he'd ever made. He went over to the far wall and knelt down to pick it up, but as he did so Gilroy had circled the room and was now pressing his boot to the sword's blade, crushing Jamie's fingers underneath just to the point of pain.

'You see, MacArthur?' he said quietly.

Jamie looked up at the man above him. That quiet voice went on.

'Your father thought he was a smart one. Oh, he had the looks, and charm enough to think himself a big fish in a small pond. But I've seen him bested in a fight, I've seen his hands all over a cheap slut while his family were sleeping in a sodding caravan, and I know he was a coward, who left you with nothing. And if you're not careful you'll go the same way. You're going to have to work hard. And if you ever manage that, to work harder still. So I'll say this to you now. I tell very few people my business, Jamie MacArthur, so if I hear anything about this on the wind, I'll know it's come from you, and you'll end up dead like a dog at the side of the road. Like your father.' Gilroy stepped back, ran a hand over his hair. A signet ring gleamed darkly on his little finger. He pointed to the sword. 'You can start by putting that over there with the rest of the metalwork. I'll be back for you in a minute.' And with that he left the room, closing the door behind him.

Alone, Jamie listened to the footsteps dying away along the corridor beyond. Unbelievable. It was – unbelievable. He was sweating, his shirt soaked, his hands damp and rage running through him like a charge. Fucking standing on my hand, he thought. One side of his face felt ready to burst into flames with the heat as he looked once again to the weapons on the wall. Stolen property, those pieces are, he thought. He thinks he's a laird already. Thieving son of a bitch. To hell with this.

He got up from the floor and went to the table, opening the envelope and staring down at the folded notes before chucking them on to the floor. He almost laughed, stepping over to lift the claymore from the floor with both hands. The steel purred as he replaced it in the scabbard that lay abandoned by Gilroy's chair. It was perfect. He put the claymore over his shoulder and moved quickly across the room to unhook the sword and the Mondegrene Dirk from the wall, tucking them under his arm.

Now to find his way out. Jamie went back to the door he'd come in by, opened it with care and walked as fast as he could down the corridor. There was no sound of Gilroy as he stepped back into the tiled room and then outside into the cool damp of the gathering dusk. He ran around to the front of the house, his feet loud as gunshots on the gravel. Ripping open the Fiesta's door, he slid all three of the weapons into the back. Then he flung himself into the front seat, started the engine and knocked the gearstick into reverse. The tyres skidded a little as he shot the car backwards, turning, and then he was accelerating down the drive.

His hands on the wheel were buzzing with adrenaline now, and the looming realisation of what he had just done. He stepped on the accelerator and the little car pelted forward. He passed the gloomy, shuttered bulk of Altnaglas House in a blur. The Fiesta's engine whined. It was only as he wrenched the wheel and turned right at the end of the drive on to the main road that he noticed, with a sickening lurch, that the arrow on the fuel gauge was swinging around the red triangle.

'Oh, Jesus Christ,' he said aloud.

Two minutes later down the peninsula road a grey 4x4 appeared over the brow of the hill behind him. It drew closer, and closer, and suddenly the headlights were switched on to full beam, flooding the interior of the Fiesta with white light.

Jamie passed one turn-off, then another. The car behind him was so close he could swear it was almost within touching distance. He knew this road well; now he leant forward, straining to see the next turn-off where he might be able to shake off his pursuer. The Balsterrick Care Home flashed past on his right and he saw the Forestry track opening up on his left. At the last minute, Jamie stabbed his foot on the brake and turned the wheel full lock. The Fiesta cornered on two wheels and for a second he was sure it was going to roll. But then he felt the bumper thud into the bank and was jolted forward, his chest thumping against the steering wheel as the car stopped dead. Behind him there was a shriek of brakes and Jamie twisted round, grabbing the claymore from the back seat before flinging the door open and leaping out.

The grey Range Rover had slammed to a halt, the headlights flaring. He recoiled in the bright, shocking light. The headlights dimmed. The door was flung open and Geordie Gilroy barrelled out of the car towards him.

Jamie turned round and started to run.

Mondegrene

He dressed carefully in his room. The blue flannel jacket with the Paisley silk lining. He combed his hair. When he was ready, he took the book of Tennyson's *Poems* from the drawer beside the bed and opened it. He removed the Luger from the hollowed-out space, checked the magazine and placed the gun in the inside pocket of his jacket. He read the words in the verse framed by the cut pages.

> *Here at the quiet limit of the world,*
> *A white-hair'd shadow roaming like a dream.*

He stood for a time, staring at those words. Then he drew his thumb and index finger across his eyelids in a pincer motion. He closed the book and placed it on the table. When he left the room, he pulled the door shut behind him with a soft click.

He moved carefully and deliberately – and slowly, of course – down the corridor. A nurse came towards him, walked past him.

'Good evening,' he said to her, and she smiled.

'On your way to watch *Neighbours*? It's already started.' And she bustled off. Ignorance, he thought. The TV lounge was blaring, bodies propped in chairs watching an old Bruce Lee film. Perhaps somebody was exercising their own quiet rebellion. Well good luck to them. Good luck to them all. He slipped in and stood beside the French windows, hands behind his back, staring out at the yellow hill, or what could be seen of it in the gathering dusk, keeping a watchful eye on the room behind him reflected in the glass. He pressed the door lever down gently to see if it was locked and it gave way at his touch. He waited a moment longer until the coast was clear, then slid the door open just enough to step outside and none of the stuffed carcasses inside, including the staff, were any the wiser.

He looked forward to this. Oh, he did, really. He'd always known, in the end, what it would come to.

He could not move fast and God knew he had little stamina left these days, but he would walk until he fell. He had only to follow one step with another, and once he reached the cover of the trees he would be undetectable for as long as it took.

It seemed he would be accompanied by old Lord Tennyson. The words from that poem from the book, one of those he'd learned in school, kept revolving in his head.

A soft air fans the cloud apart; there comes
A glimpse of that dark world where I was born.
Once more the old mysterious glimmer steals
From thy pure brows ...

Oh, they sounded good enough, those lines. He'd introduced her to Tennyson on one of those days in the library. He hadn't been able to tell what she had thought of the poetry. It had been hard to tell what Netta MacArthur thought of anything.

He let his thoughts turn to her again, as they had done ever since the young pair had visited him that morning. Looking at him as though he were a murderer.

They knew less than nothing between the pair of them.

There had been no trigger pulled, no hands about her throat. He had not looked death in the face, as he had with the rabbits he'd snared when he was a boy. He'd never wanted Netta gone, but then – she was.

He could not bear to think of it as murder – something so crass, so common. Every man his age had a story of killing, of death and the enemy. He'd spun himself different tales as his life had stretched away from the night in question. An accident, a tragedy, a mistake – never murder.

He had held in his hand the instrument of death. He tapped his fingers to his jacket now and felt the shape of the Luger. He knew as much as anyone what it was to kill: the Kraut he had shot in the throat in that Belgian cellar in 1914, the year he had put away childish things. He could see that dead German's grey face still, and thought of how that lad's whole life had been nothing but a prelude to the death he was to be dealt, lying with one eye open in a puddle of filth and blood.

Murder was something to be succeeded at, to overcome, to be done well. Kill or be killed. He had not been killed.

But what had happened to Netta had nothing to do with that. In the past, he'd questioned if it even mattered whether she had lived or died; whether she had, in the end, walked to the station after all, was even now in some other country, laughing at his memory.

But I am here, he thinks, to allow myself the truth. Once, and only once. Because I could only bear it the once.

His steps were slowing but he kept walking up the hill. Once he could have run the distance he'd travelled in under ten seconds. Perhaps that time would come again, in another consciousness.

The belief that he had done the right thing had sustained him, or at least had kept him from despairing altogether in life itself. But it had been careless of him, perhaps, not to have tidied up better at the time. Of course she was unstable, Netta, the black sheep. She was self-important, inscrutable. And then

440

there was the boy. The child he knew belonged to him, although it had never been said aloud. His son. His heir. Donald, for whom he, Mondegrene, should have provided, to whom he should have spoken the truth, before Donald's life had been taken. Some things could not be measured by any degree other than regret and sorrow.

He'd done what he could. He'd done what he thought was best, despite having little cause to. He'd arranged for Netta to spend some time away after the business with the child, trying to give him away to some pedlar woman and Lord knew what else. Her mind was disordered. It had been an unhealthy thing for her, the bearing of that child. He'd found somewhere calm, where she could recover her senses and her reason. Somewhere his own mother had once had recourse to. And he'd opened the coffers to pay for it, even visited her in the years she spent there. She had seemed peaceful enough on his visits. He told himself that peace could turn to gratitude.

But she had not been the same on her return to Altnaglas. She was unsettled, disturbed. Her eyes, where once there had been the snap of intellect, seemed clouded with the feral glaze of a wounded animal. It was as if she could no longer see what was best for her. It was as if she had no desire to make good. When she spoke – and she spoke rarely enough – she talked only of her son, now apparently in the care of her sister.

There had been no question of her returning to his employ. It would have been . . . unseemly, he thought. And besides, her mind was not fit for work in that anarchic and savage state. But she had stayed in the room at Altnaglas that he had given over to her. He visited her in the evenings, for company, as he saw fit. And when she had requested it, he had even allowed her the visit to London she had begged for, after victory had been declared in Europe. It had been against his better judgement, of course, and the thanks he'd received for his leniency had arrived in a brown envelope from the Canadian Wives' Bureau. Delivered to Altnaglas House with her name on the front.

Naturally he had opened it. Such betrayal he had felt on seeing those tickets, the passport, the details of some strangers in Newfoundland upon whom she had decided to foist herself, and them having never so much as set eyes on her. The relatives of Vincent Randall, that flash in the pan – it was madness. It was for her own good that he'd done what he had, even as he had played along with her madcap plan that night, which was to retrieve her son from the care of her sister, to take trains all the way to Plymouth, to board the RMS *Aquitania* and set sail – Canada, for pity's sake. To save her from ruinous error he had agreed to take Netta to the station. He'd been sure that he could make her see sense. But it turned out she had no sense left.

No one knew of the burden that caused him.

Then there was Donald's daughter, Anna, his own grand-daughter. Standing in front of his chair this very morning. He could have told her, then, of this pain, and this sorrow, and this life. He could have told her of her lineage. But he could not imagine a single breath without the lie that had shielded him, had cradled for him the tiny sanctuary of redemption and resolve that had allowed him to last.

The documents of travel had briefly proved a conundrum. Netta's non-arrival in Newfoundland could spark questions, he knew. But that, too, had resolved itself so sweetly it could not be but fate. He'd heard her joking with those Irish girls, once upon a time, about how they could pass for sisters. And it was true, the dark-haired one in particular did look like her, passably enough, if you discounted Netta's uncommon eyes, which did not show in the photograph. Easy enough to pass on the paperwork, the new life contained within them, to her – to Josephine Halloran.

442

The girl had taken what he had offered with alacrity. Of course she had; she had precious little else going for her. He did not foresee problems with the switch. He, with his breeding, knew a good actress when he saw one: the girl could have gone on the stage. And Josephine Halloran, at least, had been grateful. Indeed, her gratitude had taken several pleasing forms.

He'd always told himself he'd done the right thing, but today he must confront the fact that in the end he'd done nothing. That he'd made more effort each day since to dress himself than he had to save Netta the night she'd planned to leave. Of all the tales he'd told himself, the one he could never admit was that he had failed her where he had most hoped to succeed. The truth would live with him now, and the truth would die with him today.

He climbed the hill slowly, pausing after each small ascent, Tennyson's poem in his head. Tithonus, lover of Eos, Goddess of dawn, who had been granted the immortality of a god but had aged like a man.

Tithonus, who yearned for the release of death.

Thou seest all things, thou wilt see my grave:
Thou wilt renew thy beauty morn by morn;
I earth in earth forget these empty courts,
And thee returning on thy silver wheels.

He paused, his breath a weak flame in his lungs. For almost a hundred years he had walked on the earth, sleeping through the renewal of each new day, the dawn breaking pale on the yellow hill each morning. The everlasting earth would close over him when he was gone. To forget was to remember only those who still mattered. In death, he too would lie down beneath the unseeing eyes of an unforgiving eternity.

He felt tears in his eyes, as he'd supposed he would. If I knew you were here, he told her, I would not stop looking for you. I would find you, today.

Not much further now.

Anna

The sun is setting, melting into the silver dish of the loch, by the time we set slowly off to the car, hand in hand. As we drive away I lean my head against the window and narrow my eyes so the blurry pines flicker staccato in my vision. Lightdark lightdarklight.

Rod Stewart sings 'Mandolin Wind' on the tape player and beside me John Teelin hums along, one hand loosely on the wheel, the other holding mine. We are driving back to the hotel where I have my final shift in the bar tonight. He isn't leaving until tomorrow.

I look down at his hand where it rests in my lap, at my fingers laced around his. I feel as if something that was filling my vision has been lifted out of the way, and my eyes have to adjust to this new spaciousness around me.

I am thinking about Netta, and whether I'll ever know what happened to her, of what she endured, of the burden she carried.

I've been such a child, I think.

John Teelin takes his hand away to change gear, and I look at him in profile, the beauty drawn in the lines and angles of his face. I watch his eyes as they flick from the road ahead to the rear-view mirror. He's not what I thought he was, at first. He doesn't seem to make things easy, but I think he tries to make things better. He is kind. And I think I've acquired a taste for his particular brand of humour which I completely missed at the beginning.

445

'I can see you over there,' he says, breaking into my thoughts. 'Eyeballing me. What's on your mind?'

'I was thinking that I should thank you,' I say.

'What's that?' He glances over to where I am sitting.

'Thank you,' I repeat. 'I wanted to say thank you.'

'Why?'

'For sharing those things about your family with me. I never thought about family that much before. I suppose I'd tried not to think about all of that. But when you talk about it, it's something to be discovered, to be valued. It's helped me think about things . . . differently. So thanks.'

He shakes his head. 'And here was I thinking it was you helping me,' he says. 'There's two sides to every hill, as my mam used to say.' He smiles at me. 'The upside and the downside.'

'Which one am I?'

'Ah. The top of the hill, of course.'

'Very smooth.'

'Well. It's a slippery slope,' he says, and laughs at his own joke as I roll my eyes.

The road we are driving has narrowed, squeezed between the loch and the hill which towers above us and is held back by wire nets where the rock has been blasted. The loch comes to an end and we pass the care home on our right. There's a layby up ahead with a couple of cars parked in it. We are very near the Altnaglas cemetery where we found Bridget's grave, and about a hundred yards from the entrance to the care home, on the other side of the road. I think of Jerome Mondegrene, how time has twisted him around himself like ivy. I lean over, kiss John Teelin on the cheek, and he slips his arm around my shoulders and pulls me close.

'Anna,' he says, 'I'll be in Glasgow in a few weeks. Do you think maybe, if you're free, you'd like to come and see me in the town?'

He sounds almost unsure; I try not to smile. 'I'd like that,' I say.

'Yeah?'

'Yes.' I kiss his ear and he grins, and I feel happiness intense enough to name it.

As we get closer to the layby I see a large grey 4x4 with its door open near a small car, a white smudge in the fading light. I lean forward as we pass. I know that car.

'Stop.' I twist my body round in the seat; the belt tightens against the side of my neck. 'Stop. John, can we turn round? That's my mum's Fiesta.'

'What?'

'That was my mum's car back there. Stop, please. We need to go back.'

'Sure, I'll turn when I can, Anna,' he says calmly. He slows and does a U-turn in a wide part of the road and drives back to the layby.

'Oh my God, is it an accident?' I crane forward. The white Fiesta is wedged right up against the bank, the driver's door open and the keys still in the ignition. The Range Rover is parked close behind it, the sidelights still on. The interior is empty. John Teelin slows to a halt and I am out of the car before he's even put on the handbrake. It is quiet and the light is fading fast; in a few minutes it will be dark. I go over to the open door of my mum's car, my heart thudding painfully in my chest. The car is empty, but lying on the back seat is a short dagger with a handle that glints blue and a sword with a long blade.

I start back. 'Jamie?' I call up to the yellow hill that stretches above us. 'Jamie?'

John Teelin has got out of the car and is looking through the windows of the Range Rover. He looks across at me, his face as confused as I feel.

'I think it's my brother,' I say. 'He borrowed the car.' I turn, calling Jamie's name up into the dark trees on the bank.

447

There's a path to the woods at the far end of the layby and I climb up a few metres. I look down at John Teelin standing there, and then I look up at the hill. The way is stony and steep, the path narrow through the gorse. 'Jamie!' I yell. 'It's me. Are you there?'

'Anna,' John Teelin calls up to me, his voice low. 'Anna. You need to come back and—'

'Wait!' I stop, straining to hear. I'm sure I heard shouts, the breaking of sticks. 'There's someone up there,' I say. 'Listen.' I call Jamie's name again, but my voice is obliterated by the sudden crack that rings out from the hill above me. It is loud and trails a bouncing echo in its wake.

John Teelin is beside me now, seizing my arm. 'Anna,' he is hissing. 'Stop.' We stare at each other for a second.

'That was a fucking gunshot,' I say.

'Sounded like it.'

'They're not meant to be shooting stags at this time of year. What the hell is it?'

He is shaking his head. 'We should phone the police.'

'But the other car!' I stare down to the layby. 'Where are they, what's happened?'

'We'll phone the police. You can't go up there, Anna.'

'I can't just leave.' I turn away, breaking into a run up the rough track. My foot catches on a rock and I fall, sprawling forward on my hands and knees.

'What the—?' I hear John Teelin exclaim behind me.

I scramble up, wiping my smarting palms on my jeans. There's a sword lying in front of me. Its long, straight blade glints in the dying light. There is mud on its handle.

I keep running, leaving John Teelin far behind me. My breath is raw in my throat. I yell Jamie's name until my voice cracks.

And then finally I hear my brother's voice: weak, calling to me.

I scramble through the gorse, squeezing my eyes shut as the spiny twigs whip against my cheeks and hands, and I see him, lying up on the hill to my right. There is another figure in front of him, hunched over, motionless.

I'm crying out, running to him, dropping to my knees. Jamie's face and chest are bloody. I scream his name. My voice doesn't sound like mine; it sounds far-off and wavery and I can hear my pulse roaring in my ears. There seems to be blood everywhere; blood and bits of matter; it's on my hands now and the stench is heavy in my nostrils, pungent and metallic. 'You're bleeding.' I put my arms around him. 'What happened to you? Where are you hurt?'

'I'm OK,' he says. 'It's my arm. Just my arm. It's not my blood.'

The man in front of Jamie is on his knees, his head bowed to his chest as if in prayer. The face is hidden.

'Is he dead?' Jamie is saying. He tries to sit up, gasping with pain. 'Is he?'

I look and then look away quickly. The ground in front of the slumped figure is slick and dark with blood. 'Who is it?' I fight down a wave of nausea that yawns in my throat.

'It's Gilroy,' Jamie says. His breathing is laboured. 'Geordie Gilroy. Is he dead?' My brother struggles to lean forward. 'Anna. Is he dead?'

Mondegrene

He passes the laburnum that guards the dogs' graveyard. It had been lovely last summer when he had come down. In full bloom. He strokes the pods on the bush; golden, those pods, then poisonous. He thinks of the dogs that he's laid to rest here: Tip, Bax, Chaser, Ladybird, Bonnie, Felix, Alacrity, Sal – all the lovely creatures who have kept him company over the years. Always easier, dogs. Unequivocal. He'd felt their deaths more keenly than the passing of most of the people he'd known in his life.

Except her. He'd missed her enough. But all he'd done was not look for Netta, because, when it came to it, what was there to find?

Nothing.

The pistol is cocked in his hand and his hand does not shake. He stares down at the dark ground and wonders if he is able to kneel. *Nearer the earth, nearer, my God, to thee.*

There had been no trigger pulled, no hands about her throat.

He hears shouting on the wind and raises his head to see two figures out on the hill. Hunters, he thinks, from the lodge. But no, they are fighting. He stares, confused and disbelieving. The tall man is Geordie Gilroy. He would know him anywhere. Gilroy has caught the other man's arm, twisting it up behind his back and kicking the man's legs out from underneath him.

The man who has fallen is much younger than Gilroy. He cannot be sure, but if all things were equal he would swear it was Donnie MacArthur. But of course it cannot be Donnie, sprawled in the dirt, taking heavy blows, twisting to defend himself before Gilroy lifts him off the ground by one arm. It can't be Donnie, his beautiful boy, his son. Netta's son. He'd sacrificed them both, just as he had sacrificed himself, forgoing all that was good and guiltless, in order to protect and survive.

He hears the sound of a car down on the road below, and turns to see a blue Golf pulling into the layby. A young woman and a man get out. The couple who visited him earlier. They are scrambling up the path, shouting and searching, but there is no time now and he knows it is up to him.

The weight of the gun is familiar in his hand. He steadies his right with his left. He breathes out slowly, and squeezes the trigger.

Gilroy falls to his knees.

The sound echoes around the hill. Mondegrene draws breath, his lungs still burning. He turns around. Dusk is falling; he straightens his tie. There is one bullet left in the chamber.

He walks slowly up the yellow hill, the gun in his hand down low by his side.

Wednesday 29 January 1947

Netta

It started to snow as I walked up the hill track and the Land Rover drew up alongside me. He was hunched, hawk-like, in the cab.

'Where's the boy?'

'He's not coming.' I increased my pace, feeling the freeze on my cheeks. The Land Rover rolled at my side.

'Get in.' The voice of a man who gave orders as easily as breathing. I flexed my fingers inside my mittens. I concentrated on putting one foot in front of the other. He continued to crawl along beside me. I could sense his fury at being disobeyed. But when he spoke again his voice sounded gentle, wearied.

'Get back in, Netta.'

I looked up at the hill looming above; flakes of snow were starting to whirl into my face. 'Will you take me to the station?'

'Whatever you want. Get in. For God's sake.' He braked, then leant over and opened the door as I stopped. I climbed into the cab. It was hot inside; the heater at my feet blasted out fuggy air thick with the scent of petrol and dusty metal. He turned on the headlights and snow glittered in the beam. It looked darker outside now that I was in here.

The gearstick hit my knee as he shoved the Land Rover into reverse.

'No!' I made a grab for the metal rod as he turned the vehicle around. He knocked me away, humming tunelessly as we started back down the hill, tapping the slim steering wheel. He was wearing black fingerless gloves and the skin on his knuckles gleamed bone-white. I licked my lips. 'Take me to the station, please.' My tongue felt ragged and dry.

He laughed then, softly. 'I'm not a bloody taxi driver, Netta. Let's just have a little think about this, shall we? Leave your son? Piece of nonsense.' He reached forward and turned something on the dashboard, and the wipers began to arc across the darkening glass in front of me, squeaking faintly.

'I'm not going back.' I put my hand on the door lever, wrenched it upwards. The door swung out of my grip in the wind. He put his foot down; below me, the ground rushed past in sudden open space.

'I'm taking you back to Altnaglas, Netta, and we'll talk about the whole business there. You haven't thought this through. You don't even have a ticket for the boy, do you? And what about a passport? If you're determined, I can sort all that out. The money can be recouped, I'll make sure of it. There are departures every month at present. I can arrange for your passage on the next ship, once it's all straightened out. I'll go and get the boy myself if I have to.'

'No,' I said again, and heard my voice rising. 'No. He chose her. He chose Bella. I've nothing left, do you understand me? Just ghosts. Ghosts, everywhere.' I scrabbled to grasp the handle of the case by my feet. 'Let me out. I'll walk to the station. I'm going on my own.'

He didn't even turn his head, just stared straight ahead. 'If you get out, you'll die on this hill. Close the door, Netta.'

'I know the path. Let me out.'

The Land Rover slewed and skidded, the open door crashing back in, failing to catch and falling open once more. I leaned forward to grab the handle but he seized my right arm, squeezing the flesh so tightly below the elbow that I felt

456

the bones move. I twisted, yanking off my mitten and stabbing the rigid fingers of my free hand towards his neck, then
his eyes.

He roared as my nails gouged his skin. 'You damned bitch.'

There was a blow to my face, his fist, and I fell back against
the seat and spun to the left, out of the open door and into
empty space, down. My shoulder hit the ground and I turned
over once and lay crumpled, awaiting the second wave of pain
to surge through my body. When it had passed I got to my
feet, crossed my hands over my chest and staggered, trying to
run.

I couldn't see straight; there were splintered shards of white
in my eyes. A high keening sound in my ears. The hillock of
the small corrie was before me. I groped with my hands, nearly
on my knees as I made my way around its side. Then I
crouched down, spitting in the snow. A taste of old silver in
my mouth.

The lights of the Land Rover were still behind me. I heard
the door open. I pushed into an overhang on the side of the
hillock, burrowing in through the heather until I reached a
more gentle darkness that stank of sheep. Here I waited.

Silence. The snow was not yet thick enough for footprints.
He was listening for me, I knew. The curiosity of the hunted,
he had told me once, as we stood in the hallway of Altnaglas
beneath the mounted antlers of deer the Mondegrene family
had stalked and killed over the years. Wait long enough, be still
enough, he had said, and they cannot help themselves but
come closer.

I held my breath, squeezed my eyes shut and watched red
circles pulsate in time with the pounding of blood in my ears.
I began to count in my head, backwards from two hundred.
When I reached eighteen I heard his footfall, and then the
slam of the door and the resounding rumble of the engine as
he drove away.

Darkness, the secret song of snowfall.

I stayed crouched down for some time, thinking of the path over the hill. At last I hauled myself upright. My face felt heavy and thick and something I vaguely recognised as a welt of pain was throbbing in my shoulder, but if I held it with my other arm I could walk, I could last.

I'd been slow. I'd lost a mitten. And worse – much worse, my case – where was the case? The case with my ticket, with all my papers? Had it too fallen from the cab, or was it still in there, with him? 'Next time I'll kill him,' I said aloud, and the sound of my own voice was so comforting I said it again and then again, a mantra recited in time to my plodding feet. I thought my eyebrows might have frozen. Frostbite, I thought, Mallory and Irvine. Toes and fingers and the tips of a nose. That wouldn't happen to me, though, on my mountain. My mountain.

My head began to clear; my senses felt peeled to the bone. Pain, yes, but also warmth, flooding warmth like getting into a bath. I was well along the path. No. I was off the path, and the snow was thicker up here, much thicker, and coming down fast. Up to my knees in snow, and then my thighs, and I was falling forward. So easy, that falling. But struggling up again, remembering my father turning a dead ewe on frozen ground, the tiny lamb beneath her. There was someone up ahead of me, anyway. I could see their footprints.

Sing. I should sing. *Pale hands I loved* ... the rocking stone was on my right, its clefts filled with snow, the rocky banks where wild strawberries grew in sunshine, the river with its pearls and the man I once met there, the one who wouldn't tell me his name. When he'd kissed me he'd held the tops of my arms to keep my body steady, his hands tight enough to leave marks on my bare skin afterwards.

The snow was covering over the moon and the moon was a pearl. A pearl in the palm of darkness. I tried to sing again,

458

Pale hands I loved beside the Shalimar. But now my lips wouldn't move well; the snow had turned them to stone. Still in my head the song fell and rose. *Where are you now? Who lies beneath your spell?*

There were footprints now in the snow behind me as well as in front. Rapidly filling in. Who was in front? Who was behind? The tracks before me were small. Purposeful. I cried out with joy but my numb lips hushed the sound.

I knew she would be here, somewhere.

And just then, as if in answer, the dark up ahead parted for an instant like a drawn curtain and I saw, quite clearly, the girl in front of me: her jaunty, swinging stride. She had only to turn her head and I would see her, not dead, not gone, just here. Up here, all along.

My head came up suddenly against solid rock and I dropped to my knees again in the heathery snow. I ran my bare fingers up and down the rough stone. I had come to the caves. The bone caves. All would be well now.

I was on my hands and knees, groping in the snow, the flakes feather-warm on my arms. I had only to find the door. There was a fire behind it, I knew. I could sleep there; I could stay. My body was a ball, my knees to my chest. I tried to unwind myself, to stretch. I had only to find the door, and when I opened it I would see Bridget again. She'd be there, opening her eyes. I could feel the softness of her face under my hand, warmth flickering through every pore of her skin, the white of the blankets, everything kind, supple and stretching.

And now the light is everywhere, a great opening of light, the yellow hill suddenly golden when the sun took its slope just for a moment, the loch still in the evening, a swan rearing upright, beating its wings. And above the bright water, a cloud of starlings moving through the air like smoke, a flock of a thousand shadows, wheeling on the wind above the roosting place.

And I am wrapped within that bird-blanket, soft and indistinguishable in that murmuring mass, cradled in my own mother's arms.

And in my arms my child, a place of safe sleeping. A blanket for the baby.

To wrap him in.

To wrap him in.

Sunday 12 April 1998

Anna

We were not feral children, in that caravan. We washed. We watched repeats of *The Clangers* on a TV powered by a generator. We ate Frosties swimming in milk chilled in a fridge. The front of the fridge was stuck all over with colourful alphabet magnets with which Jamie and I would form silly, cryptic messages. Messages like 'toenails forever', or, memorably, 'broccoli is not the question'. Our clothes were more or less clean most of the time. We took out books from the library van and we went to school. And our dad was going to build our home: our real, immobile home.

When summer comes, I will build you a house, he would say.

You mean we, Donnie MacArthur, my mum would say. Us.

And you'll be barrowing the stones, then? He'd wink at her and tuck his arm around her shoulders. Sometimes she would let him, leaning into him and turning her face to his as if they saw eye to eye about everything. Sometimes she would shrug him off, shaking her head. His promise loomed over us all.

I remember the magic tricks, the cards he could shuffle in a blur, the coins that disappeared no matter how hard he told us to watch. I remember riding high up in his arms, or swaying on his shoulders as he made an 'inspection' of the foundations he'd laid on site in front of the caravan. He'd point out to me where my own room would be. When he'd got one of his used cars running sweet as syrup, he'd take me up to the old quarry at the back of the hill. I remember how I'd sit on his knee and

463

steer, his hands over mine on the wheel often rough and oil-stained. Black dirt pushed down deep in his nails. I thought all men's hands were like that.

I shift my weight on the lilo and my seat bones touch the floor. The tiny Scalextric car zips around the corner too fast and flies off the track, hitting the wall and landing on its back like a prone beetle, wheels still whirring. This thing is addictive. I can see why Bruce is so hooked on it.

It is Easter Sunday; we are due at Crois na Coille for lunch. In the living room next door, Mum is cooing over the baby, who is very sweet and very tiny. He is sleepy and paying precisely no attention to Mum's question of who is just the most handsome lad. Lena is having a well-earned nap. Bruce is making a snack in the kitchen. I predict paste sandwiches and pickled onions on sticks.

Jamie puts his head around the door of the room.

'Alright?' he says. 'We're planning to head off to Crois na Coille in the next wee while.' His voice is low so as not to disturb the drowsy baby. His arm is still in a cast but the black eye he's had for the past two weeks is finally starting to subside. 'You ready?'

I put down the Scalextric controls. 'I'm ready whenever you are.'

Jamie nods and is about to close the door again.

'Wait,' I say, standing, and he stops, then comes fully into the room.

I stumble around for words to connect us again, for I have hardly seen him the past couple of weeks. He was discharged from the hospital in time to go back in with Lena for the birth. I feel almost shy of him, my brother: this step he has taken into a new realm of which I can only stand on the outside, looking in.

'How are you?' I manage, at last.

He smiles. 'Grand. I'm grand.'

'How's Mum doing, do you think? I know she's been up with you a fair bit at the flat. Do you think she's doing OK?'

'Yeah, I guess so.' He scratches his nose. 'She loves having everyone here, at the house. I think she's finally forgiven Bruce for getting me involved with Gilroy and all that. So yeah. I think she's doing alright now.'

'I can see Bruce makes her happy.'

Jamie's eyes widen, and he starts forward to pretend to feel my forehead. 'You feeling OK yourself?'

'Get out of it.' I shove his hand away. 'You do know you've cut yourself shaving. Again.' I point. 'There.'

He laughs. 'Aye. Well. You try scraping a razor over these bruises.' He bends, carefully, to pick up the wee car from the floor and sets it back on the Scalextric track. 'Are you planning to stick around for a while or what?'

I tell him I'm going to the city in a few days.

'Meeting up with this lad John Teelin, are you?'

I lift my chin. 'I am, yeah.'

'Do you think you'll be staying there for a bit?'

'I don't know yet. Maybe just for a couple of days. We'll see.'

'He seems a nice enough bloke.' He smiles. 'And when do you go back to uni?'

'I'll be starting again after the summer. I just need to get my loan sorted out and find a place to stay. I'm actually really looking forward to it this time.'

Jamie nods. 'Good on you,' he says.

'Have you started your new job yet?' I ask.

He picks up the Scalextric control and sets the car in motion again. 'I've only been there a few days,' he says. 'But working with Ally at the forge, it's definitely better than going it alone. He's a good laugh. And it's good to have some steady money coming in again.'

465

'Lena seems to be doing well.'

'Lena's amazing. Amazing. She's made up with the wee one. We both are.'

'I'm so happy for you all,' I say.

'Aye, thanks.' He looks sheepish, rubbing the back of his neck, glancing back down the corridor. 'That's it. Anyway. I suppose we'd better be heading off. You coming?'

In the living room Jamie passes me the baby to hold while he and Lena gather their things. I cradle the surprisingly heavy bundle close to my chest. His sleeping face is a tiny, flawless moon. He reaches a hand from the blanket, opening and closing his fingers to cast slow and mysterious spells in the air.

Fern and Bella are waiting for us at the front door of Crois na Coille. Inside the scent of roast lamb fills the air and the table in the living room is laden with all manner of baked goods: Bella may have been cooking all week. Fern flits around, her face bright. She clasps the baby awkwardly, as if there are too many parts to get a hold of at once, but strokes his head and beams when he closes his fist tightly around her pinkie finger. Bella, on the other hand, nestles him in her broad arms and he settles at once. I have noticed that it is often the least demonstrative people who are most at ease with tiny children and animals.

'Now, before we eat,' Bella is saying, when we have all assembled in the living room, 'there is one thing we must do.'

With two hands, Fern takes down the black Bible. We all gather round as she opens the cover. I tuck my arm through Mum's. She responds with the lightest squeeze, as if drawing in a wing, and I feel at that moment flooded with love for my family, a heady tide which bears on its crest the magnitude of being only here, in the centre of this moment, with such a new one in our midst. More complicated than the ease of affection, far more tangled than friendship, this love has bulk, is heavy, is laced with pain and difficulty and is still sweet and strong as the blood that binds us.

Across the room from me, Bella is gazing at the baby, her head on one side and her eyes brimming with tears, although she will not let them escape. As I watch, she looks at me and then away, and she is soft in that moment, fleetingly stripped of the tough outer layer I am used to seeing. It is love, I think, the agony and joy and pure tenderness of love. I feel certain, in that moment, that she is thinking of my father.

I know now that we love in spite of, and beset by, the unknown. Netta's story will remain, at least for me, as incomplete as it ever was. I will probably never find out what happened to her. Jerome Mondegrene, the only person who might perhaps have known the truth, is dead. And Mondegrene himself took with him the man who was ultimately responsible for the murder of my father, if Gilroy's ravings to Jamie on the hillside shortly before his own death are true. So much for looking back, when the present erases so much.

The past lives in you, John Teelin said to me not so long ago. But the past, and what is to come, do not have to circle each other in endless revolutions. I look at the baby's face, so filled with infinite mystery, the newest link in an undetermined chain, with a hundred possible stories before him. We are only allowed such a small slice of knowledge about who we are, and where we really come from. We march relentlessly into our unknown futures, beginning anew with every second.

But right now, there is this present. I lay my head softly on my mother's shoulder, seeing the car key dangling from her fingers. *Life is a series of moments called now.*

'You're not going to use biro again,' says Bella.

Lena rocks the precious parcel of baby and blanket, humming softly to him. On my other side Jamie is twitching a little. I nudge him. It's for Bella and Fern, I'll say to him later, not your feelings about God, or the absence thereof.

467

Fern removes the lid from her fountain pen with a flourish, and in the front of the book she writes *Donald Angus MacArthur, born 2nd April 1998*.

We crowd around to see, and beyond the window the yellow hill shimmers, the gorse now in full bloom, shining and golden as if the sun has exploded and poured in shards upon the earth.

Acknowledgements

Enormous thanks to Holly Faulks and Lily Cooper for their talent, dedication and belief in this novel.

Thank you, Laura Williams and Kate Rizzo of Greene and Heaton. Thank you, Steven Cooper, Aphra Le Levier-Bennett and all at Hodder & Stoughton.

Thank you, Linda McQueen.

Thank you to Wendy Bough for giving new writers fantastic opportunities through the Caledonian Novel Award.

Thank you to A.L. Kennedy and to James Robertson for their sage advice and enthusiasm.

Thanks to Paul Macdonald of Macdonald Armouries, and to the staff at Cruachan Dam, Loch Awe. Heartfelt thanks to the staff, past and present, of Edinburgh University's School of Scottish Studies Archives and the Department of Celtic and Scottish Studies: teachers, colleagues, friends. Thank you to the singers, the musicians, the tellers of tales – and thank you to those who recorded them so that new generations can discover the rich oral traditions of this country.

Thank you to Anna Wendy Stevenson, Naomi Harvey and Rachel Harris for the music and the adventures.

Immense and heartfelt thanks to my family. To my mum Rosemary who has read the text countless times and always has something new and insightful to say. To Tanya, Bill, Allison and David for reading early drafts and offering their thoughts. To Dougie for the stories. Time for the ditty bag?

Thank you to my beautiful boy Seumas who came into the world just as this book was being finished.

And thank you, Matheu, for absolutely everything.